Happy reading !

Enjoy

MOON SHADOW

Book 2 Auriano Curse Series

by

PATRICIA BARLETTA

www.lachesispublishing.com

Published Internationally by Lachesis Publishing Inc.
Rockland, Ontario, Canada

Copyright © 2017 Patricia Barletta
Exclusive cover © 2017 Laura Givens
Inside artwork © 2017 Joanna D'Angelo

A catalogue record for the print format of this title
is available from the National Library of Canada

ISBN 978-1-77359-005-9

A catalogue record for the Ebook is available
from the National Library of Canada
Ebooks are available for purchase from
www.lachesispublishing.com

ISBN 978-1-77359-004-2

Editor: Joanna D'Angelo

Copyeditor: Kerry Genova

Dedication

To Amy, Chris, and Destiny, who never fail to cheer me on,
and keep my feet planted firmly on terra firma

Acknowledgments

Writers don't work in vacuums, even though sometimes we feel as if we are the sole occupants of the universe. We have "others", those who help shape our rough manuscripts into shiny objects. My thanks go to Mike Kimball from the Stonecoast MFA Program in Creative Writing, who was the first person to see this manuscript and taught me the term "on the nose." (If you didn't know, it's dialogue that's so obvious the reader could make it up.) I also want to send a shout out to Joanna D'Angelo, who helped me polish the manuscript into its final form. And of course, my gratitude goes to my critique buddies, the Cover-To-Cover Writers Group, who, besides critiquing my work, advise, console, encourage, and put up with my whining. This book is so much better because of all of you.

Also Available

Moon Dark
Book 1 Auriano Curse Series

Coming Soon

Moon Bright
Book 3 Auriano Curse Series

MOON SHADOW

Chapter 1

"*Arretez!*"

The command to halt came out of the black night. Antonio Valerio Cesare D'Este, Duke of Auriano, roused from his doze as his coach came to a stop. The little door in the ceiling of the coach slid open, and Piero, his driver-valet-bodyguard, his Guide, murmured, "Highwaymen, *Sior* Tonio. Two of them in the middle of the road."

Antonio sat up, immediately alert. "Do what they say, Piero," he said. "Let them take what they want. No sense in anyone getting hurt over a few coins."

He welcomed the disruption. The journey from Auriano to Paris had been long and dull. A confrontation by highwaymen would relieve the boredom. He straightened his cuffs, then checked the stiletto hidden up his sleeve. He would probably not use it, but always being prepared had kept him alive.

He heard some conversation between Piero and one of the thieves, then the *clip-clop* of horses approaching. Out the window in the hazy moonlight, he saw two horsemen. One of them dismounted and flung open the door to his coach. The fellow pointed a pistol at Antonio's heart. With his other hand, the thief took a lantern from his comrade and hung it on the handle of the door. Pale light flooded the interior of the coach.

"Bon soir, monsieur," the thief said. "Your money, if you please."

With a raised eyebrow and a wry twist to his lips, Antonio tossed a small pouch of coins to him. The thief caught it and passed it to his companion.

"You have more." The robber posed it as a statement rather than a question.

Antonio coolly surveyed the highwayman. He was a slight fellow. If his larger companion did not have that pistol aimed at Piero, Antonio could have easily disarmed him and taken back his money. Rather than being entertained by the distraction of a simple robbery, he was annoyed by the fellow's manner.

"You have all my coin," Antonio said. "Now please allow me to continue on my journey."

The thief stepped up into the coach and sat on the edge of the opposite seat. He wore a dark scarf tied across his face, exposing only his eyes, and they were shadowed by his hat. Even so, beneath the muffler, Antonio saw the outline of his chin, the plane of his cheek. Too soft for a full-grown man.

"You have more," the thief said again. The pistol hovered inches from Antonio's heart.

Antonio raised a disdainful brow. "If I did, I would have given it to you."

The highwayman ignored Antonio's statement. "Your thumb ring, *monsieur, s'il vous plaît.*"

"You are an obstinate little fellow, aren't you?" Antonio was not about to hand over the gold band, engraved in a repeating pattern with the symbol of the House of Auriano. Inside was more engraving—his full name and title.

A dagger appeared in the thief's other hand. He dragged the point lightly down Antonio's cheek, then pushed it against the vulnerable pulse at his throat.

The move surprised a laugh out of Antonio. The fellow was feisty as well as obstinate.

"Are you laughing at me, *monsieur?*" The point of the dagger dug deeper, pricking skin, drawing a bead of blood.

Antonio did not like the thief's aggression. With a flick of his wrist, the stiletto slipped into his hand, and in the same motion, he smoothly pressed it against the robber's throat. "It seems," he drawled, "we have a stalemate. I told you I have no other coin, and the ring does not leave my hand. Take what I gave you and go."

The highwayman reared back from the deadly edge at his throat, but he huffed a breathy chuckle. "No stalemate, *monsieur*. I think I will have to teach you some manners." He lowered the muzzle of the pistol and pressed it against Antonio's genitals. "I believe I have you in checkmate. Drop your weapon, and give me the ring, *monsieur. S'il vous plait.*"

Not wishing to spend the rest of his life as a eunuch, Antonio laid his knife on the seat beside him and slowly pulled the ring from his thumb. Instead of holding it out to the fellow, he let it drop to the floor of the coach. "Ah, *scusi,*" he said without the least bit of regret in his tone.

The thief bristled. "Do not move, *monsieur*. The trigger of my pistol is very sensitive."

"How very unfortunate," Antonio murmured, hoping to provoke the thief and gain the upper hand. "Your lover must find that quite frustrating."

At the insult, the robber stilled. Pressing the pistol harder against Antonio's groin, the outlaw used the point of his dagger to snag the ring from the floor, then neatly slipped it into his pocket. Once again, he placed the tip against Antonio's throat. "Do not," he said, "try any more tricks, *monsieur,* and do not move. I have little patience." Using his dagger, he cut the buttons from Antonio's waistcoat, then slid the dagger beneath his stock, sliced it apart, and slit his shirt down the front.

Antonio did not dare move with the pistol resting

3

between his legs, but his annoyance had turned to fury. Besides the fact that the fellow had ruined a perfectly good shirt and stock, the thief had uncovered what Antonio wore on a silken cord around his neck.

"*Sacre bleu*," the highwayman whispered. "Not a myth." Using the point of his dagger, he lifted the two moonstone pendants hanging on the cord. "Give these to me."

Suspicious of the thief's initial response to the stones, Antonio wanted to see what he knew of them. He shrugged indifferently. "Those stones are of little value."

"Perhaps," the thief said. "Perhaps I would like to see them decorating *ma petite amie*. Or perhaps their value has little to do with money."

The thief could be lying, or he could be ignorant of the stones' value. Either way, Antonio was not about to give them up easily. They were two parts of the moonstone that his new sister-in-law had worn when his brother first met her, the stone that had been broken into three by the sorceress Nulkana in the battle that had nearly ended his brother's life.

The thief tipped his head, and the lantern light slanted beneath the brim of his hat. Antonio caught a glimpse of the fellow's eyes. They were the color of turquoise, tilted up at the corners, with thick lashes. Beautiful. It was no wonder the fellow was so aggressive. With those eyes, he probably had been defending himself his whole life.

"What if I refuse to give you the stones?" Antonio wanted to see how brave the fellow really was.

The highwayman pressed the barrel of the pistol against Antonio's testicles to the point of pain. "How much do you value *these* stones, *monsieur*?"

"You don't have the stones to dare," Antonio taunted.

Raising his head, staring Antonio in the eye, the thief said, "You have no idea what I would dare." Despite their beauty, the youth's eyes were cold.

4

Antonio wondered what life had done to this fellow to turn him so ruthless. He had no doubt the thief would pull the trigger on his pistol. Carefully, he took hold of the cord around his neck and pulled it over his head. Dangling the stones, he said, "If you take these, be assured I will come after you to take them back."

The thief sheathed his dagger and wrapped his fingers around the stones. A smile touched his eyes. "You will have to find me first. *Bon chance, monsieur.* Enjoy the rest of your journey."

In a flash, the thief was out of the coach. He grabbed the lantern and bounded back onto his horse. The lantern was extinguished, and Antonio heard the sound of retreating hoofbeats. Then silence.

Piero's voice came through the little opening in the ceiling. "Excellency? *Sior* Tonio? Are you all right?"

Antonio breathed deeply to control his rage before he replied. "*Si*, Piero. I am unhurt. And yourself?"

"*Si.*"

"How fast can you get us to Paris? I have a score to settle with this highwayman." As he spoke, he yanked the ruined stock from about his neck and jerked his torn shirt closed.

Without answering, Piero slapped the reins and gave a shout to urge the horses into a gallop. Antonio braced himself against the side of the coach and stared out at the dark night. The gibbous moon looked swollen on one side and about to burst with something infectious. Only a few more days and the curse would take hold of him. He would turn to Shadow, when he would lose the sense of smell, taste, and touch. And on the other side of that— the ravages of the Hunger, when all his senses and appetites would demand to be fed.

The highwayman had stolen the one thing that would dissipate those wild, dark cravings of the Hunger. Two of the three pieces of the charmed moonstone. One of the stones was still with his twin brother, Alessandro; one was his; one he had been bringing to his sister. They would not break the curse, but they helped alleviate the worst of its manifestation. The blue stones themselves were unimpressive with a dull opalescence. Their gold filigree setting that he had commissioned for them was worth more than the stones to anyone who did not know what they were. But the highwayman seemed more interested in the stones than their settings and seemed to know something about them. That made Antonio suspicious.

He would find this thief. He would teach the fellow what it meant to cross Antonio Valerio Cesare D'Este, Duke of Auriano, and then he would take back what belonged to him.

* * *

Solange Delacroix leaned over the neck of her horse as they plunged at a gallop down the narrow path through the woods. Behind her, she could hear the pounding of Gide's horse and his occasional curse when a branch slapped across his face. She did not slow her headlong rush. She was anxious to see her treasures in bright lamplight. And, if she were truthful, she was anxious to be away from their victim. The man had been too arrogant, too practiced with that knife, too imperturbable. Too damned attractive. Even now, even as Solange raced to get as far away from him as she could, those golden eyes seemed to burn into her head.

The path opened into a clearing. Bursting out of the trees, she reined in her horse before the abandoned woodcutter's hut. She swung to the ground, rushed inside, and lit the only lantern. Its flame illuminated the rustic, single room with a small stone hearth in one wall, a narrow bare cot against the opposite wall, and a rickety table in the center. As she dumped the contents of her pocket onto the table, she heard Gide dismount, heard his tread on the stone step, and then his bulk filled the doorway.

"What in blazes are you thinking, Solange?" His vehement tone revealed his concern. "You could have broken both our necks."

Solange pulled the scarf from her face and stared at her brother with wide eyes. Sweeping her hand across the items on the table, she said, "Look, Gide. Look what we have."

Her brother closed the space between them in three long strides. Gazing at the pieces gleaming in the lamplight, he nudged the two pendants with his finger. "*Sacre bleu,*" he whispered. "Could one of them be the stone of the myth?"

Solange knew the myth, that a stone existed with magical powers, that it could dissipate the ravages of a terrible curse. It would not revoke the curse, but be a balm to its devastation. Their father had told them the tale of the stone when she and Gide had been little. But that seemed very long ago when Mama and Papa were alive and there had been stories and family meals and happy times. She stared at the two blue moonstones, the pieces that might buy her freedom from this life she was forced to lead. They were uneven triangles, obviously broken from a single stone and set in gold filigree. They reflected an odd opalescence in the lamplight. They fascinated her. She swept up the cord from beneath her brother's examination and dangled the stones in the lamplight. "They don't appear to be special. But our victim threatened to come after me and take them back."

"He threatened you?" Gide's brows drew together in anger.

Solange smiled at her brother's concern. "Calm down, little brother. I held a pistol to his balls, so he didn't dare move. He has no idea who I am." Her gaze dropped to the gold band lying on the table. "I wonder who he is. I didn't recognize the coat of arms on his coach."

"He is either very brave or stupid to ride in a coach in

France bearing his coat of arms," Gide said, referring to the angry prejudice of the peasants against the aristocracy since the Revolution. He picked up the ring and held it closer to the lamp. "It's engraved with the same device as the coat of arms." He looked closer. "There's engraving on the inside. *Antonio Valerio Cesare D'Este, Duke of Auriano.* An Italian duke. No wonder he proclaims his nobility. He doesn't know any better." He placed the ring back on the table and shook his head. "I don't like it. There's only supposed to be one stone, not two. How did it get broken?"

Solange shrugged. "We don't know the truth of the story. Maybe there have always been two stones."

"The myth only tells of one. Myths come from truth. And if this is the stone of the myth, why would an Italian duke have it?"

At Gide's dire expression, Solange laughed. "Why not an Italian duke?"

Gide scowled.

Solange gave him a playful push. "You worry too much." She studied the stones once more. "Remember the rhyme? The one that Papa taught us?"

Gide recited, "*Feed the hunger; Feed the pain . . .*"

"*. . . Wear the moonstone; Lose the shame.*" As Solange finished, the stones glowed dully. She caught her breath, then stared at her brother, who stared back. "They *are* real," she whispered. In a decisive move, she undid the clasp on the cord and slipped one of them off. "I think I'll keep one of these."

"*Zut!* You can't!" Gide looked horrified.

"Why not?" She shrugged.

"Because Le Chacal wants them." Her brother's tone implied she was being dense.

"He only spoke of one moonstone, so I will give him one," she said blithely. "He doesn't need to know there were two." She cast a warning glance at Gide. "And you won't tell him."

Gide's gaze slid away from her. "Why would I tell him?"

"Gide. Promise me you won't tell." Solange placed a beseeching hand on her brother's arm.

"*Zut,* Solange! What if he asks?"

Gide's last statement pulled at her heart. They had both been broken by Le Chacal, the Jackal, the king of the thieves of Paris, who ruled the Paris underworld with no mercy. Only her bargain with him allowed them any sort of freedom, and kept her brother relatively safe, away from becoming one of *les chauffeurs,* those thieves who had few compunctions about torturing their victims, then murdering them when the outlaws had what they wanted. Years ago, when they were starving orphans wandering the streets of Paris, Le Chacal had caught them stealing a loaf of bread. He offered them sanctuary—food and a dry, warm place to sleep. Only later they learned what his price was; becoming thieves for him. And for Solange as she became older, the price was much, much higher. They'd had no choice, it was steal for Chacal or starve.

She looked him in the eye. "You won't have to lie to him, Gide. He'll never suspect there were two stones."

Gide drew a breath. "I won't let him hurt you either."

Solange smiled and squeezed the muscular arm beneath her hand. Her brother was a man now, but she was still his older sister. She had raised him from the time when they were children, after their parents had been killed just before the Revolution. When she and Gide had been taken in by Le Chacal, she thought she had found a guardian angel. Instead, they had fallen into the hands of a devil.

Picking up the gold band, she slipped it back into her pocket. Perhaps, she would keep this, too. Its owner intrigued her.

"Come on, Gide," she urged. "I have to get back to the city. Vernoux will be waiting for me."

"How can you give yourself to him?" her brother demanded as he followed her out to their horses. "He hurts you."

"Not always. And he visits much less than he used to. Sometimes he does nothing but watch me." Solange clapped her hat on her head and swung up onto her horse. "Vernoux pays for the roof over our heads. Or would you prefer to sleep down in the Catacombs with the rats?"

"*Oui.* I would if it meant you did not have to be his whore," Gide said as he mounted his own horse.

She shook her head at the old argument. Being mistress to the Marquis de Vernoux meant that they lived comfortably, despite their ties to Le Chacal. Vernoux's abuse was part of the price she paid for being stupid enough to fall for Le Chacal's enticement and entrapment in the first place.

Steeling herself against thoughts of the pain the coming night might hold, she dug her heels into her horse's flanks and called, "I'll race you back to the city."

* * *

Antonio stood in the receiving room of the Panthémont Convent and waited for the Mother Superior. It was near three o'clock in the morning, and the bell for the liturgical hour of Matins would soon ring. If it had been any other religious house, he would have honored the nuns' privacy and waited until daybreak, but not here. This convent was renowned for both its education of France's royal and noble daughters, as well as its scandal. Although most of the noble daughters and all of the royal ones were gone since the Revolution, scandal still hung like a dark veil over the place. It had been the perfect spot to hide his sister, Allegra. The veneer of propriety and morality covered the tolerance of impropriety beneath. While Allegra had been taught decorum, she needed the freedom that the curse on their family demanded. The Mother Superior was a very understanding and discreet woman—for a substantial donation.

Having arrived at his Paris house not long after midnight, he had felt the need to visit Allegra. He had no piece of the moonstone to bring her, but he needed to see her to assure himself that she was safe. The letter she had sent to him and Alessandro in Venice hinted at some threat, but she had treated it lightly. As soon as he had celebrated his brother's marriage to the lovely Sabrina, he began his journey.

And been robbed. He would not leave Paris without taking back what was his and punishing the thief. Something about the fellow nagged at Antonio, but he couldn't quite grasp what it was. Yet, discovering the identity of a highwayman with distinctive turquoise eyes should not be too difficult.

He heard the scrape of a shoe against the stone floor, and then the Mother Superior entered. She was a middle-aged woman, and in deference to the laws of the Revolution, instead of a nun's habit, she wore a simple gown and a small, light veil, revealing her dark, gray-flecked hair. In spite of her age, she was still a handsome woman. Bowing respectfully, he murmured, *"Ma donna."*

She approached him with a smile and outstretched hand. *"Bon soir, mon seigneur."* After he had taken her hand and bowed over it, she said, "You honor us with this visit, but I am afraid your sister is not here."

Antonio stiffened. "Not here? Where is she? Has something happened to her?"

She waved him to a pair of simple wooden chairs near the hearth, where a small fire burned. When they had both been seated, she said, "The last time I saw her she was in perfect health."

"Then?" Antonio prompted. Having dealt with the

woman before, he knew she was circumspect to the point of exasperation.

The Mother Superior sighed. "I tried to convince her not to go, that she would be safe here." A tiny frown appeared between her brows. "Your sister can be quite headstrong." She turned to gaze at the flames.

Out of respect, Antonio bit down on the curse that sprang to his lips. He did not need to be reminded of Allegra's faults. Instead, he asked, "Where did she go, *ma donna?*"

The nun turned back to him. "That I cannot tell you." Pulling a folded parchment from her pocket, she held it out to him. "But she asked me to give this to you."

As Antonio took the letter, the bell for Matins began to ring.

"I must go," the Mother Superior said, rising. "We miss your sister. I hope when you find her, she will be well."

Antonio waited until she was gone, then he broke the seal on the letter. Opening it, he read:

My Dearest Brothers,

If you are reading this, then I have left France. Information has come to me concerning the object we seek. The others who also seek it have begun to gather here in Paris. I have felt a sense of danger for several months, and have decided to hide between the Waters and the Stones. Luisa and Ernesto are with me, so you need not fear that I am alone. Once I have established myself, I will write to tell you of my situation. Keep me in your thoughts, as I will keep you in mine.

Your Loving Sister,
Allegra

Crumpling the note in his hand, Antonio could not decide between relief that Allegra was safe, or annoyance that she did not wait for either him or Alessandro to come to her. She was between the Waters and the Stones. That meant she was in England, somewhere between the city of Bath and Stonehenge, both places of tremendous power and a logical destination. She would be safe there, and her Guide, Luisa, was with her along with Luisa's husband. They would not be difficult to find.

Yet, the other part of her note disturbed him. She had information about the object they sought, the magical Sphere of Astarte, that could bestow immortality, wealth, and power on anyone who possessed it. More importantly, it was the one thing that could break the curse on their family, so they would never again have to live part of every month as Shadow with no sense of taste, smell, or touch. So they would never again have to endure the ravages of the Hunger as they transformed back to human. He wondered why she had not shared that information. And then anxiety speared through him as he wondered if she could be in more danger than she'd let on.

He read the letter again. No, she would have used their code word for danger: *incendio*—fire, that referred back to the conflagration in their *castello* in Auriano that had sent them to live in Venice when they were young.

Those others she mentioned who were gathering in Paris had to be the diabolical Legion of Baal, a group of men who sought to return the Sphere to ancient Phoenicia in order to tap its magic. If they possessed the Sphere, the balance of power in the world would shift drastically— and not for the better.

As he strode out through the gate of the convent, he decided he would write to Alessandro to inform him of these recent events. Luisa and Ernesto would protect Allegra with their lives, so she was safe. As for himself, he would remain in Paris for a while to discover exactly what the Legion of Baal was plotting. At the same time, he would seek the highwayman and teach the thief a lesson in humility.

Chapter 2

The following evening, Antonio stepped into the salon of *Madame* de Volonté. He found it unusual that he had been announced at the door with his full title when anything hinting at the aristocracy had been banned in France after the Revolution. It was the second odd thing about the evening. The first was the existence of the social salon, one of several places Piero had discovered, where Antonio might learn the identity of the highwayman who had robbed him. He thought it peculiar that the information would be available at such a gathering, but he was willing to follow any avenue to retrieve the moonstones.

The opulent salon seemed to be transported from the decadent time before the Revolution. Crystal chandeliers lit the space and highlighted the rich clothing of the gentlemen and the diaphanous, revealing gowns of the women. Long mirrors covering the silk-clad walls reflected sultry glances, alluring eyes, caressing hands. This was not a salon of the intellectual or the revolutionary, but rather a salon of the *demimonde*, the hazy half-world of the French courtesan, where otherwise proper gentlemen could mingle with women willing to allow them access to their charms. The atmosphere crackled with the excitement of the hunt and capture, the lure of a coy prize, the gratification of an arrogant victor, the surrender of a compliant captive.

Around him in contrast to the sensual ambiance, he heard snatches of a discussion of the artist Jacques-

Louis David, whispers of scandal within the Directory, the ruling body of France, and rumors concerning General Bonaparte's victories in Italy and his invasion of Venice. Antonio wondered if the general had kept his promise and vouchsafed the *Ca'D'Este*, the Venetian *palazzo* of the House of Auriano, his home. But that concern was for another time.

His attention was drawn by quiet laughter, applause, and murmurs of appreciation from a corner of the room. The group parted. A young woman stepped forward and approached him.

Mesmerized, Antonio stared. She was tall for a woman and moved with sensuous grace. Her hair was the color of ripe wheat, upswept into mass of ringlets which revealed a long neck. Full lips curved in a welcoming smile. She wore a gown of the new fashion, high-waisted, the skirt skimming her curves. The pale green silk, shot through with gold thread, highlighted her coloring. Its tiny sleeves revealed the ivory skin of her arms, and the deep decolletage hinted at the lushness beneath. But what made him blink were her eyes. They were the color of turquoise and tilted up slightly at the corners, framed by thick lashes. They were like jewels.

Like the eyes of the highwayman.

Antonio bit down on his shock. He envisioned the scene from the night before, the thief sitting across from him, the thief's eyes shaded by the wide brim of the hat, then revealed in the light of the lantern. Looking at the woman before him, he knew. This vision of beauty approaching him lived a double life. Anger flashed through him. How could he have been so blind? The highwayman had been female. A beautiful woman. A woman whose every movement promised seduction. He had been duped as well as robbed.

"*Bon soir, mon seigneur*," she greeted him, as she held out her hand. "Welcome to my salon. I do not believe we have had the pleasure of a previous acquaintance."

Her voice was a husky purr. Despite his anger, he felt his body stir, and his ire turned to amusement at his body's betrayal. This was the thief who had stolen from him, the person he gleefully could have throttled. At the same time, he wanted to kiss those luscious lips, run his fingers across her pale skin, explore her mysteries, hear her sigh in pleasure. The irony tickled him, fascinated him, made him wary.

She showed no recognition of him and played the game of innocence. In fact, she approached as if she had nothing to fear. From the way she moved, from the coldness in her eyes on the night she stole from him, he knew she was no innocent. But two could play this game.

Taking her outstretched hand, he was stunned as soon as her skin touched his, for they hadn't touched when she'd robbed him. This woman hid tremendous power at her core. Beyond that, he sensed another force running through her. At some point, she had also come into contact with a piece of the Sphere of Astarte, the artifact that would free him from his curse. He used every ounce of self-control not to react. Was she a danger to him or his salvation?

In that moment, Antonio knew he would not leave Paris until this woman had both returned to him what was his and given up her secrets. Hiding his intentions behind a façade of civility, he bowed over her outstretched hand. He nudged her thumb away from her fingers to reveal the web of flesh between hand and thumb. There, in plain sight, was a birthmark, the starburst, indicating that she was a descendant of the sorceress Halima, whose sister, Nulkana, had placed the curse on his family. The mark was an exact replica of the one on the hand of Sabrina, Alessandro's wife. Although this woman's power was similar to Sabrina's, it held a different tone. It was darker, wilder. Without realizing it, *Madame* de Volonté had given up one of her secrets.

Satisfaction made him bold. Grazing his lips across

her knuckles, he touched the tip of his tongue to her thumb, the spot corresponding to where he would have worn his ring on his own thumb. She flinched, and he knew he had disconcerted her.

Straightening, Antonio noticed the faint line which appeared between her brows and the quick flash of fear through her eyes. He smiled. "I have heard that your salon is a collection of the jewels of Paris, *madame*."

She took back her hand and flicked her fan open. A cool smile curved her lips, and the line between her brows disappeared. "Truly? Then I shall have to make my gratitude known to the gossips."

"But surely those who collect here are merely glass in comparison to your beauty." He complimented outrageously, yet his words held an underlying truth. This creature standing before him was gorgeous.

Madame de Volonté snapped shut her fan, and her smile turned coy. "You flatter me, *Monsieur le Duc.* Come and join us." She wound her hand through his arm and steered him toward the group she had just left. Her hip brushed tantalizingly against his. "We were just discussing the duel, and the merits of the pistol versus the sword."

"Ah. The muzzle or the point," he nodded, heightening the sexual innuendo.

She introduced three men and two women, then she asked, "So which do you prefer in the duel, *mon seigneur?*"

"That depends on my intent, *madame*. Do I wish to finish off my opponent in a blinding flash, or perhaps toy and prolong the pleasure of combat?"

With a wicked gleam, she began a rhyme. "He raised his pistol and cocked his gun. His aim was sure; he needn't run—"

Antonio finished, "His finger twitched; the trigger gave. His load he shot and couldn't save."

As his taunt met its mark, her eyes widened. Antonio's lips curved innocently. She knew he was not deceived by her calm demeanor.

While the onlookers applauded his cleverness, her smile remained cool. "Bravo, *Monsieur le Duc.*"

Not wishing to make an enemy of her, he started another rhyme. "He swished his sword, and with a thrust, he plunged it to its depth—"

With a mischievous glance, she continued, "Her cry of pain was clearly heard; this virgin met her death—"

As he opened his mouth to take up the rhyme, she stalled him with a raised finger. "In this war, she lost her blood, but surely gained a stud."

Her smile was victorious. As laughter erupted around them, he played the gentleman, allowing her the win in the contest of wits, but this would be the only one he would let her have. He vowed, in the end, she would surrender everything to him. Her body, her secrets, and most importantly, the moonstones.

*   *   *

Solange watched the duke's eyes as she delivered her final lines of the rhyme. He smiled graciously in defeat, but he gave away nothing in that golden gaze. She sensed he was not pleased that she had bested him. Apprehension trickled through her. Was he aware she had been the highwayman? That touch to her thumb could have been merely a suggestion of his interest. Or it could have been something more ominous. His composure during the robbery and the fact that he had appeared in her salon indicated an audacious man who feared very little.

Across the room, she saw Gide glowering in her direction. Her brother was present to protect her, and most of the time he remained inconspicuous, allowing her freedom to flirt and act the seductress. The frown on his face did not bode well for the duke. Gide would disrupt her salon if he thought the Italian was a threat to her.

She gave a barely perceptible shake of her head to

indicate that Gide should keep his distance. Although the duke's boldness disturbed her, she would handle the situation without her brother's intervention. Auriano was, after all, only a man, and she certainly had experience enough in dealing with that species.

Yet, he was an extremely attractive member of the male side of society. The light of the hundreds of candles in the room revealed the strong planes and angles of his face. Gold streaks swept through his wavy, unbound, collar-length, chestnut hair. His lips were finely chiseled. When he smiled, those golden eyes crinkled at the corners, and a dimple appeared in one cheek. Even his skin had a golden cast to it. He was breathtakingly handsome, almost to the point of beauty.

She had dealt with other handsome men, men who were so self-absorbed they barely acknowledged others in the world, men so arrogant they treated everyone else with contempt, men who hid ugly cruelty beneath their attractive exteriors. Rarely had she met a handsome man who could be kind. This handsome man, whose muscled arm beneath her hand indicated his strength, was an enigma. If he knew she was the thief, why not openly accuse her? If he did not suspect, then why did he taunt with his words and actions? She was frustrated at his mystery and wanted to send him on his way.

But despite the danger, she felt drawn to him. His eyes in the dim light of the coach on the night she had robbed him had mocked and challenged her. Knowing he was unaware that she was a woman, she had challenged him in return and discovered he was more than a bored aristocrat. His cold threat when she stole the moonstones was no idle bluster. His appearance at her salon proved that. She sensed he would not rest until he retrieved what he felt belonged to him. Her attraction to him was madness.

While the others around them engaged in conversation,

he leaned close and murmured, "Is there someplace where we might converse privately, *madame?*"

At his proximity, she caught the scent of rosemary and citrus, lemon perhaps, an intoxicating mix. His warm breath against her ear sent a shiver through her. Annoyed at her reaction, wanting to prove to herself he was no different than any other man, she nodded. "Of course. Please come with me." Solange reasoned he would not dare harm her with so many witnesses in her salon. She led him to a small balcony that overlooked the River Seine. At the moment, it was deserted. Turning to him, she asked, "So, *Monsieur le Duc*, what is it that demands such privacy?"

He smiled, took her hand and ran his thumb down the back of her ring finger. "You wear no wedding band, *madame.*"

Unnerved by his touch, she snatched her hand away. "What jewelry I wear does not concern you, *monsieur.*"

"But you are addressed as *madame.*" He raised a brow in curiosity. "Am I to conclude you are a widow?"

"I do not believe that is any of your business." She looked away in disdain.

Huffing a laugh, he said, "But it is part of *your* business, *si?* A good way to imply experience and skill in your art."

Her gaze cut back to him. "What do you want, *monsieur?*" she snapped.

Wry speculation twisted his lips. "I want to know how much it will cost me to partake of your art."

Solange narrowed her eyes. His bluntness outraged her, and her fingers twitched with the urge to slap him. Her salon was not a place where men might find a temporary release, but where they could discover a woman who would be a long-time companion. Besides, no one ever requested her services, partly because she ran the salon, and partly because it was common knowledge that she belonged to Vernoux. Because this man was a foreigner, he most likely did not know of her arrangement with Vernoux, but he should have realized she was not for sale.

Raising her chin, she said, "I am insulted, *mon seigneur.* I do not sell myself like a common whore."

As she began to sweep past him, he blocked her way. His eyes had gone hard and cold. "Is that because you are a common thief?"

Solange caught her breath, then forced a laugh. "Oh, *Monsieur le Duc*, how droll." She tapped her fan against his chest. "You are very clever. No one has ever flirted by accusing me of being a thief." Hiding her apprehension behind another light laugh, she asked, "And where, pray, would I hide my pistol?" She indicated the revealing nature of her diaphanous gown with a sweep of her hand.

"Perhaps in the waistband of your breeches," he said, his tone smooth steel beneath velvet. "And your knife would be in a sheath at your hip."

She ran her palm down over the curve of her hip and watched his eyes narrow. With a teasing tilt to her lips, she said, "I seem to have misplaced the knife." Then with a raised a brow, she asked, "And breeches? Why ever would I wear men's clothing?"

He smiled wryly. "A perfect disguise for a beautiful woman who wishes to thieve but remain anonymous, *si?*" His words taunted while his tone seduced.

She shook her head. "I know nothing of these things."

He stepped forward, all flirting gone, and forced her to back away. "I believe you do know, *madame.*" Taking another step, he compelled her to retreat. "And I mean to retrieve what belongs to me."

Without touching her, the duke had backed her against the balustrade of the balcony. The river flowed directly below. Unlike Vernoux, who would have laid hands on her in pain, this man had dominated simply through the force of his presence. Although she feared his discovery of the truth, for some reason, she did not think he would physically harm her.

"I have nothing that belongs to you," she bluffed, feeling the stone of the balustrade dig into her. "Please, *Monsieur le Duc*, if I step back any further, I will plunge into the river."

A muscle jumped in his jaw; anger darkened his gaze. "Do not think you can escape me by a quick swim, *madame. Thief.*" His last word sliced at her.

Fear cut through her. What would he do if he knew for certain she had been the highwayman? Beyond his shoulder, she saw Gide appear in the doorway. Relief weakened her knees, but apprehension followed quickly. Her brother's thunderous expression did not bode well for the duke. There would be a scene. She could not afford that.

"Is there a problem, Solange?" Gide asked. He appeared ready to turn the Italian into a bug, an easy task for him because he had a strong streak of magic running through his veins, while hers had disappeared.

At her brother's question, Auriano blinked. Without taking a step back, his presence seemed to withdraw, turning chill and more deadly for its retreat. Then he smiled, a smile of seduction, of promised pleasure edged with devilish intent. "Solange," he said. "A beautiful name." Taking her hand, he turned it over, raised it to his lips and placed a gentle kiss on her palm. "It has been a delight. I look forward to our next meeting."

His words were more threat than promise. The touch of his lips on her palm was warm and soft. Confused by the contradiction and swift change in his manner, Solange stood frozen as he bowed, and whispered, "Solange," as if he were placing a claim on her name. He nodded once to Gide, brushed shoulders with him as he passed, and disappeared into the crowd.

Solange wilted against the balustrade. With the duke's

exit, she felt as if she had just been released from a very confined space. She could breathe again.

Auriano angered her. He alarmed her. His arrogance, his poise, his daring were qualities she would have to battle with all her wits.

His seductive charm was another matter entirely. Despite her anger, despite her alarm, she had been physically attracted to him. The memory of his lips against her palm made her skin tingle. She closed her fingers around the spot. Her heart thrummed in her chest, but from fear or excitement? She had not been physically attracted to a man in a very long time, after she had become Vernoux's property. And therein lay the danger. She could not allow herself to become attached to the duke for any reason. Vernoux would not allow it. Vernoux would kill to keep what was his, even if it meant destroying his own property. He had proven that not long ago when a young woman who had been one of his other companions turned her attention elsewhere. She had been found floating face down in the Seine.

Gide stood in front of her. "Solange? Did that Italian duke hurt you?" he asked. Then, dropping his voice, he added, "Did he suspect?"

Straightening, she smiled reassuringly. She was not going to give Gide any reason to confront the dangerous Italian. "No," she said, answering both of her brother's questions. "He was merely mistaken about the purpose of my salon. He thought perhaps I might entertain him for the evening."

"He what?" Gide flushed in anger. "I should call him out!"

Solange laughed. "Down, little brother. You can't call him out for thinking I'm a whore, because that's what I am."

The pain of the truth made her brother scowl. "You don't have to be. We could run away, hide in some other country. Vernoux would never find us."

She shook her head. "Vernoux has connections throughout the world. You know he belongs to the Legion of Baal. One of the members would find us for him and return us here. What do you think Vernoux would do then?" At Gide's frustrated silence, she linked her arm with his and turned him back in the direction of the salon. "Come, Gide. The Italian duke is gone, and we have guests to entertain. Later, we will make a visit to Le Chacal, bring him the duke's coin and tell him of that item he sought."

"Do you think, by bringing the moonstone, Le Chacal will free us?" Gide asked.

"I think," she said quietly as they returned inside, "that we won't bring it to him. We'll use it as a bargaining chip." She smiled at him.

Instead of smiling back, her brother frowned. "What of Vernoux?"

Her expression turned thoughtful. "I wonder if I could convince the Italian duke to provoke a duel with the marquis."

"You wouldn't do such a thing," Gide stated bluntly. "That would be the same as murdering the Italian. Even you wouldn't go that far."

Solange laughed. "Oh, Gide, sometimes you are much too serious."

Her brother smiled when he realized she was teasing. Yet, her words were not spoken completely in jest. The Italian duke was a dangerous man. When she had robbed him, his use of the knife he'd pressed against her throat had been masterful. If his swordplay were as practiced, if his aim with a pistol were precise, might he not be a formidable opponent for Vernoux?

To discover those answers, she would need to become better acquainted with him, a risky prospect. Although she would have to be very careful in order not to raise Vernoux's suspicions, she looked forward to the challenge of matching wits with the Duke of Auriano.

Smiling brightly, she went to speak to a gentleman who had just settled his new mistress in a very elegant suite of rooms.

*   *   *

Gide watched his sister act the impeccable hostess and ply her trade. He hated what she did and the fact that she still thought of him as a child who needed protecting. He was no innocent, not living as they did in a house provided by her protector who got pleasure from her pain; not roaming the roads as a highwayman to pay off Le Chacal. Frustration made his fist clench. Someday, he would free her from this servitude.

His gaze wandered to the far side of the room. The Duke of Auriano was making his way through the crowd to the door. Several times, women stopped him to flirt outrageously. The man charmed each woman with his smile and a few words, then bowed politely and moved on. Gide let out a breath when the duke finally disappeared through the door. Something about the man raised his hackles, something besides the fact that he had appeared to threaten Solange. He was too smooth, too composed. An element of violence smoldered beneath that calm exterior. And he had been in possession of the moonstones, which were supposed to be only myth.

"The Duke of Auriano is an interesting man, *n'est-ce pas?*" *Monsieur* Gravois said at Gide's shoulder.

Gide turned and stoically kept the disgust from his face. Gravois was Vernoux's creature, a man who lived to please the marquis and who snapped up any crumb Vernoux might throw him like a lapdog. He would report everything he saw tonight.

"I never spoke with the man," Gide said. "I have no idea how interesting or boring he might be."

"Come, now, boy, I saw the dislike in your eye. You

can confide in me." Gravois pulled out a handkerchief and wiped the ever-present sweat from the rolls of fat at his neck.

One thing Gide hated was being called "boy." He had seen too much in his two decades of life to be thought of as a naive child. Looking down at Gravois whose head only reached his shoulder, he asked, "When have I ever confided anything to you, Gravois?"

The man gave a sage nod. "You are right, of course, but what if I could make the Italian duke disappear?"

"Why would I wish that to happen?" Gide turned a bored stare over the crowd.

Gravois's smile was sly and made his features appear even more swinish than usual. "Then you would not have to worry about your sister's involvement with him. And you would gain the gratitude of the marquis."

"My sister is not involved with the Italian. She is Vernoux's woman. And I have tasted the gratitude of the marquis, a gift I would rather not have to accept again." Gide's memories of Vernoux's "generosity" made him physically ill. Every time the marquis bestowed something, he required some payback, usually in the form of Gide's painful sexual favors, a secret he had kept from Solange for many years.

"But what if this time, he would give you your freedom?" Gravois's little pig eyes flickered with cunning.

Gide snorted a laugh. "That will never happen."

With a shrug, Gravois said, "This time might be different. The Duke of Auriano might be someone Vernoux would sell his soul to be rid of."

"The marquis sold his soul a long time ago," Gide said. "Go away. Go report to your master and leave me alone before I have you thrown out."

"I'll leave," the fat little man said, "but think about my offer. Freedom would be sweet, *n'est-ce pas?*"

Gide turned away, dismissing him, but the temptation

of Gravois's suggestion of freedom was not so easy to block from his mind. What if, by doing away with Auriano, Gide could free both himself and Solange from their servitude to Vernoux? They would be able to flee Paris, perhaps buy a small farm in the country with the coins they had skimmed from their thievery. They could live their lives as they wished, without having to answer to anyone. For just a moment, he allowed the fantasy to entice him.

Solange's musical laughter drew his attention. His sister would never forgive him if he ever did anything so evil as what Gravois suggested. She was his only family, and he could not live knowing he had betrayed her trust.

Yet, the idea of freedom hovered like a seductive temptress in the back of his mind.

Chapter 3

Antonio watched the salon of *Madame* de Volonté from the shadows of a doorway across the street. Almost everyone had left. The oil lamp marking the nondescript entrance began to sputter as a man and two women emerged, chatting and laughing. They stepped up into the last carriage, and it creaked away down the cobblestones. The glow in the windows of the house dimmed as candles were extinguished. Antonio saw the pale light from a last, single lamp move from window to window as it was carried through the rooms.

He waited. The woman, Solange, would eventually make contact with someone. As he had left the small veranda, he heard snatches of her conversation with the man who had interrupted them. The young man wanted to call him out for propositioning her. All he heard of the rest of the conversation was that the two thieves were going to someone named Le Chacal and bring him coin and the moonstones. He suspected Le Chacal was the presence behind Solange's thievery and had told her of the moonstones. Antonio wanted to meet this person.

His thoughts turned to the seductive woman who'd confronted him this evening. *Madame* de Volonté. He surmised it was not her true name, but rather one that she had chosen, or one that had been chosen for her. It meant "willingness" or "will." Two words that could have different connotations. How *willing* was she to play the procurer for wealthy gentlemen looking for alternatives to their dull wives? What secret did she hide that *willed* her to the dangerous occupation of highwayman? A twinge of pity bit him at the idea that she was forced to live such a life.

Her first name seemed to be much more in keeping with who she was. Solange. A beautiful name for a beautiful woman. A beautiful woman who was deadly, who was a descendant of Halima and who had touched the Sphere of Astarte; who wielded knife and pistol like a man, yet exuded the bewitchery of a Circe. A woman who robbed with eyes of ice one night, and then seduced with glances of fire the next. He was well aware of the danger she presented. As soon as he caught his first glimpse of her as she strolled toward him this evening, he knew he would take the risk. He wanted her.

Badly.

He wanted her beneath him, above him, and in any other position he could possibly devise.

Brainless.

Madness.

The words of his twin, Alessandro, came back to him. *One of these days, Tonio, you'll find yourself with a blade in your back and floating face down in a canal.* In Venice, taking Alessandro's identity when his twin became Shadow, Antonio lived life on the edge, recklessly pursuing where he had no right to go, inviting danger along as if it were an old friend. He had done that out of frustration and desperation, hoping to lure any tidbit of information about the missing Sphere of Astarte into the open.

Unlike Venice, Paris had no canals, but it did have a river and plenty of dark alleys. Antonio was not about to end up as unidentified flotsam or refuse. In this city, he could be himself and pursue information in his own way. But he could not allow himself to become involved with a woman who might be connected with an enemy. Until he discovered whom she might be working for, he would keep his distance. And then . . .

29

He took a deep breath and let it out slowly, forcing himself back to sanity, willing away his desperate need, a need that echoed his cravings during the Hunger. Never before had anything from that insanity spilled over into his life as flesh and bone. Until now.

Across the street, the door opened, and a man stepped through. He was the one who had been so protective of *Madame* de Volonté. The man's physical resemblance to her indicated he was a relative, most likely a brother. When Antonio had brushed against him on his way out, he felt the man's energy, marking him as a descendant of Halima, just like Solange. He was young, just entering adulthood, but already he showed signs of strength in the width of his shoulders. Antonio suspected he might have been the other highwayman, the one who kept watch and aimed his pistol at Piero. Watching him move away down the street with masculine grace, Antonio knew the fellow would be dangerous in a fight, someone he would have to watch carefully.

He wondered where the young man was going, and he was tempted to follow, but his real quarry was *Madame* de Volonté. Solange. If she did not emerge soon to run to her master, he would steal inside. Then they would have a long private chat about thievery and deception and hidden power.

He did not have to wait long. The door opened once again, and she emerged, this time dressed as a highwayman. Just as she shut the door behind her, the lamp beside the entrance sputtered to its death. Keeping well back, he followed her.

She led him across the river and deeper into the city on the left bank. Occasionally, she would glance back over her shoulder, as if sensing he was behind her, but Antonio knew how to keep to the shadows. Wondering where she was leading him, he was prepared for a long trek that might take him into the slums or to the outskirts of the city. They passed through a small section of taverns, cafes, and cabarets where poets could recite their scribblings, all of the establishments dark and shuttered because of the late hour. Then the buildings turned residential, nearly rural with houses scattered here and there. She disappeared behind one of them. He followed, and beyond an open field in the scant moonlight, he saw one of the gatehouses in the crumbling remains of the city wall. She took a quick glance over her shoulder, then slipped inside.

Antonio raced across the field and stepped into the black interior of the structure. The flare of a torch from a stone archway lit a long flight of stone steps going down and indicated that she was below him and moving away rapidly. He followed.

With the torchlight as a guide, he kept well back from her. At the bottom of the stairs, another stone archway marked the beginning of a dirt tunnel sloping down, leading farther beneath the city. It was high enough for a man to stand and wide enough for a wagon to pass. Intrigued, puzzled, Antonio trailed her and wondered what this place was. Musky dampness rose up in a draft from below. He smelled dirt, rotting vegetation, and the coldness of death. His first thought was that it had been created by the sorceress, Nulkana, but he sensed no magic.

After several minutes, the tunnel opened into a small chamber. At the opposite side, Solange's torchlight moved away down another tunnel. Antonio stepped into the dim space and traced his fingers along the odd-looking walls covered in smooth rounds and long lengths, punctuated with holes and hollows. Not rock, nor any familiar building material.

Bones, he realized, and reeled back in horror. In the faint light of Solange's disappearing torch, he saw the walls had been covered with them, laid out in intricate patterns, the skulls used as delineation, borders, and focal points. He was in the Catacombs of Paris, that maze of tunnels and chambers that ran for miles beneath the city, where bones from disinterred bodies from the overflowing cemeteries had been placed. He had heard rumors of it but never suspected the stories were true.

He wasted no time on exploration. His quarry was moving quickly away and taking the light with her. Twenty quick steps took him across the chamber to the second tunnel's entrance.

As he followed her, he felt a faint thrumming through his muscles, a sensation that was familiar. Excitement rippled through him. Somewhere hidden within the Catacombs was a piece of the Sphere of Astarte. He had felt the same sensation when he had been close to the piece which his twin, Alessandro, had received from his new wife, Sabrina. He knew now that another piece of the Sphere was close. He would just have to find it in this maze. That would mean his family would have two-thirds of the Sphere.

Solange led him down several more tunnels, some lined with piles of bones, others with plain dirt walls, then the torchlight halted. Cautiously, he crept forward and peered around the edge of the tunnel. A chamber larger than the other opened before him with several tunnels leading out from it. It was empty. Solange had disappeared. She had placed the torch in a wall bracket to fool him into thinking she had stopped.

Wily beauty.

A wry smile touched his lips.

He walked the chamber's perimeter and examined the bone-covered walls as he tried to guess which tunnel Solange had taken. The workmen who'd placed the bones here had been skilled, plying their material with a grim sense of humor. He saw a skull and crossbones created with real bones, skulls set in the shape of a heart, leg bones placed to resemble water, more skulls in the shape of a cross. He stopped in the middle of the chamber and listened. No sound of footsteps reached his ears. No light came from any of the tunnels. All he heard was a distant, faint drip of water. He had lost her. An irritated sigh escaped him. He had been tricked so easily.

Staring at the tunnel which led him there, he realized he was lost. Finding his way through the maze back to the surface would be nearly impossible. A kick of fear sped up his heart. He had not planned on ending his life in the Catacombs of Paris. Despite his dire situation, he appreciated the irony. At least he was already in a cemetery of sorts.

Suddenly, the sharp, chill edge of a knife pressed against his throat. He froze. From behind him, Solange said, "Your manners are lacking, *mon seigneur*, for entering a place where you have not been invited."

He silently congratulated her and berated himself for his stupidity. "I was unaware this was private property," he said.

Without taking away the blade, she moved around to stand in front of him. "Why are you following me?" Her voice vibrated with anger.

He raised a brow in mild curiosity. "Why are you so worried I might be following you? Are you doing something illegal?" He let his gaze take in the chamber beyond her shoulder. "There are no coaches down here to rob. Or perhaps you are contemplating something illicit." His glance traveled down to her toes and then up again. "Not illicit," he concluded. "Not dressed like a highwayman."

Her mouth tightened. "How I dress is not your concern."

"But it is my concern, for I find removing the clothes of a man holds different challenges than those of a woman," he said, as if he were merely trying to convince her of some menial point.

The knife pressed harder. "Did you follow me here to seduce me?"

His lips curved teasingly.

"No," she concluded. "Not to seduce."

He showed his teeth in his smile. "How can you be sure?"

Uncertainty flashed through her eyes. The pressure of the knife eased. Taking advantage, he swept away her arm holding the knife, slipped his other arm around her waist, swung her around and pressed her into the wall. Brittle bones cracked behind her. He pinned her knife hand above her head. Beneath his palm, he could feel her power, inherited from Halima, pulsing through her wrist. He wondered if she knew how strong it was. Throwing away caution in favor of discovery, he decided to provoke her.

"I do not take kindly to anyone who holds a knife at my throat, and you have done it twice," he said.

She glared at him, her eyes like two hard jewels. "I do not take kindly to anyone who follows me and intrudes on my affairs," she snapped.

"Since you robbed me, I would say that your affairs have become my affairs." Ducking his head, he placed a light kiss on her jaw. "Perhaps what we need to do," he murmured, "is become involved in the same affair."

She jerked her head away. "I would rather die."

"Like the virgin in your rhyme?" he taunted.

"I am no virgin." She tried to squirm away.

"That eases my concern," he said with false sigh of relief. "Deflowering a virgin takes so much concentration."

She hissed and squirmed more.

He pressed her body tighter against the wall. The feel of her trapped along his length brought to mind a number of delicious images. The perfume she had worn earlier, an enticing mixture of roses and cinnamon, teased his nose. Reminding himself he was not here to seduce, only to learn her secrets, he could not help baiting her.

"Ah, *madame*," he murmured, "if you move like that, I can give you *la petite mort* right now."

* * *

Solange immediately stilled. His words both chilled and enticed. *La petite mort.* The little death. The ultimate sexual release. She had a feeling that this man could give her that with little trouble, and he would do it expertly, exquisitely, gloriously. His body pressed against her, from shoulder to thigh. It was taut with muscle and controlled strength. At her hip, his arousal subtly nudged her, but he did not act on that need. Even as he captured her and held her prisoner, he was gentle, careful not to hurt her. So in opposition to Vernoux, who would hurt her to prove his dominance, who would beat her if he learned she had been with another man, who would take her violently to mark her as his. The notion of giving herself to this Italian duke who held her with such constraint tempted with the force of the devil's allure. But she could not allow herself to be seduced into any attachment to him, for one way or another, she planned to use him to free herself from Vernoux.

Beyond Auriano's shoulder, she saw torchlight coming from one of the tunnels. Le Chacal's men who patrolled the Catacombs. Her rescuers. Their arrival forced her to dispel any daydreams of *la petite mort* with the man pressed against her. "If you do not let me go, *mon seigneur*, your death will not be *une petite*," she said.

He tipped his head thoughtfully. "Death is always a release, whether large or small, *si*? Don't you wish for release, *dolce mia?*"

Staring at him, she wondered how much he knew or guessed about her. What release did he refer to? The sensuous, sexual one he taunted her with, or the psychological, physical one that bound her to Vernoux? Before she could decide, his head went up as he heard the men. Then he smiled down at her, a soft, sardonic smile.

"Release sometimes comes sooner than we expect, *si?*" Stepping back, he let her go.

* * *

When Antonio heard the approaching footsteps, he considered running, but the tunnels were dark and confusing. He was already lost, and eluding the men who came would no doubt only drive him deeper into the maze. Besides, he had expected to meet *Madame* de Volonté's master. What better way than to be captured and brought before the man as prisoner? Later, he could easily escape, for in a few hours, he would turn to Shadow.

Behind him, he heard the men enter the chamber and then halt. Solange pushed away from the wall and stepped to the side, showing herself, the cool, detached highwayman. Before she turned her attention to his captors, she sent one last glance his way.

"Let us see how you can escape this difficulty, *mon seigneur*," she murmured, those beautiful eyes challenging, mocking.

Antonio smiled. "Ah, *bella mia*, you have no idea what I can do."

Her lovely mouth tightened, and she turned away. "Le Marteau, Roux," she greeted the thugs with a nod. "We have a guest." With a gesture, she ordered the men to take him prisoner.

The two of them made an odd pair. One was shorter than Antonio but bulkier, with a bald pate and a full beard that was braided in several places. Sporting an iron hoop through each earlobe, he wore a leather jerkin with no shirt, revealing his thick arms. The other man was taller than his companion, thin, almost gaunt. His hair hung in greasy spirals to his shoulders, and one eye was cloudy. He sported a large, red birthmark that ran up the side of his neck and splashed across his cheek.

Antonio assumed he was Roux—Red—and the other was Le Marteau—the Hammer. They each appeared capable of murder. Neither man was particularly gentle when they took hold of Antonio's arms.

"Gentlemen," he said on a sigh, "I'm very willing to go with you. You don't need to ruin my coat."

In surprise, the men looked to Solange, who narrowed her eyes at Antonio. "It's all right," she told them. "Don't let him escape." Turning on her heel, she took the torch from its bracket and led the way into one of the tunnels.

The two outlaws released Antonio, and one of them gave him a hard shove. With an arrogant glare at them both, Antonio brushed at his sleeves, then followed Solange. The thugs trailed close behind.

Even as he took notice of the way they passed, he found his gaze returning to the woman walking before him. The contrast between the male clothing she wore and the very feminine sway of her hips riveted him. Having seen her dressed as a woman only a few short hours earlier, he wished the man's coat did not hide quite so much.

The tunnel ran straight for about fifty paces, then curved abruptly to the left. Solange hopped across a rivulet, then tossed back over her shoulder, "Walk only where I walk." She kept close to the right side of the tunnel.

Antonio glanced at the floor and saw a herringbone pattern of stones down the middle. Scuffing his shoe, he sent tiny pebbles across the path. Some of them fell through cracks between the stones and echoed as they landed far below—a trap for anyone who did not know his way. After another few paces, the tunnel narrowed to the width of one man, and a gate, about shoulder high, blocked their way. Solange picked up a small square stone and pushed it into a matching hole in the wall, then she opened the gate. A mechanism above her head clicked into place. Antonio glanced up, and six feet above the gate, the sharpened edge of a guillotine blade gleamed with deadly menace.

Solange grinned at him. "A souvenir of the Terror and a way to discourage unwanted visitors if they make it past the Grave," she said, as she stepped through the open gate.

Antonio assumed the Grave was the trap in the floor under those patterned stones. Passing beneath the blade, he worked not to duck his head and hunch his shoulders. They walked for several more minutes, then the tunnel curved to the right. Ahead was an arch made of skulls. Light and voices reached him.

He followed Solange through the arch and entered a very large chamber. The walls were plain, gray stone, but the ceiling was decorated with bones and skulls, a mockery of the glorious ceilings found in the churches of Venice, Rome, and Florence. Men lounged about its perimeter and across the floor, covered in a motley assortment of tiles, no doubt pilfered from various looted mansions in the city. A few women moved among the group with pitchers. Other women curled about some of the men. Seated at the far end of the chamber on a large, carved, throne-like stone chair was a man who watched them approach with the attention of a vulture. As they came closer, he dumped the woman who sprawled across his lap onto the floor. He was not quite middle-aged, wiry, with shoulder-length hair the color of dirty straw. Clean-shaven, he had a scar that ran through his eyebrow, across his eye, and down his cheek. He was missing his right hand.

Solange stopped a few feet away. Placing a hand on her hip, she assumed a pose of arrogant unconcern.

"Solange Delacroix," the seated man drawled.

Antonio took note of her name. So, *Madame* de Volonté was an alias. Interesting.

She nodded a greeting. "Jean-Jacques."

The man leaned his chin on his tattered silk-and-lace-covered stump and graced her with a cool smile. "You know that you are the only one I allow to call me that."

"And you are the only one I come to visit in this hell," she replied.

"Then I am honored," he said, the chilliness in his eyes brightening to amusement. "What have you brought me, *ma petit vache?*"

My little bitch. Antonio stiffened at the man's name for Solange. Before he could protest, he was shoved roughly to his knees.

"Kneel before Le Chacal, *le Roi des Voleurs*," the bald man behind him ordered.

Antonio gazed at the Jackal, the King of the Thieves. So this was Solange's master, the man for whom she stole. He surmised the man seated before him held some threat over her. Otherwise, why would she bother to risk her life as a highwayman when she appeared to have a safe, easy existence running her salon? Le Chacal must be a powerful leader, for the men around him all had a look of deadly intent, each of them capable of violence, each of them capable of taking the man's leadership. Antonio realized he would have to be very careful if he wished to leave this chamber alive.

Le Chacal's rapacious gaze swept over him, then focused on Solange. "Well?"

Ignoring Antonio, Solange said, "My brother has brought our tribute."

She swept her hand to the side. The man who had protected her at her salon, who had left her house before her, stepped forward. Antonio's guess at their familial relation had been correct. The man tossed Antonio's pouch of coins—not his ring, not the moonstones—and Le Chacal caught it neatly.

The King of the Thieves weighed the pouch in his single

hand. "Heavy. A good night's work. Some rich bastard is a few coins poorer, eh, Gide?"

Gide jerked his chin in Antonio's direction. "Him."

Antonio felt the tension rise. The two men behind him shuffled closer. Le Chacal's dark eyes focused on him with a predatory glare. Although Solange had not moved, Antonio knew by the tiny pull at the corner of her mouth she was unhappy with her brother. He decided at that moment if he had to fight his way out, he would take her with him, and then the two of them would have that delayed chat.

"Why did you bring him here?" Le Chacal's question was posed in the gentlest of tones, suggesting that the one who answered should be wary.

Solange shrugged. "He followed me."

"So." Le Chacal raised a brow, stretching his scar and turning his face ghoul-like. He glared at Antonio. "Why were you following *ma petite vache*?"

"I was curious about the reason why a beautiful woman should disguise herself as a boy," Antonio said, "and rob an innocent man." He turned to gaze speculatively at Solange. "But perhaps the disguise only makes one more aware of the charms beneath." Playing the besotted suitor was the only excuse he could think of that Le Chacal might accept for his presence.

The man made a sound of disgust. "You are a fool if you think she would allow you access to those charms." His eyes hardened and cut to Solange. "Have I not taught you to be more careful when you come here? You have brought a stranger. You know what must be done."

With a jerk, Solange dropped her hand from her hip and straightened. "He had the moonstone."

Le Chacal's head snapped up as he looked from Solange to Antonio and then back to her. "Where is it?"

"It is someplace safe." Her words were flat, implacable.

A slow smile spread across the criminal's face, twisting

his scar. "Ah, *bon*." His satisfied comment revealed that he was the person who had told Solange about the moonstone. Or . . . perhaps it was the other way around.

Antonio met the outlaw's eyes and saw the next words there before the man uttered them.

"Kill him."

The bald, bulky man grabbed Antonio's hair and yanked his head back. The tall man with the cloudy eye pulled a knife. It hovered above Antonio's exposed throat. He had already felt cold metal against his skin once this night. He did not appreciate a repeat. If his blood were to be spilled, it would mingle with that of others. He shifted his arm, preparing to release the stiletto hidden up his sleeve.

"Wait." Solange took a step forward.

Le Chacal turned his annoyed gaze on her. The knife at Antonio's throat stilled.

She dug in her pocket, held up the silken cord with one of the moonstones, and tossed it to Le Chacal. Out of the corner of his eye, Antonio saw dismay cross her brother's face. So, they had been planning to use the moonstone for some other purpose than bargaining for his life. And even more interesting, they only gave up one stone.

Plucking the stone out of the air, Le Chacal examined it, turning it over several times. He bent forward and casually leaned an arm across his knee. "What can you tell me about this?" he asked Antonio in a deadly quiet tone.

Antonio wondered what the man knew about the purpose of the stone. If he drew him out, trying to gain information, he would be revealing his own knowledge. He decided to keep Le Chacal as ignorant as possible.

"Nothing," he said. "I bought it from a peddler." He could feel Solange's gaze on him and hoped she would remain silent.

Sitting back in his chair, Le Chacal stared thoughtfully at Antonio for a moment. Then dismissively, he repeated, "Kill him."

"Stop!" Solange held up her hand. "He's an Italian duke. If you kill him, you'll have many more problems with the Directory than you have now. They'll have their troops double their efforts to catch you."

With a shrug, Le Chacal said, "The Directory does not concern me, nor does one Italian duke more or less. If he knows nothing about the stone, then he is of no use."

"He's lying. He knows how the moonstone works." Beneath her bald statement lay an unmistakable note of desperation.

Le Chacal's speculative gaze landed on her. "*Ma petite vache*, I think you have some soft feelings for this man."

"That is ridiculous." She sniffed in disdain.

"Of course it is," Le Chacal murmured sardonically. "I am sure the Marquis de Vernoux would be interested in hearing your denials."

Antonio blinked at the name. He had stepped into a nest of vipers. His brother had met Vernoux when Alessandro had saved Sabrina from the Legion of Baal, and the outlaw's comment hinted that the Marquis de Vernoux was Solange's protector.

Le Chacal heaved a sigh. "Very well, you may have your plaything for now. We will see how much he knows of the moonstone." With a wave of his stump, he said, "Put him in the Chamber of Ghosts."

Antonio wondered why Solange had bargained for his life, but the thought was very short-lived. The knife was pulled away from his throat. He saw it flipped in the air. Blinding pain exploded as the hilt smashed into his skull. The last thing he saw before blackness claimed him was the furious look on the face of Solange's brother.

Chapter 4

When Antonio regained consciousness, he was immediately aware of three things: he was lying on his side on something very hard and cold, his head was pillowed on something soft, and cool fingertips stroked his temple. He knew who owned the fingers. And the pillow beneath his head was her lap. Rolling onto his back, he bit down on a groan as pain shafted through his head. The rattle of a chain and the grip of metal around his ankle told him he was shackled. He would deal with that later. Gingerly, he opened his eyes. Total blackness confronted him.

"I think I'm blind," he muttered dolefully.

He heard Solange chuckle. It sounded hollow as it reverberated in the space. "No, not blind. It is very dark." She continued to stroke his brow.

The touch of her fingers soothed the pounding pain in his skull. Her statement reassured him.

"You saved my life," he said. *"Grazie."*

"You are most welcome, *mon seigneur.*" Her tone was tinged with amusement.

He decided the blow to his head must have addled his brain, because he could not dredge up a single good reason why she had become his savior. "Why didn't you let Le Chacal kill me?"

"I thought you would prefer that did not happen." Her words were spoken lightly. He knew she would not give a true answer if he probed further.

"Why are you here?" he asked instead.

She sighed. Her fingers did not stop their caress, but they trembled. "This is my punishment for allowing you to follow me."

Guilt pinched him, but if he had not followed her, he would not have met Le Chacal and discovered several interesting items. For instance, the Marquis de Vernoux, Solange's protector, was connected to the outlaw. Antonio suspected that the marquis, as a member of the Legion of Baal, was behind the theft of the moonstones and aware of their ability to relieve the Hunger. With the Legion in possession of the moonstones, the Auriano family would be weaker because they would have to deal with both the curse of becoming Shadow and the Hunger as they emerged from that state. The information confirmed what his sister had said in her letter. The Legion was becoming more aggressive in their attempts to gain the pieces of the Sphere of Astarte.

Was the woman who so gently caressed his brow an agent of the Legion, or was she an unwitting pawn? Was her presence in the dark a ruse to get him to disclose information, or truly a punishment for her carelessness? He needed those answers quickly. Very soon, he would turn to Shadow, revealing the curse to her. He was not about to give her that knowledge.

He would have to Thought Bind with her, to get inside her mind to discover her loyalties. The idea of invading her private thoughts made him cringe, but his situation was grave. He wrapped his hand around Solange's wrist. Her soothing caresses stopped, and he pressed his fingers gently against her pulse. It raced beneath his touch.

"You are afraid," he observed.

"No." Her pulse jumped, revealing her lie.

He could relieve that fear to discover more about her. "What has frightened you?" His thumb moved in soft circles against the back of her hand.

"We are in the Chamber of Ghosts, *mon seigneur*. It

44

is said that the spirits that live here can suck your soul. That is only a myth. The ghosts are here because of the rats. The rats will eat you alive. I am not frightened, but I do not wish to be here." Despite the bravery of her words, her trembling contradicted them.

"You speak as if you have personal knowledge of this place," he said.

"I have been here once before." Her tone was wry.

"You have obviously escaped," he observed.

She gave another soft chuckle. "In a way. Le Chacal cannot afford to allow me to be disfigured by an attack of rats. He would lose a hefty stipend, perhaps even his life."

"By the Marquis de Vernoux," he guessed.

"*Oui.* Their relationship is complicated. And I . . . well . . ." She took a breath as if gathering courage. "Le Chacal will release me when he hears my screams of terror."

His brow wrinkled in confusion. "Why don't you scream, then, and get released?"

She paused, then gave a little sigh. "He knows if the screams are false. So I wait to be horrified, and he waits to hear me scream."

Her punishment was real, and her courage touched him. Even if she were an agent of the Legion of Baal, she had put herself at risk to bargain for his life. Yet, her fear gave him an opening into discovering her motives. "Let me help you," he said.

She chuckled wryly. "How can you help me, *Monsieur le Duc*? You are in the dark with me, and you are chained to the floor."

He could hear the rats beginning to gather at the far side of the chamber, scrambling along the ridges of bones. The click of their claws, the rush of their bodies in the thick dark was disconcerting, even to him. He needed to hurry, but Thought Binding was not a process to rush. Taking a breath, he forced his heart rate to slow.

He laid her hand against his chest and continued to caress her pulse.

"You have no idea what I can do, *bella mia*," he murmured, repeating the words he had spoken earlier. "Don't be afraid. Let me help." Ruthlessly, he lured her in.

* * *

To Solange, his fingers against her pulse were reassuring. His thumb stroked the back of her hand, across her knuckles and then around in circles. She could feel his heartbeat beneath her palm, and somehow, it matched perfectly with her own.

"Let me help, *dolce mia*," he repeated in a whisper.

His words were more than mere sound. They seemed to be a comforting cushion inside her head. In the dank chamber, she felt warmth seep through her. She gasped at the sensation, then released a sigh as her fear receded.

How had he done that? She could not allow herself to be seduced by soft words and a tender touch. Too much was a stake. Her life and that of her brother's.

"I am here with you, Solange." His voice was gentle, subdued. "Don't be afraid. I won't let them get you."

For some reason, she believed him, she trusted him. Logically, he should have been the last person to trust. She had stolen from him, and he had reacted with chilling boldness, pursuing to exact revenge. Yet, even when he had the chance, he had not hurt her.

She sensed another presence in her head, one that surrounded her with security, safety. It seemed to rock her softly, holding her in a warm embrace. No one had held her like that in a very long time. The sensation was bitter-sweet, reminding her of what she had lost, making her want it again. Tears stung her eyes. She blinked them away. The presence in her head demanded nothing, only soothed and cradled her. As it consoled her, she dropped her defenses. She sensed a gentle probing.

"Show me, Solange."

No, she couldn't. Horror crawled through her, shriveling her insides.

"I will keep you safe."

His murmured words came at the same time she felt that presence grow softer, wider, more encompassing, encasing her in a cocoon of protection.

Safe.

She could not remember a time when she had felt safe, although she knew that once, long ago, she had not expected to feel any other way.

"Show me, Solange."

His whisper was not a command, but rather an enticement, an offer to share her burden. So she opened her mind and brought out the memory that haunted her, that made her tremble and sweat, that brought her awake screaming in the middle of the night.

She was in the Chamber of Ghosts. Gide huddled close beside her. They were children. Jean-Jacques had put them here, had betrayed them, tricked them. He had wanted them to steal for him, and she refused. So she and her brother sat on the cold stone floor, in dark so black it was like a weight on her eyes.

Then she heard them. The rats. The patter of their feet on the stones. Their scurrying. The scrunching of their teeth on the bones. She remembered what came next. Their tentative approach. Gide's cries of terror as he kicked out at them. Her own horror when she felt their snouts against her ankle.

The scream built in her throat.

"Shh . . . Solange. You are safe. I won't let them hurt you."

His voice curled around her, calming her. She had survived, but the memory continued.

The rats had come then, swarming around them. At the sharp bite just above her ankle, she had flung out her arm, and the power ripped from her fingers in a flash. Astounded at what she had done, she sat very still. Until they came again, and once more that energy jumped from her fingers. She killed dozens of the creatures, but the flare of light revealed hundreds more, their eyes red and hungry. And then as the creatures slowed their attacks, around the walls, she saw in the flashes what she had not seen before—skeletons, bodies, decimated, chewed, chained to the floor. Past feasts of the rats.

Horror clawed at her. Panic at what would happen to her, to Gide, snagged at her. The power in her froze.

After a time, the rats attacked again.

All she could do was scream.

Solange.

Her name whispered in her brain. Like that presence that cushioned her, his voice calmed her.

Brave Solange.

She shook her head in denial, even though she knew he could not see.

They cannot hurt you. You can destroy them.

She shook her head again.

You can. You have tremendous power.

She knew that. Somewhere deep inside, she knew she was powerful. But she had forgotten.

He had gifted her with the memory. The memory of her magic. Something she thought she had lost. Vernoux had taken her, used her, made her believe she had no power.

But this man had caught a glimpse. Instead of taking, he had given. Without thought, she leaned down and placed her lips against his. His mouth was warm. He accepted her kiss pliantly, willingly, yet she sensed restraint as well. That presence in her mind swirled with color, but then receded as if holding back, as if waiting to see what she would do. He did not deepen the kiss but allowed her to take it in any direction she chose. Vernoux had never done that. She and Vernoux had never kissed.

Drawing away, she felt tears of gratitude sting her eyes.

"Do not thank me yet." His quietly spoken words were like a splash of water on her face.

What had she done? She wanted to erase that moment of weakness, take back that kiss. She wanted to pull back the memory she had shown him and smother it beneath layers of denial. With a jerk, she tried to break free from his grasp. He would not allow it.

The presence in her head grew softer.

Solange. Trust me.

She heard the voice in her head. "Why?" Her question whispered in the dark.

The presence in her head receded until it was only a thin filament.

"I want Le Chacal to release you so that I can escape," he said aloud.

Reality hit her. Laughter bordering on hysteria bubbled up at the absurdity of his statement. "There is no escape from here, *mon seigneur*."

"There is," he assured her. "But I have to do it alone. You have to scream, Solange, so Le Chacal will release you."

"He will know it is deception."

"He won't know. Trust me, please, Solange."

She contemplated his request. She had no reason to trust him, except that he had reminded her of what she could do. And he had not inflicted any pain. But she had stolen from him. He had every right to be angry, to seek revenge.

On the other side of the chamber, she could hear the rats gnawing, scratching, scrabbling in the dark. Soon, they would gather, and one or two would venture out seeking food, and then the rest would come.

He spoke again. "The rats won't hurt you. You have the power to destroy them. But you have to remember the horror. You have to make Le Chacal release you. You have to scream."

"So that you may escape? That is impossible." She shook her head even though he could not see.

I'm in your head, Solange. Do you truly doubt what I can do?

As he said the words, she felt a caress through her mind. It sent a wave of warmth through her body, tender, sweet. She gasped. He had to be very powerful to be able to do that. Perhaps he could escape.

He had not taken advantage of his ability to invade her thoughts, to strip her emotionally naked. Instead, he had comforted her. He did not force her, and she knew he could. That fact alone convinced her.

"*Oui.* I will scream," she said.

"*Bene,*" he whispered, as his fingers pressed firmly against her pulse. "I'm sorry. This will be frightening."

Before she had time to change her mind, his presence filled her head again, at first gently, softly, reassuringly. It grew and turned menacing and dark. She wanted to escape, but there was no place to go. It dragged at her memories and pulled out the one she had just showed him. The rats. She heard them, their feet, their claws, their teeth. She heard them gathering. She felt them brushing against her, their paws on her, their bodies wriggling over her. As she tried to push them away, they only came faster. This was worse than her memory. That presence had changed it, twisted it to something more terrifying, more horrific than it had ever been. She whined as panic claimed her. No, no, no. Get away.

She fought for breath. They covered her, suffocated her. Their teeth nipped at her ankles. Her legs. Her arms. They bit at her face.

Screeching, she lashed out.

* * *

Antonio winced at the pain that lanced through his head. Not his pain, but hers. The rats held her, but something else threatened as well. Dark, looming, menacing, it whirled through her mind as if it were alive. It fed on her fright.

Startled at the chaos and her flailing arms, Antonio became disoriented, almost losing both his physical and mental connection with her. He wished he could help. He knew he could not. She had to scream so that Le Chacal's men would come for her.

He restrained her hand against his chest and latched onto the thin, bright line that was their mental connection. Shoving away that other malevolent thing, he concentrated on her memory of the rats, exaggerated it, made it more horrific. He culled his own dark recesses to amplify the threat. The rats multiplied, grew larger, more aggressive.

She shook. And cried. She brushed wildly at the invisible rats. Antonio squeezed his fingers around her wrist, anchoring her to him. Gulping air, she screamed, and her terror expelled itself. The walls echoed her fear, amplifying it until her screams became a mantle of noise. The palm of her free hand sparked. Flinging it wide, her energy flashed, exploding on the opposite wall, again and again.

Antonio caught her other wrist, found the source of her power in her mind and smothered it. He could not let Le Chacal know what Solange could do. With her power shut down, Solange's screams turned to whimpers. Slowly, she started to shrink into herself, retreating to a place in her mind where he would never be able to retrieve her. Before she closed herself off from everything, at the last moment, he wrapped a thin cord of sanity around her, grounding her.

I am here, Solange, he told her.

Her whimpers turned silent, and he felt tears hit his cheek.

He saw the flicker of torches coming from the tunnel. Their jailers, coming to release her. Relieved that he could finally give her respite from her terror, he pulled back the darkness and surrounded her with comfort.

Shh . . . Solange, dolce mia. The rats are gone.

He sensed her surprise before the effects of shock took hold of her. The pulse beneath his fingers raced unevenly. Her skin turned cold, her breathing fast and shallow.

Solange, you are safe. Sleep now.

With a final swirl through her mind, he erased everything he had just done, making her forget. As if he were pulling draperies across windows, he shut down her awareness, and then gradually broke their connection. Scrambling up, he caught her just before she collapsed into a boneless mass and laid her gently on the floor.

When Le Chacal's men entered to retrieve her, he was kicking at the few rats that had crept too close.

The two outlaws ignored him as they gathered up Solange as if she were a piece of baggage. He watched as they retreated back down the tunnel, Solange slung like a sack over one of their shoulders. The flare from the torch receded, finally leaving him in total darkness.

And just in time. He could already feel the curse taking hold.

Chapter 5

The next night, Antonio blended with the shadows beside her bed as he watched her sleep. Solange. So beautiful. So deceitful. So brave. So terrified.

The full moon had come the night before, and with it, the curse. He welcomed it, for it allowed him to slip the shackle on his leg and escape from the Chamber of Ghosts. He had followed the faint torchlight from Solange's rescuers and melded with the shadows at the edges of Le Chacal's salon. When one of the outlaws left to go above ground, Antonio had trailed him.

Before him now, Solange murmured, but she was still caught within her slumber. Antonio let his gaze travel around her bedchamber, over the dark shapes of furniture, into the black corners. He had searched the room for the other moonstone and his thumb ring. That had been an exercise in futility. She had hidden them very well, perhaps somewhere else in the house, perhaps somewhere in the city or in the woods. He suspected she had not disposed of the second stone. With her power, it must call to her, forging a connection. But when the Hunger took him over, he would need it more than she. The stone dissipated the dark, savage cravings he experienced when he transformed from Shadow to flesh and bone. That would happen in a fortnight. He hoped he could find it before then.

The missing thumb ring puzzled him. She had not given it to Le Chacal, and he wondered why. It was gold, valuable. He doubted she had sold it on her own.

He had a feeling that the King of the Thieves would learn of any deception. So where was she hiding the two pieces she had stolen? He would need to gain her trust in order to get her to reveal where she had secreted them. Not an easy task. The woman lying before him, despite her sweetly soft appearance, was complex and wily.

The moonlight streamed through the window, skimmed over her, turned her into an ethereal creature. Curled into a tight little ball, she grasped a pillow to her as if it were the only thing keeping her alive. Perhaps it was, at least at this moment.

The night before in the Chamber of Ghosts, after he had terrified her by using her own memories against her, he had seen not only her strength but also her vulnerability. He had gained some understanding of this woman sleeping before him.

He regretted making her scream, but the outlaws had taken her from the chamber just as he began his transformation to Shadow. He wondered what Le Chacal's reaction had been when he discovered his prisoner had disappeared, leaving behind a pile of clothes and a locked shackle. Amusement rippled through him.

Solange murmured again and gripped the pillow tighter. Her dreams were not pleasant. Guiltily, he wondered if the nightmares she suffered were magnified by what he had done. If his brother, Alessandro, ever discovered how he had used Thought Binding against her, his twin would bestow on him a tongue-lashing of epic proportions. The irony was that he himself had been angry when Alessandro had used it on Sabrina. That had resolved itself when Sabrina learned of her power. And then Alessandro had married her.

Watching Solange sleep, Antonio wanted to reach out and comfort her. He raised his hand to soothe away her distress. And stopped, curling his fingers into his palm. He looked down at his hand, dark, no longer flesh and bone.

He was Shadow now. He could taste nothing, smell nothing, feel nothing. Except, perhaps, this woman.

His hand dropped to his side. He refused to touch her. He would not fall into the same trap as his twin, even though that had ended happily. When Alessandro had been Shadow and touched Sabrina, he had been able to feel her, and so he craved her to the point of madness when he entered the Hunger.

Antonio did not want to crave this woman sleeping before him. He would not go mad over a woman, not even one as alluring as the one before him, not even one who could bring him closer to his ultimate prize, the piece of the Sphere of Astarte. He meant to use her until she gave up her secrets. All of them—her connection to the moonstone, her power, the location of the piece of the Sphere.

He would gain her trust by helping her to steal. Then he would get her to help him retrieve the piece of the Sphere. He merely had to convince her.

It was time to wake her.

* * *

Solange.

She heard her name as if from a far corner of her mind.

Solange.

The voice dragged her away from her dream, a confusion of darkness and swirling colors, menace, pain, and fear.

Solange.

Her eyes snapped open. She blinked, and focused on the dark room, the shapes of furniture in the moonlight. Nothing threatened. Everything felt familiar, and she lay still while her heartbeat slowed. She was alone.

Solange.

She gasped. Not alone. A voice called in her head. She remembered another who had done that, but she had left him behind in the Chamber of Ghosts. Guilt pricked her, but she could not afford compassion. He was a threat to the precarious safety she had woven around her life and Gide's.

Solange.

This time, the voice held just the tiniest exasperation. Slowly, she rolled to her back. Curious, afraid of what she might see, she peered into the shadows. Out of the night, at the side of her bed, a form appeared, hovering there like some dark angel. With eyes like molten gold, it was blacker than the night around it, as if all light had been sucked into its form. It was a shadow of the dark.

Her breath left her lungs in a rush.

Hello, Solange.

She stared, frozen, not daring to move. The frightening vestiges of her dream still clung to the borders of her mind. What if something from that dark realm had materialized?

I won't hurt you.

Illogically, the creature's reassurance calmed her. The vague memory of another voice calming and reassuring hovered in the back of her mind, but that was in the Catacombs. The shadowman's voice sounded familiar, but she knew she had never seen nor heard such a creature before.

Will you scream?

The question surprised her. She should be terrified but found she was not, only apprehensive at finding such a creature in her bedchamber. Her scream would certainly rouse Gide, sleeping just across the hall.

"I'll scream if I feel the need," she said.

I won't hurt you, the shadowman repeated more emphatically.

"How do I know that?"

Amusement tinged the shadowman's reply. *If I wished*

to harm you, I could have done so before now. You dream deeply.

Annoyed, embarrassed that this creature had been watching her sleep, she snapped, "You take liberties." She wished she had some weapon close at hand.

He laughed. *Si.*

At that single word, her eyes widened. The creature was Italian? Was it somehow connected to Auriano? "What are you? Why are you here? What do you want?" Her questions tumbled one after the other.

So many questions. It tipped its head thoughtfully. *If we are to have a conversation, would you mind if I make myself comfortable?*

She paused, bemused at his courtesy. Not quite sure how such a creature could make itself comfortable, she gave a vague wave of her hand. At her gesture, it stepped up onto the bed and half-walked, half-floated to perch on the footboard. It had exerted no weight on the mattress. She could see the faint outline of its muscles rippling as it moved. Powerful. Beautiful. Frightening. Naked. Definitely male.

Feeling vulnerable lying on her back, Solange pushed herself up and clutched the covers to her. She took stock of anything near that she might use as a weapon—the candlestick on the table next to the bed, a glass that Vernoux had left. She regretted that her dagger lay in the bottom of the wardrobe across the room.

You will not need your knife, he said.

She gasped. "How did you know . . .?"

With a soft chuckle, he said, *You can hear my voice in your head. I have many talents.*

"If you can read my mind, why are we bothering with a conversation?" she demanded.

I never said I could read your mind. Then he teased, *I know that you are more comfortable with a knife in your hand.*

Irritated at his arrogance, she said, "You seem to know a great deal about me, while I know nothing about you."

What would you like to know, Solange?

His question was straightforward, but when he said her name, she felt a light caress across her mind, as if fingers gently brushed against her. The sensation raised the tiny hairs on her arms, and the nape of her neck tingled. She pulled the covers closer and higher.

"Stop that," she ordered.

He said nothing, but she sensed his amusement.

Scowling, she said, "If you are going to play games, then get out."

He chuckled. *But games are so delightful, bella mia.*

She lapsed into confounded, annoyed silence at his teasing. She was surprised that he had not pointed out the absurdity of her making him leave.

Sobering, he said, *I will behave. Ask your questions.*

"What are you? Why are you here? What do you want?"

You can see what I am. I am here because of you. I think we might be able to help each other.

She sat up straighter. "How can you help me?"

You are a thief. I can help you steal.

Narrowing her eyes in suspicion, she asked, "Why would you want to do that?"

Instead of answering, he asked, *Wouldn't you like to steal more than a few trinkets from weary travelers?*

"I get more than mere trinkets," she said mulishly.

What if I could help you steal more in one night than you could get in months of stalking the highways? He asked his question as if he were murmuring sweet enticements.

Solange refused to be persuaded. "What do you get out of helping me?"

I am looking for something. You can help me steal it. His tone was serious.

"What are you looking for?" Suspicion mixed with curiosity in her question.

Something quite valuable. The flatness of his statement revealed that he desperately wanted this thing, whatever it was.

"How valuable? Like gold? Jewels?" She kept her tone level, hiding the surge of excitement at possibly acquiring a fortune.

Do you truly think I need your help to steal such things? He chuckled again and shook his head. *What I am looking for appears to have little value, but is quite precious to me.*

His circumspect response made her wonder what the item could be. Then the memory of the moonstones popped into her head. Could he be after those as well as Le Chacal? Instead of revealing her knowledge of the stones, she asked instead, "Why did you choose me?"

Because you are beautiful.

She hissed in annoyance at his flippant answer.

Do you not know how beautiful you are?

His question was a seductive murmur, and she felt warmth color her cheeks. She had not blushed in a very long time. Embarrassed that he had been able to provoke such a response from her, she snapped, "I don't need help. I work alone."

No, you do not. Your brother thieves with you.

She scowled and glanced away.

I have seen you play the highwayman, dolce mia.

"The duke," she gasped.

Si.

"You are his ghost?"

Hardly, he said, his word drier than a summer's drought. *He and I are . . . acquainted. He would like his property returned.*

"Then he's not dead?" She worked to sound merely curious instead of pathetically hopeful.

Were you grieving for him, Solange? he taunted.

"Hardly." She mocked his own word to cover her

relief. "He can come get his property himself." Despite her brave statement, Solange was not anxious for that confrontation.

Did you not leave him a prisoner in the Catacombs?

She avoided his molten, accusing gaze as guilt twisted through her. "I should think you would be able to help him escape."

He prefers to do things on his own terms. I believe he has already caused Le Chacal to rethink his imprisonment. Sly humor ran through his words.

"Is Auriano free then?" She could not control the note of hope in her tone.

He tipped his head. *Are you pining for him, Solange?*

She ignored his baited question. "Did Auriano send you? Is that what this visit is about?"

His amusement vanished. *What this visit is about, little thief, is finding something that I want. In return, you gain my help. Do we have a bargain or not?*

The steeliness of his tone suggested that he might be losing patience. With his voice in her head, Solange wondered what other abilities he might have. She was not about to make him angry. His acknowledged connection to the Duke of Auriano also made her wary, for that man was a formidable opponent. But if the item he sought had any value, then why would she be foolish enough to turn it over to him? Perhaps she would steal it and sell it herself for a fortune. She and Gide could buy off Le Chacal and then disappear. Vernoux would never be able to find them, even with the Legion of Baal.

Giving a jerky nod, she said, "*Oui.* I will help you."

Bene, he said. Satisfaction replaced his tautness. Standing, he took one step across the mattress, then floated to the floor. He swept an elegant bow. *I look forward to our partnership. Buona sera, dolce mia.* Then he moved to the door.

"What do I call you?" she said just before he slipped out.

He turned back to her, and she heard a riffle of laughter in her head.

Tonio.

At his name, a warmth invaded her brain. It seeped down through her body, and then disappeared, like the teasing caress of a lover. Gasping at the exquisite sensation, she closed her eyes. By the time she opened them again, he was gone.

* * *

Antonio stood for a moment on the street before his house on the *Ile Saint-Louis*. After he had left Solange, a sense of evil had followed him to his door. He knew that evil. It was Nulkana, the ancient sorceress who had placed the curse on his family centuries ago. It was the reason he turned to Shadow when the moon was full until it became dark once more; why he lost the sense of taste, smell, and touch. The reason he would have to endure the Hunger when he returned to his flesh and bone form.

He was surprised that the sorceress had been able to find him. His sister-in-law, Sabrina, had battled with the sorceress over the life of Alessandro, and Nulkana had been severely wounded. He was amazed the sorceress had healed enough to be able to search for him.

He scanned the street to either side. Seeing nothing, he looked up. There, atop a house several doors down, he caught movement. An owl. If he had not been Shadow with his heightened sense of sight, he might not have seen it. The bird blinked at him, then turned its head as if uninterested. But Antonio knew better. It was Nulkana's pet. He had hoped for more time in Paris before he would have to do battle with her.

He entered the house, and the sense of malice dropped away. Like all the other residences of the Auriano family,

L'Hôtel des Vénitiens, their Paris residence, was shielded from the sorcery of Nulkana. The entry hall was empty and dark as he knew it would be. The few servants would be asleep. Ascending the stairs, he moved silently to his bedchamber. The door was slightly ajar, and he slid in through the opening. A single candle burned low on the mantle and caused shadows to waver around the room. A man lay on the floor at the foot of his bed.

Crouching over him, Tonio whispered silently, *Piero.*

The man jerked upright, wide-eyed and fully awake. "*Sior* Tonio. *Scusi.* I was meditating on the Seven Deadly Sins."

Amused, Antonio teased him. *Of course you were. Why are you sleeping on the floor?*

"An owl attacked one of the serving girls earlier. I thought I should warn you." Piero rubbed the sleep from his eyes.

I saw the bird, Antonio said. *Nulkana has found me.*

"The sorceress is healing quickly. She is more powerful than we thought."

Si.

"Was your evening successful?"

Si

Antonio evaded the searching gaze of his Guide. The bargain he had struck with Solange would grate against his Guide's code of honor. Members of the House of Auriano were not common thieves, at least not in recent centuries.

"Are you going to ask me to kidnap the woman?" Piero grumbled, scowling.

With a laugh, Antonio shook his head. *No. I have not touched her, and I am not planning on doing so. One kidnapping in the family is enough, si?*

When his brother had touched Sabrina while he was Shadow, he'd craved her to the point of madness during the Hunger. Antonio and their two Guides had no other choice but to kidnap her so Alessandro might touch her again. Only the moonstone pendant she had been wearing had soothed his brother's frenzy. Antonio was not about to make the mistake of touching Solange. He had no moonstone. She had stolen it.

The sound of a coach entering the courtyard drew his attention. Going to the window, he saw his family crest on the side of the larger coach he had left for his brother's use. Alessandro was supposed to be on his wedding trip with his new bride, not here in Paris with the threat of the Legion of Baal so close. Concern propelled him to the door, but resentment against his brother's presence knotted in his chest. Alessandro did not need to come to Paris. His twin, the prince and older by two minutes, usually thought Antonio was unable to handle matters on his own. Antonio had yet to convince his brother that he was just as dangerous, even though their training skirmishes with rapier or stiletto were usually a draw.

Piero, come, he alerted his Guide. *It's Alessandro.*

While Piero went to rouse the servants, Antonio met his brother at the top of the stairs. Alessandro carried his new wife in his arms, her eyes closed, her head on his shoulder.

What's wrong? Antonio asked, anxiety coursing through him.

As soon as he spoke, Sabrina raised her head and smiled sleepily at him. "Oh, Tonio, I'm so glad you're all right."

Si, he answered, confused. Of course he was well. Her head dropped back to her husband's shoulder, and she closed her eyes again. Antonio gave his twin a puzzled look.

"She was worried about you." Smiling apologetically, Alessandro moved past with Sabrina in his arms and disappeared into one of the bedchambers farther along the hall.

Perplexed, Antonio retreated to the drawing room.

Alessandro appeared not long after, poured himself a brandy, and flopped into a chair. Taking a sip, he sighed and let his head rest against the high back of the chair. "It's been a long trip, and we traveled fast. Sabrina has been feeling ill lately."

She is unwell? Antonio was even more confused. He could not understand why his brother would allow his wife to travel if she were sick.

Merely the pregnancy, Tonio, Alessandro assured him silently. *Morning sickness.*

Relieved his sister-in-law's illness was not serious, Antonio's annoyance surfaced. *Why are you here?*

Alessandro raised a brow. *You sound angry.*

I'm very capable of attending to matters without you, Antonio said.

Alessandro glanced away. *I apologize for intruding.*

He took another sip of brandy, and Antonio waited silently for an explanation.

Sabrina is very fond of you, Alessandro said.

Confused once more at his brother's comment, Antonio answered, *As I am of her.*

A pleased smile curved Alessandro's lips.

Antonio could no longer contain his impatience. *Sandro, you should be on your wedding trip with her, not racing here to Paris.*

Sitting up straighter, Alessandro studied the brandy in his glass. Aloud, he said, "My bride can be very persuasive. She would give me no peace until we came to . . ."

To do what? Merda, Sandro! What is wrong?

"Evan told her you were in danger." Alessandro shrugged. "You know he has special gifts."

When Sabrina's son, Evan, Alessandro's stepson, matured, he would be a potent sorcerer. Even now as a child, his abilities were amazing. But Antonio was still waiting for his brother's explanation. *What is this danger that I am supposed to be in?*

Alessandro fidgeted. *Evan mentioned it was from a woman.*

Staring for a moment, Antonio burst into silent laughter. *I am in danger from a woman?*

Alessandro did not share his humor. Instead, he frowned. *I think you should take this seriously, Tonio. Evan saw you stabbed through the heart. By a woman.*

Still amused, Antonio put his hand to his chest. *If I had a heart, I might be concerned, but you know I am heartless where women are concerned.*

I thought the same of myself once, Alessandro countered.

I'll keep your advice in mind. Although he teased his brother, he could not help but be reminded of a pair of turquoise eyes that had mocked him while the woman who owned them held a knife to his throat. But then she had saved his life down in the Catacombs. He wondered if Solange would ever be desperate enough to kill him.

Alessandro distracted him with his next words. *How is Allegra?*

Gone. To England. Antonio proceeded to tell his brother of the events since arriving in Paris and what he had discovered about their sister. And his bargain with Solange. But he left out some details, like his Thought Binding with her. And his desire as Shadow to touch her and possibly feel her skin beneath his fingers.

When he finished, Alessandro was silent, staring at him thoughtfully. "I think," he finally said aloud, "that Sabrina and I will leave for *Le Chateau des Ombres* in a few days."

The Chateau of Shadows, their estate just north of the city, was where they retreated when they endured the Hunger and transformed from Shadow to human while in France. Antonio was surprised that his brother would leave him alone, but grateful.

"I don't like the arrangement you have with this woman,

Tonio," Alessandro said aloud. "Break it off. Use some other way to find the missing piece of the Sphere."

Just as you broke off your pursuit of Sabrina? Antonio needled.

Alessandro frowned. "Sabrina was not a desperate highwayman. This may be the woman that Evan saw in his vision. How do you know you can trust her?"

With a shrug, Antonio grinned. *I can't, but isn't that part of the sport of dealing with a woman?*

"I've learned that not all women are treacherous, but then there are others . . ." Alessandro murmured. "Be careful, Tonio." He tilted his head. "You know I'd kill you if you died."

Antonio snickered. *Then I'll come back to haunt you. How do you think Sabrina would like living with the two of us?*

Looking appropriately horrified, Alessandro said, *Merda. I'd probably wind up as a ghost as well.*

Chapter 6

"I don't see how we're going to get in," Gide said in an undertone to his sister. "We've never robbed a house this large. Just because he says he can help us doesn't mean we aren't going to get caught." He jerked his chin in Tonio's direction.

They were standing in the shadows. The moon lit the ornate gate across the street from them. It opened into the courtyard of *L'Hôtel Carnavalet*, one of the few mansions in the city still occupied by a wealthy family. The nobility had fled or been executed during the Revolution and the Terror, but the *nouveau riche*— merchants and bankers—had slipped into the void. Tonio had convinced Solange that robbing such a place would bring her more wealth than any attempt on the road as a highwayman. She had been intrigued by the idea. Her brother had been suspicious.

Tonio heard Gide's remark and regarded his sullen face. *Afraid?* he taunted the young man.

Gide's head snapped in Tonio's direction, then he turned away as if he could not bear to look at what he saw. "No, I'm not afraid," he grated. "But I don't want my sister spending the rest of her life in *prison*—or worse."

Tonio allowed his gaze to rest on Solange, then murmured, *I would never let that happen.*

Solange ducked her head at his words, and Gide lunged at him. "Don't you dare look at her like that! You're an abomination!"

Solange grabbed at her brother. "Gide, stop. Don't get

him angry." She cast an apprehensive glance at Tonio.

Si. Listen to your sister, amico mio, Tonio said, motioning to Solange to release her brother. *I will not place you or your sister in danger, and I will not tolerate any disrespect.*

"What can you do to me? You're nothing but a shadow," Gide scoffed.

Tonio flicked his fingers. Without touching, he jerked Gide's dagger from its sheath and allowed the point to hover mere inches from the young man's chest. *I can do many things.*

Gide stared at the blade floating in the air so close to his heart, then raised his shocked eyes to meet Tonio's gaze.

Take the knife and put it away, Tonio ordered. *Do not doubt me again.*

As soon as Gide wrapped his fingers around the hilt, Tonio turned away as if unconcerned, but he was very aware of what the young man was doing. When he heard the hiss of the blade sliding home in its sheath, he turned his full attention on the mansion. He had not been completely certain that Gide would comply. The younger man's dagger in his back would have ruined his plans for the evening.

Irritation made Tonio frown. Solange's brother was uneasy about him and therefore dangerous. This association with the brother and sister was more difficult than he had anticipated. If they had not stolen the moonstones, if Solange did not have that power running through her, if she had not come into contact with a piece of the Sphere of Astarte, if his desire to touch her were not so strong, he might have heeded Alessandro's warning and dissolved the agreement he had made with them. So many ifs.

He was not about to let these two go. He needed to find the piece of the Sphere of Astarte. The only way he knew to do that was to gain Solange's confidence so she would reveal its location. For now, the only way to gain her confidence was to help her steal.

The plan was madness. And desperate. The Duke of Auriano stealing? How absurd. Yet, here he was. He shook his head at himself. Then focused on their objective.

He moved across the road, then leaped to the top of the wall and crouched there. The stone-paved courtyard before him lay empty in the moonlight. Beyond that, the mansion sat quiet and dark, its inhabitants asleep. The imposing front edifice was broken by long narrow windows, but no balcony offered a place to stand so he could open one. He sighed. Solange had not chosen the easiest target. Gaining a foothold on a narrow windowsill was not impossible for him, but he would have preferred a steadier perch. Perhaps the back of the mansion provided an easier way in.

As he studied the mansion a moment longer, he sensed something was not quite right. Although there was no sign of anything out of the ordinary, he felt uneasy. It was one of the few mansions that had not been ransacked during the Terror, and he wondered why it had suffered so little damage. Unable to determine the source of his disquiet, he glanced back at the two dark figures waiting in the shadow of the building across the street.

Stay there, he told them. *I'll open the gate for you after I've looked around.*

* * *

Solange saw him disappear to the other side of the wall, then felt Gide shift beside her.

"He gives me the shivers," he muttered. "How can you tolerate looking at him?"

"I think he's beautiful," she said.

She felt her brother's disbelieving gaze, but she would not meet his eyes. For some reason, she felt compelled to defend the shadow creature—Tonio. When he had visited her bedchamber, his seductive caress across her mind was beyond anything she had ever experienced. His proposal of the bargain to work together intrigued her, and the object he sought roused her curiosity. His desperation to find it hinted that it was valuable. What if she could convince him to share its wealth?

"Don't you find his name odd?" Gide asked, breaking into her thoughts.

"It's Italian." Solange shrugged.

"Like the duke we robbed," Gide said. "Auriano. His given name is Antonio."

Solange stared at her brother as she realized what he was suggesting. *Tonio* was a shortened version of Antonio. She remembered the name engraved inside the man's ring. But it was impossible that the Shadow figure and the duke were the same. How could the flesh and bone duke turn into a shadow?

The gate in the wall opened, and Tonio stood there. *Come*, he beckoned silently.

Solange put aside the puzzle as she and her brother hurried across the road and through the gate. Tonio shut it behind them, then, keeping to the shadows, led them along the wall and around to the back of the mansion where a garden and manicured lawn spread out in the moonlight. A pair of glass-paned, double doors stood ajar, inviting them into the dark interior of the house.

We'll separate, Tonio said. *Solange will come with me. We'll meet back here. Be quick. Don't take anything too large.*

Gide's mouth flattened at the warning, and he stepped inside. Solange followed. She felt Tonio behind her but ignored the tingle of awareness as she gazed about the room. They had entered the main salon. Most of it was in darkness, but enough moonlight came through the windows that she could make out chairs and settees

70

covered in silk, a chandelier dripping with crystals, and a huge Aubusson carpet covering most of the floor. Above the mantle, a large bare area indicated a portrait had once hung there. Solange knew the house had once belonged to a noble family, now all dead because of the Terror. The missing portrait had probably been of one of the noble ancestors.

She wasted no time on any further examination of the room. What she sought would be in the library or study. Following Gide, she headed for the door in the far corner of the room, stepped through and found herself in the entrance hall. Gide climbed the wide staircase to the floor above, but she was interested in the several closed doors around the perimeter. She opened two before she found the room she sought. A large desk sat in one corner. Behind it, a small ladder of shelves with a scattering of books gave the room its designation as the library.

Crossing the room, she made directly for the desk. Tonio trailed her but remained silent. He seemed merely curious about what she was doing. She ignored him. One of the lower drawers in the desk was locked, but the key was in plain sight on the desktop. Pulling open the drawer, she found the money box she sought and placed it on the desk. It was black metal with simple gold filigree at each corner and firmly locked with no key in sight. Spying a penknife next to a quill holder, Solange grabbed it and tried to pick the lock, but after several minutes of effort, the box still remained closed.

May I try? she heard in her head.

Glancing up, she saw Tonio watching her from the other side of the desk.

"I suppose you think you can do better," she muttered.

He said nothing, merely waited for her answer.

With a scowl, she held out the knife.

I won't need that, he said.

Reaching across the desk, he placed his hand on top

71

of the box with his fingers curled down on top of the lock. She watched his eyes become unfocused, then the lock clicked.

E vai, he said with a grin and raised his hand. There you go.

Although grateful for his help, Solange was annoyed at his arrogance. Sending him a quelling glance, she raised the lid of the box. A large pile of banknotes sat on top of gold coins scattered across the bottom. Wasting no time, she scooped everything out and dumped it into a small sack.

With a nod, she indicated she had finished. As she started around the desk, a small dark cat streaked in front of her. Tripping, she grabbed at the desk. As she did, she brushed against Tonio. He jerked away as if he had been burned.

She felt a warm tingle on her skin where they had touched. Looking down at her hand, she expected to see a trail of sparks, but she saw nothing unusual. She must have imagined the sensation. But when she raised her head, Tonio was staring at her.

His gaze was shocked, intense. She knew then she had not imagined the sensation. He had felt it, too.

He took a step toward her. With a wave of his hand, her hat floated from her head and landed on the desk. He stepped closer. Those molten eyes held her immobile. Reaching out, he traced his fingers down her cheek and stopped at her jaw. A warm tingle erupted in their wake. The sensation was like nothing she had ever felt before, as if tiny stars had landed on her skin and left a sparkling trail. She breathed out a sigh.

Tonio's eyes closed and his head fell back as if he were savoring the sensation. His fingers stroked, back and forth. Tingling followed along her skin in their wake. The sensation enthralled her.

He dropped his hand and opened his eyes again. That

golden gaze mesmerized her, held her. She knew without a doubt that he was going to kiss her. And she knew she was going to let him.

One small part of her wondered what it would feel like. How did a person kiss a shadow? The rest of her waited with anticipation. She barely knew this creature, what he was, who he was. He was using her to accomplish his own ends. Yet, she was drawn to him. His abilities, his teasing, his soft seduction wreaked havoc on the wall she had built around herself to guard against men's advances. But he was not a man. He was only a shadow. Then why did she tremble in expectation?

He stepped closer, framed her face with his hands, and that warm tingle made her cheeks glow. The heat slowly spread down her neck, over her breasts and down her belly, swirling deep inside her. She gasped at the throb of desire.

Are you afraid? he asked.

"No." Her word was barely a breath.

I am. Wry amusement tinged his statement. He traced his thumb across her bottom lip, making it pulse with warmth. *I've never kissed a woman as . . . I've never felt . . .* His words trailed off, and he gave his head a tiny shake. *I've never wanted to kiss a woman more than you.*

His words warmed her, and she felt a blush rise in her cheeks. Anticipation made her breath hitch. Her lips parted, and she stared into those molten eyes. Lowering his head, he placed his mouth gently against hers. Her eyes slipped closed. She felt no pressure, but the tingling sensation marked where his mouth touched. It was exquisite. She felt giddy, light-headed. A moan of pleasure escaped her. Although she wanted to wrap her arms around him, she was not quite sure if his body had mass or if she might wind up clutching at air. She was afraid to discover which, and she was afraid to move, lest he stop.

Tentatively, she touched her tongue to his lips. He needed no further invitation. The feel of his tongue in her mouth as he caressed, as he left a trail of that warm tingle, made her whimper with pleasure. She arced up, opening herself, offering herself to him. One part of her observed that she had never—should never—offer herself to any man. Another part of her wanted Tonio to do whatever he wanted. She was more than curious about kissing this shadowman. She was eager to learn his kiss, his touch. The few innocent kisses she had shared with the boys of the streets had never aroused her. But Tonio was making her feel things with just his lips and tongue that she never dreamed possible.

The tingles he created in her mouth radiated out, down through her body. Her lips pulsed. She felt moisture between her thighs. Her breasts ached to be touched. She throbbed. Heat and desire pooled in her center, then spiraled through her. The spiral grew tighter. It arrowed down into her womb. Her body clenched in response. And held in suspension for just a moment.

The wave of release hit her before she realized what was happening. She could not stop the ecstasy that shot through her. A part of her realized she should remain silent, and she bit down on her cry of pleasure. Throwing back her head, she rode the passion. The intense explosion washed through her again and again until it ebbed on her tiny whimper.

Spent, she slowly opened her eyes. She felt as if her body had been taken apart and rearranged. She had never experienced anything like it. Sucking in a breath, she attempted to orient herself back in the world.

Tonio stood close before her. His hands circled her waist. Somehow, she was sitting on the desk. He gazed at her with an odd combination of surprise, awe, and male pride.

It was good, si? he said.

She dragged in another breath. When she could speak, she asked, "What did you do to me?"

He tipped his head thoughtfully. *I kissed you. Would you like me to do it again?*

"*Oui.* No." Befuddled, she closed her eyes and shook her head to try to clear it. Looking at him again, she said, "Get away from me."

He stepped back, but as he did, his fingers traced across the back of her hand. She hissed at the tingling sensation and jerked away.

I asked if you were afraid, he said.

"I wasn't. I'm not." She lied. Drawing another deep breath, she tried to gather her scattered thoughts. She had never experienced anything like what had just happened. Vernoux delivered only pain, never pleasure. But this shadowman had given her *la petite mort* with only a kiss. What would he be able to do if they actually made love? Her imagination cringed at the possibilities. The ramifications scared her to death. The possibility of such a thing happening was nil. Yet the idea made her toes curl with want.

The sound of Gide's furtive footstep in the hall brought her back to reality. They needed to leave before they were discovered. Tonio backed away. She slid to the floor, and her knees buckled, weakened from the earth-shattering release he had given her. As she grabbed at the desk for support, she felt her feet leave the ground as he held her up with merely a sweep of his hands, without even touching her. Irritated that she had allowed herself to be so vulnerable, she glared at him. He gently lowered her until she felt the floor beneath her feet once more. Stiffening her knees, she edged around Tonio and headed for the doorway.

Just before she reached it, she heard in her head, *I'm looking forward to our next kiss, dolce mia.* Laughter edged his words. Her hat settled lightly on her head.

Pressing her hat down, she turned on him with a scowl.

"Don't think you can now take liberties because we shared one little kiss."

Si. It was a very little kiss. His dry tone and sober expression mocked her. Moving around her, he preceded her into the hall. *I will do better next time.*

There would be no next time. She wanted to pound on him. Instead, forced into silence so they would not be heard, she gritted her teeth and followed. Despite the fact that this creature was a shadowman he could annoy and provoke her as well as any man—better than any man. If she did not think he could be useful, then she would dissolve the agreement between them. But he had helped to break them into this house, and she had come away with a small fortune. If Gide had been as successful, then they would be well on their way to buying out of their servitude to Le Chacal.

Lost in her thoughts, she almost walked into Tonio when he stopped short. He was staring at a carved molding above the main entrance. The moonlight barely penetrated the shadows in the hall, so she could not see what had arrested him.

Whose house is this? he demanded without taking his gaze from the crown above the door. All amusement had fled.

Flustered at his abrupt change, she did not answer immediately.

He spun to face her. *Whose?* Those molten eyes pierced her.

"It-it b-belongs to *Monsieur* Gravois. He owns a silk manufactory and does some work for the Directory." She hated the stutter, but he had suddenly become rather frightening.

He pointed back at the molding without taking his gaze from her. *Do you know what that is?*

She could not see whatever he indicated. It was too dark. She shook her head.

A frog glyph. It's not part of the original decoration. And it indicates the owner is a member of the Legion of Baal. Have you ever heard of them?

Solange stared at him. When she had chosen this house, she had no idea that Gravois was a member of the Legion. She disliked the fat little man and thought stealing from him would be a lark. If Vernoux discovered that they had been here, he would be enraged.

"We have to get out," she whispered urgently. "Hurry."

His eyes narrowed. With an abrupt gesture, he waved her back to the garden door of the salon where they had entered.

She hastened in the direction of their exit. If he had not stopped her, if he had not kissed her, they would have been out of the house by now. Fear sat like a clawed predator between her shoulder blades. She expected them to be discovered at any moment. Wanting to run, she knew they would be quieter if they crept slowly, so she followed Tonio's deliberate progress through the salon and out into the garden. Gide waited for them there. Seeing her, he gave her a triumphant grin, then silently fell in beside her.

* * *

Tonio led Solange and her brother back to the courtyard at the front of the house. He understood now why he had felt uneasy. *L'Hôtel Carnavalet* had remained untouched during the Terror because it was protected by the Legion of Baal. No doubt after the noble family who had been living there had been disposed of, Gravois had placed his mark on it, keeping it safe. Allegra's words in her letter came back to him—that members of the Legion of Baal were gathering in Paris. He already knew that the Marquis de Vernoux was a member, and now he had evidence that another member lived in the city—

Monsieur Gravois, powerful through his work with the Directory. How many more members of the Legion were here? Why were they gathering? What did they know that he did not?

And what was Solange hiding? Her fear had been obvious when she discovered the mansion held a connection to the Legion. Perhaps she was not in league with them, despite the fact that the Marquis de Vernoux was her protector. Or perhaps she was, and robbing this house was a betrayal. Either way, he knew she was anxious to be away, as anxious as he was.

In his haste to retreat from the grounds of the mansion, he led the two thieves from the corner of the house and across the stone courtyard instead of keeping to the perimeter near the wall. Solange was nearly abreast of him, but Gide trailed behind. Just as he and Solange reached the shadow of the wall, three footmen burst from the front door.

"Stop! Thief!" one of them yelled.

Gide tried to outrun them, but they cut him off and surrounded him. They were big, hired no doubt for their strength. Solange took a step toward her brother, but Tonio blocked her way.

Back, he said. *Against the wall. Don't move. Don't make a sound.*

She began to protest.

He cut her off. *You can't help him if they catch you, too.*

She pressed against the wall, and he caged her with his arms and legs. He would be invisible to the men in the courtyard, and Solange would be hidden between him and the wall. He was careful not to touch her. This was not the time to experience that uncanny rush of sensation when he came into contact with her skin. She stared up at him with wide, frightened eyes. He wanted to reassure her, but knew that would be pointless. Gide was caught, and he could not help him now. That would have to wait.

Behind him, the men were questioning Gide. "What's in the sack, boy?" one of them asked.

"Nothing." Gide's tone was sullen.

Tonio heard the sound of knuckles against flesh. Solange cringed at the noise. Glancing over his shoulder, he saw Gide reeling from a blow. A dark trickle of blood appeared at the corner of his mouth.

"We asked what you had in the sack," one of the footmen asked.

"Flowers," Gide said.

The three men glanced at one another, then moved in closer.

"We're not going to ask you again," the first one said, raising his fist.

Gide cringed. "I told you. Flowers." Backing away, he held up a defensive hand. "Look." He upended the sack.

Tonio was amazed to see a bunch of flowers fall out of the sack. Why had he stolen flowers? The three men looked just as surprised.

"They're for . . . there's this girl." Gide shrugged. "I wanted to bring her flowers."

Tonio turned back to Solange with a glare. Had her brother wasted his time by picking *flowers?* Solange had her hand across her mouth, and her eyes held laughter. Why was she so amused? Angry at the two of them, Tonio turned back to the courtyard in time to see one of the men knock Gide to the ground with a blow to his head. A boot landed on Gide's ribs, and he grunted in pain.

"Get out, boy, and don't ever come back." The order was growled as one of the men grabbed Gide by his hair to force him to meet his eyes, then flung him away.

Solange's brother gathered up the flowers, stuffed them into his sack, and scrambled to his feet.

"Oui, monsieur. Pardon." Bowing, Gide backed away toward the gate, then turned and fled.

Tonio waited, silent and fuming, while the three men returned to the house. When he was sure they were inside, he backed away from Solange. Relief and amusement made her eyes glow. He was not entertained at all.

Did I risk my neck for you so your brother could steal flowers? he snapped.

Solange shook her head, and a ripple of laughter escaped her. "No," she whispered. She slipped away from him and skipped out the gate.

Tonio watched her go. Irritated with them, disconcerted at finding himself on the grounds of a house belonging to a member of the Legion of Baal, he jumped to the top of the wall, bypassing the gate. He saw Solange meet up with her brother in the shadows across the street. Putting their heads together, they shared a laugh, then ran off down the street. Solange glanced back over her shoulder, met his eyes, then disappeared around the corner with Gide. Tonio did not follow. He would allow them their triumph tonight, but tomorrow, he would lay down some rules. He was not about to put himself in danger while they played childish pranks.

Chapter 7

The morning after the robbery, *Monsieur* Gravois was ushered into the dressing room of the Marquis de Vernoux. The day was bright with sunshine, and it streamed in through the long windows, making the room glow. Bolts of cloth—navy blue, dark brown, black worsted, lengths of pale ivory brocade, red-striped satin, yellow silk—lay piled on the settee and draped across every available place to sit. The marquis, an elegant man, slim, proud of his carriage, was standing before a glass as his tailor fitted him with a new frock coat.

Vernoux still used his title, despite the fact that the use of such trappings of the nobility were discouraged and even dangerous since the Revolution. He had allied himself with the revolutionaries, said the correct things, acted in the appropriate manner during the Terror to save his skin—and his head from being separated from his body on the guillotine. As a result, he had been granted this one indulgence. Although officially he was called *Monsieur* Moreau, to those who knew him well, he was still the Marquis de Vernoux. Gravois had known the marquis for a long time.

"Ah, Gravois, just in time," Vernoux exclaimed. "That yellow silk you sent me will make an excellent waistcoat. I believe it will go well with this new frock coat, *n'est-ce pas?*"

Gravois ran his eye over the burgundy wool draped across Vernoux's shoulders. "*Oui, mon seigneur.* It will go very nicely." He watched the tailor tuck and pin, then cleared his throat. "Vernoux, I have come on quite another matter. A rather delicate matter."

The marquis met Gravois's gaze in the mirror. Vernoux's eyes snapped cold and dark. "You know I despise being bothered with problems this early in the day. Come back later, when I have fortified myself with a cup of chocolate." He paused. "In fact, don't come back at all. Handle it yourself." Striking a pose, he surveyed himself in the glass.

Monsieur Gravois bowed his head and sighed. "I'm afraid I cannot, *mon seigneur*. You see, it has to do with a frog."

The marquis went very still, stared at his image in the glass, and gave no indication that he had heard. With an abrupt gesture, he snapped at the tailor, "Get out." He pulled at the skeleton of the frock coat hanging on him. "And get this infernal rag off me."

Gravois watched the frightened tailor ease the lovely burgundy wool from the marquis's shoulders, bow, murmur an apology, and scurry from the room. Vernoux was a frightening man when he was disturbed, and *Monsieur* Gravois had deeply disturbed him. The silk merchant swallowed in a dry throat. What he had to say would make the marquis furious.

Slowly, Vernoux turned to face him. Gravois thought the man had the eyes of a snake—deadly, cruel, without feeling, completely amoral. Those eyes pinned him where he stood.

"What, Gravois, about the frog?" Vernoux said very quietly.

Clearing his throat, Gravois said, "A thief broke into my house last night."

Vernoux hissed with impatience. "I told you to hire more men. I don't know what you expect me to do. Don't waste my time."

"He stole the Silver Arrows."

Once again, Vernoux stilled. Gravois felt those eyes on him as if they were two fangs biting into his skin. The Silver Arrows were magical artifacts that could help the Legion of Baal find the pieces of the Sphere of Astarte. He had been entrusted with their keeping when Vernoux discovered that one of the pieces of the Sphere was here in Paris.

After what seemed like an eternity, the marquis drawled, "You never cease to surprise me, Gravois, with your stupidity. I am amazed the Lord High still allows you to remain a part of the Legion and has not sacrificed your heart to the god before now."

The idea of being sacrificed to Baal struck terror into his soul, but Gravois had a card up his sleeve. He decided the time had come to produce it. Bowing his head as if he were humbly contrite, he said, "The thief was someone you know, Vernoux." He paused dramatically. "The brother of your mistress, the lovely *Madame* de Volonté." Gravois glanced up in time to see the fury run through Vernoux's eyes, then an expression cold enough to lower the temperature of the sunny room.

"How do you know this?" The words of the marquis were uttered so softly that Gravois had to strain to hear them.

"Three of my footmen, ones that you recommended to me, caught him, then let him go. They said he had only plucked flowers from the garden. I recognized the boy's description."

"Flowers." Vernoux's expression became shuttered. "Young Gide has become quite the talented sorcerer, *n'est-ce pas*, to be able to transmute silver arrows to flowers?" He wandered to the window to look out at his own garden with its riot of blooms. After several moments, he turned back to the silk merchant. "I want you to send *Madame* de Volonté some flowers, Gravois, cartloads of them. Denude your garden if you must. But do not allow her to know they came from you. I will retrieve the Silver

Arrows for you and save your miserable heart from the Lord High's sacrificial knife."

Gravois bowed low, thanking Baal and whatever other spirits watched over him that all he had to sacrifice were the flowers from his garden. "*Merci, Monsieur le Marquis.*" Straightening again, curiosity made him ask, "What will happen to *Madame* de Volonté?"

With an arrogantly raised brow, Vernoux said, "She will be staggered with delight at such an extravagant display of generosity, and then I will show my overwhelming affection for both herself and her brother. Especially her brother."

With another quick bow, Gravois took his leave, sorry he had asked.

* * *

Solange greeted the Marquis de Vernoux in her drawing room the night after the robbery. Dropping into a deep curtsey, she murmured as she always did when he arrived, "*Monsieur le Marquis.* I am honored by your presence."

"*Ma petite putain.*" My little whore. Vernoux's words purred with the satisfaction of a contented cat.

Uneasy at his apparent good mood, Solange cast a quick glance at him. His mouth smiled, but his eyes held a dark glint. She had seen that expression before, and it did not bode well for her safety. Rising from her curtsey, she pretended she had not noticed.

"May I offer you some refreshment?" She indicated the tray holding a decanter of brandy and a selection of bonbons.

Ignoring her question, he said, "I see you have a generous admirer." He cast his gaze pointedly at the abundance of flowers scattered about the room in many vases.

Solange gave a nervous laugh. As soon as the flowers

had arrived, she knew they were an ominous message. She'd fought panic all day. Now, as her heart galloped in her chest, she feigned ignorance. "I have no idea who they are from. They arrived this morning by the cartload." She paused as if an idea had just occurred to her. "*Mon Dieu*! Vernoux! They are from you!" Grabbing his hand, she kissed it. "Oh, *merci*! They are beautiful!"

"Do you like them?" Vernoux asked blandly.

"Of course I like them." Solange pouted. "How could I not like them? You know how much I adore flowers."

"Are there enough flowers to satisfy your craving?" His tone contained only mild curiosity.

Solange knew he was leading her into a treacherous quagmire. She could do nothing but respond. "I am humbled at your generosity, Vernoux."

"You did not answer my question." Vernoux's eyes glittered dangerously.

"*Oui*. Of course there are enough. But now that you have been so generous, you know I will expect such gifts again in the future," she said coyly as she tried to distract him by swaying closer and running her finger provocatively down his chest.

"Oh, I intend to be most generous," he murmured. "Since I have gifted you with all of these flowers, perhaps you could ask your brother not to steal them from the gardens of others."

Solange fell back a step, once again feigning innocence. "I beg your pardon?"

Cold, deadly fury turned Vernoux's eyes black. Grabbing her by the wrist, he pulled her toward the door of the drawing room. "Let us go speak to him now, shall we? And perhaps we will also explain that he should not steal from the houses of those who protect him and his sister."

Terror clutched at her. Having seen that look in his eyes before, she knew it foreshadowed pain. She did not wish to see him inflict it on Gide. Yanking against his grip, she fought to slow his progress. "Vernoux. No. Wait. Please."

Surprisingly, he stopped and turned to her, and appeared to be merely the calm gentleman. Solange knew he raged beneath that exterior.

"The robbery last night was my idea. Gide wanted nothing to do with it. He went along because I convinced him. Please. It was not his fault. Don't hurt him. Please." She hated to plead, but she knew that humbling herself before this man was the only way to dissuade him from his intent.

"Why should I not hurt him? He stole the Silver Arrows. They are very valuable." His flat, unemotional statements only underscored to Solange how enraged he was.

Desperate to protect Gide, she blurted, "We will return them."

"Of course you will." Vernoux once more dragged her toward the door.

Resisting, she said, "If you must punish someone, then punish me."

Stopping again, Vernoux's lips curved into a tight, cruel smile. "*Ma petite putain*, did you think I would forget you?" He ran his finger down her cheek like a caress. It threatened rather than seduced. "You know how much I like to hear you whimper." Tapping her lips, he said, "Tonight, I feel the need to hear you beg." His smile disappeared, and his eyes took on the black, cold-blooded expression of a snake. "You will beg me for mercy, first for your brother and then for yourself. You will learn that you may not do whatever you wish. You are allowed to thieve because it amuses me, but you have gone too far. You have stolen from the Legion of Baal."

Discarding caution, she snapped, "We thieve because Le Chacal demands it."

"Ah, yes, Le Chacal." Momentary amusement flitted

through his eyes. "Who do you think protects Le Chacal? If it had not been for me, the scum would have lost both hands."

"And if it had not been for Le Chacal, your precious *l'hôtel* would be rubble, trashed and looted by the revolutionaries." As soon as the words were out of her mouth, she knew she had pushed too far. "Forgive me, *mon seigneur*," she said with head bowed. "I do not know where these words come from."

Vernoux's eyes narrowed to slits. "Do not try to distract me. I know your charming tricks."

He dragged his nail across the swell of her breast that peeked from her gown. She clenched her jaw at the scratch of pain, a minuscule reminder of what lay in store for her. His gaze heated. He jerked her close and drew her hand to his crotch where his erection strained against his form-fitting doeskin breeches. Only rage aroused him that much.

"I am anxious to begin, and I am tempted to bugger your brother," he said. "You would not wish to watch that, would you, *ma petite putain*? Because I can easily accomplish it before I bugger you."

Solange swallowed and shook her head.

"*Bon*. Then let us get on with it. Your brother will learn his lesson, and then it will be your turn."

As he pulled her toward the door again, she resisted. "No, please, Vernoux. I beg you!"

Swinging around to face her, he lifted his arm, his hand a hard fist. His sleeve fell back, exposing the frog glyph tattooed on the inside of his wrist. It glowed faintly. Solange flinched away. It was not his blow that she feared, but the burn that glyph could inflict. She had felt it before. It scalded like nothing she had ever experienced. It bit under her skin and into her brain, where it seared away everything else until it was the center of existence.

"Do not force me to use this on you. I would regret

marking you in such a manner, but I will do what is necessary. You have mocked the Legion of Baal, and you will be punished." Cruel lust flashed across his face, and again he jerked her close. "And after, when I take you, you will remember exactly who your master is." His hand came down and clamped on her breast. At her wince of pain, he smiled thinly. "There, you see? You have already begun to learn your lesson."

As he dragged her through the doorway, Solange closed her mind against the torment that was to come.

* * *

The night after the robbery, Tonio entered Solange's bedchamber through the window. Flowers were scattered everywhere—across the floor, across the furniture, trampled underfoot, clinging to the draperies, strewn across the bed, some even dangling from the sconces on the walls. Although the covers on the bed were rumpled, Solange was not in it. Puzzled at the disarray of the room, surprised that she was not abed at this hour of the night, he crossed the room to search for her. He had come with the intent of venting his irritation at what Gide had done the night before. He would not leave until they came to an understanding.

A whimper from a dark corner beside the bed drew his attention. Glancing over, he saw a small form curled into a tight ball on the floor. When he moved closer, he realized it was Solange. Something was very wrong.

Solange? he asked. He crouched down and reached out to touch her. When his fingers brushed her shoulder, she cringed away. The warm tingle he had felt before was barely perceptible.

"Don't. Please." Her words were thin with pain.

What is wrong? Are you ill? Concern made the questions tumble from him.

"Please, see to my brother. The room across the hall."

What has happened?

She drew a shaky breath. "It's nothing. I'm all right."

Uncurling, she sat up. Pain flickered across her face. Her lashes were spiky from tears. With an effort, she tried to pull herself to her feet. Tonio held his hands out on either side of her and used his mind to support her until she could stand. As she grabbed the bedpost, he saw the shredded back of her nightdress. Dark stains speckled the material. Blood.

Solange, what happened? Anxiety ripped through him. *Who did this?*

She would not look at him. "Please, go to my brother. He needs help."

Tonio was reluctant to leave her but realized he would get no answers until he did as she asked. *Let me call your maid.*

She did not respond, did not move. Her shoulders drooped, and her head hung down. As angry as he was with her, he ached to see her in such pain. He wanted to ease her suffering. Stepping back, concentrating, he held his hands out in front of him, palms up, and lifted her from the floor. She gasped, and panic rose in her eyes. *It's all right*, he reassured her. *I won't hurt you.* Slowly, gently, he floated her above the bed where he allowed her to settle, face down. He heard a muffled sob.

Resting his hand on her head, he asked, *Did I hurt you?*

"No. Please. My brother." Her words were barely a breath.

He gave her a last, light caress, then did as she asked. With a twist of his wrist, he forced the bell pull beside the bed to dip, calling her maid as he exited the room. He found Gide in his room, slumped against the bedpost. His wrists were tied above his head, the back of his shirt ripped open, his back a bloody mass of welts. Beside him on the floor lay a switch from a thorn bush. He was barely conscious and in much worse condition than his sister.

With several quick flicks of his fingers, Tonio untied the drapery cords binding him and eased him gently to the floor. Gide moaned in agony. A burn in the shape of a frog glyph marked his shoulder. Whoever had done this was a member of the Legion of Baal. Tonio suspected he knew who it was.

He bent over Gide, and placing his fingers against Gide's pulse, entered his mind quickly, inducing him to sleep. He could at least give Solange's brother that small relief. Both Solange and Gide needed help. He bounded to the window and jumped to the rooftop of the adjoining building.

Tonio raced home, his rage bubbling inside as he flitted from rooftop to rooftop. He first roused Piero, then stood outside his brother's bedchamber. Alessandro would not be happy being pulled from the bed he shared with Sabrina, but Tonio could think of no other alternative. As Shadow, he was not about to expose himself to the fright, speculation, and gossip of servants. Alessandro would have to step in and take control. For this moment, he was glad of his twin's presence in Paris.

Sandro. He sent the call through the heavy wood of the door. Tonio sensed his brother awaken, then his reluctance to leave the side of his beautiful wife. *Sandro, I need you.*

After a moment, the door opened. Looking annoyed, Alessandro stood naked in the opening. "I hope you have an excellent reason for rousing me from my bed."

I need you to take my identity. There's trouble.

Tonio explained the situation, and when he had finished, concern darkened Alessandro's face. "I'll wake Sabrina. She'll be able to help." He paused, and Tonio felt his twin's searching regard. "This woman . . . Have you touched her?"

Antonio shrugged and let his gaze slip away.

"*Christo!*" Alessandro's word was a quiet explosion. "Do you understand what you have done?"

Tonio glared at his brother. *What I have done is*

endanger this woman's life. Will you help or not?

"*Si.* Of course. But you must promise me you will not touch her again." Concern tinged his words.

Tonio remembered the madness that had taken hold of Alessandro during the Hunger after he had touched Sabrina, the madness that had prompted Tonio to kidnap Sabrina for his twin. If he did not touch Solange again, would he be able to avoid the same kind of madness? Would he be able to restrain himself from touching her again? He shook his head, both in answer to his twin and his own questions.

If you'd had more time as Shadow, would you have refrained from touching Sabrina? he asked quietly.

Alessandro sighed. "This is not going to be easy, Tonio. Please, don't get yourself killed."

With a grim smile, Tonio said, *I'll do my best.*

*   *   *

Solange lay quietly, blocking out the dull throb that radiated up her back and down the backs of her legs. Tonio had returned with the Duke of Auriano, his servant, and a lovely woman named Sabrina, who was wed to the duke's brother, the prince. The duke was very much flesh and blood, so Gide's suspicions that the shadowman and Auriano were one and the same had been wrong. But he was not the magnetic, sensuous man she had met at her salon, despite his beauty, nor the dangerous man who had trailed her into the Catacombs. He was polite and solicitous, but cool. Perhaps he had lost interest in retrieving his property. Or perhaps he had lost interest because of what he had learned about her connection to Vernoux. Although she was relieved she did not have to deal with his advances, a tiny part of her regretted the loss of his interest. But she hurt too much to give the matter much thought.

Patricia Barletta

The three of them had taken control of the household. Sabrina had applied an ointment to the welts across Solange's buttocks, which had blunted the sharp knives of pain, and had made her swallow some vile concoction that would help her sleep. But Solange's humiliation at the abuse Vernoux had inflicted on her would not recede, nor the memory of the torture he had inflicted on Gide.

The others had gone, and only Tonio remained standing at the side of the bed. She could feel his eyes on her, those golden, molten eyes. She wanted him next to her. At the same time, she could not bear to look at him. Her degradation sat in her chest like some dead thing she could not cut away. She did not want to see pity in that golden gaze. Keeping her eyes closed, she hoped he thought she was sleeping.

She sensed him stretching out beside her. His weight was nothing on the mattress. She felt his hand at the base of her neck, and the touch soothed her. The warm tingle she had felt before radiated outward, trickling down her spine, dulling the pain.

Solange, who did this to you? His words in her head were quiet, but she heard the underlying anger.

Not willing to reveal her misery, she opened her eyes and smiled. "Thank you for taking care of Gide."

Why would I not take care of your brother? The tone of his words was cool.

Realizing she had insulted him, she tried to smooth his feelings. "I know you do not trust him."

Annoyance rippled across his features. *Did you think I would leave him to suffer?*

"I . . . No." She lapsed into silence, closing her eyes against the affront that lingered in his gaze. At least it was not pity.

What of you, Solange? Should you not also be grateful that I took care of you? he baited.

Trying to deflect his anger, she looked at him and

92

smiled seductively, slipping forgetfully into her role as *Madame* de Volonté. "I will be when I have recovered."

His hand lifted from her back. *You will not play the whore for me. You know that is not what I meant.*

She sighed, regretting that her words pushed him away. "I have always taken care of Gide first."

Perhaps that is his problem. Perhaps that is why he foolishly stole flowers.

Surprised, Solange stared at Tonio. He did not know. She debated for a moment about telling him, then decided he deserved the truth. "Gide did not steal flowers. He stole the Silver Arrows, artifacts that are supposed to locate something called the Sphere of Astarte."

Tonio went completely still, then he rolled from the bed. He looked around the room, at the flowers scattered everywhere. When his gaze landed on her once again, she saw he had put all the pieces together. *When your brother thought he would get caught, he turned the Arrows into flowers,* he said.

"*Oui.*"

And whoever did this to you took back the Arrows.

"*Oui.*"

The Marquis de Vernoux. Tonio's statement was flat.

Solange did not answer.

I know of Vernoux. You played a dangerous game by robbing a house belonging to a member of the Legion of Baal, he scolded.

Stung at his accusation, she snapped, "If you'll remember, you were the one who urged the theft of a grand house. I had no idea *l'Hôtel Carnavalet* was owned by a member of the Legion." In her agitation, she moved against the sheet covering her and sent slivers of pain radiating up her back and down her legs. An embarrassing whimper escaped her throat, and a tear trickled from the corner of her eye.

Shh . . . Solange. Dolce mia. Tonio crouched beside

her on the bed. His hand brushed her cheek and cupped her head. His thumb rubbed lightly just below her ear.

At his touch, calm settled on her once more. Sleep began to pull at her, the effects of the tisane she had drunk. Before she slipped into unconsciousness, she murmured, "He did not get all of the Arrows. One seems to have gone missing."

His amusement rippled through her mind like a warm breeze. She smiled, satisfied that she had pleased him. When he brushed his thumb across her lip, she felt his emotions turning solemn.

I'm sorry, dolce mia. The words were barely a whisper in her head. The touch of his lips at the corner of her mouth sent warmth through her and cradled her as she descended into sleep.

*   *   *

Tonio stood in the doorway of the kitchen of Vernoux's *l'hôtel.* His anger had overridden his good sense in going there; but as he watched the two people in the otherwise empty room, he was glad it had. Before him were Vernoux, still clothed, and a young woman, naked. She was younger than a woman. A girl. No doubt one of the scullery maids, the most vulnerable of the Frenchman's staff. The marquis had her bent across a work table, splayed out on her stomach, her toes barely touching the floor. He supported himself with one hand. The other crushed her cheek to the table and held her down. He used her brutally, remorselessly. Every thrust pushed her frail hip bones into the stone-like wood of the table. Every thrust wrung a cry of misery from her.

Tonio's revulsion fueled his rage at the Frenchman, whose cruelty had evidently not been sated with his punishment of Solange and her brother. He was taking it out on his servants. It was time to teach him some restraint.

Tonio wanted to kill the man right there but did not wish to traumatize the girl any more than she already was. With a controlled movement of his hand, he slid a knife from the wooden block where they were stored. Turning it in midair, he let it fly with deadly accuracy. It thunked into the worktable a scant inch from Vernoux's hand. The marquis froze. The girl screeched. Tonio stabbed a second knife into the table on the other side of the Frenchman's hand. Vernoux's head snapped around in astonishment. Tonio sent a third knife through the air, stabbing it down between the Frenchman's spread fingers. The marquis jerked his hand away from the deadly blades. With another quick movement, Tonio flung him sideways, away from the girl. The marquis landed in an inelegant sprawl on the floor.

He immediately surged to his feet. Tonio observed with satisfaction that his member hung limp within his unbuttoned breeches.

"Who's there?" Vernoux demanded. "How dare you . . ." His words trailed off when he saw Tonio emerge from the shadows.

I dare. Tonio stepped farther into the room. *Didn't you get enough sick pleasure from abusing Madame de Volonté and her brother?*

Vernoux's eyes widened, then hardened. Grabbing the girl's arm, he pulled her from the table and flung her away. "Out," he commanded her, keeping his eyes on Tonio.

The girl picked herself up and scurried to collect her clothing. As she hastened past Tonio to the door, he saw bruises along her arms, more on her tiny breasts. Her lip was swollen and split, her cheek mottled purple, and the dark smudge of a black eye was beginning to form. She cast a quick glance in Tonio's direction, and her mouth dropped open. He sent a gentle nudge into her mind, urging her to run. Gratitude replaced the shock in her eyes. In her hurry to escape, she left the door ajar. Tonio closed it with a subtle movement of his hand.

Casually, Vernoux rearranged his clothing. "I know

what you are," he said as if he were having an informal conversation over a glass of brandy. "The curse. I always wondered if all the rumors were true."

Then I am pleased I could provide some enlightenment. Tonio's answer dripped sarcasm. *I think we have a few things to discuss, Monsieur le Marquis.*

"I have nothing to discuss with a monster." Vernoux pulled one of the knives from the table and tested its sharpness with his thumb.

Ah. A monster. I've been called worse. But which of us is the true fiend? Tonio watched Vernoux's movements closely.

The marquis chuckled. "Oh, I have no difficulty in pinpointing the culprit." He flipped the knife in his hand and caught it by the blade.

Excellent. Tonio nodded. *Then you will not mind if I teach the monster a few manners.*

"I think not." Vernoux flung the knife. It whistled past Tonio's ear and stuck into the wall behind him.

Really, Vernoux, is your aim truly that bad? Tonio sauntered closer, daring the Frenchman.

Anger narrowed Vernoux's eyes. He wrenched another knife from the table and examined its sharpness. "Does a shadow bleed?" he asked, mildly curious. He flipped this knife also, catching the blade, the handle, the blade. "Can a shadow die?" Without warning, he threw the knife.

Tonio jumped easily out of the way. *Pathetic,* he observed, as he flicked his hand, giving the marquis an invisible push.

The Frenchman stumbled backward. Glaring, he said, "You do not scare me with your silly tricks."

Not tricks, Tonio disputed. *A warning.*

Vernoux sneered. "A warning of what?"

Tonio swiped his arm through the air. The pots hanging on a rack over the table tumbled from their hooks and crashed onto the marquis. Vernoux uselessly tried to protect his head.

You will not touch Madame de Volonté, Tonio said, moving to within a few arm lengths of the Frenchman. With another flick, he pushed the man again.

"She is my whore," Vernoux said scornfully.

She is no one's whore. Tonio whipped his arm in an arc and sent the Frenchman crashing into an *étagère* piled with crockery. The pots and dishes exploded into pieces.

Vernoux scrambled up. Small cuts on his neck and ear showed red. "I own her." Scooping up a pile of broken pottery, he flung it.

Tonio stopped it in midair and threw it back at him. *You do not.* He stalked closer. *She is owned by no one. If you hurt her again, know I will come after you. Next time, I will not be so gentle.*

With another wide sweep of his arm, he propelled the marquis forward, against the table, where he sprawled across it in the same position he had held the girl. As his genitals slammed against the wood, he let out a bellow of pain.

Not so much fun when you are on the receiving end, si? Tonio taunted.

Vernoux's hand closed around the handle of the knife still sticking into the tabletop. In a single movement, he jerked it free, surged upright and swept it in an arc. Tonio jumped back, but it raked across his ribs. He felt nothing but knew he would have a scratch there when he turned to flesh and bone. It would probably hurt like Hades.

Annoyed he had allowed the marquis to surprise him, he swung out his arm and slammed him onto the table. The Frenchman's head hit the hard wood with the crack of a pistol. His eyes glazed as he sprawled across it. The knife skittered to the edge and hung there.

Tonio jumped up onto the table and crouched beside him so he could look into the man's eyes. *You will not abuse Madame de Volonté in any way.* He flicked his fingers to collect the knife. It flew into his palm. *Nor,* he said, *will you flog her brother.* He let the Frenchman see the blade. *Do I make myself clear, Monsieur le Marquis?*

Vernoux glared at him but refused to answer.

Tonio wanted to stab the knife into one of those glaring, snake-like eyes or perhaps into the Frenchman's ugly heart but refrained because he surmised that Solange might be considered suspect. No suspicion would fall on her over what he did this night. Instead, he held his free palm in the air over the Frenchman's groin, slowly closed his hand into a fist, then twisted. Vernoux grabbed his crotch and his face convulsed in pain. He let out a strangled groan. Tonio tightened his hold on the man's privates. Vernoux's groan escalated in tone and volume.

Am I making myself clear? Tonio sent his words stabbing into the Frenchman's mind.

"*Oui,*" Vernoux gasped. The hatred in the man's eyes simmered.

Bene. He released his hold on the man's privates. The Frenchman's hand relaxed open on the table near Tonio's knee. *Just to remind you to behave . . .* Tonio said, then he jabbed the blade through Vernoux's palm.

Vernoux howled a combination of pain and outrage.

Too late, Tonio saw the flash of intent in the man's eyes. He caught the upward movement of his arm out of the corner of his eye, the glowing frog glyph on his wrist, and jumped away, but not soon enough. The Frenchman's wrist caught his shoulder, and the frog glyph grazed his skin. The burn seared him.

Cazzo! he swore, surprised that he felt the sensation. Was that frog glyph lethal while he was Shadow? He should have felt nothing. Tendrils of icy-hot pain began to twine across his shoulder.

Vernoux emitted an ugly laugh.

From beyond the kitchen door, Tonio heard the sound of running feet, the cries of alarm. The altercation had roused the household. It was time to leave. Perhaps he would have the opportunity to kill the man another time. Besides, his shoulder needed attention.

Satisfied the Frenchman had learned his lesson, Tonio said, *I am so glad we had this chat.* He pulled the knife from Vernoux's hand and stuck it into the table far from his reach.

The marquis bellowed in pain. His dark eyes burned in his bloodless face. "You will pay for this," he rasped. "The Legion of Baal will destroy you."

Ah. Well, they will have to catch me first. Ignoring the poisonous sting from the burn on his shoulder, Tonio executed an elaborate bow, then lightly stepped across Vernoux's prone form, and floated to the floor. *Buona sera, Monsieur le Marquis.*

As he slipped out of the kitchen, he heard Vernoux calling for his footmen to catch the intruder. Chuckling, Tonio disappeared into the shadows.

Chapter 8

A week after his encounter with Vernoux, Tonio was crouched on the low branch of a tree in the same woods where Solange had robbed him. Below him, she sat on her horse as they waited for a coach to pass, one with wealthy passengers whom they could relieve of their valuables.

He rolled his shoulder, easing the stiffness from the poisonous burn Vernoux had inflicted. Usually, nothing hurt him while he was Shadow, a dangerous condition because he could be severely injured and not realize it. But he and his brother had been shocked at the effects of the frog glyph. By the time Tonio had returned home, he was sick and shivering. Fortunately, Piero had been able to counteract the poison before it destroyed his Shadow body. The slice across his ribs would have to wait until he returned to flesh and bone, and besides, he could not feel it.

Solange shifted on her horse. "How long have you been Shadow?" Her voice drifted up to him in the quiet night and broke the silence that had stretched between them since arriving at this spot.

During the week that had elapsed after he had discovered her trembling and hurt in her bedchamber, Tonio had visited her every night, sometimes allowing her to see him, other times just watching her sleep. Guilt over urging her to steal from one of the great houses had been part of what drew him to her bedchamber, but only part. Her connection to the Sphere of Astarte had lured him. And his overwhelming craving to touch her. But he had restrained himself. After the abuse by Vernoux, he knew she would not welcome the advances of anyone. During the week of her recovery, she had been cool and polite, with no evidence that they had ever been the least bit intimate. That they had never shared that shattering kiss in the middle of their robbery.

It was only the two of them there in the dark. Her brother was still too ill to join them. Her question surprised him. It was gentle, tentative, intimate, spoken as if they lay in bed together; spent, after making love. Her cool reserve was gone.

He looked down at her upturned face. Only the curve of her cheek, the point of her chin, and the darker bow of her mouth were visible beneath the shade of her hat. The light of the waning moon was filtered beneath the trees, and the shadows of the leaves created a lacy pattern on her skin, making her appear like some wood-bound nymph. The urge to trail his fingers across her cheek, her lips, made him clench his fist. It was not the time. They were there to thieve.

When he did not answer, she tilted her head. "Am I being too forward?"

He laughed. *Si.*

She faced forward again so he could not see her face. "If I asked *how* you became Shadow, would that be less intrusive?"

If I asked how you became a thief, would you tell me?

She said nothing.

He smiled at her silence. *Ah, dolce mia, I guard my secrets just as you do. Perhaps, in time, we will learn to trust and share, si?*

She was quiet for so long he thought the conversation was at an end, then he heard her ask, "Can you at least tell me if you are human?"

That, he decided, was a very good question. He glanced down at her upturned face. *What else would I be if not human?*

Her hat dipped and shielded her face. He knew she was trying to come up with an answer. Throwing away caution, he dropped down to land lightly on her horse behind her. His thighs bracketed her. His chest rubbed against the coat across her back. He projected enough force to make her aware that he surrounded her. *I am male, dolcezza, and every time I look at you, I want to touch you.*

He felt her stiffen and knew she was thinking of Vernoux's abuse. Keeping his hands on his thighs, he said, *My touch will never cause you pain, Solange.*

Her head dropped forward, exposing the nape of her neck. "I can't forget . . . I can't make it go away."

May I help? Apprehensive, he waited for her answer. If she refused, he would abide by her wishes, even if it meant madness when he entered the Hunger. Despite the fact that he did not entirely trust her, he would not inflict any more pain upon her.

Finally, she gave a tiny nod.

Grazie, he murmured.

Lightly, he traced his fingers across the nape of her neck, where pale tendrils escaped from the braid she had tucked up under her hat. That warm tingle erupted beneath his touch, and he felt her shiver in response. Trailing his fingers across the pulse below her ear, he felt it quicken. It would be easy to Thought Bind with her, to give her pleasure with nothing more than a bit of pressure, but he needed to feel her, to let her feel him. He moved on to her cheek and teased the corner of her mouth. Her lips parted. As he rubbed his thumb across her bottom lip, she drew in a breath.

I think you enjoy my touch, he whispered in her head.

She expelled her breath in a soft whimper of acknowledgment.

Pressing his lips against the back of her neck, he closed his eyes as he savored the feel of her. He felt her bones go soft. As she yielded to him, visions of making love to her in his Shadow form blossomed in his mind. He imagined the feel of her, naked beneath his length, the tingle of her skin skipping along his body.

Aroused, unnerved by what he saw and felt, he drew back. He had never before wanted a woman while Shadow. If he made love to her in his present state, what would happen once he entered the Hunger? Would his craving for her drive him closer to madness? Or would he be able to control it better because he had been satisfied while still Shadow? He let his hand fall to his thigh.

She stiffened in response to his withdrawal. "Why did you stop?" Her question sounded like a plea.

Because this is not the time for such things. He swung back up to the branch.

"I disgust you." She did not look at him, and her shoulders sagged.

No. Never that.

Her silence told him she did not believe him.

If we make love, it will not be when part of my attention is listening for what is coming down the road. If we make love, I wish all my attention on you, dolce mia.

Despite the fact that she ducked her head, he could see the corner of her lips curve up in a tiny smile. He had pleased her, and that pleased him. Even though questions churned in his mind about entering the Hunger, he knew that his answer to her about making love had contained the wrong word. It was not *if,* but *when.* Making love with this woman was inevitable.

He forced the thought away as he crouched on his branch and focused on their task.

* * *

Solange stared out at the moonlit road and tried to ignore the little skitter in her chest at Tonio's words. Anticipation at feeling his hands on her made her wet her lips. How could she possibly be looking forward to making love with him? He was Shadow, not flesh and bone, not solid. She was not even sure if he was human, for he had answered her question with one of his own. But his touch made her feel things she had never experienced. It made her forget the harshness of Vernoux's hands and the pain they inflicted. It made her think about pleasure, something she had not contemplated with a man. It caused the moisture between her thighs even now, after such a short encounter. She wanted more.

Stupid, stupid, stupid. She could not afford to allow herself the luxury of pleasure with him. He was using her for his own ends, just as she was using him.

Someone is coming.

With relief, she heard his warning in her head. They were here to do a job, not to flirt, certainly not to tantalize each other with arousal. Peering down the road, she could neither hear nor see anyone coming, but she knew his sight and hearing were better than hers.

After a moment, he added more information. *A single rider, coming fast.*

With a nod, she pulled her scarf up over the lower part of her face and urged her horse forward into the road. The sound of galloping hooves reached her ears before the rider rounded the curve. At first, she thought they were going to collide, then the rider pulled up so hard that his horse reared. He swore violently as he tried to get his horse under control. She kept her own horse under tight rein with one hand and the pressure of her knees. When the rider's horse came down hard on its front hooves, and she was sure she had the man's attention, she showed her pistol.

"Your money or your life, *monsieur*," she said.

He stared at her in astonishment as his horse pranced. "You are robbing me?"

His amazement was so complete that she laughed. "*Oui.* I am robbing you." She saw Tonio move out into the road behind him, cutting off his retreat. Becoming serious again, she ordered, "Throw your money on the ground, *s'il vous plait, monsieur,* and I will let you pass unharmed."

The man's horse paced in a circle, and he caught a glimpse of Tonio. His attention was immediately riveted, and he forced his horse to quiet. Turning his back on Solange's lethal pistol, he expelled a curse. "Auriano? Is that you?"

Solange was not sure she heard correctly. Her gaze cut to Tonio, standing in the middle of the road, and she watched as he executed a graceful bow.

Buona sera, General Bonaparte, he said, humor rippling through his tone. *It seems we keep running into each other.* He glanced around as if looking for something. *Did you lose your army, General? Where are your aides?*

"I'm traveling incognito," the general snapped.

Aren't you aware that the roads are dangerous? You never know when you might fall in with robbers, Tonio taunted.

Shocked into silence, Solange's mind raced. Their victim was none other than the hero of the Italian Campaign that the French were waging, and he and Tonio obviously knew each other. But what had really caught her attention was what the general had called Tonio. Were Gide's suspicions correct? Was Tonio truly the Duke of Auriano? And if he were, then who was the man who had come that night to help her and Gide after Vernoux had inflicted his punishment? He certainly had looked like the duke, the man she had robbed, the man who had appeared at her salon. But if Tonio was the real duke, how had he become Shadow?

Her attention snapped back to their victim when the general asked, "Have you turned to highway robbery since you left Venice, Excellency?"

Tonio shrugged. *Merely a sideline, general. I trust you left our palazzo in good condition?*

"It was untouched when I left, although I can't say the same for the rest of the city. The Great Council needed to be taught some manners. I admired the four bronze horses of St. Mark's."

You stole them? Tonio's tone was half astonished, half amused.

"Among a few other baubles. They are being transported to France as we speak."

That special weapon that we gave you, do you still have it?

"*Oui.*"

Is it with you?

"*Oui.*"

Annoyed at being ignored, Solange snapped at Tonio, "Are you done catching up on old times? I thought we were here to rob him."

Bonaparte glanced at her and the pistol still aimed at him. "Are you going to rob me or shoot me?"

"I won't shoot you if you drop your money on the ground," she told him.

Solange, let him go, she heard in her head.

Her astonishment at Tonio's request jerked her gaze from their victim. Experience quickly brought it back to focus on the general.

"A woman?" Bonaparte's surprise turned to a chuckle. "Now I know why you have turned to thievery, Auriano. I would bet my last *sou* that under all those clothes, she's beautiful."

Irritated at what Bonaparte implied, Solange said scornfully, "Does the fact that I might be beautiful have anything to do with the fact that I am holding you at gunpoint and about to rob you, General?"

The general bowed. "My apologies, *mademoiselle*. You have the advantage."

"Your money, *monsieur le general, s'il vous plait,*" she bit out.

No, Solange, not him. Tonio's words were adamant.

Solange glared at him. She was astounded that Tonio would let their victim go, no matter how important he was or how well he knew him. And she was furious that he had deceived her about his identity. "I'm not letting him go. I need to show something for tonight. You know Le Chacal's demands. *Excellency.*" She twisted the title into an insult.

Solange. Her name was half warning, half request.

Tonio took a step toward her, and she leveled her pistol on him. She felt General Bonaparte's gaze dart between the two of them.

Swinging the pistol back to the general, she said, "I have no problem with shooting either one of you."

Faster than she could have imagined, Tonio was astride the horse behind her. His hand covered hers where she held the gun. She felt that warm tingle where his Shadow skin touched hers, but there was something else there besides, some power that exerted pressure.

Don't make me force you to drop this, he said, his voice sounding intimate in her head. *You have to let General Bonaparte go. If you rob him, he can bring the authorities down on both you and Gide. I won't be able to protect you.*

"Will you be able to protect me from Le Chacal and his Chamber of Ghosts?" she fumed. "Will you be able to protect me from going insane?"

Si.

His answer surprised her so much, she let the pistol dip. That pressure on her hand pushed it down to rest on her thigh. It was done gently, but she knew that if she threatened Bonaparte again, he would not hesitate to use that force to restrain her. She could feel it thrumming through the long legs that bracketed hers, the expanse of

107

chest at her back. He gestured to Bonaparte. She watched mutely, impotently, as the general tipped his hat to her, then spurred his horse back into a gallop.

"*Merci*, Excellency, *mademoiselle*," he called as he sped past. "*Au revoir!*"

Solange did not move as she listened to the hoofbeats fade into the night. Tonio remained silent, sitting behind her. His presence overwhelmed her, overloading her senses. She was furious, and she needed to be away from him, from that thrumming that enveloped her.

"Get off my horse," she spat.

His hand fell from where he held her. She felt him slide away, and then he was beside her on the ground. Before he could say anything else, before he could placate her, before he could seduce her with his words or his touch, she wheeled her horse, dug in her heels, and galloped off into the woods.

*   *   *

Tonio watched her go. She was heading in the direction of the shack where they were to meet after the robbery. He would give her some time, and then he would follow and try to explain. Letting Bonaparte go without robbing him had been the lesser of two bad alternatives. He needed the general's goodwill, for the Frenchman still held the Crystal Dagger, the weapon that had been created by the Legion of Baal to destroy Nulkana. If he and Alessandro ever needed the man to give it back to them in their war with Nulkana, then robbing him at gunpoint would not help to convince him.

Tonio had to make Solange understand that the sorceress was a bigger threat than the King of the Thieves. In order to explain it to her, he would have to tell her about Nulkana. He would have to reveal some of his secrets. And then endure her anger.

He was not looking forward to their conversation.

As he started toward the edge of the road, he sensed the evil watching. Nulkana had found him again. He searched the area as he tried to find the owl he had seen before, but he saw no round eyes staring at him from the canopy of trees. The evil reached out for him, curling around his soul, sending icy tentacles through him. Clenching his fist against the pain, he swung out his arm as if he were pushing away a physical attacker. The evil receded, then came again, this time gently, almost like a lover.

Back away! he ordered.

He heard a malevolent laugh, as if from a great distance. It was toying with him, letting him know it was coming. A cold caress twined around his soul, then with icy claws, it ripped away, leaving him swaying.

He hunched up against the emptiness that engulfed him. Tonio knew that void was a mirage. Nulkana wanted him to believe that her evil was the cure for the curse, and she wanted him aware that she was nearly strong enough to attack. The sorceress had tried to kill his brother's wife several times, and he was suddenly afraid for Solange's safety—Solange, who had the same powers as his sister-in-law. She had run into the woods alone and was now massaging her anger at the solitary shack. Without wasting any more time, he raced into the trees.

* * *

When Tonio arrived at the clearing, the shack was in darkness. Solange's horse stood docilely before it. The door was wide open. He could sense no evil. Evidently, Nulkana had enjoyed her fun with him and then retreated. At least he would not have to deal with an evil sorceress, only an enraged woman. But then, interacting with an evil sorceress seemed like child's play in comparison to placating an enraged woman.

Carefully, he approached the doorway. As soon as he stepped to the threshold, a dagger sliced through the dark. It thunked into the doorframe only inches from his head. Alessandro's warning about a woman stabbing him in the heart flitted through his brain.

Your aim is off, dolce mia, he said.

Another dagger whizzed out of the night and smacked into the wood on the other side of him.

"If I wanted to hit you, I would have." Her voice emanated from the darkest corner of the single-room shack.

Ah. He nodded, pretending to understand, then gave in to his bewilderment. *Why didn't you?*

She was silent for so long, he thought she would not answer. Finally, she said, "I need to know why you deceived me."

He thought that over for a moment. *It was not deception. I was being judicious.*

"Judicious." Her repetition of the word was flat, as if all of her anger had deflated. "I suppose you might call Vernoux's abuse the other night judicious. After all, he was only teaching me a lesson."

Remorse shot through him at her barb. *Ah, dolcezza, no.*

"Don't call me that." Her voice was low and vibrated with her anger.

As you wish, he acceded. *I need to explain some things to you.*

"*Oui.* You do. You need to tell me why General Bonaparte called you Auriano. You need to tell me how you know him. You need to tell me why you agreed to help me, and then let our victim go." She paused, and her next words were released in a shout of anger and frustration. "You let him go!"

He heard the rush of air as she attacked. Raising his

hand, palm outward, he halted her just as she reached him. Her fist drew back, but when she would have swung at him, her arm froze as she hit his invisible wall. Antonio was not afraid of her blow. Rather, he feared the effect of her skin against him, the feel of the warm tingle that enticed. He feared he might be distracted enough to try to seduce her. And he very much wanted to seduce her. But this was not the time for seduction. She would hate him for that, and he did not want her to hate him. At least, not yet.

Solange, will you listen to my explanation?

She struggled against his restraint. He held her immobile, watching the play of expressions across her face in the scant moonlight. Astonishment to apprehension to anger. Her eyes blazed at him.

"*Salaud!*" she spat.

I think my parents might disagree with you that I am a bastard, he replied mildly. He watched her struggle another moment, then said, *I will let you go if you promise not to hit me.*

With a glare that held enough heat to cook him, she gave a jerky nod.

Slowly, he lowered his hand. Her fist dropped to her side, and she took a step back. Narrowing her eyes, crossing her arms, she tilted her head, suspicion written plainly in every lovely curve.

"So? Explain." She bit out her words as if each syllable was from a valuable horde.

Shall we get comfortable? Perhaps light the lamp and sit? He swept his arm toward the dark interior.

With a hiss of annoyance, she spun on her heel and moved to the table. After a moment, a light flared. In the lamplight, he saw the only place to sit was a small cot against one wall. He drifted in the other direction, to the table top and sat, tailor-style. As he did, she pointedly stepped away, back toward the door, as if she might flee if he provoked her. Seeing him settled, she pulled one of the daggers from the doorframe before moving to the cot and perching on its edge.

"All right, Excellency," she said, once again giving the title a sarcastic twist. "We're sitting. And I'm listening."

He reminded himself that she had every right to be furious and fought not to lose his own temper at her verbal darts. The urge to push her to her back and punish her with a kiss, to remind her he was helping her made him close his eyes for two heartbeats. Behind his eyelids, the vision of her writhing in passion beneath him made him open them again.

His wild craving for her unnerved him. He had lusted after other women, but never this intensely, never with such single-mindedness, and never while Shadow. In comparison to what he felt towards Solange, his feelings towards those other women were as pale as air. He wondered if Alessandro had felt so out of control around Sabrina, and then remembered his brother's mad need during the Hunger. Tonio was determined to avoid that at all costs. A cool explanation of the danger they were in would help.

Solange, do you know what you are? he began.

Her eyes widened fractionally in surprise at his question, then she shuttered them again. "This is not about me. This is about you. Why did you let Bonaparte escape?"

Because he is holding a valuable artifact for us . . . for me. I can't make an enemy of him.

She immediately picked up his error. "*Us? Who else* is he holding it for besides you?"

Realizing his mistake, he hesitated. He had not planned on revealing who he was quite so soon. *My family*, he said.

*   *   *

Solange saw him glance away and knew whatever he was about to tell her would reveal much. Either he was preparing to lie, or the truth was something amazing. At first surprised he had a family, she realized that of course he must if he were truly the Duke of Auriano. But she rejected any soft feelings he might evoke. She fueled her anger, played with the dagger in her hand, and refused to be swayed by seductive words or pity. She had counted on his help, and he had betrayed her. Now, she had nothing to give Le Chacal, and Vernoux had given the Jackal permission to be remorseless. Only the thin line of Vernoux's protection had kept her from becoming the outlaw's whore as well as Vernoux's. If that changed, she would have no compunctions about covering her dagger in blood—Le Chacal's, Vernoux's.

Tonio's.

Those molten eyes turned back to her. *My family*, he began, *was cursed generations ago by a sorceress named Nulkana. She wanted something that we had—the Sphere of Astarte.*

Solange's lips parted in surprise. Tonio nodded at her recognition.

Si. The artifact that the Silver Arrows are supposed to locate. The Sphere was broken apart by my ancestor and the pieces scattered. Only finding the pieces, returning them to Auriano, and connecting them again will completely break the curse.

"What does this have to do with General Bonaparte?"

He is holding the Crystal Dagger. It was created by the Legion of Baal to kill Nulkana.

"The Legion of Baal?" Solange stared at him, wide-eyed. "They are merely an international group of wealthy men." Wealthy men who were able to inflict pain with a frog tattoo.

Tonio shook his head. *The members are more than wealthy men. I think you know that. The Legion also seeks the Sphere. They are very dangerous.*

Silently, Solange admitted what she had been denying

113

for many years, what her experience with Vernoux had shown her—that he had some sort of magical power. "But why would these men want the Sphere of Astarte?"

Because it contains strong magic. It will impart wealth and power beyond imagination to anyone who owns it. The members of the Legion of Baal want to rule the world.

Suspicion narrowed her eyes. "Is that the real reason you wish to find the Sphere? So you may become powerful and wealthy?"

He shook his head sadly. *No, dolce mia. My family already is wealthy, and the only power we seek is to walk the earth as normal men.*

Solange glanced away from the pain in those golden eyes. Even if she had not believed his words, his naked expression revealed the truth. Not wishing to delve deeper into his soul, she turned to another subject. "Why is General Bonaparte holding onto this Crystal Dagger? Surely after so many centuries the sorceress is dead."

No, she is still alive.

"How can that be?"

She lives by sucking the life out of young women.

Appalled, Solange sucked in her own breath.

Nulkana wants the Sphere because it also bestows immortality.

Stunned, Solange stared at Tonio as she tried to digest everything he had just told her. She had always known that Vernoux was more than a lucky aristocrat who had escaped the guillotine. The frog glyph that gave such pain was proof of that. But she had no idea that there was other evil in the world worse than his.

"I always thought the Sphere of Astarte was a myth," she said.

Like the moonstone? he taunted.

She felt the heat rise in her cheeks.

Do I look like a myth, dolce mia? His words swirled softly through her brain.

Chapter 9

Solange studied him. He did look like a myth, like something from a fairy tale, dark and mysterious, sensuous and seductive. He was all those things. But he was also more. In the lamplight, the faint definition of features, of muscle and sinew were visible. Beyond those golden molten eyes that were so arresting, she could see the shade of the face of the man he was, that beautiful man of flesh and bone who had entered her salon and challenged her, the one whom she had robbed. The same one who, as Shadow, had kissed her in the middle of a house theft and brought her such pleasure that she had shattered.

"Auriano," she whispered.

He dipped his head in acknowledgment. *Si.*

"Then who was the man who came to help the other night?"

My brother.

Although she had been in pain, she remembered the man who had brought help after Vernoux's abuse. He looked *exactly* like the duke, not like a brother with a family resemblance. Anger whipped through her. "You lie. He is the duke."

No, Solange, he is Alessandro, Prince of Auriano. His gentle words were solid with truth. *He is my twin.*

Her eyes widened. Twin brothers. Two devastatingly beautiful men walking the world. "Does he become Shadow, also?"

Si. When I am not.

Fascinated, without thinking, she stood and approached him. "May I touch you?"

His lips twisted wryly. *That would be the fulfillment of my deepest desire.*

Untangling his legs, he let them hang over the edge of the table. Solange stepped between his knees. Hesitantly, palm out, she lifted her hand and let it hover a minuscule distance from his chest. She felt a faint tingle, like an echo of what she felt when he touched her. Her gaze dropped to his chest and followed the ridges and curves of the muscle and sinew that would be visible beneath his skin if he were solid.

Fascinated by the tickling buzz on her palm, she moved her hand through the space over his chest. She wondered what he was feeling and peeked at him from beneath her lashes. His lips were parted, but he appeared to be clenching his jaw, as if holding back some powerful feeling. Those golden eyes were intense, watching her. Afraid suddenly of what he might feel like, she froze. What if she found him repulsive?

Touch me, dolcezza.

His seductive murmur enticed. Her apprehension was foolish. Whenever he had come into contact with her, she had felt only pleasure. Closing her eyes, she placed her hand flat against his chest.

"Oh," she breathed.

At the moment of contact, she sensed a warmth slip through her mind, as if he had expelled a mental sigh. Beneath her hand, besides that tingle, his skin was fluid, yet not. It felt like floating her hand on the surface of warm water. It supported and enveloped at the same time. Yet, there was tension to his skin, so she could push no further than the surface. Beneath, she sensed the muscles and sinews, the bones, but they, too, seemed to be fluid. When she moved her hand to the center of his chest, his heartbeat pulsed under her palm, like a steady wave on water.

Her eyes opened. "You feel beautiful," she whispered.

He smiled. *Grazie.* His fingers slid along her jaw, then cupped her neck. *You also feel beautiful to me.*

The tingle of his touch sent a delicious shiver down her spine. He drew her closer and placed his lips gently against her mouth. Solange stood perfectly still, not wanting to disturb the moment. Her eyelids fluttered closed. With her hand against his chest, his hand at her neck, their lips barely touching, time seemed to stand still. The moment balanced precariously before it tipped, either in a slow slide or a wild rush downward into pleasure.

Perhaps you should remove your coat, si?

The suggestion was barely a whisper in her brain. With their lips still touching, even before the words stopped, she was stripping out of the garment. Her waistcoat went next, and then the stock around her neck beneath his hand, leaving her skin bare to his touch. The feel of him, that warm tingle on her skin, his thumb against her pulse, made her suck in a breath.

He drew back, and his hand slid from her neck. Holding his hands on either side of her, without touching, he slowly pulled her shirt from her breeches. Her eyes were locked into his gaze, unable to look away, falling into the heat in those golden eyes. She felt his fingers skim under her shirt across her ribs, and she shivered. Then he stilled as he came into contact with the strips binding her breasts.

Ah, bella mia, this is wrong, he murmured.

In a flash, the strips were undone and laying on the floor at her feet. When she felt his hands cup her breasts, she released an audible sigh. His fingers sought out her nipples and teased. Pleasure shot through her, pooling in her center. She threw back her head with a moan. Leaning in, he kissed the hollow of her throat, his tongue licking where his lips had been. While she had been distracted, somehow, her breeches had come undone, and she felt his hand slide down across her belly. His fingers tangled in the curls below and stopped.

Will you allow me to give you pleasure? he asked.

A soft laugh escaped her. "You did not ask the last time."

He shrugged, a wry smile tilting his lips. *A surprise for both of us.*

Running her hands up his thighs, she asked, "May I give you pleasure?"

Uncertainty flickered across his face, then his expression smoothed out. His gaze heated with an intensity she could feel in the back of her brain. He slid from the table to stand, his body brushing down the length of her. As he did, one hand splayed across her back, while the fingers of his other hand curled deeper into the triangle of hair between her thighs. That warm tingle pulsed against her tiny nub, echoing as a throb deep inside her. She whimpered her joy.

Watching you shatter is pleasure for me, he said.

Barely able to make her mind work as his fingers slid inside her, she gasped, "I want to see you shatter."

Ladies first, he murmured and kissed her.

His mouth came down on hers with an explosion of tiny shocks. She welcomed him, invited him to partake. His tongue danced counterpoint to his fingers. She had never felt such delicious sensations. They invaded her, wrapped around her, building in strength. She slipped her arms around him, one tiny part of her marveling at the fluid feel of him. Moaning in pleasure, she wriggled closer. She wanted to crawl inside him, have him crawl inside her. Never before had she felt such need. And all the while that throbbing at her core, rising, rising, until it crested, flinging her apart with a cry of unbridled passion.

Her knees buckled, and she sagged against him. He supported her, not with pressure, but some other force that made her feel weightless. Resting her cheek against his chest, she felt that warm tingle pulsing. While she had found release, he had not. Despite her pleasure, she was still in need, and she wanted to return his gift.

He touched his lips to the top of her head. *You shatter beautifully, dolce mia.*

Playfully, she traced her fingers over his ribs and was rewarded by a responsive shiver. "How do you shatter, my Shadow?"

Ah, that is a question we will have to explore.

Trailing her fingers down, she outlined his hip, but when she slipped to its hollow, his hand stopped her. His head went up. He became very still.

Do you sense that? he asked, his tone wary.

At the same time, she felt an icy tentacle curl about her heart. She gasped. "What is it?"

Without answering, he let her support her own weight, and with a flick of his hand, put out the lantern, plunging them into darkness. Something drew her gaze to the doorway of the shack. Beyond, the moonlight shone on the clearing, but nearer to the door, a mist gathered. An unnatural cold seeped out from it, edging across the floor. It reached her ankles and crawled up her legs.

Nulkana, Tonio said.

As he spoke the name, the mist filled the doorway, and in its middle, a dark, indistinct figure appeared. Tonio pushed her to the floor and covered her with his body. Peeking beyond his shoulder, she saw the figure's outline sharpen. Its face was hidden, and it was darkly cloaked and hooded, lethal in its stark simplicity. Menace emanated from it like a cloying fog. That one icy tentacle about her heart turned to two, then three, and they wound inside her chest, writhing, squeezing.

Use your power, Solange, Tonio urged.

She gaped at him. Power?

Like the rats, he said.

119

The rats. In the Chamber of Ghosts. "I can't," she gasped as those tentacles twisted tighter. "I don't remember how."

You do.

He placed his fingers against the pulse in her throat. Immediately, she saw herself in the Catacombs, and she saw the power flashing from her fingers. She did know. Lifting her hand, she sent a wave of power out toward that figure. It flared with a satisfying zap and surprised her with its intensity, for she thought she had lost that ability. She knew she had hit the figure, but nothing happened. It still stood in the doorway. The energy seemed to go right through it. She heard an evil laugh.

"Did you think you could harm me?" the figure asked derisively. "And you, whelp, do you believe you can protect your little slut from me?"

Nulkana laughed again. The abrasive sound made Solange clench her teeth in fear and discomfort.

"I will have you both," the sorceress said. "Not now, but when I am ready. And you won't be able to stop me."

Atop her, Solange felt Tonio stiffen, then tremble, as if he was enduring some terrible pain. Then he abruptly went limp, his head dropping to her shoulder. The mist in the doorway began to recede, and the figure of Nulkana grew smaller. After a moment, both Nulkana and the mist disappeared with a *pop.* Beyond the door, the moonlight still shone on the peaceful clearing.

Tonio did not move. What had Nulkana done to him? "Tonio."

He did not answer. Giving him a little shake, Solange tried to wake him. No response. What was wrong with him?

"Tonio." She gave him another shake.

I'm all right, dolce mia. His words finally came, weak and strained.

"Are you hurt? What can I do?" She had never had to help a Shadow before. She had no idea how to go about it.

Please, just let me lie here for a moment.

His request was no hardship. Solange relaxed and wrapped her arms about him. His body was weightless and covered her like a sensuous blanket. That warm tingle leaped between them. She rubbed her hand soothingly over his shoulder.

"What did Nulkana do to you?" she asked.

I felt as if she were trying to pull out my heart. He nuzzled her neck. *You make me feel whole again.*

Glad she was able to help, she absently rubbed his back while her brain churned with questions. "Why did she leave so suddenly? I didn't hurt her. She could have killed both of us."

He kissed the pulse below her ear, then circled his tongue around the spot. *Using your power has made you taste like plums,* he murmured. He propped himself up and stared down at her. *I can taste you.* That golden gaze held astonishment and awe. *Dio mio, I can taste you!* Dipping his head, he ran his tongue up the side of her neck, then across her lips. *Mmmm, definitely plums.*

Annoyed, she tried to push him off. "Will you please stop licking me like some bonbon?"

He grinned. *But you are a bonbon, dolcezza.*

Solange wriggled out from beneath him and sat up. "We've just been attacked by an ancient sorceress. Could you please explain what happened?"

Reaching out, he let his fingers drift down her throat and across the bare skin revealed by her open shirt. Solange swallowed at the delicious sensation, then slapped his hand away. She was not going to let him distract her, despite the fact that echoes of her arousal still throbbed.

His lips twitched, but he dropped his hand. *I will explain if you promise we can finish what we started.*

She scowled at him.

Tell me you are not curious about making love with a Shadow. Lifting her hand, he kissed her palm, then tickled with his tongue. Licking his lips as if he had just tasted the most decadent morsel, his gaze became wolfish.

Solange felt the tingling effects of his tongue ripple all the way up her arm, and the effects of that gaze deep in her center. Snatching her hand away, she ordered, "Explain."

A mocking sigh wafted through her brain. *You have no mercy, bella mia.*

Reaching behind her, she grabbed her dagger off the cot where she had left it. "I have a weapon." She waved it under his nose. "Explain."

Tonio held up his hands in surrender and became serious. *That was only a projection of Nulkana's form. That's why you didn't injure her.*

"But if that was only a projection, how could she hurt you?" she asked.

She has the power to hurt, but she's not strong enough to attack yet. She wants me to know she's watching. Both of us.

"Why is she watching me?"

Don't you know what you are?

"You asked me that before. Of course I know what I am. I'm a thief and a whore." She spat out the words in a cold voice laced with a lifetime of agony and abuse.

Ah, Solange, he said, shaking his head sadly. *That is not what you are. You know that in here.* He placed his finger softly over her heart. *You are magical. And you are just as powerful as Nulkana.*

Solange stared at him. Not wanting to believe him, she reverted to her role as cool, insulted temptress. "You have a very odd manner of seduction, *monsieur*."

His eyes narrowed. *If I wanted to seduce you, I would not be telling you that you could reduce me to ash with a flick of your hand.* He paused. *If I wanted to seduce you, I would tell you that you are the most beautiful woman I have ever met. That your eyes remind me of the summer sky, and your lips remind me of plump, sun-kissed fruit.*

I would take your hand and worship each finger.

He laid her hand, palm up, in his. Then he touched his lips to each fingertip. He followed that by sucking on every one.

Solange was mesmerized. She knew she should be asking more questions, but she could not form the words. The tingles against her skin distracted her. Each time he sucked on a finger, she felt the pull up her arm and into her chest. Once again, he tickled her palm with his tongue. Her body throbbed with such intensity that she moaned.

Shocked at her visceral response, she jerked away from him. "Stop that."

Instead of his teasing amusement, he turned serious. His steady gaze held hers.

You are powerful, Solange. Nulkana knows that, and she will do everything she can to destroy you.

She shook her head in denial. "I'm not powerful. She has nothing to fear from me."

She does. Because you are descended from her sister, Halima, who was also a sorceress.

"That's impossible."

Hold out your left hand and spread your fingers.

Solange thought the attack by Nulkana might have unbalanced him.

Please, humor me, he requested.

Apprehensive, she did as he asked.

Unerringly in the dark, he touched the web between her thumb and first finger. *You have a mark here, like a starburst.*

"How can you see that? It's black as pitch in here." She had always been self-conscious about the birthmark, so dark against her pale hand.

I saw it before, at your salon. It's the mark of Halima. You are her descendant. And powerful.

Suddenly terrified of everything he was saying and

what it implied, Solange scrambled to her feet. "I'm not. Don't tell me that. I'm a whore. Vernoux's whore. I thieve for a man who answers to him. And I have nothing to show for tonight. Because you let our victim get away."

With jerky movements, she stuck her dagger into its sheath. Her hands shook. She could not seem to catch her breath. Stalking to the doorway, she pulled the other dagger from the frame. By the time she turned back to the room, Tonio was also standing. The moonlight flowed from the open door behind her and illuminated his figure. He floated several inches above the floor. She closed her eyes, denying what she was seeing.

"I've gone mad. You're not real. The story you just told me is my imagination."

Solange, you're not making any sense.

A wild laugh escaped her. "Of course not. Because I've lost my mind. I'm having a conversation with a Shadow."

His words came, undeniable, into her mind. *A Shadow who can give you la petite mort.*

She opened her eyes at that. Her body still wanted. Him.

But she was not going to succumb to those words that echoed so seductively in her head. He was myth, fairy tale, while Le Chacal's implicit threat was real.

"I'm going back to the city. And I don't want you to follow me." She stalked to the middle of the room. Waving the dagger at him to force him back, she swiped her waistcoat and coat off the floor. Shrugging into the garments as she moved back to the doorway, she tried to ignore the feel of his eyes on her. He was not real. Everything was a lie.

Solange, I'm sorry.

His words halted her just before she stepped across the threshold.

I will make amends for letting the general go.

A warm caress floated through her brain, and she

shivered. She had to get away. From him. From what he had told her. From the insanity that her life had suddenly become. She shook her head, not willing to reply to something—to him—that she was trying to deny with every fiber of her soul.

Forcing her feet to move, she walked out into the night, mounted her horse, and spurred him to a gallop. She would ride through the dark and try to forget the heat that pulsed in her core, and the warmth of his touch against her skin. She would not imagine that her body was alight with a sparkling trail left by the imprint of his fingers.

And she would deny that she was descended from a powerful sorceress.

Chapter 10

Having dismissed her maid for the night, Solange stared into the mirror above her dressing table without seeing her reflection. Her salon this evening had been a disaster. One of the men had tried to take advantage of one of the women. Another couple had indulged in a very public argument. Vernoux had arrived in a steely, cold rage, his hand wrapped in a bandage, barely healed scratches vivid along his cheek. He left with a young woman who was too innocent to take on a protector. Solange had tried to stop him, but when he directed that frigid gaze on her, she knew she had no choice but to let him go. She did not want to think what condition the woman might be in when the marquis finished with her.

This morning she had received a message from Le Chacal demanding that she produce spoils from her thefts, or he would force Gide to join *les chauffeurs,* those remorseless thieves who tortured their victims. Her life seemed to be falling apart, and it all had begun with her thievery of the Duke of Auriano. She wished she could rewind time.

The flame of the lamp on her dressing table flickered from a draft, as if someone had moved through the space behind her, but she was alone, and she had heard nothing. Only one person could move so silently. She focused on the reflection of the room in the mirror. The faint outline of one side of his body was visible on the far side of the room. Tonio. He had come like she knew he would. She covered her eyes with her hands.

Hiding won't make me disappear, dolce mia, he said.

"Go away." She did not drop her hands. Covering her eyes somehow gave her a sense of fragile safety.

Something upsets you. His voice sounded closer, as if he had moved up behind her.

Refusing to look at him, she felt a near hysterical laugh bubble up in her throat. What escaped sounded more like a sob. "Why should I be upset? My life is falling apart, and I just learned I am somehow related to an evil sorceress. I'm trying to convince myself you're not real, but if I open my eyes, I know I'll be able to see you."

I am sorry, dolcezza.

A warm caress floated over her mind. Soft and sweet, comforting, it brought her to the point of tears. She would not cry. So she resorted to anger. "Stop that." Dropping her hands, she glared at him in the mirror. As she suspected, he was close behind her.

He shrugged. *I am only trying to help. Would you prefer I seduce you?*

Gritting her teeth, Solange fought the compulsion to say yes. She had wanted him since the other night when Nulkana had attacked them. When she had learned who he truly was. When she had learned who *she* truly was. No, she had wanted him since the first time he appeared in her bedchamber and made that bargain with her to steal.

He chuckled at her silence. *Ah, so you do prefer seduction.*

"Do not mock me." Jumping from her seat, Solange swung to face him. She had expected him to move back, but he remained where he was, so close that her night rail brushed him. With only a slight sway of her body, she would be rubbing against him.

His sigh wafted through her mind. *Solange, you cannot fight what you are. Anger will not change it. We must talk about this.* He paused, and his tone turned teasing. *Then I will seduce you, si?*

Before she had a chance to react, he walked away, releasing her from an answer. Surprised, she watched him. She admired the perfect form of him, the play of shadow and light that rippled across the darkness of his muscles as he moved. She yearned to run her fingers down that long back.

He settled himself, tailor-fashion, on the bed. *Come, bella mia, sit and talk with me. Let me help you understand.* He held out his hand in invitation.

His words seemed sincere, even though he sat on the one piece of furniture in the room that Solange wanted to be furthest from. She was not going near the bed, not until she could unravel the confusion of who she was. Of who he was. Of what they were.

Ignoring the invitation of his hand, she turned the little chair before her dressing table around, sat, and faced him. She folded her hands in her lap, crossed her ankles, and kept her back straight.

His fingers fisted around air, and he dropped his hand. That golden gaze mocked. *Afraid?* He spoke his single word mildly, without force.

"Judicious," she retorted. "I think you used the word yourself."

His amusement riffled through her brain.

She raised her chin in challenge. "So. Let us talk."

Tell me about your parents.

Surprised at his request, she hesitated. This was not how she expected the conversation to begin.

I need to understand them before I can explain what is happening with you, piccola mia.

Little one. He had never called her that before. It made her feel innocent, something she had not been in a very long time. Tears threatened again. How could he make her cry so easily with kindness?

Swallowing, she took a breath. "My parents—" Her voice broke, and she could not go on.

How did they die?

He surprised her again with his insight. Her throat clogged. She had pushed their death into a tiny back corner of her mind. Remembering would bring grief, and that was weak. Swallowing again, she straightened her shoulders and raised her chin. She would not give in to weakness.

"They died in a fire." Glaring at him as if he had been involved, she said, "Murdered."

He was quiet for several heartbeats. *That is very sad,* he finally said. *Tell me about it.*

She had told no one of the manner of her parents' death. It was too painful, too personal to share. For some reason, she wanted to tell him, to share with him what she had been holding in for so long. The words began to spill from her.

"My *maman* loved to sing. She was kind and gentle, and she and my papa loved each other very much. My papa was head gardener for the Comte d'Aucoin. He could make the most glorious flowers bloom. His orchards bore huge, sweet fruit. The comte referred to him as his magician." She shrugged. "I guess he was magical, for I often found him chanting verses to his plants in the orangery. He made me promise never to tell anyone. When he found I could scare away the little animals that would nibble at the plants with a flash from my hands, he swore me to secrecy.

"We lived in a comfortable house on the comte's estate, and as long as we did not bother anyone or allow ourselves to be seen, Gide and I could play in the comte's gardens. One day, a stranger arrived in the village. He was a member of the *sans-culottes*, the revolutionaries who were behind the overthrow of the king. This stranger convinced the villagers that my father had bewitched the comte into taking over most of the common land for his gardens. This was land the villagers used for firewood and grazing their livestock, and so it was my father's fault they were hungry.

"The anger started slowly—hard looks, charging us more for things at the market than they were worth. Then the shopkeepers would close their shops if they saw us coming. The other children threw manure at us. One day, Gide and I had gone to pick strawberries, and when we returned, our house was in flames. Neither of my parents escaped." She swallowed past the lump in her throat, then went on.

"The comte had no use for two children, and no one in the village would have anything to do with us. Gide and I had nowhere else to go, so we came to the city."

She swiped at a tear.

I am sorry, dolcezza. That must have been very hard for you.

She shrugged away his sympathy. "We survived." She did not tell him that they survived by becoming thieves for Le Chacal, who gave her to Vernoux when she was old enough. By that time, Vernoux had solidified his influence with the Committee of Public Safety that ruled France and could have Le Chacal thrown into the *Conciergerie* on a whim. She had been a bribe.

He shifted on the bed as if he sensed what she held back. *You get your power from your father.*

Not willing to accept his statement, she said, "It was just a toy, something I could play with."

Until Le Chacal put you and Gide in the Chamber of Ghosts with the rats.

She let her gaze slip away from him. "*Oui*," she said, trying to forget the horror. "I was sick for days after that, and when I got well, I thought I had imagined it."

Your gift is not a toy.

She would not answer.

You are very powerful.

She refused to meet his eyes.

Solange.

He stood before her. Swiftly, silently, he had moved from the bed without her being aware of it. When she tipped her head back to look at him, his fingers grazed across her cheek. That warm tingle erupted so intensely she gasped.

Your power calls to me, he said.

"No." She shook her head, still trying to deny him, herself, and what she was. She had become an orphan because of the power passed down to her from her father. Fear of what she was had ruled her life since. Her ability was a dangerous, knife-edged legacy. And then Vernoux had made her feel powerless.

His hand cupped the back of her head, and effortlessly, he brought her to her feet. Their bodies brushed. Even through the light gauze of her night rail, that tingle bolted through her and ended in a throb of fierce need.

Tell me you do not desire my touch, he murmured.

Looking into those golden eyes, she was lost. "I . . ." She could not form a thought, much less a sentence.

His lips curved seductively. *I want to touch you, dolce mia. I want to feel you beneath my fingers. I want to feel your body pressed to mine. Please.*

Lowering his head, he placed his mouth chastely against hers, and then he placed a tiny kiss at each corner. His touch was exquisitely gentle. Solange was so focused on what his mouth was doing, that she did not realize the tie at the neckline of her night rail had been loosened until she felt the material slip from her shoulders. As soon as the skimpy barrier fell to the floor, using only the hand at the back of her head, he pulled her tightly against him.

His sigh, as if from tremendous relief, slipped through her mind. *I have been starved for your touch.*

As she felt the warmth of him pressed against her breasts and along her thighs, Solange realized that she thirsted for him. She felt as if she had been in the desert for days, and he was her oasis. He had not forced her, coerced her, or beaten her into compliance. He had asked. Even now, standing so close together, he waited for permission. She knew if she denied him, he would respect her wish. But denying him was the last thing she wanted. Wrapping her arms about his ribs, she squeezed against him. He enfolded her as if she were wound in a sensuous blanket. Every inch of her skin tingled with delicious warmth.

"Kiss me," she whispered.

He complied. Slowly, he lowered his head and merely grazed her lips. His tongue licked delicately and traced their contour.

I can still taste you, he said. *Like plums.*

And then he plundered, his tongue swooping into her mouth, teasing, arousing. Solange drowned in the sensation. All that tingling, inside her mouth, surrounding her, arrowed down to her core where she throbbed, deeper and harder. Until she exploded into stars. With only a kiss.

When she returned to reality, when she was able to take a breath and open her eyes, she was lying on her back on the bed. Weightless, he was lying atop her.

"How did we get to the bed?" she asked.

He looked very pleased. *I very much enjoy giving you la petite mort*, he said.

She very much enjoyed having him give it to her. Vernoux had never given her pleasure. He had never allowed another man to touch her. But she was not about to allow this man to gloat.

She assumed a stern expression. "You did not answer my question."

He shrugged. *It seemed to be a more comfortable place to be.* His gaze turned mischievous. *We could stand again.* He glanced sideways. *If your knees are too weak, there is a wall I could—*

132

She did not let him finish. Pushing him off her, she rolled over and reversed their positions. She registered the sense of him beneath her but did not let the odd yet pleasurable feel of it distract her.

"If we stand," she said, "I think you will need the wall because it will be your knees which will be too weak." She punctuated her statement by running her fingers across his ribs. The quiver of his muscles rewarded her.

I do not require my knees in order to stand.

"But you do need to concentrate." Ducking her head, she sucked one of his nipples. The tingles from his fingers curved around her hips became stronger. Smiling coyly, she said, "I think I might destroy your concentration."

Is this a challenge, dolce mia? He trailed his hands up over her back and rubbed his thumbs along the sides of her breasts. *Because I can distract you with little difficulty.*

He was already proving his statement true. She wanted his hand on her breast. She wanted his mouth on her breast. She wanted his hands and mouth all over her body.

And she wanted to touch and kiss everywhere on his body.

She grinned. "No challenge. I win."

Proving her point, she sucked on the other of his nipples. She felt him draw in a breath. Pleased with his reaction, she moved lower, licking, kissing, and nipping her way down his body. The exotic feel of him riveted her. Pliant, warm, fluid, all at the same time, she could not get enough. When she reached his erection, she stopped, only because she was fascinated. Reverently, she took it in her hand.

His half sigh, half moan wafted through her head. *I surrender, dolce mia.*

She tapped his thigh with her finger. "I have only just

begun." Taking him into her mouth, she hummed with pleasure at the tingle.

Madre di Dio. His fingers curled into her hair and halted her. *My concentration is slipping, dolcezza.*

Pleased that she had such an intense effect on him, she allowed him to draw her back up across his body. Quickly, he flipped her to her back.

Let us test your concentration, he said as he took her nipple into his mouth.

Pleasure shot through her. "Ah" she breathed.

Moving lower, he worshiped her body as she had worshiped his. Then he was between her thighs, and his tongue was caressing her nub. The tingles from his touch were so intense, he had barely begun before she convulsed in bliss.

His chuckle sounded in her head. *No concentration at all.*

"I was concentrating very hard," she panted.

She lost the thread of the discussion when he slipped inside her. The sensation was incredible, extraordinary, for there was no pressure, only that warm tingle. Feeling that inside her, feeling his body rubbing against her was delightful torture. She never wanted it to stop.

She heard his murmur in her mind as a counterpoint to each thrust.

Velvet.

Sweet.

Hot.

Perfect.

Those molten eyes held her gaze. She dissolved into them, spiraling into infinity. And then a million suns exploded in her. Her cry of ecstasy gave voice to his silent yell of exultation.

She fell into reality with his lips against the pulse at her throat. It was more than a kiss. It was a connection to his soul. She sensed great power, intelligence, as well as great sorrow and pain. Wanting to know more, twining her fingers in his hair, she pressed him more firmly against her. Like the desire of her body, she felt the need to connect with his mind. It opened before her as soon as she had the thought. It was majestic, potent.

But all she caught was a glimpse.

Raising his head, he broke the connection. *No, tesoro mio, not yet*, he said gently.

Although disappointed, she was not upset by his denial. For he had called her his treasure. His lovemaking had been gentle and sweet. She felt cherished, not used like an object as she always did with Vernoux. And he had given her the most intense pleasure she had ever experienced. She reached up and touched his cheek.

"*Merci,*" she whispered.

Prego figurati. My pleasure. He smiled, slipped off her and cuddled her against him.

* * *

Antonio felt her slide into sleep. They lay together like two spoons, her cute bottom curled against his thighs. The touch of her skin against him felt heavenly. Lovemaking while Shadow was definitely a memorable experience.

Easing away from her, he stood by the bed and watched her sleep. He wondered how their relationship would change when he returned to flesh and bone. He would once again become the Duke of Auriano, wronged victim of her thievery, a human, visible rival of the Marquis de Vernoux. Glancing to the window, he saw the soft moonlight reflecting on the sleeping city. Soon the moon would be dark, and he would enter the Hunger. Another two days. He pushed that thought away.

His gaze dropped to the window sill where a small object lay. He had brought her a gift to make up for the loss of plunder on the night they had let General Bonaparte go. With a small movement of his hand, he lifted it through the air and allowed it to settle on the pillow next to her.

Buona sera, dolcezza, he whispered.

She sighed and snuggled closer into the covers.

Trailing his fingers one last time across her cheek, he left her.

Chapter 11

The afternoon after Tonio's visit, Solange arrived at *L'Hôtel des Vénitiens*, the magnificent Paris home of the Auriano family. It had remained untouched during the upheaval of the Revolution and the Terror, while other mansions in the city had been looted and destroyed. She wondered if it had anything to do with the curse on the family. Unlike the mansions of Gravois and Vernoux that exuded a chilly, arrogant, forbidding atmosphere, this *l'hôtel* felt welcoming, serene, and calm.

She let the lion's head doorknocker fall and heard it echo inside. Her insides churned as she waited, both from nervousness at attempting to gain entrance to such a majestic place and from emotions that had nothing to do with grandeur. After a moment, the door swung open. She was cool and gracious to the servant who held the door for her, but on the inside, she was furious. She had come to spill that wrath on Tonio's head.

When she entered the foyer, she saw signs that someone was about to leave on a trip. Several trunks were piled to one side, and two footmen were bringing another down the stairs. As she was led across the black and white marble floor, she was intercepted by the majordomo, the servant who had come with the people Tonio had brought to help her and Gide after Vernoux had beaten them. He had also been the coachman on the night she and Gide had robbed Tonio.

"Pardon, *Madame* de Volonté," he said with a bow. "*Ma donna* wishes a word with you. Please, come this way."

Curious about the many roles this servant played, she said to test him, "I have seen you before."

The man nodded. "*Sì*. If I may say so, I am glad to see you fully recovered." He gave her a tiny smile. "His Excellency was also relieved that you recovered so quickly."

He made no reference to the night of her highway robbery. His statements were a strange combination of boldness and respect, not quite servant-like. Solange wondered what his true relationship was to the House of Auriano.

He led her up the curving staircase to a small receiving room, then left her with another bow. She examined her surroundings while she waited. Each of the panels of the room was painted with an Oriental motif, of a woman wearing a kimono and walking through a garden. Exquisitely executed, they were set off by gilt frames and borders of ivory-colored lacquer. The gilt armchairs upholstered in ivory brocade, inlaid tables and chests were Italian, yet the furniture complimented the painted panels.

She turned from her examination when the majordomo announced, "The Princess of Auriano."

The woman who had gently applied the healing balm to the wounds Vernoux had inflicted appeared in the doorway.

Curtsying, Solange murmured, "Your Highness."

"No, no," the woman said as she entered. "You must call me Sabrina." She sat in one of the chairs pulled into a group before a small table. "Come, sit with me." She turned to the servant. "Please send tea, Piero, and perhaps some hot chocolate for our guest." Smiling at Solange, she explained, "I am English, you see, and I enjoy my tea, but I understand not everyone cares for it. My husband loathes it, in fact. He says it tastes like the canal water of Venice." Her smile turned to a grin.

Solange found herself liking this woman immediately.

"I think I have inconvenienced you," she said. "It appears you are preparing to leave on a trip."

"Nonsense." Sabrina waved away her apology. "Your timing is perfect. We are leaving, but only to our chateau outside the city. If you had come later, you would have missed us."

Solange had mixed feelings when she heard that— relief that she would be able to speak to Tonio before he left, and fury that he would be leaving without informing her. How could he be so cold? Ducking her head, she hid the anger in her eyes.

"I know you have come to see Tonio," Sabrina said, "but I wished to speak to you first."

"There is nothing you can say that will change what I have to say to him," Solange told her.

Sabrina shook her head. "I do not wish to interfere. Men can sometimes be so—" She was interrupted by the arrival of the tea tray. After pouring for both of them and taking a sip, she placed her cup back on the table. "Tonio has told me of your reluctance to accept your bloodline."

Solange caught her breath, both because Tonio had shared a confidence and because the woman before her spoke so calmly of it.

"You see," Sabrina went on, as if she were merely discussing the ability to paint or do needlework, "I also have the same ability." Holding out her hand, she produced a glowing orb of energy.

"*Sacré bleu,*" Solange breathed.

The woman curled her fingers into a fist, and the energy flickered out. "I only recently learned what I could do."

Solange's cup rattled in the saucer, so she placed it on the table. She clasped her fingers together to hide their shaking. "My ability has just returned to me. And my brother's —" She choked, unable to go on.

Tipping her head, Sabrina asked, "Is your brother able

139

to cast spells, perhaps make objects disappear?"

"*Oui.*" Solange found herself breathless at the woman's insight.

"I have a young son who is able to do the same," Sabrina said with a smile. "He is always hiding my gloves and playing other tricks on me." Picking up the cup of chocolate, she held it out. "Perhaps you should take another sip for strength."

Solange sipped at the chocolate while her mind raced. To know there was another woman in the world who could do the same things as she could was a gift beyond measure. Yet, if Sabrina could also produce energy, where did she get the ability?

"Are you also descended from a sorceress?" she asked.

"Halima," Sabrina said. "The sister of Nulkana." She held out her hand again and revealed the delicate birthmark on the web between her thumb and first finger.

Solange stared at her. "We are related." Mimicking the princess, she held out her hand and showed her own birthmark, which mirrored the one of the woman sitting across from her.

With a smile, Sabrina picked up her cup. "It would seem so. I have always wanted a cousin."

Being related to this woman warmed Solange, yet she could not understand how Sabrina could be so calm about her heritage. "But sorceresses are . . ." She floundered, searching for words.

"Wicked?" Sabrina supplied. "Evil? Brides of the Devil?" She touched the back of Solange's hand. "Are you wicked?"

Solange could not meet her eyes. "I have done some terrible things."

"Sometimes we must do certain things to survive. That does not make us evil." She paused as she took a sip of tea. "But we are descended from a good sorceress, and our abilities are what we make of them, good or bad.

140

We can use them to help the ones we love, and that makes us more powerful than those who use their abilities only to gain wealth or influence." Placing her cup back on the table, she stood. "I must go. My husband is waiting for me, and sometimes he is very impatient." She grinned. "Men, you know." Her smile turned sincere. "Thank you for speaking with me. I enjoyed our chat. I will send Piero to bring you to Tonio. I'm sure you're anxious to see him."

Solange watched her leave. Stunned at what she had just learned, she stared at the empty doorway, her mind reeling. She was startled when Piero appeared in her line of vision.

Bowing, he said, "*Madame*, if you would follow me, please?"

The majordomo led her down a long corridor that veered sharply to the left into one of the wings of the house. Stopping before a door at the end, he rapped on it and called, "*Madame* de Volonté to see you *Sior* Tonio." Listening a moment, he turned to Solange with a smile and opened the door for her.

Solange stepped into a dim receiving room. The drapes had been drawn across the windows, allowing only slivers of light through. Even in the low light, she could see that this room was more masculine than the one she had just left. The walls were of natural waxed wood panels framed by deep molding. One wall consisted of built-in shelves crowded with books. Paintings by various artists dotted the panels, and the overstuffed furniture was covered in dark red brocade. Beneath her feet, a thick Oriental carpet in rich jewel tones muted her steps.

At first, she did not see Tonio. Then shadowy movement from a chair in a corner of the room caught her eye. She watched him rise and approach her. The grace of his movements once again took her breath away.

Buongiorno, dolce mia, he said, smiling as he bowed.

141

I am honored at this visit. Please excuse the dimness of the room. He swept his hand in a broad motion. *Sunlight sometimes hurts my eyes.*

For a moment, she forgot why she had come. His gaze captured hers. His words wound about her. He could distract her as easily as taking a breath. Blinking, she forced herself to disregard his magnetism.

"One does not usually get paid for *making love*," she said.

Che cosa? What's this? Confusion drew his brows together. *I do not understand.*

Digging into her reticule, she pulled out the small object she had found on her pillow when she awoke that morning. It was a tiny, exquisite glass sculpture of a peacock, its tail open, the colors vibrant, the feathers and features picked out in minute detail. She held it out in the palm of her hand.

"I am not for sale, *mon seigneur.*" Walking past him, she placed the bird on the table next to the chair where he had been sitting. "Besides, if you wished to purchase my services, you would have to come to an agreement with my protector, the Marquis de Vernoux." She started past him on her way to the door.

Solange. Tonio blocked her way. *You misunderstand.*

Stopping, she glared at him. "I understand very well. You wanted me, and I pleased you."

Si, but—

"Since I performed so well, you decided to reward me." She narrowed her eyes. "I suppose I should be flattered. After all, I have worked very hard at my craft." Tears threatened as the hurt she had felt that morning returned. Blinking them away, she said, "Of course, getting a male in rut to perform is not so difficult." Stepping around him, she stalked to the door. When she tried to open it, the handle would not turn.

Solange.

She refused to face him. "Please open the door," she said.

Not until you hear what I have to say.

She turned to him but remained where she was. "Do not use your tricks on me. I have some of my own." Raising her hand, she produced a ball of energy like the one Sabrina had shown her earlier.

Ah. His gazed cooled. *Piero told me you were having tea with my sister-in-law. I am glad she helped you understand.*

She jerked a nod. "*Oui.* She made me understand very well."

Not everything. He moved closer, his anger a tightly held thing between them. *The sculpture was a gift to make amends for allowing General Bonaparte to escape.*

His explanation melted her anger a little, but the hurt was still there. She had learned very early that accepting gifts from men was dangerous, and this complex Shadow was especially perilous, a threat not only to her life, but also her peace of mind. "Your amends are a little late. Le Chacal has already informed me of his displeasure."

He was silent for two heartbeats. A chill seemed to congeal in the air around him. *You have other items you could have given him. Those surely would have pleased him.*

Solange stared at him. He meant, of course, the second moonstone and his thumb ring. She had not forgotten about them, yet for some reason could not bring herself to part with them. Revealing that to Tonio was the last thing she wished to do. "I have given them to Le Chacal already." Her glance slid away at her lie.

His eyes narrowed fractionally, then with a smile like a knife, he turned away. *Of course you have.* He shrugged. *I have helped you all I can, dolce mia. If you will not accept my gift, there is nothing left for me to do.*

She raised her chin. "I never asked for your help. What we had was a business agreement. Not a friendship. You made that clear when you left that trinket." She tilted her head in the direction of the glass bird.

He lifted the tiny bird and floated it before him. *This is truly a remarkable piece. Murano glass from Venice. Sculpted by a master craftsman. A pity you won't accept it.* He allowed it to sink back to the table. Then he focused on her, his gaze piercing. *There is one thing which you seem to have forgotten.*

She frowned at him. There was nothing else.

Our agreement, he reminded her. *I would help you steal in return for your helping me find a certain object.*

"Your help has been a disaster," she snapped.

My help has given you knowledge of who you are. The truth in his statement glared at her.

She waved her hand in dismissal.

If you do not help me find the piece of the Sphere of Astarte, then Nulkana will find it, he said, calmly. *That will make her stronger, and she will come after you and your brother. She wants you dead as much as she wants to destroy my family.*

Her eyes narrowed. "Are you threatening me?"

He settled into the chair. *I am stating a fact. It is your decision.*

Solange seethed. Once again, she'd been backed into a corner by a man. She had to protect Gide, and after witnessing what the sorceress could do without her full power, she was sure Nulkana would have little trouble destroying them once she gained the piece of the Sphere and her power returned.

The Marquis de Vernoux would also like to find the piece, he added. *I wonder how he will treat you once he has what he wants.*

The veiled threat and the knowledge of Vernoux's cruelty took her breath. "You are reprehensible."

He shrugged. *You were the one who declared this a cold business arrangement, Madame de Volonté. No feelings.* Pausing, he flipped his hand, and the little peacock floated into the air once more. *Are you sure you won't accept my gift?*

"Damn you," she seethed through clenched teeth.

A cold smile curled his lips. *I am already damned, dolce mia.* With another twist of his hand, the door opened. *Piero will see you out.*

Solange wished for the dagger that lay in her wardrobe in her bedchamber, for she could have plunged it into his cold heart with glee. Instead, she lifted her chin, turned, and left with as much dignity as she could muster.

Just before the door closed behind her, she heard in her head, *I'm looking forward to continuing our partnership, dolcezza.*

* * *

In the gloom of twilight, Le Chacal stepped gingerly over fallen sections of ceiling and holes in the parquet floor of the once magnificent mansion in the Marais. This area of the city was a wasteland now, the beautiful palaces that had housed the royals and nobles looted and burned out by the rioters of the Revolution. He felt a sense of satisfaction at the destruction around him.

At one time, he had been as comfortable in the opulent surroundings as any aristocrat, for he had been the first footman for the Chevalier Boucher. That had changed suddenly when the chevalier discovered he was a member of the *sans-culottes*, the revolutionaries who believed in equality. He found himself turned out onto the street by his employer, his belongings and the few livres he had saved confiscated, his prospects for marrying the girl of his dreams dashed to pieces. Desperate, he had attempted to retrieve what was his and was caught. The Chevalier Boucher decided to impose punishment himself rather than turn him over to the authorities. He had chopped off his hand. Only the intervention of the Marquis de Vernoux, who happened to be a guest of the chevalier's at the time, had saved his other hand. For that, along with protection from the authorities for being the leader of the thieves of Paris, Jean-Jacques Bayard, now known as Le Chacal, was indebted and tied to the crafty aristocrat. An arrangement he hoped this meeting would terminate.

Entering the main salon, Le Chacal glanced up at the once magnificent ceiling. It was a mural, depicting the four seasons with flowers, trees, nymphs, and cupids. Water stains and singed spots marred its beauty. An empty hook in the center indicated that a great chandelier had once illuminated the room.

Lowering his gaze, he came face to face with a man standing only several feet away. Le Chacal halted. He had not heard the man's arrival. Cadaverous, the man was dressed in a dark brown robe of Oriental design, the fabric rich and heavy. His hands were tucked into his sleeves.

The man bowed stiffly from the waist. "I am Kek. My mistress awaits. Please follow me."

Intrigued, at the same time he was slightly repelled by the man's appearance, Le Chacal nodded. Kek led him to a far corner of the salon where he muttered a few words, waved a hand, and a door opened in the wall. Without a backward glance, Kek descended a set of stairs that led down into darkness. Le Chacal hesitated at the top step. There had been no door in the wall when he had first entered the room, and these stairs should not have been present.

"My mistress has many talents." Kek's voice floated back up to him as if he had heard Le Chacal's thoughts. "She also is not a patient person."

Throwing away caution, Le Chacal followed. As he

descended, the area around him seemed to be lit, but not from any ordinary source, and the light followed as he moved. He heard a shuffling sound behind him, and as he turned, saw the door closing by itself. A chill shot down his back. He was not easily frightened, having experienced numerous dangerous moments in his life, but this meeting unnerved him. If it turned bad, he would have no escape route.

Light showed at the bottom of the stairs. As he stepped down onto the floor, a large room opened before him, a replica of the salon above, not destroyed as it now was, but restored to its magnificent beauty. He only glanced at his surroundings, for at the far end of the room a woman watched him. She was a gorgeous creature with dark hair piled high on her head, dark eyes, and ruby lips. She was dressed in the new fashion of the high-waisted dress, and its white material was so filmy that it hid nothing. Le Chacal swallowed and felt himself go hard immediately. The woman sauntered closer.

"Jean-Jacques Bayard," she murmured. "Le Chacal. Your name is well known in Paris."

Le Chacal swept her a bow. "*Mademoiselle.* You have the advantage of me since I do not know your name. An oversight that I would like to amend."

She laughed, a throaty sound that wound through Le Chacal's brain. "So, the thief has charm. Shall we see if he has wits as well, Kek?" Kek merely bowed his head and said nothing. The woman stepped closer. "My name is Nulkana. I give it to you because you will hear of me eventually. I am looking for something, and I think you might be able to help me find it."

"I am able to find many things, *mademoiselle*," Le Chacal said.

"Yes. I have heard, which is why I chose you." Her lips curved in a sly smile.

Le Chacal bowed again. "I am honored."

147

Nulkana raised an arrogant brow. "As you should be. But we shall see if I have chosen wisely."

"I am the best at finding hard-to-find items. Everyone in the city knows that." He could not help bragging a bit.

Her gaze narrowed. "Unfortunately, others are also searching for this item I seek."

"Then the item is valuable, *oui?*" Le Chacal's greed raised its head.

"In a way, it is quite valuable, although its appearance is deceiving. People have been killed in the search." She sighed sadly.

"And so, to look for and find this item is dangerous, *nest-ce pas?*" He wondered how high he could push his finder's fee.

"Yes." Nulkana swayed nearer. "Does that frighten you, Jean-Jacques Bayard, Le Chacal?"

Her fragrance, rich, musky, spicy-sweet, like nothing he had ever smelled before, swirled around him. He thought he detected a barely perceptible undertone of decay but decided that could not be possible. The scent clouded his head until everything else around him disappeared. Only the woman before him remained solid. At that moment, Le Chacal would have run through the fires of Hell for her.

"No," he said, "I am not frightened."

"Good." She smiled and stepped back.

As soon as she did, his head cleared, and his thoughts became clear once again. "If I am to put myself in danger to find this item for you, what do I get in return?"

"What is it that you would like, Le Chacal?" she asked coyly.

Again, he wondered how much he could ask for without incurring her anger. If the item she sought were as valuable as she implied, if he were to put himself in danger to seek it, then he should be royally rewarded.

But of course, there was one thing he wanted more than anything else.

Before he had a chance to answer, she nodded. "Ah. I see what would please you. You wish me to dispose of this man, the Marquis de Vernoux."

Surprised that she knew his thoughts, he gave a short nod. "*Oui.*"

"But what if I could give you more?" Her words were a husky whisper.

Le Chacal was mesmerized at the same time a part of his brain flashed a warning. He was too canny to believe a beautiful woman's promises and too wary to be deceived by an overgenerous offer in negotiations.

She waved her hand and fluttered her fingers. Le Chacal felt a burning down one side of his face and an odd warmth at the stump of his arm. Looking down, he saw a hand where no hand had been for years. Touching his face, he felt no puckered skin where a scar had run from forehead to jaw.

"*Mon Dieu,*" he whispered in awe.

"It is illusion only, for now. Payment will be given when the item is received." She gazed at him thoughtfully. "Without the scar, you are a rather attractive man. Perhaps when this is over, I will keep you."

From the corner of the room, Kek cleared his throat.

Nulkana raised her hand and made a fist. "Kek, sometimes you annoy me."

Kek doubled over, either in a bow of obeisance or in pain, Le Chacal could not tell which. "Yes, mistress." The man's voice sounded strained.

Nulkana smiled. "When this is over . . ." She shrugged, a graceful lifting of one shoulder. "Well, that is for later." She placed her hand on Le Chacal's chest. "Is the reward satisfactory?"

"*Oui.*" He had trouble speaking, for the spot burned where her hand lay. The reward was more than satisfactory, and he was aware she knew it. He also knew that he would have to pay dearly for it. "What is it you wish me to find for you?"

"A piece of the Sphere of Astarte." She dropped her hand from his chest.

Filling his lungs again allowed his brain to work. "I do not—"

"You do," she snapped, stepping very close. "You do know what it is. Do not lie to me. Others have given you the task of finding it." Her lips curved in a menacing smile. "In fact, you know *where* it is, don't you, *Monsieur Le Roi des Voleurs?* You will not give it to them. You will give it to *me.*"

Her words were cold, but her eyes were colder. That gaze was ancient, cruel, amoral. Fear crept up Le Chacal's back and sat like a cold snake on the nape of his neck. He kept his lips firmly pressed together. He knew the artifact she wanted. He had kept it, secret and hidden from Vernoux, to be vindictive. Now, he realized its value was much greater than it appeared or what he had been led to believe. Perhaps he could negotiate to raise the price.

Her red lips pouted, and her gaze turned sultry. "Do not make me punish you, Jean-Jacques Bayard. I would much prefer to reward you." Leaning in, she ran her finger down his cheek where his scar should have been.

The trail of her finger left a warm tingle, and her scent erased the fear. In its place, arousal came swift and hard, close to pain. Le Chacal gasped.

"Mmm, I think you would make a delightful playmate." Her hum vibrated along his skin. "Do we have a bargain?"

He hesitated.

The sorceress sighed as if she had given in to great persuasion. "Oh, very well. I will also give you wealth. Will that please you?"

"*Oui.*" The single word took an enormous amount of effort.

"There is one other little thing I ask." She made a little moue of distaste.

There it was, that catch in the bargain, the reason for her generosity. Everything came with a price. This one, he knew, would be high.

"I want the woman who calls herself *Madame* de Volonté dead. That is if I have not already killed her myself." Her eyes had once more turned cold and lifeless.

Le Chacal stared. Despite his ruthlessness, the thought of killing Solange did not sit well. He had become attached to her, perhaps even held some affection for her. He would regret having to kill her.

Nulkana spoke again. "Remember the reward, Jean-Jacques Bayard. What I ask is such a little thing compared to what you will receive. Will you agree to do this?"

To have his hand again. To have his face again. And wealth. What was the life of one insignificant girl in comparison? Perhaps he could fake her death. He was, after all, Le Chacal, *le Roi des Voleurs*. And finding the perfect moment would be easy, for he had a network of beggars and street urchins who could watch her.

He gave a curt nod. "*Oui.* I agree."

Nulkana smiled, a world of promise in the curve of those ruby lips. "You have made me very happy, Jean-Jacques Bayard." She turned away. "Now get out. And next time, bathe before you come here."

A sense of emptiness opened in his chest at her retreat. He gazed hungrily at the outline of her hips and the shape of her bottom through the filmy dress. A dark flowing cape materialized from nowhere and covered her. The loss of the sight of her body weakened his knees. Befuddled, he stared stupidly at Kek when the man appeared at his side.

Kek gestured to the stairs behind him. "I will show you out."

Le Chacal stumbled after him up the stairs, where, at the top, the door opened once more. As soon as Le

Chacal stepped through, the door closed behind him and disappeared once more. He was alone in the ruined salon of the vandalized mansion. Only then did the consequences of what had just taken place register. He had just met with a woman, a powerful sorceress, who could repair his broken body, who could arouse him with her scent, who could create a palatial salon out of nothing. Staggering a few steps, he sat down heavily in the middle of the floor. Drawing up his knees, he dropped his head on them. Fear and arousal warred in his body, and he shook as if he had the ague.

And then Le Chacal, the Jackal, *Le Roi des Voleurs*, the King of the Thieves, broke down and sobbed.

*   *   *

As soon as Kek returned and stepped off the bottom step, the beautiful salon returned to its normal state, the kitchen of the *hôtel*. Swags of cobwebs hung from the ceiling. A rat scampered across the uneven floor. Thick dust covered every surface. All the cooking utensils were gone. Only a long preparation table covered with an assortment of bottles and vials, and two rickety, straight-backed chairs remained.

Nulkana slumped into one of the chairs. She was no longer the beautiful seductress with sleek, dark hair and porcelain skin. Instead, her hair was matted and gray, her skin wrinkled with age spots. She placed her hand over the wound through her side that she had received when she had battled that annoying creature in Venice who was a descendant of her sister, Halima. She had learned the little slut had wed the whelp who was head of her enemies, the Prince of Auriano. Nulkana sighed. She would wait and have her revenge one day.

She turned to the silent, black-robed and cowled figure in the corner. "I need to feed, worm," she said.

The figure did not move.

"Do not think of defying me." The sorceress raised her hand and slowly curled her fingers.

The figure jerked, then bowed and glided into the dark hallway beyond.

"Your worm is becoming more resistant," Kek observed.

"He serves his purpose," Nulkana shrugged. "I will deal with him when I see the need." Her gaze sharpened. "You will leave him alone, Kek. He is mine to toy with and torture."

Kek bowed. "As you wish, mistress."

Nulkana moaned. "This wound is taking a very long time to heal," she said. "The whelp's slut is very strong."

"But soon you will have a piece of the Sphere of Astarte, mistress." Kek poured a bilious green potion into a glass, then added a clear potion. As he mixed, the solution turned violet and started to bubble. He handed the glass to the sorceress.

"I will not have the piece of the Sphere if I die from this wound." Nulkana threw the drink down her throat. She gasped and coughed. "Or I might die from your healing potions."

"Now, mistress, you know you are gaining back your powers," Kek soothed. "You have been able to project yourself over great distances, and what you just did for this unimportant thief, well, it was magnificent."

"He is not unimportant." Nulkana's eyes blazed. "He holds a piece of the Sphere that is hidden in this city, and he has power over that slut who is another descendant of my weak, do-good sister. If I weren't suffering from this wound, I would retrieve the piece myself." She groaned and pressed her hand harder over the black blood that oozed from her side. "Where is the worm with my meal?"

As she spoke, the screams of young women echoed through the cellars.

"I believe he is coming now," Kek observed.

"What power might I have if I could feed from Auriano's wife, and this other who is like her?" she mused. "That pesky Legion of Baal would be insects beneath the toe of my shoe."

"You would be glorious, mistress," Kek assured her.

The robed figure appeared in the doorway and dragged a young woman before the sorceress. The girl's eyes were glazed, but she trembled violently. With a touch, the figure calmed her.

Nulkana made a sound of disgust. "Weak," she spat. "You will be punished for that, worm. You know I like to feed when they are filled with terror. They have more spice."

The figure bowed his head and stepped back.

Nulkana rose from her chair and grabbed the girl by the back of the neck. The sorceress's fingers elongated, up the back of her victim's head. She placed her hand against the girl's chest where it seeped through her skin. The girl's eyes widened, and then her screams of terror and pain filled the room.

When the girl dropped to the floor, her hair was gray and thin, her face sunken and wrinkled. Breath no longer passed her lips.

But Nulkana glowed with vigor.

*   *   *

Naked, Gide shivered in the chill air. No fire on the hearth for warmth, no candle to shed light. The windows had been boarded over. Keeping his hand on the wall for guidance, he paced the perimeter of the tiny dark room as he tried to stay warm. The space was bare except for a chair in its center. He had discovered that piece by banging his shins on it. He had no idea what time of day it was or how long he had been there, nor even why he was being kept prisoner. He was thirsty and hungry. Frightened, he realized he had made a terrible mistake.

After he left Solange's salon, no longer able to watch his sister accept Vernoux's verbal torment, he had gone to Gravois and accepted the man's offer to get rid of Auriano. He had watched his sister become fascinated with the Italian, and his jealousy gnawed at him. He and Solange had always done everything together. Auriano had taken her attention. Although the Italian duke had disappeared, the shadowman who had appeared in his place was having too much influence and becoming much too intimate with Solange. He had put them in jeopardy with Vernoux and had caused Vernoux's latest punishment. The connection between the Italian duke and the shadowman was eerie, unholy, and made the hairs on the back of his neck rise. Gide had no liking for Vernoux, hated him in fact, but he was not about to let Auriano or his shadow counterpart ruin the delicate balance of Solange's existence.

Gravois had asked if Gide would be willing to join the Legion of Baal. The offer was more than he had hoped for. If he agreed, he would have the same power as Vernoux. He would be able to free Solange from her servitude to the marquis. They could leave Paris, buy that farm, and live their lives freely. He had agreed.

Stupid.

He had been shown to this room by several men who had thrown him to the floor, taken away his clothes, tied him to the chair, and left him. At intervals, one of them would return to ask him questions. What did he want? What was he willing to do to achieve it? Would he follow orders without question? Over and over, the same questions. They never let him sleep, gave him nothing to eat. He lost count of the minutes, hours, days perhaps, that he had been in this prison. Consciousness slipped away, came back, retreated. He had been given something to drink. He slept, dreaming of strange creatures, terrifying places, none of which he could actually recall, only the fear. And then he had awakened untied, sprawled on the floor of his prison. That had been . . . how long ago?

He heard footsteps outside the door, and it swung wide. Three men stood in the opening, outlined by dim lighting. One held a lantern. Gide held up his hand to block the glare. The men all wore dark green silk robes, a frog glyph embroidered in red on the left breast. Their faces were obscured by hoods.

"Who are you?" he demanded. "Why have you kept me here? Why do you keep questioning me?"

"We needed to be sure you truly want what we can offer." Gravois's voice came from the depths of one of the cowls. "What are you willing to do to achieve your goal?"

Gide hesitated. He thought he had known when he had approached Gravois. Before, he would have answered, "Anything." Now he was not so sure.

"Release him. He does not suit," a disembodied voice from the hallway said.

"Wait." Gide stepped forward. He was not going to lose this chance. "I'll do whatever you want."

"You will be tested," that voice said. "If you perform satisfactorily, then your request shall be granted."

One of the men tossed a plain green robe to him. Quickly, Gide put it on, thinking it would warm him. The thin material only seemed to capture the room's chill in its folds. Or perhaps it was his soul that was chilled.

Another of the men held out a gold, jewel-encrusted chalice to him. Once again, Gide hesitated. Despite the fact he was parched, the hint of menace that surrounded these figures made him suspicious of what the chalice might contain. Drug, or poison, or merely wine? He had already been drugged once. The man shoved the chalice at him. Realizing he would be forced to drink its contents whether he wished to or not, Gide accepted it and drank it down. It was wine, cool, sweet, yet something else swirled in its depths. Even as it quenched his thirst, his apprehension grew.

He handed the chalice back. The two other men took him by the arms and escorted him out of his prison. The third followed. Gide was led down a bare corridor sparsely lit by sconces on the wall. At the end of the hallway, a narrow door stood open, revealing a staircase leading up. A cold breeze fluttered the robe around his ankles, swept up his legs and made him shiver. The two men holding him propelled him up the stairs. By the time he reached the top and stepped out onto a roof, everything in his perception was distorted.

The night sky above him whirled with a million stars. The moon sparkled and hung like a huge dinner plate just above the unusually high balustrade around the perimeter of the roof. Beneath his feet, symbols painted in red on the stone shifted. He felt as if he walked on a cushion of the softest down. The men on either side of him seemed like angels. When one of them reached up and pulled off Gide's hood, the touch felt like the caress of a lover.

Anticipation replaced apprehension. Excitement replaced fear. Whatever was about to happen was his destiny.

His two guides brought him to stand before another figure who was robed in deep purple. The figure appeared to grow in size until he towered above Gide, and then in a blink, he returned to normal. The moon just above the man's shoulder cast his face into invisibility within his hood. Beyond him, a small brazier glowed with blistering embers.

Whatever was about to happen, Gide was ready. He drew a breath, inhaling everything, filling his lungs, and then filling them more until he felt his chest might explode. He could smell the ashes from the brazier, the remnants of a meal from the house next door, the detritus in the street gutter, the filthy beggar who slept in the alley. He could smell the two men beside him, the man behind him, the man before him. Especially the man before him. He smelled of green things, growing things, of storms and sunshine, of animals that roamed forests, of stones older than time.

Gide was drawn to him with such force he took a step forward. His two guards jerked him back. Amazed at the expansion of his senses, uncomprehending what his senses were telling him, Gide stared. He felt the man's return stare, a bit puzzled, as if he had suddenly come upon a new species of animal and did not know what to name it. Then whatever connection there was between them was shut down. The black inside the man's hood shifted, swirled. Two eyes appeared, red with slitted black irises. In a far corner of Gide's mind, he knew this was illusion, yet uncontrollable fear clutched at him. He dropped to his knees. Each of his guards placed a restraining hand on his shoulders.

The man in purple spoke. "You have a desire to join the Legion of Baal." His voice contained many layers. On the surface, it was quiet, English-accented, but it was surrounded by deep booming levels of different tones. It hurt the inside of Gide's head. He wanted to cover his ears but knew that would be a mistake.

One of the guards dug his fingers into Gide's shoulder. "Answer," he snarled.

"*Oui,*" Gide said.

"You will abide by the laws of the Legion."

Gide had no idea what those laws might be. When he hesitated, fingers once again bit his shoulder. "*Oui.*"

"You will follow the Lord High's commands, even unto death."

Death? Would he give his life for these men? Who was the Lord High? What was he getting himself into?

All Gide wanted was to get rid of the Italian duke. And to be free.

At his long hesitation, the man in purple said with annoyance to someone behind Gide, "You waste my time. He is not ready."

"He is," Gravois responded nervously. "He wishes the death of Auriano."

"That is the Lord High's privilege," the purple-robed man stated.

"This one does not care who accomplishes the task," Gravois said.

Gide felt the attention of the man in purple turn back to him. "Is this so?" the man asked. His words compelled an answer whether Gide wished to respond or not.

"*Oui.*"

"Joining the Legion of Baal will bring you knowledge of many things. Unimaginable secrets. Your life will change. It will no longer be your own but will belong to the Lord High. Is this what you wish?"

Gide felt his life had not been his own for a very long time already. To agree would not change much. "*Oui.*"

"Then answer this. Will you follow the commands of the Lord High even unto death?" His words held soft temptation.

Gide had never before been seduced by a man, but at that moment he would have done anything this man asked. It was the drug, he told himself, or magic, but that made no difference to his body.

"*Oui.*" Gide nodded to emphasize his answer.

"I am The Messenger," the man in purple intoned. "I speak for the Lord High, and I accept this novice into the Legion of Baal."

A small, low table was placed before Gide. One of his guards took his left arm, laid it, palm-up, across the surface and pulled back the sleeve of his robe. Then each man held Gide's forearm against the table. Gide

Patricia Barletta

observed curiously, dispassionately. He stared at the pale skin of the inside of his bare forearm and wondered what was about to happen.

The man in purple picked up a quill, dipped it into a small pot, and held it over Gide's arm. "You will not cry out. You will utter no sound. Your silence will be a test of your obedience." A drop of the ink fell onto Gide's arm. "I mark you with the frog," he said. "You will be known by all those who wear this mark. As a novice, you will do their bidding." Then he touched the quill lightly to Gide's skin and began to draw.

At first, Gide could feel nothing, and he watched, fascinated, as the simple lines appeared beneath the quill. Then the lines seemed to waver and squirm. He felt a sharp prickle. As the man in purple finished the glyph, Gide saw his skin begin to ripple, as if something were just beneath the surface and trying to get out. Excruciating pain erupted under the glyph. Gide clamped down on his cry. He tried to move his arm, to shake off whatever was happening. The two men held his arm to the table. He grabbed and clutched at them with his free hand, but someone twisted that arm behind him. He was in agony. A scream tore at his throat trying to escape. In terror, he watched as his skin split where the lines had been drawn. No blood seeped from the wound, but the exposed flesh and muscle glowed red.

Slowly, a small frog emerged from his flesh.

Horrified, he squirmed. "What have you done to me?" he yelled. "Get it off! Get it off!" He tried to stand, but the men held him down. He could only stare, terrified, at the creature that had erupted from his skin. Torturous pain sliced into his arm. He gritted his teeth against the scream building in his chest.

What had he done?

"You scream like a child," The Messenger said. "You were ordered not to do so. I will not complete the ceremony."

The words cut through the haze of pain. Gide wanted this, needed this, to save Solange, protect her from the Italian duke. "I won't cry out again," he promised on a pant. "I'll be quiet."

The Messenger was silent. Gide felt his gaze, studying him, analyzing. Finally, the man turned to the brazier and, with a pair of tongs, picked up one of the glowing embers. He placed it against the back of the frog. It sizzled. Then, as if it were made of wax, it melted, burning into Gide's flesh. He clamped down on the tormented scream that climbed up his throat.

Colors swirled. The purple robe of The Messenger bled into the indigo of the night sky. The green robes of the men who held him seeped into the weathered stone of the balustrade around the roof. The pale flesh of his arm glowed with a bluish light. Dizzy, nauseous, overwhelmed, Gide closed his eyes. He felt a hand on his head. A sudden peace descended on him. The pain in his arm receded. Soft darkness draped over his mind.

And he floated away, borne on a gentle breeze, that took him to a beautiful place of flowers and streams and waterfalls.

Chapter 12

Solange stood in the bright light of the full moon and stared up at the façade of *le Chateau des Ombres*, the Mansion of Shadows. She could understand why it had such a name, for large, ancient trees stood sentinel around the house and cast long, deep shadows on the building. She suspected that was not the true reason why it had been called such. This was the country home of the Duke of Auriano. It was fitting that he would have a house named after his secret.

She was dressed as a thief, having come to steal, not silver or gold or jewels, but knowledge. And she had come for help. As much as she hated to admit it, Tonio seemed to be her only recourse. Gide was missing, and she was worried. She refused to go to Vernoux for help, and Le Chacal had dismissed her inquiry with casual neglect. When she had gone to *L'Hôtel des Vénitiens* in Paris, she had been told no one was in residence. So she had come here.

The house before her was dark, its inhabitants having retired for the night. A window above her stood open, and she suspected it led to one of the bedchambers. Vines climbed the wall beside it. She would have easy access to the mansion. More difficult would be finding Tonio's chamber.

Grabbing the vines, she started up and eased through the window. She found herself in a dressing room, lined with drawers and doors, an immense wardrobe towering against one wall, a dressing table adorned with perfume bottles and small boxes, a chair with articles of clothing thrown negligently across it, and doors leading to the right and left. The door to the left opened on a lady's bedchamber, and from its opulence and size, appeared to belong to the mistress of the house, but it was empty. The one to the right was the master's chamber. Solange could see two forms snuggled together between the covers of the immense bed. Sabrina and her husband, the prince. Quietly, she retreated and closed the door.

She searched all of the other rooms on the floor but did not find Tonio, although she did discover what appeared to be his room, large, masculine, decorated in dark woods and heavy furniture. Open trunks displayed men's clothing. The bed linens had been turned down, but the bed had not been slept in. Thinking he might be on the floor below, she crept down the wide, curving staircase, but a search of salons, drawing rooms, morning rooms, receiving rooms, ballroom, library, and other rooms whose functions she could not name did not reveal his presence. Until she came to a small sitting room in a corner of one of the wings of the house. One wall of the room was a series of French doors which led out to a moonlit garden. In the scant light of the waxing moon slanting into the room, she noticed a panel standing ajar in the wall next to the fireplace. Investigating, she saw a set of stone stairs leading down. A lamp hung just inside the opening. Lighting it, she started down the stairs.

At the bottom, she came to another door, but with no handle or latch. She pushed against it, but it did not budge. Placing the lamp on the floor, she examined the wall around the door. There had to be some way of opening it. Then she noticed a stone about eye-level in the wall where the imprint of a hand had been carved. She pressed against it. The door receded into the wall, she heard a click, and it swung inward. She stepped through into softly lit space.

As she moved into the room, the door closed behind her. Spinning around, she saw that it had disappeared. What had once been a door was now only a wall panel, covered in a rich, blue, watered silk. Nothing indicated an opening had ever been there. Realizing she had no escape in that direction, she turned to survey the room. It was a bedroom, opulent, dominated by an enormous canopied bed. On it were four people, and what they were doing made her stomach clench. A man lay on his back, his limbs spread in lethargic ease, while three women twined about him, their mouths all over him. Not all that long ago, she might have been one of those women, forced to cruelly service Vernoux, but on the rare occasion now when he felt the need for her, he preferred her by herself, easier for him to torment.

The man on his back languidly turned his head to look at her.

Antonio! Transformed to flesh and bone.

As soon as he saw her, he murmured something to the others. They slid away from him, and he swung off the bed. He stood magnificently, unabashedly naked. His broad shoulders curved down to narrow waist and hips that flowed into long legs. The dim candlelight played across his chest and around his ribs, obscuring and then defining the muscles that rippled there. A pink line, the mark of a healing wound, sliced down across his side and marred the symmetry of his body. She wondered when he had received it, and from whom. Between the hollow of his hips, his erection stood proudly. Expressionless, he stared at her. Solange wanted to look away. She wanted to run and hide, but she remained glued where she was. She could not drag her eyes away from his perfect form.

Grabbing an open bottle of wine that stood on the bedside table, he took a long swallow, then wiped his mouth on the back of his hand. Mesmerized by the strong curve of his throat, the sharp slant of his jaw,

Solange told herself to move. This was a chance for escape, but her feet did not obey her brain. He turned his gaze on her again, prowled closer, his swagger full of masculine arrogance. She realized there was no sign of recognition in his eyes. Instead of that hypnotic golden gaze, his eyes were as black as the depths of Hell.

He stopped before her. Solange felt his examination from her head to her toes. She blushed, grateful for the floppy hat that shaded her face.

"What do we have here? A little thief come to steal my treasures?" With a swipe of his hand, he knocked the hat from her head. He expelled a breath of sarcastic laughter. "What have you come to steal this time, thief?"

With her identity revealed, she did not hold back. "You disgust me," she spat.

He blinked, a lazy, insolent motion. "Do I really? Is that righteous anger I hear, or perhaps jealousy that I did not invite you? Would you like to join us?" He waved his hand in the direction of the bed.

Solange carefully did not follow the line of his hand. "I'd rather have my toenails pulled out."

A dark eyebrow quirked up. "That's a rather painful alternative."

"Better than being your whore," she snapped.

"Ah, I see." He glanced back over his shoulder at the three who had continued their activities without him. When he turned back to her, sardonic amusement curled his lips. "They come to me freely, of their own will. They are not forced by anyone, least of all me."

"But you pay them," she accused.

"I reward them," he corrected mildly.

"With coin," she argued.

"Not always." His voice dropped to a seductive murmur. "Sometimes our mutual satisfaction is reward enough." His hand snaked out, and he grabbed the back of her neck. As he touched her, his breath hissed through his teeth. His gaze turned feral. "Sometimes, our satisfaction is mingled with a small amount of affection. You do know what affection is, don't you, thief?"

Solange stared up into those hard, black eyes. She could not move, for his hand held her in a velvet vise. "I—" Swallowing, she could not answer. She had never allowed herself to feel affection for anyone besides Gide, but he was her brother. Was it affection that she felt for this man when he had been Shadow? Is that why she had been so furious, so betrayed when she had found that exquisite glass sculpture on her pillow? Was it jealousy that made her so furious now? No. She had no feelings for this man. What had passed between them had been merely lust.

His eyes bored into her. They were hungry, angry. They held no mercy.

Once again, his lips curled in a smile, but there was no amusement in that demonic gaze. "Allow me to explain. Affection is the care between two people. It is a gift given and received. Accepting affection is a grace. But perhaps you know nothing of that. Perhaps you don't wish to know. But you do know about mutual satisfaction, *si?*"

His barb made her flinch. Two nights ago, their mutual satisfaction had been incredible. But that was before the delicate balance of their relationship had tipped into something cold and business-like. Solange tried to shake her head, but his grip would not allow it. She was not sure if she was responding to his question or denying something else in the depths of that gaze.

His eyes narrowed. Then, without warning, he stepped forward, pushing her back against the wall with his body, and trapped her there. His mouth came down on hers, seducing and plundering at the same time. Surprised, she froze, allowing him to have his way. He took full advantage, slipping his tongue between her lips, caressing, stroking, expertly kindling a throbbing heat deep inside her. Without volition, she found herself writhing against him.

He could have violated her. He did not. Instead, he awakened a yearning for more of him, for wanting to be naked against his bare skin, of a desire to feel him pressed against her, inside her. God forgive her, he made her want to do to him what those women had been doing, her mouth all over him, tasting, sucking, needing. Her knees went weak. She grabbed his arms for support. And kissed him back.

As soon as she did, he retreated. She felt bereft and stupid for being so weak. He stared at her. Some emotion flashed through his eyes, but she was unsure what it was. His jaw tightened, and a muscle jumped there. Straightening, he dropped his hand from her neck, releasing her.

"Go away, little thief," he said.

He raised his hand, and she recoiled from the threat she imagined in that movement. All he did was reach beyond her shoulder. She sensed the slide of the door opening behind her.

He huffed a sarcastic laugh. "Did you think I would harm you?"

She opened her mouth but found she could not utter a sound.

Anger tightened the corners of his mouth. "Not all men are monsters. I have never hit a woman." Bending down, he swept up her hat from the floor and plunked it on her head. "Get out." He spun her about and gave her a nudge into the passageway. The door slid shut behind her.

Solange grabbed the lantern and raced up the stairs. Extinguishing it, hanging it back where she had found it, she slipped back into the sitting room and headed toward the doors leading to the garden. She wanted to be away from *Le Chateau des Ombres*, away from *him* as fast as possible.

Before she was completely through the door, she heard a voice ask, "Leaving so soon?"

Spinning about, she saw Antonio sitting in a chair not far away. He had donned a dressing gown and slippers. How had he arrived in the room before her? Rising, he stepped towards her. She fell back a step. Annoyed with her cowardice, she halted and straightened her spine.

"I would not have thought you would run away," he observed.

"I'm not," she lied.

He raised a skeptical brow.

"I need to see to my horse."

He said nothing, but his silence revealed his disbelief.

Digging in her pocket, she pulled out his thumb ring. She had been planning to use it as a bribe to get him to help her find Gide. Now, she just wanted it out of her possession. Flipping it to him, she said, "I am returning this to you and severing any ties between us."

He caught it deftly, then examined it, turning it over in his fingers. A small smile played around his lips. He stepped forward, took her hand, placed the ring in her palm, and closed her fist around it. "You might want to give this to the person who owns it."

Puzzled by his comment, she stared a moment. Then her mouth fell open. Of course. This was the prince who stood before her, Antonio's twin. Her supposition that Tonio had reached the room before her was silly.

A crash from below brought a frown to his face. "It sounds like my brother is not faring too well. What did you do to him?"

"Nothing." She shook her head for emphasis. "I did nothing."

He raised a curious brow. "You seem to have quite an effect on him."

She was not about to take the blame for Tonio's bad behavior. "What is wrong with him?"

"He is experiencing the Hunger, an unpleasant period of time between Shadow and flesh," he said.

She huffed in disbelief. "He didn't appear to be in any distress when I saw him."

The prince was silent for a moment, then he said, "Antonio has told me of your forced relationship with the Marquis de Vernoux. Like you, my brother is forced to certain actions, not by another, but by the Hunger. He experiences cravings that he cannot deny. Sometimes those appetites make him violent. He cannot help himself, and he despises what he must do in order to survive." His concerned gaze swept over her.

"He didn't hurt me," she said. "He only—" He only what? Frightened her? Made her angry? Made her want him? Solange closed her eyes, fighting back the memory of his kiss filled with desire—dark and wild. She had understood even while it was happening that something demonic lurked beneath the surface, something that he had been holding on a very tight leash.

"My brother is an honorable man," the prince said. "And I believe he cares for you. He touched you while he was Shadow. That is why—"

A howl echoed up the staircase. Of rage or pain? Her eyes snapped open.

"He needs your help," the prince said.

The idea frightened her. "I won't be used."

"*Si.* I can understand that." He paused. "Why did you come here tonight?"

Uncomfortable with the truth, Solange shifted her weight and let her gaze slide away. "I had my reasons."

"I'm sure you did." He tipped his head thoughtfully. "Perhaps the two of you can work out some bargain. He can help you; you can help him."

She raised her chin. "I never said I came here for his help."

His glance slid over her clothing. "I don't think you came to seduce Antonio," he said drily.

Annoyed at the prince's insight, she snapped, "Why I came is none of your business." Then bit her lip at her insolence towards a prince.

He raised a brow at her tone. "My family seems to attract outspoken women," he observed mildly. When she started to apologize, he waved it away, saying, "The reason for your being here doesn't matter. You're here. Go to him. Help him."

Solange remained where she was. Quiet came from the room below, and she wondered if Tonio had gained control of whatever demons were eating at him. Then she heard the sound of glass shattering against the door. A wine bottle, perhaps? He was obviously in torment, but the thought of going to him scared her. He was too seductive, too humanly male. She wanted him too much. She could not afford to become entangled with him.

"Help him just for tonight," the prince urged. "Please."

His tone was earnest and just shy of pleading with her. Solange looked toward the open panel but did not move from her spot.

At her hesitation, he said, "*Mademoiselle. . .* Solange— May I call you that?—I am not asking you to bind yourself to him. I am merely asking that you go speak with him. Surely, visiting with a sick man is a gesture of charity."

Put that way, the prince made her descent below to Tonio's chambers seem harmless. Antonio was sick, and she understood he suffered. Compassion for his plight weakened her resolve. She could help him, for just one night. After all, being with him, having him touch her was the most pleasurable experience of her life. Why not allow herself this one enjoyment? Coming to her decision, she started for the door in the wall.

As she put her foot on the first step, the prince said, "You might want to return the moonstone to him. It helps to dampen the effects of the Hunger. Mine seems to do little to help him this time." He paused. "If my brother does not get what he needs during the Hunger, he will remain Shadow for the rest of his life." Solange stopped in midstep. The effects of the curse were dire. She certainly did not wish Tonio to remain Shadow for the rest of his life, despite the exquisite sensations he created when they touched. But the moonstone called to her. She was not sure she could easily give it up.

"Good luck, *mademoiselle*," he said. Then he wandered to the glass doors and stared out into the garden as if she were not there.

Solange looked down the dark staircase. Silence came from the room at the bottom. Lighting the lantern again, she descended and halted before the door. Apprehension tickled her middle. What would she find on the other side? What exactly did Tonio need? The answer to that last question scared her. She placed her hand on the stone. The door opened, and she stepped through.

Tonio swung to her with a snarl of rage. His fingers curled into the bed hangings. With a wrench, he ripped them from their rods. They billowed and flopped around his legs. The empty, disheveled bed revealed he was alone.

"You again." His accusation whipped at her. "Didn't you get enough of a performance, little thief? Or did you wish to join in?" He shook his head. "Too late. I sent my friends away."

"I came to help," she said, and took several steps forward, stepping over the leg of a broken table. Glass crunched underfoot.

His head snapped back as if she had punched him. "At what price?" He whipped the bed hangings out of the way. "I don't need your help." Grabbing the wine bottle on a nearby table, he raised it to his mouth and took several large swallows.

"Tonio—"

He turned on her, his eyes angry, demonic in their darkness. "What do you want? You were the one to declare our relationship a cold business arrangement. An unemotional give and take. Why should I let you help me when you'll only ask something in return? Something I may not be willing to give?"

Of course, he was correct. She needed to keep her dealings with him unemotional. Otherwise, she could see herself falling under his spell. What she wanted to do was turn around and run. Yet, his declaration that the ancient sorceress wanted to kill her and Gide, and the fact that the man before her might be the only way to find her brother and keep him alive rooted her where she was. That and his obvious torment. "Why did you send the others away?"

His eyes narrowed, and he took a step toward her. "So, you did wish to join in." His lips curled in a chilly smile. "I apologize for disappointing you." Turning away, he raised the bottle to his mouth again. His hand shook.

"No, Tonio. Truly, I just want to help you." She reached out and touched his arm. It trembled beneath her fingers.

He sucked in a breath at her touch. "*Madre di Dio*," he croaked.

Afraid she had done something to hurt him, she dropped her hand and fell back. He swung to her, his eyes black and hungry. Tossing away the bottle, he approached, one stride, then two.

Solange retreated. He was a lethal predator stalking his prey. His hand whipped out and grabbed the front of her shirt. It ripped. She halted. His fist closed around the moonstone she wore beneath the garment. A groan escaped his lips. His shoulders hunched. Pain contorted his face. His eyes clenched shut. Solange was afraid to move, not sure what was happening, not sure whether he was in extreme agony or whether he might at any moment become violent.

His eyes snapped open. The black color had leached from them. They were not the beautiful gold they had been when she had robbed him, but they were a more normal shade of brown. Despite that, his gaze bored into her, his mouth a thin line.

"Give it to me."

His command demanded obedience. Frozen by the transformation of his eyes, Solange could not move.

He shook her. "Give it to me."

When she still did not comply, he took her shirt in both hands and ripped it open. Grabbing the moonstone in his fist, he jerked it from her neck, breaking the cord. The other hand he kept tightly wound in the material of her shirt. His eyes closed. His head dropped forward. A sound, halfway between sigh and groan escaped from him. When he staggered, Solange came out of her daze and grabbed him. His arm slipped around her shoulders, and he leaned on her.

"I need to touch you," he croaked.

She shook her head. "No."

"I need to touch you." This time, it was a growl.

Without waiting for her consent, he snaked his hand under her coat, grabbed the back of her shirt and ripped it away from her. She cried out. Before she could pull away, his palm flattened against the skin between her shoulder blades and crushed her against him. He curled around her, his head nuzzling the crook of her neck, his lips against the pulse beneath her ear.

"I don't want to hurt you," he murmured. "Don't move. Please." His tongue circled gently against her skin.

Something in his tone beguiled her. Something in his touch dissolved her defenses. Instead of struggling, she tentatively wrapped her arms around his ribs and spread her hands across his back. That tingle she had felt while he was Shadow was gone, but the warm solidity of him beneath her fingers was just as enticing.

He sighed. "Ah, *dolce mia*, your touch is like heaven."

His touch, too, was divine. The flat of his hand against

her back, the warmth of his breath against her skin, the tickle of his tongue below her ear swept away any thought of refusal. Closing her eyes, she held him. The swirl of his tongue enthralled her. Calm settled over her. She felt her muscles loosen, felt herself go slack as she leaned into him. And she drifted.

After a time, she felt him draw away. Forcing her eyes open, she watched him tie the cord holding the moonstone around his neck. Her brain was fuzzy, and she felt unconnected to reality. When he slowly pushed her coat from her shoulders, she put up no resistance. He untied her stock and pulled it from her neck. He ripped the shreds of her shirt from her shoulders. The cloth binding across her breasts seemed to unwind by itself. She was bare from the waist up, but somehow that was unimportant. He scooped her up in his arms.

"I don't think—" she began, but whatever she was going to say died.

"Shh. Don't speak, *dolcezza.*"

His murmur reassured her. Gently, he laid her on the bed. Her boots slipped off. His fingers tugged at the buttons of her breeches. That garment whisked away. When she was naked, she lay unmoving, her limbs relaxed, waiting for whatever he wanted to do. All her arguments, all her denials, all her reservations had dissolved to nothing.

He crawled onto the bed and knelt beside her. Reaching out, he ran his hand up her thigh, across her hip, over her ribs. Her skin responded as if it had a life of its own. It quivered beneath his touch. She sighed. He cupped her breast and stroked across her nipple. She purred with pleasure.

"My touch will never hurt you, *dolce mia.*" His words were spoken more as a vow than a mere statement.

His hand continued its upward journey, trailing across her collarbone, her shoulder, up her neck, where it wound softly. His fingers cupped the back of her head. His thumb brushed across her ear. Leaning down, he placed a gentle kiss at the corner of her mouth.

"*Grazie, dolcezza*," he whispered.

Stretching out, he rolled her to her side and snuggled her against him. Her bottom fit comfortably against his thighs. Her back pressed against his chest. His arms encircled her. She felt safe, cherished. He pulled the covers over them, and she felt him place a kiss on her shoulder. The moonstone pendant grew warm against her back.

A wisp of curiosity curled through her brain. Why had he only touched her? Why had he not joined with her, brought them both to shuddering ecstasy? What had restrained him, when clearly he wanted to ravage her the first time she descended the stairs?

Finding the answers proved to take too much energy. Lethargy stole through her limbs. Fogginess clouded her brain. Cocooned with him, she fell into sleep.

Chapter 13

Solange drifted awake. She felt comfortable, cozy, well-rested. Opening her eyes, she gazed at the unfamiliar surroundings. The dim light revealed the dark blue and gold of the coverlet, the rich blue watered silk on the walls, the thick pile of the Aubusson carpet on the floor. The disarray of the room, the ripped swath of gold brocade hanging from the rod above her head, indicated some sort of disturbance. Where was she? What had happened here?

Rolling to her back, she gazed up at the ceiling, visible because the canopy had been torn down. Slowly, a memory formed of a warm, hard body curled around her, of her feeling of security. Of being wrapped in Antonio's embrace. Oh, *mon Dieu.* Lifting up the covers, she peeked at herself just to be certain. Yes, she was naked.

Memory flooded back. Of his rage. Of his reaction to her touch. Of his taking the moonstone. Of his stripping her. Of his tender touch. Of her compliance. She winced. Her memory faded at that point. What else had she allowed him to do?

Throwing back the covers, she slid out of the bed. She knew exactly where she was. The room around her was lit only by a single candle on the mantle. Since it was below ground, no windows let in any light, but she could see the broken table pushed against one wall, the glint of broken glass from the wine bottle he had thrown. The wine-stained panel door in the wall was slightly ajar, and a thin stream of daylight seeped through. She winced again. She had slept through the night. Probably with him.

"*Mademoiselle, s'il vous plait,*" a young woman's voice spoke from a dark corner.

Solange swung to the voice. A maid approached, holding up a dressing gown.

"*Monsieur le Duc* asked that I assist with your toilette," she said.

Solange allowed the girl to slip the wrap onto her shoulders, then glanced around. Her coat, waistcoat, breeches, and boots had disappeared. "Where are my clothes?"

"They are being brushed and cleaned."

A moment of panic set in. What would the servants do if they found Antonio's ring? "I had put something in the pocket."

The young woman moved to the mantle and handed Solange a handkerchief tied with a white ribbon. "We found this in the pocket."

Unwrapping the small bundle, Solange was relieved to see the gold band. She nodded. "Thank you."

"*La princesse* has offered one of her own garments until yours are ready." The maid indicated a gown laid out on one of the chairs.

"That's very kind of her, but I will wait until my clothes are ready," Solange said.

The girl bit her lip and bowed her head. "Forgive me, *mademoiselle*, but *Monsieur le Duc* requested that you break your fast with him. He waits for you."

Of course he did, the arrogant rogue. She knew his request was more of a command. Even if she refused the invitation, he would come find her. Despite her memory of his gentleness as he had run his hand over her body, the rage in his eyes that had preceded his emotional shift unnerved her.

Something about the night before nagged at a corner

of her brain. Something about the way he had so easily undressed her, something about her complete acquiescence was not right. She had no idea what that was. But she intended to find out.

With a nod, she agreed to the maid's assistance.

When she was dressed, the maid showed her to the dining room. She felt a bit uncomfortable and wished she had refused Sabrina's kind offer of the loan of her dress. The princess was several inches shorter than Solange, and so the hem of the garment hung above her ankles. Even though the clothes she wore on the evenings of her salon were much more revealing, she felt exposed. She had to keep her composure if she were going to confront Antonio and if she were going to convince him to help her find Gide.

As she approached the dining room, she heard voices in conversation and quiet laughter. Stopping in the doorway, she was surprised to discover it was not the formal dining room as she had thought, but a much smaller, more intimate room with two walls of long windows that looked out over rolling lawns and allowed in bright sunlight. The other two walls held a mural of a quaint farm scene. A wrought iron chandelier hung from the ceiling. Seated at one end of the small, oval table was Sabrina, leaning intimately toward the man Solange had met last night, Antonio's twin. At the other end of the table was Antonio, dressed impeccably in a dark blue jacket, pale yellow waistcoat, snowy white shirt, and stock. His face was in profile as he stared out the window, the light behind him turning his unbound hair into a bright aureole, making him appear like an angel. Solange bit down on the ironic laughter she felt bubble up. The man was far from angelic.

The two men stood when they saw her in the doorway. The princess smiled warmly.

"I'm glad you could join us," she said. "And I'm so glad that my dress was fitting."

Solange smiled back, but she could not help trying to twitch the garment longer. Out of the corner of her eye, she saw Antonio tilt his head to peek at her exposed ankles.

"It is quite perfect," he said with a smile.

Solange scowled at him and felt the heat rise in her cheeks. She was actually blushing! Not having blushed at anything for years, she was both amazed and annoyed. That was the second time he had made her blush. How could this man unnerve her so easily?

He pulled out a chair for her to his left and sat himself after she was seated. When the footman approached to ask what she wished to eat, she told him merely hot chocolate.

Antonio added, "The lady will have croissants with peach preserves, strawberries, perhaps a slice of ham and some cheese, the wonderful Brie that arrived yesterday."

When the footman retreated, she hissed at the overbearing rogue, "I don't want all that."

"You must keep up your strength, *mademoiselle*," he murmured.

Turning away, he locked gazes with his brother. Solange watched as some sort of very brief, silent communication went on between them. His brother gave a quick nod, rose from the table, and held out his hand to Sabrina.

"Come, *cara mia*," the prince said. "It is a beautiful morning. I would be pleased if you would walk with me in the garden."

The princess sent Solange an encouraging smile before she left with her husband.

As soon as they were gone, Tonio said, "Did you sleep well, *mademoiselle*?"

She pinned him with her eyes. "I think you know the answer to that."

The corner of his mouth lifted. "I also slept well."

"What did you do to me?"

"Do?" Mischief flashed through his eyes, eyes that

had returned to their glorious golden color. "Don't you remember?"

"Of course I remember." She was not about to allow him the upper hand by revealing she could not.

"Ah. Then you remember my doing this." He reached out and trailed his fingers along her jaw. "And this." His fingers curled around the nape of her neck, and his thumb brushed beneath her ear.

His touch fuzzed her brain. "I don't—" she began, but had no idea what she was going to say.

"And you must remember this," he said, as he pulled her close and placed a kiss at the corner of her mouth.

Her eyes closed and her lips parted.

"And certainly you remember this," he murmured against her mouth. His tongue tasted the outline of her lips. "Tell me what else you remember, *dolce mia*."

Solange searched her brain for an answer. All she could find was the ability to take in a breath and let it out.

"Surely you remember the delight, the pleasure. *La petite mort*," he whispered.

La petite mort. No. Despite the fact that she had a blank in her memory, she sensed that had not happened. Her body would have remembered if he had given her such exquisite pleasure. He was toying with her. Jerking back, she glared at him.

"Villain," she spat. "We did no such thing."

He huffed a laugh. "No, we did not."

"You made me think . . . You took my memory and made me believe . . ." She was so angry she was sputtering.

"I did not take your memory. You remember everything that happened between us."

She blushed again as the image of his stripping her formed in her brain. What was it about this man that made her react like a virgin?

"You undressed me," she accused.

"*Sì*." He smiled. "A very pleasant experience."

"But I—You forced me."

His gaze turned cool, and a single brow arched up. "I would never force you. Whatever I did last night, you wanted me to do."

"But I felt . . . something."

He shrugged. "You were frightened. I merely calmed your fears."

Her eyes widened at the implication of that statement. "How did you do that?"

A servant arrived with the food and prevented him from answering. When the basket of croissants, the bowl of strawberries, the plate of sliced ham and wedge of glorious runny cheese had been placed within her reach, when her chocolate had been poured and the servant had left, Tonio took her hand.

"You know I have the ability to enter your mind, *si?*"

Solange stared. Although she had known some of her interactions with him had been unusual, especially his ability to speak in her head, she had not consciously thought about what that implied. Now, all the times she had felt that other presence in her mind came rushing back to her. She jerked her hand away.

"You violated me!"

His eyes narrowed. "I never took advantage of you. If you had wanted, you could have shut me out."

"How could I have done that? I have no knowledge of these things. You are lying."

He sat back in his chair. His gaze turned chilly. "I may be many despicable things, but one thing I am not is a liar, *Madame* de Volonté." He paused as his eyes impaled her. "As one who has lied herself, you should know truth when you hear it."

Defensive anger made her chin go up. "I have not lied to you. I have merely omitted telling you some things." She stabbed him with a look. "As you omitted telling me things."

He stared, immobile. She could envision that brain behind those incredible eyes whirring and clicking as it plotted and planned the next step in their intricate dance. Finally, he gave a solemn nod.

"Very well, *madame*, we each have our secrets." Then he smiled.

Solange was dazzled by the drastic change in his manner. The smile itself was enough to stun her into muteness. The fact that it was a complete switch from his offended attitude made her reel. Her overwhelming attraction to him shook her to her soul.

He pushed the plate of cheese toward her. "You must try this cheese. It is *delizioso*."

Needing to find her emotional footing, like a marionette, she scooped a chunk from the runny wedge and placed it on the plate before her. Then she spread a bit on one of the croissants and took a nibble. The buttery flakiness of the croissant, the creaminess of the cheese, was a symphony in her mouth. The sensual experience distracted her from both her anger and her dismay at her inability to best him at seduction, a game at which she was expert. Surprised into relishing the food, she spread more cheese on more of the croissant and ate the whole thing. He was silent the entire time.

Finally finished, she wiped her mouth and sat back in her chair. His gaze was warm, knowing, and he chuckled.

"It is *buona, si?*"

She nodded. "*Oui.*"

Reaching out, he rubbed his thumb across her bottom lip. "*Scusi*, you have a crumb . . ."

Instead of wiping the crumb off on a napkin, he sucked it off his thumb, his eyes caressing her face as he did so. A throb of desire caught her by surprise. Annoyed at her response to him, she dropped her gaze to her lap.

"So, *dolce mia*," he said, his voice swirling around her like syrup, "why did you decide to visit our chateau last night?"

Solange's head snapped up. She had almost forgotten. His thumb ring was still clutched in the fingers of her left hand. He had said nothing about her awkwardness in breaking and holding the croissant, using only her first finger and thumb. Now, she placed the gold band on the table and pushed it toward him.

Without a word, he snagged it with his forefinger and let it slide to his knuckle. Placing his elbow on the table, he held up his hand, gazed at the ring for a moment, then turned an inquiring look in her direction.

"So, you came to return my ring? All this way just to be contrite? Surely you could have done this before I left Paris. Perhaps instead of lying when you told me you had given it to Le Chacal."

Solange let her glance slide away to the windows. He had caught her—a double lie, for she had lied about not lying. Guilt twisted through her. She had not wanted to lie, had not meant to, but he churned up her insides and made her feel things she had never felt before. They were so foreign she had no name for them. She only knew they spawned a need for him she had never felt for anyone. They confused her and addled her brain. And that made her say and do things she thought she would never do.

She focused on the peaceful scene out the windows. Beyond the panes of glass, the serenity of the lawns, the copses of trees, the lovely folly with its tiny dome and delicate columns mocked her. She would never find such peace. Taking a breath, she turned back to Antonio.

"My brother has disappeared," she said. "I came to ask you to help me find him. Please."

Tonio gazed at her a moment, then he sat back and slipped the ring onto his thumb. Focusing on his hand, he turned the band round and round. The silence in the room stretched out. A bird landed in a bush outside the window and twittered. The sound seemed loud in the utter quiet.

Solange wanted to know what Tonio was thinking. She wanted to shift in her seat but dared not move for fear that any movement would tip his answer against her. Coming here last night, she had been confident that she could get him to help her. Now, she was not so sure.

He raised his head. Those golden eyes bored into her. "Your brother," he said, "does not like me. Why should I suffer discomfort, possibly even place myself in danger looking for him? Surely, he is old enough to do as he wishes."

"He would never just disappear," she told him. "And he wouldn't leave without saying goodbye."

"Why did you not ask the Marquis de Vernoux to help you? Or Le Chacal?" He tipped his head. "Or did they turn down your request? Am I your last resort, *madame*?"

She opened her mouth to deny the charge, then closed it again. She could not lie to him. Not in this. Gide was too precious to her. "*Oui*," she whispered, hanging her head. "I did not ask Vernoux, and Le Chacal would not help."

"If I give you my help, what are you willing to give in return?"

Solange drew in a breath. "I gave you the ring."

He huffed an unamused laugh. "Something that was mine to begin with."

"And you took the moonstone," she reminded him.

"Which you stole from me and had no intention of returning."

Indignation made her stiffen. "Of course I—"

"Stop. Another lie will not help you."

Solange wilted.

He leaned forward on the table. "If I expend my time and my energy and my talent looking for your brother, what price are you willing to pay, *Madame* de Volonté?"

What was she willing to pay? Stupidly, she had assumed that returning his ring might be enough, but she should have known better. She'd made it clear that their relationship would be strictly business. Cold, unemotional. Why then, did she think he would so easily agree to help her just because she asked? Just because they had shared exquisite pleasure?

He sat back. "You were quite definite that affection plays no part in the relationship. Since that is so, I feel I have the right to demand payment in return for finding your brother."

"I have little coin, but I will pay whatever you ask."

Barking a laugh, he swept his arm wide, indicating the room, the chateau, the grounds beyond. "Does it look to you as if I need your money? No, *Mademoiselle* Delacroix. What I want from you is far more precious." He paused.

Afraid of what he might ask, Solange stared at him.

Quietly, he said, "What I want, little thief, is your time. You will make yourself available to me whenever I wish."

"But I cannot! Vernoux—"

His hand sliced through the air, cutting her off. "You will. Or I will leave your brother to rot wherever he is." He shrugged. "Vernoux will have to accommodate me."

"You snake!" she hissed.

His brow curved up. "Ah. Well, I have been called many things. I believe that is the first time I've been named a reptile, particularly for agreeing to help someone. Do we have a deal, *madame*?"

She glanced away, this time to the idyllic scene of

the farm mural painted on the wall. That, too, mocked her as much as the peaceful rolling lawns beyond the windows. She and Gide would never have the small farm which had always been their dream. She would always be subject to the desires of a man until she grew so old no one would desire her, and her dreams could never be fulfilled.

Turning back to Antonio, she nodded. "*Oui.* We have a deal."

He smiled like a pirate who had just discovered a cache of gold in the hold of a ship. "*Bene.*" Standing, he said, "If I am to return to Paris to search for your brother, I must make preparations. Please, stay and finish your meal. I am sure your clothes will be ready soon, so you may return to the city as well. Unless you would like me to accompany you?"

She shook her head vigorously.

"I thought not."

"Wait," she said, as he began to move from the table. "You never told me . . . How do I shut you out of my mind?"

His smile turned soft. His gaze turned seductive, enticing. Stepping away from the table, he moved behind her. He whispered in her ear, "Just by thinking it, *dolce mia.*"

Solange stopped breathing at his revelation.

He trailed his fingers across the back of her neck as he left.

She shivered. The caress of his fingers, the feel of his skin against hers was an aphrodisiac. Each touch gave her pleasure, and the lack of that touch made her crave it more. How could she keep this consuming passion from Vernoux? How could she keep her sanity if all she wanted was to be near him? How could she keep her soul?

Something dug into her palm, and she realized she

186

was gripping the bowl of a spoon so hard the edges bit into her skin. The pain helped clear her head, and his last bit of information finally registered. If all she had to do was think him out of her head, then that is what she would do. She would be cold and calculating, clever. She would not give him the chance to seduce her. Their association would be cool, business-like, just as they had agreed.

He would find Gide, and in return, she would give him some of her time. Relieved she had finally worked out a plan, she plucked a strawberry from the bowl and went to see if her clothes were ready.

It was time to return to Paris.

Chapter 14

Antonio hopped across a stream of sewage running down the middle of the street. He heard a grunt as Piero stepped across beside him.

"Disgusting," Antonio's Guide mumbled. "At least in Venice the tides wash everything out to sea."

Tonio smiled. "You could have stayed at the chateau in the country with Alessandro instead of coming back to Paris with me."

"*Sior* Alessandro doesn't need me. *Donna* Sabrina is very capable of looking after him while the curse takes hold, since it has been partially broken after they found a piece of the Sphere of Astarte." Piero picked up his foot and examined the bottom of his boot where something mushy and smelly clung.

Antonio nodded. "*Si*. He has told me that remaining flesh and bone during the day and becoming Shadow only at night has made his life much easier. And he has the moonstone to dampen the Hunger. And a beautiful wife to ease him through it each morning . . ." He frowned and shrugged to cover the wistfulness that crept into his tone.

"Don't despair. You will find the piece of the Sphere that is hidden here. I can feel it." Piero scraped the mess off the bottom of his boot. "Just please find it quickly, *Sior* Tonio. I long for the clean air of Auriano or the salt air of Venice." He checked the bottom of his boot again, and his expression turned gloomy. "I fear my boots are ruined."

Antonio chuckled. "You will have a dozen new pairs when I find the piece of the Sphere. But first I have to find this stupid man-boy who has upset his sister."

Piero gazed down the dark alley before them. To the east, the sky was beginning to brighten into dawn, but the light had not yet reached the dim streets of the city. "You'd think the young man would have found a more comfortable place to hide."

Tonio raised his lantern and followed his Guide's gaze. The alley before them ran between the back entrances of two abandoned mansions and behind several shops and poor, humble residences. Debris lay scattered down its length, and small piles leaned against the walls of the buildings. The stench of garbage and excrement lay heavy in the pre-dawn stillness. From where he stood, he saw no niches, no nooks where a man could hide, but that did not mean there were none. In the past two days, their search had uncovered many hidden places where the poor and the homeless of the city lived, not any better off than before the revolution that was supposed to make every man equal. In fact, one of those unfortunates had directed them here, after Tonio had proffered a few coins.

Stepping forward, he said, "Come, Piero. We'll look down here, and then we'll go home for something to eat and a rest."

Piero heaved a sigh. *"Grazie, Sior* Tonio. My humble bed is calling to me."

"Your bed is not that humble, Piero," Tonio remarked drily, "but I agree that sleep would be very welcome." He took several steps, then halted. "Do you hear that?"

Coming from somewhere down the alley was a quiet male voice singing. Or chanting? It stopped suddenly, and the sound of breaking glass punctuated the silence. Sobbing reached their ears.

Antonio hastened forward with Piero close behind. He came upon someone huddled into a small alcove where the wall of one of the mansions met the building next to it. The man rested his head on his knees, and his arms wrapped about his head. Glass crunched under Antonio's boots, and the ground was slick with something wet.

"It's better this way," the man sobbed. "She'll kill me anyway."

"Gide." Tonio set down the lantern and squatted before him. "Gide, I've come to take you home."

"Go away," he mumbled, alcoholic fumes clouding every word. "Go away. She won't want me."

"Gide, pull yourself together. Your sister is worried about you. She sent me to find you."

Gide's head rolled back and forth against his arms. "She won't want me after she finds out what I've done."

Antonio wondered what Gide could have done that would make him so miserable. "Of course she'll want you. You're her brother."

"No." The word came on a sob.

"Gide, come. I'll take you home." Antonio touched his shoulder to urge him along.

Gide's head snapped up. "Get away from me," he snarled. "This is your fault."

"*Merda!*" Antonio breathed when he saw the man's face. Dirt mixed with wet blood streaked across his forehead and both cheeks. " You're hurt. What happened?"

"Nothing I'd tell you about." Gide's eyes glinted like hard stones in the lantern light.

Antonio bit down on his exasperation. "Then don't tell me, but we have to get you home."

He reached for Gide's arm to help him to stand, but the young man jerked away. A stain darkened the ripped cuff of his shirt and spread beneath the sleeve of his coat, which was pushed partway up his arm. A jagged, diagonal wound cut across his wrist and flowed with blood.

"*Cazzo!*" Antonio caught Gide's arm and held it to get a closer look. "What did you do?"

Gide laughed mirthlessly. "Getting rid of the one thing I thought would get rid of you. What a joke, *n'est-ce pas?*" Once again, he jerked his arm away.

Antonio tried to grab him with one hand and untie his own stock with the other to use as a bandage, but Gide struggled away from him. Piero caught hold of him and wrestled him to his back. He pinned his arms and kept him quiet with a knee across his chest.

"Thought Binding, *Sior* Tonio.," his Guide panted. "Quickly. I can't hold him much longer."

Antonio wrapped his fingers around Gide's throat and pressed against the pulse points. Almost instantly, he was inside the man's head. A dark fog hovered in one corner of Gide's mind, and Antonio sensed something spiteful, menacing. He did not stay long enough to discover what it was. He was more concerned with calming Solange's brother and getting him home. Inducing him to unconsciousness, he retreated quickly. Gide fell slack against the dirt of the alley.

Before Solange's brother could make any more difficulty, Antonio pulled his stock from his neck and bound Gide's wrist. Blood saturated it immediately.

"It needs sewing, Piero, or he'll bleed to death," Antonio said. "We have to get him home fast."

They hoisted the young man to his feet and supported him between them. Gide moaned when he was upright.

"I think I'm going to die," he mumbled. Then he vomited all over Piero's boots and passed out.

* * *

They arrived at Solange's door by the time gray, predawn light was beginning to brighten the city. After banging several times, they were able to rouse a servant to allow them entrance. Antonio sent the servant scurrying for hot water, bandages, needle, and thread.

They carried the unconscious Gide to his room where they placed him on the bed. Antonio stripped him to his waist. By the time he had finished, Solange appeared in the doorway.

"You found him," she said, relief coloring her words. Then concern verging on panic made her tone rise. "What has happened? What's wrong with him?"

Antonio turned to her. "He has met with an accident. Piero will do what he can to help."

He watched her approach. She moved carefully as if she were in some pain. He surmised Vernoux had visited her during the night and handled her roughly. He had warned the marquis about touching her. The thought of that man's hands hurting her made him want to kill. But he would bide his time. His immediate concern was with Gide.

Solange moved closer and caught a glimpse of the blood and filth that covered her brother. With a gasp, she grabbed the bedpost. The sleeve of her dressing gown fell away, and Antonio saw the raw, red lines around her wrist that spoke of cruel bindings, and the three dark bruises on her neck that looked suspiciously like fingerprints. He tried not to speculate what that French pig had done to her. He clenched his teeth so the violent words that hovered on his tongue would not escape his lips. With effort, he returned his focus to Piero as his Guide cleaned Gide's wrist.

Despite the fact that Gide's wound still pumped blood, enough had been cleaned away that Antonio was able to make out faint ridges on his wrist. The wound sliced across them and the blood blurred them, but they appeared to be some sort of design.

"*Sior* Tonio," Piero said, "please, I need you to hold the wound closed for me so that I may sew it."

Antonio knew that Piero needed no such help, but he complied with his Guide's request. As soon as he did, he

192

saw why Piero had asked. Held together, the ridges formed the glyph of a frog. Sometime in the recent past, Gide had become a novice of the Legion of Baal. He exchanged a glance with Piero. The stakes in the race to retrieve the piece of the Sphere of Astarte had just been raised.

"*Grazie,* Excellency," Piero murmured. "If you would be kind enough to send in the young sir's man-servant, we can get him cleaned up and made more comfortable."

Antonio cleaned his hands, then took Solange by the arm and guided her out of the room. She looked like she was on the point of collapse. After sending for Gide's man-servant, he steered her to her sitting room. She sank slowly onto a chair and tried to hide a grimace of pain. Tonio ignored it for the moment, reminding himself their relationship was purely business. But his insides churned with rage at what had been done to her.

"Is Gide. . .?" she began, swallowed, and started over. "Will he be all right?"

Antonio kept his tone cool and remote. "I am no physician, *madame*, and he has lost a great deal of blood." He did not need to show her the large, dark red stains all over his own clothes. And he was not about to reveal what her brother had been trying to excise on his wrist. Enough had been done to her in one evening. She looked too fragile to learn such news. Besides, he felt it was Gide's confession to make. "Piero will do what he can. He is quite talented in caring for wounds."

She nodded. Without meeting his eyes, she said, "I am very grateful for your help."

"I told you I would help." He kept his words mild, leashing the frustration that ran through him.

"*Oui.* You did." Exhaustion underlined her words.

As she fell into silence, Tonio could not contain the need to comment on her condition. "Are you unwell, *madame*?"

Her gaze flew to his face. Panic swept across her

features. Then those marvelous turquoise eyes turned chilly as stones.

"I am quite well, *Monsieur le Duc. Merci.*" She glanced at the windows where dawn lightened the edges of the closed draperies. "I have been consumed with worry over Gide and have not slept well, that is all." Turning back to him, she graced him with a cool smile. "Surely you can understand a sister's concern for her brother?"

Her distant and reserved manner annoyed him. He wanted her to throw her arms about him and weep on his shoulder in gratitude and relief. He wanted her to confide the atrocities Vernoux had committed on her, so he could gently undress her and kiss her injuries into pleasure and forgetfulness. Instead, he nodded curtly.

"Of course. I won't bother you any further, *madame.* Piero should be finished by now. I'll leave you to rest. If you need further assistance, please send for me." He bowed and turned toward the door. With his hand on the handle, he stopped. "I will be here tomorrow evening, *madame*, to collect payment."

She stared at him as if she did not understand.

"You promised your time in return for finding your brother," he reminded her coolly.

He watched her wilt, then in the next second, she straightened.

"I always pay my debts, *mon seigneur.*" Her chin went up a notch. "I will honor our agreement."

Antonio allowed himself the tiniest of smiles. "Of course you will," he murmured. With another bow, he left, anticipation for the next evening already bubbling through him.

* * *

Solange paced her bedchamber as she waited for Antonio to arrive. She rubbed her damp palms down the skirt of her dressing gown. Her stomach fluttered. Part of her wanted this night to end as quickly as possible. The other part wished it might go on forever. She hated Auriano for forcing her to play the courtesan for him. At the same time, the memory of his touch made her heart race.

She was grateful that he had found Gide, although she worried about her brother. He had developed a fever. She should be by his bedside, laying cool cloths across his head, giving him sips of water, spooning up broth for him. Instead, she had to prove her gratitude to Auriano by keeping her part in their bargain. Annoyance brought a frown. She did not dare defy him. He could destroy her by going to the authorities and revealing her identity as a highwayman, or he could reveal Le Chacal's hideout in the Catacombs, which would bring the wrath of the outlaws of Paris down on her. Neither was an attractive option. So she waited for Antonio to come and claim her.

Anticipation of his arrival, his seduction, made her throb. She drew a breath. She was being a fool. Their relationship was a chilly business arrangement. No soft feelings, no sentimentality. Auriano had reminded her of that quite well on the morning they had sat together in that intimate dining room at *le Chateau des Ombres*.

The aches from Vernoux's abusive treatment the other night, had faded. At least she was able to walk without pain. She wondered how well she would be able to hide the marks of his cruelty from Antonio. She wanted no pity from the duke.

A knock on her door halted her, and she heard her maid's voice telling her that Auriano had arrived. Straightening her shoulders, raising her chin, she forced a smile and went to greet him.

He was not in the small drawing room where she expected him to be. Instead, she found him wandering through the dim salon. His dark figure reflected in the rows of mirrors on the walls. He turned at her entrance, all of his reflections turning with him, that graceful, muscular body, that handsome face replicated thousands of times. She wanted to stand and stare, drink him in. Instead, she dropped into a deep curtsey, greeting him in the same manner she greeted Vernoux.

"*Mon seigneur*," she murmured. "I am honored at your visit."

He did not respond immediately, and she remained in her awkward position with her head bowed while she waited for him to speak or make some move. As she did, she realized he had not removed his cape and still held his hat. Irritation at her maid's negligence flickered through her. Apprehension at his immobility swiftly replaced it.

Finally, she raised her head. "*Mon seigneur?*"

* * *

Antonio stared, speechless, astounded on many levels. The beauty, the sensuality of Solange mesmerized him. Her dressing gown fell off one shoulder, revealing the pale, soft skin, enticing with its suggestion of abandonment. The material was translucent, and the light from the doorway behind her threw her lithe figure into silhouette. The memory of those curves beneath his fingers catapulted him into an immediate erection. Her hair was loose and hung in a wavy tumble across her shoulder, ending at her waist. He wanted to wrap that silk around his hand, bury his fingers in it, inhale its fragrance.

But she had greeted him in the most humble, subservient manner imaginable. This was not the bold highwayman before him, nor the brave woman who had matched wits with him. This was, rather, the submissive female who played the whore for her master. She expected him to use her, to take advantage of her, and she would comply with whatever he wanted of her. Her night rail and dressing gown were meant for private seduction, not fit for being seen in public. His demand for her time had been entirely misconstrued. That realization made him furious at the man who had so subjugated her.

Stepping forward, he took her hand and raised her to her feet. "*Mademoiselle* Delacroix," he said. "Your beauty has made me speechless." He brought her hand to his lips in the most respectful of greetings.

A faint blush colored her cheeks, and her lashes swept down over those incredible eyes. "You compliment me too much, *mon seigneur*," she murmured. Withdrawing her hand, she stepped back. "My maid has been neglectful and has not relieved you of your outer garments. Please, allow me to take your hat and cape for you. Then we can proceed to my drawing room where I have refreshments waiting."

Instead of handing her his garments, he took her hand. "No, Solange, you may not take my hat and cape."

Her eyes widened. Anxiety flashed through them.

"Solange." Gently, he demanded her attention. "I did not come here tonight for your sexual favors."

A tiny line of confusion appeared between her brows.

"I came to spend time with you, to be with you, to enjoy your company." He remained perfectly still, not wishing to alarm her.

"But—"

"You agreed to give me your time, *si?*"

"*Oui,*" she said hesitantly.

"Then I may demand anything I wish." He watched his words instill apprehension in her eyes, and spoke again to erase that expression. "I wish to take you out into the city for the evening. I want to escort you, have you on my arm. I want other men to be jealous of me." He paused. "Solange, I want to make you laugh."

She stared. Tears filled her eyes, and she turned away. She ducked her head to hide from him, but he could still see her reflection. Her lips trembled in her effort to control her emotions.

"You mock me, *mon seigneur*," she said, her even tone belying her struggle. "I do not parade about in public. I know my place. It is here, on my back, or in any other position a man may wish."

Violent fury swept through him so fast he lost all sense of where he was. He wanted to kill that monster Vernoux for what he had done to her.

"*Mon seigneur*? Antonio?"

Her words cut through the red mist that clouded his vision. Blinking, he focused on the woman before him. Wide-eyed, trembling, she stared at him. Her gaze dropped to his side, and he realized he had allowed his stiletto to slip into his hand. Taking a breath, he forced his rage away. The woman before him was not the subject of his anger. She was the victim who had been made into an object for a man's abuse. And he had frightened her.

He took a step back, sheathed his knife up his sleeve and bowed. "*Scusi, ma donna*," he murmured, berating himself for being so stupid. "This misunderstanding is my fault. I should have made myself clear from the beginning." He smiled. "Let us begin again, *si*?"

She gave a tiny nod.

He took a breath, allowing both of them to regain their footing. "We have a business arrangement, *si*? Payment for services. So. For delivering your brother to you, I demand payment. That is, I am asking to spend time with you, to entertain you, to escort you to the theater or the gaming tables or on a cruise on the river. I am asking for your company."

She stared at him for the length of three heartbeats. He thought she still might not understand his intentions, and he was about to explain further when she shook her head.

"I cannot leave here."

Frustration made him sigh. She was very stubborn.

She spoke again. "My brother's fever rages, and I should be here if he needs me."

198

"Ah, did I not tell you? Piero came with me. Even now he is with your brother. He will stay until we return."

Her brows curved up in surprise. "Piero?"

"*Si.*"

"He will care for Gide? Stay with him?"

"*Si.*"

Antonio watched as she comprehended that she was free for the evening, that a man wished to escort her through the city, to show her off in public. She clasped her hands, and her eyes sparkled.

He grinned. "Although what you are wearing is alluring, *dolce mia*, I don't think we should take you out in it. Go put on something glorious. I will wait."

With a little jump, she turned to hurry away, then swung back. She ran to him, placed her hands on his shoulders, and standing on tiptoe, placed a kiss on his cheek.

"*Merci,*" she whispered. "*Merci, beaucoup.*" Then she skipped out the door.

Chapter 15

Antonio took Solange to the *Tuileries* Gardens, where respectable young women, dressed in the latest fashion, strolled with their *mamans* to catch the eye of admiring young men. The *Tuileries* had belonged to the royal court before the Revolution, and the people had only been allowed onto its grounds one day a year, the Feast of St. Louis. Now, anyone could stroll its paths. Solange delighted in the statuary and tightly shaped shrubs in the moonlight, and the sense of intimacy afforded by the shadows of trees and bushes.

Antonio leaned close. "We must be very careful walking these paths," he murmured.

Solange glanced around her, apprehensive. "Why is that?"

"Because a highwayman may jump out at us at any moment," he teased.

Her eyes twinkled as she said, "Or perhaps a Shadow might suddenly step from the shades of the trees."

"*Touché.*" Antonio chuckled.

After they explored the gardens, he directed her to the *Palais Royal*, renamed again after its short life as the *Palais de l'Égalité* during the Revolution. It had been the extravagant home of Phillippe, Duc d'Orléans before his execution. Now, it was a place where the fashionable and wealthy of the city mingled with the scoundrels and villains. One could find anything from shops to gambling casinos, theaters, taverns, or ladies of the evening.

Although Solange ran a salon where wealthy, famous,

and infamous men gathered, and although she directed young women in the art of becoming mistresses to those men, she had never been taken to the *Palais Royal*. She had only seen it as a thief, dressed in her thief's clothes, on the lookout for an easy victim, and attempting to dodge the *gendarmes* who patrolled in pairs to keep order. Now, as a fashionable young woman on a man's arm, she enjoyed the spectacle.

They wandered for a while through the shops. Solange admired the trinkets displayed on the shelves, the lovely bonnets, and the multihued shawls of oriental silk. Antonio bought her a fan of silk, painted with a bucolic scene of shepherdesses and swains frolicking in a meadow. It was a beautiful thing, and she snapped it open and fluttered it coquettishly. When they tired of window-shopping, he took her to *Le Grand Vefour*, a restaurant in the *Palais Royal* that had previously been a café where royalists would gather during the Revolution. He obtained a table in a small alcove, private, but with a view of the rest of the room. Solange was fascinated by the other patrons—men entertaining their mistresses, dowagers chaperoning their young charges, groups of men out for an evening's entertainment. The waiters followed a precise protocol and were as arrogant in their service as any aristocrat had ever been. Antonio ordered for them both, and they were served fish, partridge, fruit, cheese, and custard, washed down with a delicious wine from Burgundy.

When Solange could not possibly eat another bite, she sat back in her chair and fluttered her fan. "This has been a wonderful evening. *Merci.*"

Antonio smiled. "The evening is not over yet, *dolcezza.* I have one more surprise for you."

Solange was touched. She had never felt so cherished. Certainly Vernoux had never treated her in such a way. When Auriano had bargained with her, this night had been the last thing she had expected. The heat rose in her cheeks, and she lowered her eyes. "You have been most kind, *mon seigneur.* I do not wish to take advantage of your generosity."

He leaned across the table and covered her hand with his long, graceful fingers. "Solange, you agreed to give me your time. I am not done with you yet."

Of course. He would expect what every other man would expect—the benefits of her talents. Despite what he had told her earlier, he would have her play the whore for him.

"Solange, do you know how to waltz?" he asked.

His question shocked her. Had she heard correctly? She gaped at him in disbelief.

He chuckled. Taking her hand, he raised it to his lips. "You look like a startled deer," he said. "Has no one ever taken you dancing?"

She shook her head, caught between surprise and the feel of his lips against her fingers.

"We must put that to rights," he murmured. "We will waltz to wonderful music."

"I don't know how to waltz," she said. "I've never seen it done."

"Then come, *dolcezza.* Let me show you." Smiling, he rose and pulled her to her feet.

* * *

Antonio took her to one of the many *bals publics* that engaged the city. These were places where all classes of the people of Paris gathered to dance, particularly the waltz—that new craze imported from Germany. This one was held in a modest *l'hôtel* in the *Invalides*, across the river from the *Palais Royal*. Despite the smaller scale of the dwelling in comparison to its neighbors, the interior dazzled with crystal chandeliers, gilt-framed paintings on silk-covered walls, and intricate parquet flooring. The mingling crowd buzzed with conversation and glimmered with finery. Many of them wore a thin red ribbon around their throats which marked them as *à la victime*, a relative of someone who had been sent to the guillotine. Music swept through the air and enfolded the crowd like a fur wrap.

Antonio, having shown Solange the basic steps of the waltz before they arrived, escorted her onto the dance floor. She was a quick study and a graceful dancer. The feel of her in his arms as she followed his lead was intoxicating. After she became accustomed to the steps and the natural beat of the music, she smiled up at him. Her eyes sparkled. Her lips curved in abandoned joy. Something clenched and unfurled in his chest. He found that giving her this bit of happiness made him happy, perhaps the happiest he had ever been. And that astounded him. At the same time, he became wary. He could not allow himself to become emotionally attached to her. He needed to stay detached, to use her to find the piece of the Sphere and then leave her, despite his reluctance to do so.

They had danced three waltzes in succession when he led her off the dance floor to catch her breath. As they stood together at the edge of the crowd, she looked up at him shyly.

"Why are you doing this?" she asked.

Surprised at her question, he answered with one of his own. "Are you enjoying yourself?"

"Very much." she nodded.

"Then you have your answer." Smiling, he tucked her hand into the crook of his arm.

She pulled away. "When a man entertains a woman, he usually wants something in return."

Her refusal to accept his generosity irritated him. "Your time this evening was in payment for my search for your brother, or have you forgotten our bargain?"

"But you have been kind." A thin line of confusion appeared between her brows.

Her incomprehension tweaked his heart. "Has no one ever been kind to you, Solange?" he asked gently.

She glanced away. "Not for a very long time." Her quiet words were nearly lost in the music. Then the line of her jaw tightened, and she turned back to him. "We have a business arrangement. You have no need to be kind."

"That's true," he agreed. Lightening his tone, he said, "Would it surprise you if I said I liked you?"

Her eyes widened, and she gave a small laugh. "Even though I have stolen from you and threatened you with a knife?"

He smiled. "I find your spirit exhilarating."

"You have very strange taste in women, *Monsieur le Duc*." She snapped open her fan and fluttered it.

He saw she did not believe him. And he had been a fool to admit to any soft feelings towards her, for that gave her an advantage in their arrangement. The music, the gay atmosphere, her laughter, and her playfulness had lulled him into complacency.

Taking advantage of her skepticism, and relieved he had been saved from emotional entanglement, he said, "Perhaps I have other reasons for enjoying your company."

She turned a cynical glance on him. "Of course you do. You want what every other man wants from me."

"No, not every other man," he said mildly. "You know what I want, Solange."

Her fingers tightened on her fan. He watched understanding flit through those glorious turquoise eyes. He referred to the piece of the Sphere of Astarte. And she knew it. Instead of acknowledging his statement, she said, "I would like a cup of lemonade, *monsieur*. I find I am quite parched."

Amused at her evasion, he smiled, bowed, and left

to elbow his way through the crowd and forage for her refreshment.

*   *   *

Hours later, Antonio guided Solange around the corner into the narrow street which would take them to where their coach waited. Antonio enjoyed the feel of Solange on his arm. She was humming a few bars from one of the waltz tunes when the scuff of a shoe alerted him to someone at the end of the street. A figure blocked the small lamp that glowed on the house at the corner. He glanced over his shoulder and saw two others block off the other end of the street.

Solange's steps faltered.

"Stay behind me," he ordered quietly.

"I am far from helpless," she said acerbically. She bent, raised her skirt, and pulled out a dagger she had strapped below her knee.

He grinned. "*Bene.*"

The man before them was joined by another. As if a signal had been given, the four men rushed them. Antonio flicked his stiletto into his hand and nudged Solange out of the way.

Two of the men came after him. Two went after Solange. He stabbed and kicked, sliced and jabbed. In moments, his two attackers were bloody and unconscious. Their defeat had been easy. Solange was having a more difficult time. Her two attackers were bigger, more vicious. She swiped at one with her dagger, then the other. Antonio stepped forward to help her, but one of the outlaws on the ground grabbed him by the ankle and jerked. Tonio thudded to the dirt, the wind knocked out of him. Black spots appeared before his eyes. He shook them off in time to see a knife slicing down toward his chest. Thrusting up, he slammed his stiletto into the attacker's

Patricia Barletta

throat. As the man collapsed on top of him, he heard Solange cry out.

Antonio struggled from beneath the body sprawled across him and rolled to his knees to see one of the bandits slash at Solange. The knife caught in her cloak.

"Solange, use your power!" he shouted.

She glanced at him blankly, as if she had not understood.

One of her attackers grabbed her. Antonio watched in horror as the other swept his knife in an arc toward her heart.

"Your power," he yelled again. He leaped to her aid.

Solange brought up her hand. A flash blinded him. He heard a howl of pain. When his sight cleared, one of her attackers was lying on the ground. The other was running out of the alley. Solange slumped against the building and slowly collapsed.

Antonio reached her just before she crumpled to the ground. Her eyes were closed. Her skin was cold. Her pulse barely fluttered beneath his fingers.

He could see little in the dark, but blood stained her clothes. Panic ripped through him as he searched for a wound, but she appeared uninjured. Cradling her against him, he tried to warm her. Her hand twitched. She drew a deep breath, and her eyes opened.

"Are you hurt?" he asked.

She shook her head.

"You vanquished them, *dolce mia*," Antonio said, as he brushed a stray curl from her face.

Her gaze went to the man lying on the ground near her. A large hole was burned through his chest. "Did I do that?"

"*Sì.*"

She shivered and turned her face into Antonio's shoulder. "Take me home, *s'il vous plaît*."

Antonio helped her stand. He was about to guide her away from the spot when she halted. She bent over the man near her, gasped, then studied the other two nearby.

"What is it?" Antonio asked.

"Nothing. It's . . . nothing," she said, turning away.

Antonio knew it was not *nothing*. Something about those men disturbed her.

He was about to ask her when she cried out and clutched her chest. Before he could help her, icy tentacles grabbed at his heart. Solange swayed, and he barely caught her as he fought off his own pain. Nulkana was once again taunting them. He glanced around but saw nothing else threatening from either end of the narrow street. But there, atop the building, sat *her* owl silhouetted against the night sky. As he watched, it spread its wings and silently took flight. The sense of evil retreated with it.

"The sorceress," Solange said.

"*Si.* Come, *dolce mia.* We must get you home where it is safe." He hurried her back to his carriage.

Once safely inside the vehicle, Solange slumped into the corner. Antonio wanted to comfort her, keep her safe and forget their agreement to keep their relationship cool and practical. She kept her eyes closed, and Antonio knew she was avoiding conversation, either because she was too spent after using her power, or because she had no wish to reveal who their attackers were. Their ride through the streets was fast. When they finally reached her door, she allowed him to help her from the coach and swept into the house. Grimly, he followed. Now he could question her about the identity of their attackers, for he had a suspicion that it was no coincidence that Nulkana's bird appeared at the same time as the attack.

* * *

Solange's first thought after stepping through her front door was for Gide. She feared that her brother might also have been a target this night. Ignoring Antonio, she raced up the stairs to Gide's bedchamber, where she found him sleeping peacefully.

Antonio's servant, Piero, rose and bowed. "Your brother's fever has broken, *ma donna*. He will surely return to good health in a few days." He glanced from her to Antonio, who stood close behind her. "You have been attacked. By Nulkana?"

Solange realized they must look a sight. Her gown was ripped and filthy. Locks of hair had escaped from their pins and hung in tangles down her back. Antonio's breeches were covered in mud. The ivory satin lining of his cloak was torn and dragged on the floor. A scrape reddened one cheekbone.

He shook his head. "Not Nulkana, but she sent her bird to watch. Merely some outlaws." His tone was carefully level.

Solange ignored the prick of guilt at his words. She was not about to draw him deeper into her world by revealing her suspicions about the attack.

He shifted, as if uncomfortable. It was an odd movement for him. She caught sight of a red stain on his waistcoat. "You're bleeding!" Solange pushed open his coat to reveal the slice through his clothing and across his ribs.

"It's nothing, merely a scratch." He shrugged it off, then lightly touched his fingers to her cheek. "You have also been injured, *dolce mia*."

Solange covered the spot, surprised to find a bruise. "I'm fine. But we must take care of your wound."

"Piero will see to it later," Antonio said, as he took her by the elbow and steered her out of the room. "Besides, I heal very quickly. Come, let me help you to your room and then call your maid to look after you."

Solange caught the glance he sent to Piero, a silent message. He was hiding something. Annoyed, she allowed him to escort her into her bedchamber. He had her sit, then poured water into the washbasin and wet a cloth. Crouching before her, he pressed it against her cheek.

"I am sorry you were injured," he said as he dabbed the spot. "I shouldn't have allowed those thugs near you."

His touch was gentle, and the coolness of the cloth felt good against the bruise. For a moment, she allowed herself the luxury of his ministrations. But she could not fall under his spell. Their relationship was supposed to be practical, unemotional. That glance he sent Piero underscored the many secrets he still kept, secrets that could cost her her life. She pushed away his hand.

"I am fine, *mon seigneur*," she said.

"No, you are not fine. You are hurt." He pressed the cloth against her cheek again. "The evening is not quite over. You still owe me your time, and I wish to spend it caring for you."

Solange subsided into stillness. The less she objected, the sooner he would leave. Then she would not have to fight to retain control of her senses.

"Do not look so put out, *dolce mia*. I am trying to help you." Amusement threaded his words. "Did those ruffians hurt you any other place?" He reached up as if to brush her jaw, but instead of touching her, his fingers hovered a minuscule space above her skin. The sensation mimicked his touch as Shadow. Her jaw tingled. Warmth spread across her cheek, down her neck.

She gasped. "What was that?"

The corner of his mouth twitched up. "Did you not like it?"

"I—" Of course she liked it. But she was not about to reveal that to him. She stood. "I think you should go, *Monsieur le Duc*."

Antonio also stood. He traced the air above the contour of her bare shoulder. Those tingles sparkled on her skin.

"I think," he said, "you liked it very much, *si*?"

Yes, she did. So much that she wanted to curl into his

hand, lean against him, have him wrap his arms about her. Instead, she turned away.

"If you want my services, then please just say so, *mon seigneur*," she said. "I believe our agreement stipulated that you wished my time. I have given that to you already this evening."

His hand dropped. He took a step back. His warmth chilled. "I told you that was not the purpose of this evening. I wanted to give you pleasure. To enjoy your company."

She swallowed, fighting back tears. He *had* given her pleasure. He had treated her like a lady.

"You did. *Merci*," she said, her words barely above a whisper.

His manner softened. "Solange, who were the men who attacked us?"

She hesitated. Le Chacal had sent those thugs. If she revealed that, he would seek the outlaw in the Catacombs and get himself killed. She could not allow that. She very much did not want Antonio to die. She could not imagine her world without him.

"The men, Solange," he prompted. "Who were they?"

She straightened her shoulders. She could not tell him who they were. She would deal with it on her own. Le Chacal had betrayed her.

She gave a little shrug. "I don't know who they were."

He expelled a breath. "Do not lie to me."

"Why do you say I am lying?" She looked him squarely in the eye and tried not to blink.

"Solange." His fingers traced across the pulse below her ear. "You know I can easily get the answer from your mind."

"And I can just as easily think you out of my mind," she snapped.

"Only if you truly don't want me there," he murmured. His fingers floated down to her collarbone, then back up and across her shoulder.

She took a shuddery breath at the warm tingles that made her throb.

"I do not think you would deny me," he whispered.

She would not give in to his seduction. She forced herself to knock his hand away and broke his hypnotic gaze. "I told you I don't know who they were."

His eyes narrowed. "But you have an idea who they might be," he guessed.

Her mouth tightened, and she turned away.

"Le Chacal's men," he surmised.

She pinned him with her gaze. "You don't know that."

"But you do," he said with conviction.

Her glance slid away. She was unable to deny it.

A puzzled line appeared between his brows. "Why would he send men after you?"

"I don't know." She gave a casual shrug as if Le Chacal's maliciousness meant nothing.

His chin rose. "Then I shall go and have a chat with him."

"No!" Panic made her breath catch. Le Chacal would kill him. She could not, would not have Antonio's death on her conscience. "I will go myself. I can do this on my own."

"Of course you can, *dolcezza*," he agreed, "but I wish to accompany you."

That was not going to happen. She needed to confront Le Chacal alone. Her position within his gang of thieves demanded it. Besides, she needed to keep Antonio safe. If necessary, she would deceive him to keep him from going with her.

He reached out and let his hand hover above her jaw. "Do not even consider doing this without me, *dolce mia*. His hand wafted down her neck, across her shoulder, down her arm.

Solange wanted to close her eyes and revel in his magical touch, to feel that tingly warmth. Instead, she forced herself to turn away.

"Deceiving you is the last thing I would do." How easily the lies fell from her lips.

He took her arm and turned her to face him. "Deceiving me is the first thing you thought of, *dolce mia.*"

Solange gritted her teeth, then released a sigh. "I will go to Le Chacal tomorrow night. Meet me here, and we will go together. At midnight."

Tipping up her chin with his finger, he placed a small kiss at the corner of her mouth. "I will be here." He kissed the other corner. "If I find you have gone without me, well . . ." He rubbed his thumb across her bottom lip. "I have the most pleasant means of punishment." He kissed her jaw. "Pleasure can be exquisite torture," he murmured.

Solange shivered, not sure whether it was from fear or anticipation.

"*Buona sera, dolce mia,*" he whispered. "Until tomorrow evening."

With a gentle smile and a trace of his fingers across her shoulder, he was gone. Several heartbeats later, Solange remembered to breathe.

Chapter 16

Solange slipped out her front door and glanced up and down the street. She saw no one. It was well before midnight, the hour she had told Antonio to come, but she would not wait for him. She needed to confront Le Chacal on her own. Even though she was dressed in her breeches and man's coat, she knew her disguise would not fool Antonio, if he were watching. But she had outsmarted him by leaving early. He was nowhere to be seen. With a grim little smile, she settled her hat more firmly and headed down the street.

She was not going to the Catacombs. Instead, her route took her deep into the poor section of the city, where the houses leaned on each other like drunken friends, where harlots enticed, where pickpockets roamed, where taverns spilled out staggering patrons. Few gendarmes patrolled here. She turned in at the entrance to one of the rougher taverns.

The customers were a motley mix of cutthroats, thieves, whores, and drunks. The place smelled of sour wine, boiled mutton, sweat, and filth. The men kept their eyes lowered, casting surreptitious glances at those around them. Only the light-skirts approached with boldness.

Solange made her way to the back of the public room. She stopped before a table angled into a corner between a dingy window and a curtained doorway that led to the kitchen. Le Chacal relaxed in a chair with a pitcher and a tankard before him.

His chief henchman, Le Marteau, hunched over his

own tankard at the next table, his bald head gleaming, his leery eyes scanning the crowd. Next to him, Roux sprawled face down across the scarred wood. A man at the bar turned away as she passed and pulled his hat lower over his eyes. She ignored him, merely another outcast wanting to be invisible. She stopped before Le Chacal's table. Rage, betrayal, and fear were a twisted knot in her chest.

The outlaw had taken in two homeless children, had fed them and given them a warm, dry place to sleep. She and Gide had returned the favor by stealing for him, first as pickpockets and then as highwaymen. Le Chacal had been the man who had deflowered her because he was charming despite his deformities and she thought she'd loved him. She had realized her mistake when he decided to give Gide to the violent *les chauffeurs,* and she had been forced to bargain with him, the bargain that found her as Vernoux's mistress. Le Chacal had been her only comfort in those first months. Their relationship was complicated, built on equal parts trust and mistrust and respect for the other's talents. But she had never expected the man before her to try to kill her. She forced herself to remain calm.

"*Ma petite vache*," Le Chacal greeted her. "What brings you to this elegant place?" He waved his arm in irony at his surroundings.

"Jean-Jacques." Solange nodded a greeting. "I see you are well."

"Is there a reason I should not be?" he asked.

"No reason at all." She shrugged. "Enjoy your good health while you still have it."

Le Chacal tipped his head, amusement lighting his eyes. "You seem to be implying that my good health will not last. Are you able to see the future?"

"Oh, yes." Trembling in outrage, she leaned over the table. "I am going to kill you."

Le Chacal lounged, rested one arm on the back of a nearby chair. "Why would you wish to kill me?"

"Because you tried to have me killed." She forced the words past a stiff jaw.

From the corner of her eye, she saw Le Marteau jerk. She disregarded him. He would do nothing without Le Chacal's direct order, but she kept part of her attention on him. Her hand hovered near her dagger.

"Solange." The King of the Thieves tsked. "Remember what I taught you: control is everything."

"Oh, I am very much in control," she said. "Why did you send your men to kill me?"

Le Chacal poured himself some wine. "Understand, it was a business arrangement."

"You're not denying it?" She vibrated with outrage.

"Why should I?" The King of the Thieves shrugged. "You know I was behind it."

Solange whipped out her knife. "Snake," she hissed and leaped across the table. The point of her dagger dug into Le Chacal's throat. A drop of red appeared and slid downward.

Le Marteau and Roux, suddenly very alert, jumped from their chairs. The King of the Thieves waved them away.

"Would you be able to kill me, Solange?" Le Chacal asked. His voice crooned and coaxed. Using his finger, he gently pushed the blade of her knife away from his throat. "Would you be able to look me in the eye and stab me through the heart?"

Solange faltered. She was not a cold-blooded killer.

Le Chacal's mouth curled in a chilly smile. "Of course you can't, *ma petite vache*. You have a very soft heart."

Before she could respond, Le Chacal's thugs had her by the arms. Roux grabbed the knife out of her hand.

"Take her to the Catacombs," Le Chacal ordered. "I'll decide how to get rid of her later."

215

Solange delivered swift kicks with her boots and violent jabs with with her elbows, surprising her captors into releasing her. Instead of running, she brashly squared her shoulders and stood her ground. Ever since she was a child, she'd always believed that Le Chacal possessed a certain kind of loyalty to those who were loyal to him. And she'd always believed she and the outlaw had a special relationship. She swallowed down the bile in her throat at his betrayal. "Why, Jean-Jacques?"

The cutthroats grabbed her again, but Le Chacal waved them off. "I told you," he said. "It was business."

"I have always done as you asked," Solange spat. "You have no reason to get rid of me."

He leaned across the table. "But I do, *ma petite vache.* A very lucrative reason.

Who would pay for her death? she wondered. She raised her chin. "I will double it."

He chuckled. "How will you do that? Your thievery brings in little. You are Vernoux's *putain.* Will you beg him for coin? Do you think he will give it to you?" He shook his head. "Your death will bring more to me than I could ever imagine." His voice turned flat. "Take her away." He waved his stump at his men in dismissal.

Le Marteau and Roux grabbed Solange by the arms, picked her up, and hauled her toward the door. She yelled and kicked, but this time they held on fast. The tavern patrons ignored her. She should have used her power on Le Chacal and burned him to a cinder. His thugs held her arms in a vise. Her power was useless.

"Wait," Le Chacal called.

His men stopped. Solange hung between them like a rag doll. When they turned back to see what their leader wanted, Solange saw the tall stranger who had been at the bar bent over the outlaw. A stiletto dug into Le Chacal's throat. The stranger's head tipped up, allowing her to see beneath the broad brim of his hat. Recognition flashed through her like fire. Antonio! How had she not seen him follow her?

Antonio's knife pressed harder against Le Chacal's throat. "Tell them to let her go," he ordered. A trickle of crimson leached out from beneath the point of his weapon and soaked into Le Chacal's dingy stock.

A strangled sound came from the King of the Thieves.

Antonio bent close, threatening. "Tell them." Even though he spoke quietly, Solange could hear the menace in his voice.

"Let her go." Le Chacal's command came out as a hoarse croak. He motioned with his stump.

Le Marteau and Roux released Solange so quickly she staggered. Rage flashed through her. Now that her arms were free, she would let Le Chacal know that he could not dispose of her like garbage. She took a deep breath to calm herself, letting her surroundings fade away, and focusing her mind to access her power.

"Solange. Go." Antonio's voice plucked at her attention.

Her gaze twitched to him. She stared, hearing him, but unwilling, unable to respond. She felt the energy gathering, building, the prickle down her arms, the sparks at her fingertips.

"Get out of here." Antonio jerked his chin toward the door.

Yes, she would leave, but not before she incinerated Le Chacal.

"Solange." Antonio's voice was calm but demanded her attention. When she focused on him, he asked, "Are you sure you want to do that?"

Her resolve was hard as stones. "*Oui.*"

"Don't." Antonio's single word broke into her dark reverie.

She turned to him in anger. "He was going to have me killed. I have been loyal to him since I was a child. He betrayed me!" Tiny sparks erupted from her palm.

Antonio went very still. "Killing a man in cold blood is different than killing in self-defense or in the heat of anger."

"I know that. I *am* very angry." The sparks jumped from her hands. She felt no mercy toward Le Chacal. She would make him suffer.

The outlaw shifted. "Solange, *ma petite*. You know what I am doing is only business. Perhaps we can come to some understanding."

Solange raised her chin. "I understand very well, Jean-Jacques. Someone wants me dead and is paying you to make that happen." As soon as she spoke the words, she knew. Nulkana. Her gaze snapped to meet Antonio's.

"*Si*, Solange." He gave a short nod. "You know who that is. Get out. Now."

She abruptly realized the danger she was in. Her power evaporated as fear clutched at her. She spun about and fled.

*   *   *

Relief washed through Antonio like a cold cascade as he watched her escape. With stony resolve, he turned to complete his task.

He noticed men inching toward him from both sides. But before he could make his own retreat, he needed Le Chacal to understand how closely death stalked him.

He bent close to the outlaw's ear. "I should run my blade through your throat," he murmured. "But unlike you, I draw the line at cold-blooded killing. If you ever threaten Solange again, know that I will find you and kill you very slowly and painfully. She is done with you, and you with her." He dug the tip of his stiletto deeper. "Do I make myself clear?"

"It's not that simple, *mon ami*." Le Chacal attempted to draw away from the blade's point.

218

Antonio clutched the shoulder of the man's jacket and held him immobile. "It is very simple. I don't care what Nulkana promised you, and I don't care what she threatened to do if you did not do her bidding. See what I have planned for you."

His fingers flew to the outlaw's pulse at his throat and pressed hard. Antonio entered his mind quickly, ignoring the dark corners that crawled with cruel images. Instead, he placed another image in the man's brain, of the thief hanging against the wall of the Chamber of Ghosts in the Catacombs, of rats swarming down his body, nibbling, nibbling, nibbling. Of the horror Le Chacal would experience. Only when the blood had drained from Le Chacal's face, when his scar stood out starkly red against his ashen skin, did Antonio relent and withdraw.

He whispered against the outlaw's ear, intimate as a lover, "Crawl back into your hole." He flung the man into the two brutes who approached from his left, and swung his blade in a wide arc at the men to his right. In a single spinning jump, he leaped through the curtained doorway behind him.

Antonio ran through the kitchen and out into the alley behind the tavern. He could hear men pursuing. Hiding behind a pile of empty crates and wine casks, he crouched in the filth as they raced past, halted, shuffled about when they realized they had lost him, then returned inside. Waiting a few more moments to be sure he wouldn't be seen, he emerged from his hiding place.

He was angry. Solange had gone after Le Chacal herself, something he had specifically requested that she not do. This break in her relationship with Le Chacal complicated matters. He needed her to lead him through the Catacombs to help him find the piece of the Sphere of Astarte. Now, that would be more difficult, for Le Chacal would show no mercy if she ever returned. If only she had heeded his warning about staying away from the outlaw.

219

Seeing her dragged away by Le Chacal's two thugs had horrified him. The sense of helplessness that swept through him was unnerving. The fact that he might never see her again except as a lifeless corpse made his gut twist and his heart clench. He never wanted to feel that way again, and he was angry she had provoked it. He was angry at himself for allowing her to slip beneath his defenses. His jaw clenched. He would figure out his next step later. For now, he needed to deal with Solange.

*　*　*

Solange stepped into her dark bedchamber and ripped off her hat and frock coat, pulled her shirttails from her breeches. The garments reminded her too much of what she had been for Le Chacal. His betrayal wounded her. His cruelty terrified her. Her death had become far more useful to him than her life. If Auriano had not appeared . . .

"Did you truly believe that you could go after Le Chacal on your own?"

The softly menacing question came from the shadows just outside the window. Solange spun to meet the threat. She knew Antonio would come eventually.

He stepped from the ledge that marked the first story on the exterior of the house, into the frame of the window, and landed noiselessly inside. His silhouette blocked the starry night sky and the glow of the half-moon. He was Shadow, but not. He was no longer the mystical, ethereal figure with the molten eyes. Now he was solid—flesh and bone and dangerous.

Now he was the man she had deceived.

He approached silently, prowling across the carpet like some jungle animal. He had discarded the wide-brimmed hat and the *carmagnole,* the coat of the revolutionary, that he had worn in the tavern. The

220

moonlight behind him limned his outline, the white of his shirt glowing along the breadth and curve of his shoulders, down the muscular ripple of his arms, enfolded by his sleeves. His hair was tied back severely, emphasizing the angle of his jaw, the slant of cheekbone. He looked like a demon, dark, vengeful, seductive.

Solange knew he could see her. The white of her shirt marked her. She fell back, coming up against the bedpost. She reached behind her to grab the carved wood to steady herself, then slipped farther into the shadows. Her courage was quickly seeping away. She had spent most of it when she confronted Le Chacal. What little she had left would not last long. Soon, she would be a trembling pile on the floor. But not before this man. She could not let him know how weak she truly was.

"Why did you not wait for me?" His question curled out to her from the dark.

She shook her head, speechless, and came up hard against the wall.

"I told you to wait for me. You said you would not deceive me." His accusation was like a needle through her heart.

All she wanted to do was hide. He had saved her again. She had deceived him again. Even in business, such as the one she ran, especially like the one she ran, one did not betray a client. Yet, he was not a client. He was merely the man who had given her the joy of being a normal woman for one night, who had given her exquisite pleasure, pleasure like she had never known, nor, most likely, would ever know again.

He paced closer. Solange stiffened her spine when he stopped before her. She could not let him know how much he affected her.

"I had to see Le Chacal on my own," she said. "If I hadn't, then I would have lost all respect with him."

He tipped his head. "Ah, I see. Keeping his respect is

more important than staying alive." His words dripped with sarcasm.

"You mock me." Her observation came out small and sad.

"*Sì*." Antonio gave an abrupt nod. "For your foolishness. For your stubbornness. For your deceit."

She stared up at his obscured face. With no light in the room, she could barely make out the gleam of those golden eyes. She knew if she could see them clearly, they would glitter with his wrath. Despite his calm tone, she could feel his anger, tightly leashed, rippling off him.

She swallowed. Words would not come. She could find nothing to say to defend herself. Because her other reason for going alone, the one she barely admitted to herself, had been to keep him safe. She would never reveal that vulnerability.

Antonio stepped closer. Solange tried to melt into the wall.

"Your deceit doesn't surprise me," he said. "I expected you to trick me."

"You did?" She blinked in surprise.

"*Sì*. What else would a thief do?"

She expelled a breath. "A thief no longer, it would seem."

"Your regret at losing such a part of your life is touching." His tone was as dry as week-old bread.

"You mock me again."

"*Sì*. You should not be thieving at all." His flat reprimand grated.

Solange raised her chin. "I've done what I had to in order to survive. You have no right to tell me what I should or should not be doing."

His shoulders stiffened. "Of course. My mistake," he said coolly.

She tensed, expecting him to react like Vernoux, waiting for his blow.

The silence stretched. He let out a breath, shifted. "Solange," he murmured, reaching up. She flinched away. His hand froze in midair, inches from her. "*Bella mia,* I told you, my touch will never hurt you." He cupped her cheek. "It will bring you only pleasure."

Despite his tender caress, despite his reassuring words, she trembled. This was when Vernoux would be most cruel. The marquis would entice with his words, then lash out just as she let down her guard. Solange let her gaze wander as she sought out her options for escape.

His thumb grazed her bottom lip. "Do you know what I felt when I heard Le Chacal's order to kill you? When I saw his men start to drag you away?"

The softly spoken questions drew her eyes back to his face. "What did you feel?" she whispered.

"I wanted to murder them all, tear them apart with my bare hands. I . . ." His words trailed off, the violence in them raw.

Wondering what else he was about to say, astounded at his confession, she drew in a breath. "Did you? Kill them all?"

"No." A rueful chuckle rumbled in his throat. "I should have, but I didn't. Nulkana will not be quite so merciful."

"The sorceress will kill Le Chacal," she surmised.

"Eventually." He shrugged off the admission. "Will his death upset you?"

She had no answer. Her relationship with the King of the Thieves was twisted with hundreds of threads. Although she had wanted her own revenge on Le Chacal, knowing the sorceress would be merciless caused her some hesitation. As furious as she was, the idea of his murder made her stomach churn. She did not want to think about it. Yet the peril she had been in chilled her. If it had not been for the man standing so close before her . . .

Chapter 17

"You saved me." She acknowledged finally what he had done for her, and swallowed in a tight throat.

"*Si.*"

"*Merci.*" She spoke her simple thanks quietly.

"*Non c'é di che.*" Don't mention it. His casual reply held an undertone of pleasure in her gratitude. The pad of his thumb teased the corner of her mouth.

The gentle words and touch broke through her defenses like no yelling ever could. The enormity of what she had done, what could have happened to her, and that she still lived overwhelmed her. Tremors shook her.

"Ah, *dolce mia*," he murmured.

His hands cupped her face. Their warmth seeped down into her heart, thawing her icy fear. She reveled in that warmth for a moment, then with a shaky sigh, she released her terror. This man had saved her. Perhaps she could help him in return.

Solange pulled back, away from his hands. She needed all her wits, for she was not about to offer too much. She still needed to keep herself and her brother safe, and this man's touch fogged her brain.

"What can I do to thank you?" she asked.

* * *

Antonio blinked at her sudden, composed question. Her fear had seemed real, but this abrupt composure made him suspicious. His eyes narrowed. He wondered what game she was playing. Perhaps he would play along to see how far she would go.

His lips tipped up in a sly smile. "I can think of a number of ways you can thank me." He traced his fingers along her jaw. "But we already have a bargain, *dolce mia*. You have not held up your side."

He watched understanding flash through her eyes.

"The piece of the Sphere of Astarte," she said, her tone flat.

"*Si.*"

She shook her head. "I have no idea where it is."

"I do."

Her eyes widened, then narrowed in distrust. "It is someplace dangerous." She shook her head again. "No. I've had enough of danger for now." She pressed back against the wall.

He was not about to let her off that easily. He was desperate. She had made an offer. "Do you think I would let harm come to you?" he asked.

She remained mute, but her gaze slid away.

"What if I sweetened the bargain?" As he enticed, he placed his hands against the wall on either side of her.

Her mouth thinned into a mutinous line. But her eyes darkened in response to his closeness.

He leaned in and kissed a corner of those lips. "What if I could give you something more valuable than wealth?"

Her eyes closed. He nearly had her. He needed her help, but he could not let her see that. With her thief's heart, she would take advantage. But her offer to thank him for saving her had given him an opportunity to remind her she still owed him. He would not let her forget.

* * *

His silky tone wound around Solange like a spider's web. The touch of his lips made her want to melt. She forced herself not to succumb to his wiles.

"What if," he murmured against her mouth, "I could free you from Vernoux?"

Her breath hitched. Her thoughts closed down. For just a moment, she believed him. Then reality kicked in. She pushed him back. "You can't. He's too powerful."

"Solange." He gave her braid a gentle tug. Amusement rumbled beneath her name. "Remember what I am."

Of course. He was Tonio. Shadow sometimes. Other times, not. Like now, when he was flesh and bone and arrogance and male and heat. Deadly. Potent. She shut her eyes against that seductive golden gaze. The bargain was already made. He knew it. She did, too. She merely had to admit it.

* * *

Antonio knew the moment she conceded. He felt it in the loosening of her muscles, the tiny sway toward him. All that remained was for her to speak the words.

Instead of agreeing, she asked, "How do I know you'll keep your end of the bargain?"

"How do I know you'll keep yours?" he countered. Leaning into her, thigh to thigh, hip to hip, he traced her jawline, his fingers hovering just above her skin. He wanted

Her eyes darkened with the tingles he created. She blinked, swallowed. "I told you—"

"Shh." He placed a finger across those luscious lips. "No excuses, *dolce mia*. No conditions. Agree or not."

She stared at him. Her mouth pulled tight. She jerked a nod.

"*Bene.*" Despite her agreement, he still did not trust her. "I think we need to seal the bargain."

A line appeared between her brows. "I'll not sign anything. I can't have Vernoux discovering what I am doing."

"No, nothing so obvious," he said, smoothing that line away with his finger.

"A blood pact, then," she bit out. "You can use the stiletto up your sleeve so we may both open a vein."

He refused to be baited. "Much too messy." Thoughtfully, he traced the delicate arch of her brow and allowed his fingers to wander down her cheek, back around her ear, down her throat, and up again to her jaw. Her eyes began to lose their focus. *Bene.*

"I think a kiss," he murmured. "*Si*, the perfect solution." He tipped up her chin. "Not obvious, but very effective. A reminder of what we can do for each other." He touched his lips to the corner of her mouth. "A pleasurable reminder, *si?*"

Her lips parted. She seemed not to hear him. Then, quietly, "*Oui.*"

"*Bene.*" He smiled. *Molto bene.* Very good. This agreement would be one she would remember.

He kissed her, gently, a soft brush of his lips against hers. And another. Sweet butterfly kiss. Her mouth was pliant beneath his. Cautious. Expectant. Wary. She waited for him to claim her. He would. But not yet.

He ran his tongue across her bottom lip. She still tasted of plums. Her tongue flicked out, searching, wanting. He withdrew, kissing one corner of her mouth, then the other. She sighed. Her shoulders softened. He wrapped his arms around her, tugged her against him. Her body fit itself closely, molded against him. Ah, this woman could make his blood sing. His arousal snuggled in the hollow of her hip. Eventually, it would find a warmer sheath. But not now. Now, was the time for her.

He slanted his mouth across her lips. One hand cupped the back of her head. The other hand cupped her bottom. She rotated her hips, once, then halted. Her stillness spoke of her battle. She did not reject him, but neither did she encourage. He slid his fingers over the curve of her bottom and slipped them between her thighs. She wore no undergarments beneath her breeches. Her disregard for convention pleased him. Her moist heat told him all he needed to know. He rubbed his fingers back and forth. Once. Twice. A tiny shiver slipped through her.

With a soft breath, her reluctance crumbled. Her arms wrapped around his waist, and he felt her hands on his buttocks, holding tight, digging in.

Ah, *si*. This was just how he wanted her. He slipped his tongue between her lips. She welcomed him, playing, stroking. There was no reluctance in her now. Her hands crept beneath his shirt, caressed his back, kneaded his muscles, and then slid around his ribs to lay on his chest. Her expert fingers teased his nipples. Ah, heaven. But he would not indulge himself. He clasped her tighter against him. Then one stray little hand slid down to cup his arousal. He groaned. *Madre di Dio*, he wanted her. The blood pounded through his veins.

No, she was not going to distract him with her practiced wiles. Gently, he took her wrist and held it behind her.

She stiffened into an inflexible rod.

Merda. A mistake. He lifted his head but kept her wrist lightly bound.

Her gaze accused him. "You said you would not hurt me."

"Have I hurt you? Am I hurting you now?" He traced the fingers of his free hand lightly across her cheek, around her ear.

She turned her face away.

"*Dolcezza,*" he whispered. "I won't hurt you."

He kept her wrist loosely in his hand. If she truly wished, she could easily slip his hold. He hoped she would not. And her other hand was free. He wanted her to trust him. He wanted to dissipate her dark cloud of suspicion, of her fear that hovered just behind. He wanted to kill the man who had put it there. But the killing was for later.

She turned her profile to him. That presented a challenge. Although she remained quiet in his grip, she was not engaged as she had been only moments before. He wanted her engaged, consumed by pleasure.

He placed a kiss on her jaw. And another.

"You are very brave," he murmured. Another kiss. "Strong."

Kiss.

"Magnificent."

Kiss.

"Beautiful."

Kiss.

She faced him. "I'm not."

"You are. You took my breath away the first time I saw you at your salon."

She stared at him, the disbelief in her eyes evident even in the lack of light.

He placed his hand over her breast. "You have the heart of a lioness."

Beneath his fingers, the cloth strips bound her breasts. Antonio's quick concentration of thought loosened them. Her brows flicked together at the sudden freedom. To distract her, he let his hand hover above her cheek in that minuscule space where those charged tingles appeared. Her lips parted.

"May I worship the lioness?" he murmured.

A huff of sardonic amusement left her.

Antonio smiled. *Bene.* He had her.

*   *   *

Solange wanted to believe him, wanted to soak up the outrageous compliments he showered on her, but Vernoux had taught her too well of trickery and pain. Antonio's fingers still gripped her wrist, but lightly. Testing, she pulled away, and his hand dropped. *Sacré bleu.* He released her with no struggle. So unlike Vernoux. Perhaps what Antonio said was true. No man had ever complimented her courage before.

But she needed to test his truth. She leaned back against the wall, all teasing seductress. "I think perhaps you had too much cheap wine at the tavern, and you are just a little bit drunk, *non?*"

"No." He braced his palms against the wall on either side of her. Leaning close, he whispered in her ear, "You will not play the siren with me." He traced the shell of her ear with his tongue. "But you will remember not to deceive me again." One hand slid beneath her shirt, up her ribs and cupped her breast. His thumb stroked across the nipple.

Solange gasped at the pleasure that arrowed through her. A war bloomed in her head between desire and irritation. She wanted him. Too much. And that annoyed her. But she could also play this game.

She ran her hands up his thighs and curved her fingers around his lean hips. Her thumbs stroked in the hollows. His head dipped. He dragged in a breath. She hid her smile.

"So, you battle with me," he murmured. "We shall see who wins."

His hand left her breast and slid to her back. His other hand cupped her bottom and pulled her tight against him. His arousal pressed against her. He nipped her earlobe.

The breath hissed through her teeth. "I have much practice at this game, *mon seigneur.* You should retreat now before I vanquish you." She snaked her hand beneath his shirt and toyed again with his nipple.

A reflexive rumble came from deep in his throat. He kissed her jaw. "We shall see who will be vanquished."

Swinging her around, he backed her to the bed. "Be prepared to cry peace, *dolcezza*." With a little shove, he laid her flat, her legs dangling. He leaned over her, kissed the corner of her mouth.

"I will never cry peace," she said.

He smiled. "You are only raising the stakes, *dolce mia*. I enjoy a good challenge."

His weight dropped onto her, and he captured her mouth. Solange tried to remain stoic. He would *not* arouse her. He would *not* make her mindless. But his tongue stroked. His hands were beneath her shirt. His fingers traced up and down along the sides of her breasts. She shivered and felt moisture between her thighs.

This man could seduce Venus herself. He rained kisses down her throat and captured one nipple in his mouth through her shirt. As he sucked, he rolled the other nipple between forefinger and thumb. A whimper escaped her. Ah, *oui.* Her eyes closed in delicious delight, and for the moment, she forgot her determination to win this battle.

He pulled her shirt over her head. The loosened bindings for her breasts quickly fell away. But her arms were caught in the shirt sleeves, tangled in the material. Only partially bound, but enough to keep her hands from him. She could free herself if she wished. But she did not wish to. The sensation of his mouth, his hands was too delicious. For now, she would let him have his way.

She stretched beneath him and opened herself to whatever he wanted. He kissed his way down to the waistband of her breeches and back up, fastening on one of her breasts. His tongue teased, his teeth nipped. His thigh slipped between her knees and rubbed against her center. The pressure made her want more. She writhed against that solid muscle.

"What do you want, Solange?" he whispered. "Tell me what you want."

"I want—"

The rest of her words were lost in a moan of intense desire as his fingers slipped between her thighs and the heel of his hand rested over her mound. Pressure. Release. Pressure. Release. She wriggled her hips and squeaked in frustration. The buttons on her breeches came undone. With a tug, he had the garment down around her ankles. His fingers trailed up her bare thigh, across her hip, circled her navel . . . and stopped.

She peeked at him through her lashes. Why had he stopped?

"Tell me what you want, *dolcezza*." His murmur held dark promise. The light of the moon silvered his face and made him appear a wicked angel, a spirit who would give her whatever she wished. For a price.

What did she want? She wanted him to bring her to mindless ecstasy. She wanted *la petite mort*. With him. What would it cost her?

His fingers circled her navel again, slipped lower, teased the curls between her thighs. So close. She held her breath. He slid one finger across that small nub. She whimpered. Her hips bucked.

"What do you want, Solange?"

His question came again, soft, sweet, wafting inside her head like the aroma of flowers on the evening breeze.

She swallowed, trying to put thoughts into words, trying to tell him without having to say anything. Without having to surrender.

His finger moved again, pressing deeper. Almost inside her, not quite. He was driving her mad.

"Tell me what you want."

His demand was barely a breath. She wriggled against that hand. His finger withdrew.

"Tell me. What . . . Do . . . You . . . Want?" More insistent this time.

"I want—" She broke off her thought before she

revealed her weakness. No man had ever taken the time to pleasure her. But this man could pleasure her with a kiss. He could give her *la petite mort* as Shadow. What would he be able to do as flesh and bone? Her body wanted him so badly she trembled.

But she had deceived him. He would hurt her as Vernoux always did.

"Pleasure," he said.

She looked into his eyes, warm, golden, inviting. They promised passion. Not pain. She was lost.

"*Oui.*" She breathed the single word into the night.

He smiled. The appearance of that male dimple in his cheek struck a warning bell deep in her brain. But it was forgotten in the single stroke of his finger across that sensitive nub. Pleasure convulsed her. She bit down on her cry, drawing blood from her lip.

* * *

Her quick response to his touch and immediate climax surprised Antonio. She was as sensitive as a virgin, and he began to wonder about her relations with Vernoux. Did the man only use her for torture? That thought confirmed his desire to commit murder. He pushed away the rage.

He remembered their lovemaking while he had been Shadow. She had been very responsive then, too, but he had thought it was because of the strange tingling sensation they created when they touched. He was mistaken. Evidently, *Madame* de Volonté, the woman who portrayed herself as worldly wise, experienced in the ways of love, had very little experience of pleasure. The idea made him smile in anticipation of what he could teach her.

Her eyes opened, and he waited for them to focus before he wiped the drop of blood from her lip. Deliberately, he sucked the salty moisture from his thumb.

Her gaze sharpened. "Why are you looking so pleased?" she asked.

He ducked his head and kissed her shoulder. "Because, *dolcezza*," he said, kissing her neck, "I am going to teach you about pleasure." He gently sucked on her pulse. "I am going to worship your body." Moving lower, he took one nipple into his mouth, flicked it with his tongue. "I am going to please you." He transferred to the other nipple.

She moaned.

"I am going to make you whimper." He kissed his way down to her navel.

She gasped and squirmed.

"I will make your body sing." He ran his hands down her sides, over her hips, to her thighs.

She breathed out a sigh.

"And then, perhaps do it again." He pushed her knees wider apart and crouched between them. The scent of her was an aphrodisiac. He wanted to breathe her in forever.

Her arms came down, and she rested the shirt caught between them on his neck, stopping him. "I can't . . . I don't think—"

"Shh. Don't think." He smiled at her, ran his thumbs up the silky insides of her thighs. He was rewarded with her quick intake of breath. The shirt she held around the back of his neck relaxed. "My touch will never hurt you. Do you believe me?"

Silence. Then, in a whisper, "*Oui.*"

"A kiss then. To seal our bargain."

Her eyes widened in understanding. Before she could protest, he dropped his head down between her thighs and tasted her. She was intoxicating. Desire slammed into him. His arousal was fierce, almost to the point of pain. He nearly spilled his seed, and only at the last moment was he able to halt that indignity. This was for her, not him. One day, he vowed, this would be for both of them.

But now, he would concentrate on Solange because he needed her to know that bargains were made to be kept.

* * *

Solange felt his tongue, rough velvet, slide against her, inside her. His touch was exquisite. Soft, gentle one moment. Demanding, the next. She had reached *la petite mort* with just a tiny swipe of his finger, but that had not been enough. In fact, it had made her want more. He made her crave him. Like someone who had been lost in the desert for days and craved water. When he touched her, she lost her sanity. He became her *raison d'être*. Her reason for being.

His hand and fingers had delivered pleasure, but now his tongue, his lips, his mouth worked magic. Desire pulsed, pounded, grew intense. She groaned, an uncontrolled sound. Was it to make him stop or urge him on? Her fingers tangled in his hair. To hold him back or direct him? Her hips writhed. *Oui. Oui. Oui.*

He slowed. Retreated. Raised his head.

She yanked his hair, tried to push him down.

He did not budge.

She opened her eyes and peeked at him. What was wrong?

"Why did you stop?" she asked.

He rose up, then braced himself on his elbows above her. "You wish me to continue, *si*?"

She jerked her head in a nod.

Gently, he brushed a strand of hair from her cheek. "Sometime, very soon, I will give you the pleasure you seek. But not tonight. Tonight, we seal a bargain." His eyes glittered.

Before she had a chance to say a word, he kissed her. Still drugged with desire, she kissed him back. The taste of herself on his lips sent a throb through her that was so

235

intense, her hips bucked. His weight dropped on her, holding her still. His hard arousal pressed between them. He wanted her as much as she wanted him.

He raised his head. "We are finished here tonight."

"But . . ." she began, baffled.

"Do you understand that I will never hurt you?" he asked.

What he had just done was the furthest thing from pain that she could imagine. She nodded.

"So we have sealed our bargain, *si*?" He raised a questioning brow.

Oui. The kiss. A kiss like she had never expected. But she had agreed. She jerked another nod.

"Then we are done." With a wry twist to his mouth, he pushed himself to his feet.

Understanding finally hit her. He had brought her to the brink of *la petite mort* and now would leave her unfulfilled. Anger whipped through her. At him for enticing her. At herself for allowing him.

"*Enfant de putain!*" She shot upright and struggled to get her shirt back on. He was a son of a bitch. A beast. A snake.

He chuckled. "I never said I was a gentleman."

Solange finally got her shirt straightened and whipped a pillow at him. It was a very unsatisfactory weapon, but at the moment, the only one at hand. "You made me trust you."

"*Si*," he agreed coolly. "Just as I trusted you. Perhaps a mistake on both our parts."

She stood and jerked up her breeches. He stood between her and the wardrobe where her sword lay. The desire to run him through almost overcame her desire to have him pleasure her. Almost. "You will never touch me again." She lied. If he came close this very moment, she would melt into him.

One brow went up sardonically. "Your decision, of

course. But do you truly wish to deny my touch forever?"

The thought of never feeling his hands on her again, of never having them pleasure her, turned her cold.

At her silence, his lips curved. "No answer, Solange?"

His arrogance and mocking tone fired her temper. She threw up her hand and sent a pulse of power at him. But instead of stinging him as she intended, she watched it slip across his cheek, curl around his neck, and trail down his chest like a lover's caress. It hugged his erection, and then faded away.

His head jerked back. His eyes squeezed shut. His hands fisted. He sucked in a breath, then it escaped in a hiss through his teeth. A muscle pulsed in his jaw. A heartbeat passed, then another, and another. She watched him struggle for control. When he focused on her again, his eyes caught the moonlight, and they glittered. In anger or arousal? she wondered.

His voice was strained when he spoke. "It would seem, *dolce mia*, that your actions belie your words. You do want my touch. That little demonstration of your power was quite . . . delightful."

Her power had delivered seductive pleasure, not pain. Embarrassed at revealing her arousal, she snapped, "I never want to see you again."

"I think you may have to," he said quietly, "for we have sealed a bargain and are locked together now like two links in a chain."

She turned away, trying to deny the truth of his statement. "Get out."

"As you wish." He walked to the window and hopped up to the sill. Turning back to her, he said quietly, "This night was punishment for us both, *dolcezza*." Then he dropped from sight.

Solange heard the soft thud as he landed on the ground. He was gone. She licked her lips. She tasted her and him. Lifting her hands, she sniffed. His scent filled her. She wanted him. She thirsted for him, hungered for him. Her knees went weak, and she sank back to the bed. He had tricked her. He had left her so frustrated she could have cried.

And so angry, she could have screamed.

Chapter 18

Solange sat in a straight-backed chair against the wall of her drawing room and brooded. Before her, arranged roughly in a circle, were the Marquis de Vernoux and seven other men. Associates, he had told her, men who had gathered to discuss important matters, things that she would forget she ever heard. Or forfeit her life.

She did not understand why Vernoux had forced her to have this meeting in her drawing room. If it was so secret, then why allow her to listen? What she did understand was that all of these men were members of the Legion of Baal. They had revealed the tattoo of a frog glyph on their wrists to each other. All except one.

Besides Vernoux, she only knew Gravois. The others were foreigners. The *Cavaliere* Tenaglia was from Italy. A middle-aged man, he was plump with heavy jowls and fleshy lips. Every time he glanced her way, her skin crawled. Another was from Prussia, the Baron von Frei. He was about the same age as Vernoux, younger than Tenaglia. Sharp-featured, he exuded no emotion and peered down his knife of a nose at the world.

A Spaniard, a Greek, and two other Frenchmen rounded out the group.

One man did not sit in the circle, as if he did not share the same status as the other men, but Solange could not decide if he was higher up or lower. Instead, he stood relaxed with an elbow propped on the mantle. He was English, referred to by the other men as The Messenger. His black hair was brushed back severely and clubbed thickly at the nape of his neck. She suspected it was quite long when loosened from the black ribbon that wove around it. The bones of his face were elegantly handsome. He was not as broad as Antonio but just as tall, and his movements were graceful, suggesting controlled strength. Dressed impeccably in various shades of gray, he appeared as sleek and lethal as a jungle cat. His eyes were the truest, deepest blue she had ever seen. Those eyes held cool amusement in their depths, and when he glanced at her, seemed to convey some sort of shared knowledge between them.

Solange was baffled and unnerved by him. So she evaded his gaze. Besides, she had other things on her mind.

Her brother concerned her. Gide, kneeling, sitting back on his heels, was at the feet of the marquis. Vernoux rested his hand possessively on her brother's bowed head as if he stroked a pet. Gide's subservience puzzled her, and Vernoux's inclusion of him in the circle alarmed her. What had her brother done?

Ever since Antonio had brought him home, Gide had been acting strangely. He had become reclusive and uncommunicative and had even refused to allow her to change the dressings on the wound on his wrist. Something had happened to him in those days he was missing. Something terrible. Something that had changed his relationship with Vernoux.

The conversation among the men began with the Italian and Prussian complaining about General Bonaparte, who had invaded one country and was threatening the other. The men listened quietly for a time.

Vernoux shifted. "Gentlemen, we understand this general of ours annoys you, but we are here for a more serious matter. Once this pressing matter is dispensed with, I believe your problems with Bonaparte may disappear."

"You invited us to meet with you, *Marchese di Vernoux,*

but you have not explained why," the Italian said. "Perhaps you could give us your reason for having us journey so far, *si?*"

Vernoux's gaze traveled around the circle. A slight smile curved his lips. "It has come to my attention, gentlemen, that a piece of the Sphere of Astarte is here in the city of Paris."

Solange kept very still. Antonio had told her the same thing. Just before he reminded her of the bargain. Just before he seduced her. Just before he aroused her to the point of mindlessness. And left her unsated and ravenous for his touch. The villain.

Antonio had told her that he wanted her help to find this piece. Was that why Vernoux held his meeting here? Did Vernoux need her help as well?

But she had no idea where this elusive piece of an ancient artifact was.

Vernoux's announcement stunned all the men, all except the Englishman. If he was surprised, he hid it well. There was silence for the space of three heartbeats, and then they all spoke at once. The marquis held up his hand.

"Gentlemen, I understand your excitement," he said. "We are very close. But we also must be mindful there are others searching as well, and they are here in Paris."

"Auriano is on his wedding trip," the *cavaliere* said. "He will cause us no trouble."

Solange hid her surprise. These men did not know that twin brothers carried that name.

"There is no wedding trip. Auriano is here," Vernoux snapped. "The reports of a wife are false, or he has her stashed away. The cur is sniffing around what is mine. I have seen the Shadow. The curse is real."

When did Tonio show himself as Shadow to Vernoux? Solange wondered.

"Then we will do away with him," the Prussian announced coolly.

Vernoux waved away his statement. "He is only one of our concerns. The sorceress is also here in the city."

"Have you seen her as well?" Tenaglia asked sarcastically.

"I have seen her bird." Vernoux shot a look of venom at the Italian. "It watches the house of Auriano. The bird goes wherever Nulkana goes and never strays far from her."

The Italian heaved a gusty sigh. "If only we had the Crystal Dagger. Auriano was very clever stealing it from my villa."

Gide's head came up. He met Solange's gaze. She had told him about the meeting with Napoleon on the road and the botched robbery. She shook her head, warning him to silence. His glance slid away, focusing on the floor once again.

"I know where the Crystal Dagger is," Gide said.

Disappointment slid into a heavy pile in Solange's chest.

The Englishman straightened, all amusement gone from his eyes. "Where is it?"

"General Bonaparte has it." Her brother threw the statement into the room like a prize.

"Bonaparte is in Italy," the Prussian scoffed. "That does us little good."

"He's here," Gide contradicted. "My sister has seen him."

Every pair of eyes turned in Solange's direction. She sat up straight in her chair and refused to be cowed by these men. Inside, she quaked and repressed the urge to beat her brother about the head.

"My dear Solange," Vernoux said silkily. "Have you been keeping secrets?"

"No, *Monsieur le Marquis*, I—" she began.

The Prussian interrupted. "How do you propose to get the Crystal Dagger, Vernoux? Surely Bonaparte will have secreted it well."

Vernoux stroked Gide's head, and his gaze landed

thoughtfully on Solange. She sat back on her chair as if she could evade whatever he was considering. She knew it would be distasteful.

He smiled. His eyes became hooded as if an erotic desire had been fulfilled. "I believe I have just the solution," he said. "It seems fate was guiding my hand when I decided to have you all gather here. My lovely Solange and her brother can retrieve the Dagger for us."

She knew that had been coming. "No. I won't do it." Rebelling against Vernoux was unwise, dangerous, but she refused to deceive Antonio again.

Vernoux's nostrils flared, a sure sign of his ire. Before he had a chance to rebuke her, Gide spoke up. "I'll do it. I don't need her help."

"No, Gide." Solange stood, prepared to dissuade her brother from his rash offer and protect him from Vernoux. "You'll not do this."

"Solange, your resistance does not please me," the marquis said quietly. His mild words were in direct proportion to the sharp rage in his eyes.

"You do not frighten me, Vernoux." Unwisely, she threw up her arm and allowed a burst of energy to flare out. It hit a small table and toppled a vase that crashed to the floor.

A surprised chuckle escaped from the Italian. "*Marchese di Vernoux*, you have been keeping your own secrets. You did not tell us you had found another descendant of Halima."

"I was saving that piece of information," Vernoux replied. He never took his stony eyes from Solange.

She fought to keep surprise from her face, to show no weakness. How had he known about her power?

His hand drifted down the back of Gide's head and cupped her brother's neck. His fingers rested lightly at the front of his throat. The gesture might have been a caress. Solange knew it for the threat it was.

"Your brother," he said to her, "might disagree with

your decision. You see, his life is mine now."

Gide would not look at her. He closed his eyes and gulped.

What had her brother done?

Stymied, she sank back to her chair. With Gide threatened by Vernoux, her power was useless. She would not see him tortured or murdered by the marquis.

"I will do as you ask," she said.

"Excellent," Vernoux said, lifting his hand from Gide's neck. "Now, why don't you serve some brandy?"

Solange did as he asked, passing glasses from a tray. The last man she served was the Englishman, the one known as The Messenger. He took the glass, then deliberately dropped it. It shattered on the hearth.

"How clumsy of me," he said. "I fear I may have spattered your gown." He took her by the elbow and steered her away from the broken glass and puddle of brandy. As he did, he leaned close and whispered, "Do not touch the Dagger with your bare skin."

Surprised, Solange stared at him. He merely raised a brow, prompting her reply to his apology.

Recovering, she said, "I'm afraid it was my fault, *monsieur*. I will get you another glass."

As she did, she puzzled over what had just occurred. Why had he warned her about the Crystal Dagger when he appeared to be part of the group that wanted it? Why should she not touch it? What power did it hold?

* * *

Her questions still fluttered in the back of her mind two nights later, as she and Gide approached the apartments of General Bonaparte and his new wife, Josephine. How had she ever put herself in this mess? She only wanted to be done with this task. This theft was too dangerous. If she and Gide were caught, they would be thrown into prison, perhaps sent to the guillotine. Not even Antonio in his Shadow form could save her. She doubted Vernoux would bother to try.

She followed Gide up a drainpipe and inched along a ledge that marked the height of the ground floor. An open window allowed them entry into the first-floor apartment. They stepped into a small drawing room. In the moonlight, Solange could see the usual fixtures—a few chairs, a sofa, a fainting couch, several small tables. Gide moved deeper into the apartment. She followed. Nothing indicated where the Crystal Dagger might be. She wondered if the general had hidden it outside of Paris in a safer location. If they did not retrieve it, what would Vernoux tell his friends in the Legion of Baal? What would he do to Gide? Solange did not want to think on that. They would find the Dagger and deliver it.

They reached a foyer, the black and white marble squares of the floor creating a patchwork of light and void. To one side was a small pile of baggage, well-worn with hard use. It appeared waiting for someone's departure. Gide went to it immediately.

"The general's luggage," he whispered. He proceeded to unbuckle straps and open bags.

Solange felt uncomfortable as she watched. They should not be doing this. She was violating General Bonaparte's personal belongings, as well as Antonio's trust. Only Vernoux's threat against Gide's life kept her from dragging her brother away from this place.

"Solange, a light. Help me search." Gide's impatient whisper prompted her to move.

She pulled out a stub of candle and lit it, set it on the floor, then knelt beside him.

"You were stupid to get involved with the Legion of Baal," she muttered.

"It's done, Solange." He began feeling through the bags.

His dismissal angered and hurt her. "I've cared for you

since we came to Paris. We were going to leave here, escape to someplace safe. We were going to escape Vernoux. How could you let yourself become so tangled with him? He's never going to let you go."

"I've got a plan." He tossed a confident smile her way. "Trust me. I just have to find the Dagger."

"A plan? What plan?" She doubted he had thought any of this through.

He glanced around. "Not now. We have to be quick. Help me search."

Giving in, she felt through one of the bags. Shirts, stockings, neckcloths, shaving gear. Nothing like a dagger, crystal or otherwise.

"It's got to be here," Gide said a little desperately.

"Maybe he didn't bring it to Paris," Solange whispered, frantic to get away. "Maybe he left it in Italy."

Gide stopped rummaging. She felt his gaze on her, accusatory, angry. "I thought you told me he had it with him."

Solange shrugged. "I might have misunderstood." She tugged at his sleeve. "Come, Gide. I want to leave."

"What of Vernoux?" he demanded. "What do you think he'll do if we come away without the Dagger? Besides, I want it."

She scowled. "You don't need the Dagger. You shouldn't touch it."

"Why not?"

"The Messenger said not to."

He scoffed. "Maybe he wants it for himself. Besides, what about Vernoux?"

"I'll take care of Vernoux." Solange made her words much braver than she felt. Vernoux's rage at their failure would be murderous.

Gide made an impatient noise and stood. Solange watched him survey the dark foyer. Something caught his gaze, and he strode toward a corner. He grabbed the object, then turned into the light from the candle. He held a long, cylindrical map case. With a twist, he had it open, then upended it. A cloth-wrapped object slid into his hands. Solange caught the glitter of excitement in his eyes as he glanced at her in triumph. The Crystal Dagger. She could feel its pull from across the space. It wanted something from deep inside her. She wanted to give in to that drag on her soul at the same time she knew she should not. The conflict made her ill.

Gide unwrapped it.

"No, Gide, don't touch it!" she whispered in panic.

Gide ignored her. As soon as the cloth came away, the Dagger pulsed in rainbow colors. Her brother curled his fingers around the hilt, and the colors exploded. Solange flinched and curled her arms around her body. The pull of the Dagger twisted away and wrapped itself around Gide. It circled him like a lover. Then it was gone, appearing to sink into his body. He gasped and stiffened as if experiencing intense pain. Then he relaxed and looked at her like nothing had happened.

The Dagger lit the foyer, splashed colors on the walls. The light pulsed—red, blue, green, yellow. In the reflected light, her brother's face became something else, something hard, demonic.

Gide stared down at the Dagger. Dropping the map case, he caressed the blade with his other hand, as if it were the most beautiful thing he had ever seen. It probably was, except that beauty was evil, demonic. Sabrina watched helplessly as her brother fell under the weapon's thrall. Then he raised his eyes. They were wild, a bit mad, and not really seeing her.

"Gide." She stepped forward, holding out her hand in supplication, not completely sure what she meant to do, only wanting to save him.

He reared back with a hiss and ran out of the room.

"Gide, wait!" she whispered as loudly as she dared.

"What is this?" a man demanded from behind.

247

Startled, Solange swung to face him. It was General Bonaparte himself, in a nightshirt, obviously roused from sleep by all the commotion. He narrowed his eyes at her.

"Well, the little highwayman," he said. "Come to rob me after all?"

Solange shook her head, in shock at what had just occurred.

"Where's Auriano?" Bonaparte glanced around.

Solange shook her head again, unable to find any words. Her brain finally sent the message to her feet that she should move.

"Forgive us, General Bonaparte. Please."

She turned and fled through the drawing room, scrambled out the window and shimmied down the drainpipe. She did not stop running until she was behind her own bedchamber door. She did not stop shaking until much later.

* * *

Solange stood in Antonio's dark bedchamber and watched him sleep. Even in slumber, he made her want him. He was on his back, his head turned to the side, one arm outstretched. The covers hid the lower part of his body. Moonlight revealed his naked chest, the strong muscles clearly defined. She wanted to run her hand over his skin, feel his warmth beneath her fingers. That would be a mistake. Sleep softened his jaw, his mouth, making him appear vulnerable. That was illusion. She drew a breath, gathering her courage. She had betrayed him—again. Guilt twisted in her chest. She had come because she had no other recourse. Somehow, he had snuck beneath the icy cage she had built around her heart. If he denied her, she would be lost. She had never felt so alone.

She removed her slouch hat and let it drop, then moved

to the bed. With a leap, she landed on her knees and straddled him so he would be forced to listen.

His eyes opened lazily as if he had expected her. "Solange," he murmured.

"I need your help." She hated the way her words came out breathless. Desperate. Afraid.

His eyes lost their sleepy languor, and he came fully awake.

Before she lost her nerve, she blurted, "Gide and I stole the Crystal Dagger from General Bonaparte tonight."

"Why would you do that?" he asked. His words were cool and calm, but she could feel his muscles tense between her knees.

"Vernoux forced me."

"You told him of the Dagger?" His disbelief and betrayal were evident in his tone.

She could not meet his gaze. "Gide told him."

"*Cristo!* Does your brother have no brain?"

Her chin went up defensively. "He had no choice. He did what he had to do." That was coloring the truth. Gide could have kept the secret she had confided in him. He chose instead to ingratiate himself with Vernoux.

Antonio stared at her, anger hardening his eyes, pulling his mouth into a tight line. "You mean he did what he had to do to make himself important to the Legion of Baal."

He lifted her off him as if she weighed nothing, rolled out of bed, stalked across the room, turned, and stalked halfway back, completely serious now. The moonlight shifted across his nakedness as he moved.

He stood very still in the middle of the room. "They have gathered, *si*? How many of them?" he demanded.

Solange did not need any explanation to know whom he meant—members of the Legion of Baal. "Vernoux, Gravois, an Italian, a Prussian, a Spaniard, a Greek, two other Frenchmen. And an Englishman, but I'm not sure what his position is." She remained sitting on the bed, feeling she was safer there than standing on the floor where he could come perilously close.

Antonio bowed his head in thought. He was silent for a moment, then he gazed at her. "Did you touch the Dagger?" he asked quietly.

"No." The memory of the pull of the weapon made her shiver. The drag on her soul made her hug herself.

He studied her a moment in silence. "No, of course you didn't," he concluded. "You would not be here if you had. What happened?" His question demanded her truth.

"Gide touched it." She stopped, the horror she felt at the look on his face resurfacing, closing off her throat, turning her stomach.

"And?" he prompted.

She closed her eyes, not wanting to relive that terrible moment. "He ran away with it."

"To Vernoux?"

"No. I don't know. I don't think he went to Vernoux." Solange was not sure about anything anymore. "Gide is just . . . gone." She pulled a pillow to her and hugged it as if it could substitute for her brother.

Antonio frowned. "What do you mean?"

"I've always had a connection with him. I've always known when he was hurt. Even when he ran away the last time, I could sense him." She placed her hand over her heart. "Here. I could always feel him here." She dropped her hand. "Now I can't feel him at all. I'm afraid something terrible has happened to him."

"Something terrible *has* happened to him. He has touched the Crystal Dagger."

Solange drew a breath at his cool tone. She had expected his anger. She had not expected his indifference.

This situation required some negotiation. She tried to reason with him. "I understand that you are angry. Please, can you help me find him?" She hated to plead for anything else, especially with this man, for she had asked so much of him already. But she had no other recourse.

He huffed a sardonic laugh. "Another bargain, Solange? What are you willing to give me this time?"

She had nothing left to bargain. "I said I would help you find the piece of the Sphere of Astarte," she said a bit desperately.

"*Si.* And I agreed to help free you from Vernoux. But this . . ." He made an impatient gesture. "This is something different."

"I'll give you anything you want." Solange could not imagine what else he might demand of her. Whatever he wanted, she would give it.

He was silent and very still for so long she thought he would not answer. Finally, he shook his head. "No. I'll not bargain with you."

"But—"

He held up his hand, stopping her. "Gide has done this on his own. He is a grown man. It is time you treated him as such."

"He's my brother. He's the only family I have." Tears made her words waver. She swallowed them down.

He said nothing.

"What if it were your brother who had done such a thing?" she demanded.

He made an impatient sound. "My brother would not be so . . . impetuous."

She knew he had been going to use another word. Like foolish. Thoughtless. Stupid. The weight of Gide's betrayal and Antonio's refusal sat like a stone in her chest.

"Then you won't help me?" She had to try one more time.

"I did not say that. I said I would not bargain with you."

Confused, she frowned. "Then . . .?"

"I will help find your brother, Solange," he said quietly. "He is a danger now."

Relief swept through her, and just the tiniest bit of hurt. He would help her, not because she asked, but because Gide was dangerous. Why had she expected anything else? Those traitorous tears clogged her throat, filled her eyes. She turned her head to hide them.

"Ah, *dolce mia*, do not cry." His gentle words chafed her sore heart.

"I am not crying." Her denial was a ridiculous lie.

He approached the bed, wrapped his hands about her arms, and pulled her to her feet. "Of course you're not crying," he agreed. "I have complained often about the leak in the ceiling when it rains."

The giggle that bubbled up surprised her.

He smiled and framed her face in his hands. "There, you see? I knew you weren't crying."

Chapter 19

Something twisted in Antonio's chest at her tears. The response was foreign to him. He had watched other women cry, women who'd shed tears to gain a trinket or inspire an emotional response from him. Those women meant little to him beyond mild affection, sometimes not even that. He felt nothing at those dribbles. But Solange's tears made him ache, and he wanted to make them go away.

He wiped his thumbs across her cheeks. "Your brother," he said, "must live his own life."

She sniffed. "But I still worry about him."

"*Si*. He is lucky to have such a sister."

She shivered, shook her head in denial at his compliment.

He wrapped his arms about her, drawing her close. Her forehead rested against his chest. She did not resist his embrace, but she did not melt into it either.

"You can do nothing else for him tonight, *dolcezza*," he said, not adding that there might never be anything she could do for him.

He kissed her temple and gently rocked her. Slowly, she relaxed into him. Her arms came up and hugged his waist. That gesture, more than anything, revealed her vulnerability. But her hands remained fists against the small of his back.

Antonio wished he could take away her anxiety. He wanted to protect her from what her brother had done, but it was too late for that. Gide had sealed his fate, whatever that might be, as soon as he touched the Dagger.

"What will happen to him?" Her words were muffled against his chest.

"I don't know," he said.

She looked up at him. "You have a suspicion."

He shook his head. "I only know that the Dagger has a flaw. It will not kill Nulkana unless it is infused with the power of a descendant of Halima, her sister. Since your brother is a descendant and he has touched it, the Dagger is at its fullest power." He would not tell her what Sabrina suffered when she was near the Dagger, her nausea, her lapses of memory, the drag on her power and her life. "Did you feel anything when you were close to it?"

Solange snuggled closer. "It seemed to pull at me. But Gide was closer. As soon as he touched it, I felt nothing." Her fists opened and splayed across his back as if she were trying to gather as much heat from him as she could.

The touch of her skin against him was exquisite. Her lithe warmth enticed. Her softness pressing against him made his pulse pound. The barrier of her male clothing frustrated him as if he were in the throes of the Hunger. He craved the touch of her skin. He used all his will not to rip the garments from her.

He forced himself to concentrate on the conversation. "Then the Dagger has Gide," he said. "I will have to find a way to free him." He wondered if perhaps Piero would know of something.

Solange trembled against him. "I am afraid," she whispered.

He lifted her chin with his thumb and gazed down at her. "I will protect you, *dolcezza*. Do you believe me?"

She studied him a moment, then ducked her head. "The other night . . ."

"Ah. The other night. The other night was between us. Our bargain, sealed with a kiss. These other things, the Crystal Dagger, Nulkana, the Legion of Baal, those are bigger things, deadly things. I will do everything I can to protect you from them."

She stared up at him, suspicion sharpening her gaze. "How can I believe you? You will only demand another bargain."

A twist of hurt pricked his heart. And a touch of anger at her mistrust. But he buried that. Dropping his arms, he backed a step out of her embrace. "Have I lied to you? Deceived you? Have I not protected you?"

Her gaze slid away.

"Perhaps," he purred, "I should ask when I might expect the next deception from you. Perhaps I should question your presence here tonight. Perhaps Vernoux is using you as part of some elaborate scheme he concocted with his friends from the Legion of Baal."

Her wide eyes swung back to him. "No!"

He shrugged and walked away. "I have only your word, little thief, and that gives me little confidence."

Antonio stared out the window as he waited for Solange's response. He noted the moon was more than three-quarters full. In only a few more days, it would wax full and bright, and he would be Shadow once more. He needed to find the piece of the Sphere of Astarte before then. Gide's stealing the Crystal Dagger and Le Chacal's defection to Nulkana complicated the matter. But that problem was for later. He brushed away the thoughts like annoying insects.

Behind him, Solange was silent. He disliked himself for causing her more distress. He was pressing her, forcing her to be truthful, dangling her brother's danger—and the possibility that he might rescind his agreement to help—before her. His accusation that she was Vernoux's pawn had been conjured out of the air and had shocked her. He did not believe she would willingly do Vernoux's bidding, except the one she'd stated. Her anguish was too real to be feigned. But he wanted to unnerve her enough that she would let down her defenses and trust him. Trust him enough to be truthful and not deceive.

She spoke finally. "What can I do to make you believe that I came here on my own?"

He turned from the window. The moonlight silvered her, leeched all color from her. Those marvelous turquoise eyes were dark and troubled in her pale face.

"That is up to you," he said.

Her head went down, then came back up. "The other night . . ."

"*Sì?*"

"Why did you stop?"

"I told you. To teach you a lesson."

She shook her head. "That is not the only reason."

"No?" He wondered where she was going with this conversation.

"Just before you left, you said it was punishment for both of us."

"*Sì.*"

"You wanted me." Her statement demanded his confirmation of a truth.

He laughed. "Of course."

"Another man might have used a different means to teach a lesson."

"*Sì.* Another man might have." He gave a short nod.

"You didn't hurt me."

"I told you I never would."

"You could have taken me, used me for pleasure."

Antonio hesitated. Confessing what he had done would reveal his ruthlessness, not a quality he was proud of. His confession would also reveal his softer side, something she might be able to use against him. It might also give her the confidence to trust him.

He kept his voice level as he said, "I seduced you, *dolcezza.* I aroused you to the point where you could not say no to anything I wanted. I would not take advantage of you like that."

She did not move, barely seemed to breathe. Her eyes held him as much as her hands might have. The silence stretched.

"You are an honorable man," she finally said.

Antonio dipped his head. A self-mocking laugh escaped. "No, but I like to retain the few scruples I have."

"Tonio." She stepped forward one pace.

He raised his head. *Dio.* She was beautiful.

She took another two paces toward him. "Antonio, make love to me."

He stopped breathing. Had he heard correctly? He knew, of course, that making love with this woman was inevitable, but he always thought he would be the one to initiate. A tiny suspicion bloomed in his head.

She stepped closer, reached out and placed her hand on his chest. It trembled against his skin.

"Make love to me," she repeated in a whisper.

Her touch sent heat spiraling through him. He covered her hand. "Why are you doing this?"

A tiny line appeared between her brows. Uncertainty clouded her eyes. "Because I want you."

"How do I know you aren't deceiving me again?"

Anger flared across her face. Just as quickly, it was gone. Her lashes swept down. "Then look into my mind. See that I am telling the truth."

Was she offering to open herself to him because she knew he would not take advantage? Or was she being sincere? He wanted her so much he ached. He wanted her more than anything he had ever craved during the Hunger. He discarded those scruples he had just mentioned. Wrapping his fingers around her wrist, he matched his heartbeat to hers and entered her mind.

Her arousal circled her mind in rosy shades and violet tints. She wanted him—badly. His seduction had worked very well. Guilt pinched him, and he shoved it away. He had accomplished what he wanted, forced her to remember him and what he could do, forced her to be aware that his honor demanded that she match it with her own.

That dark, joyless form of her fear and suspicion was not visible. Around him, her mind was open. He could have explored anywhere he wished. Nothing was closed to him. That alone told him all he needed to know. It was time to relieve her consuming need.

*   *   *

Solange heard him calling to her in her head. She could feel his presence, strong, gentle, protective, tender. He stroked against her arousal, a soft brush that felt like the touch of a rose petal. Her mind shivered in response. Colors popped around her—gold, blue, red, purple, silver. He spiraled around her, invited her to dance. With barely a thought, she joined him.

They twined together. Each of her senses was flooded. She smelled ripe berries, tasted sweet honey, heard the lilting song of birds. Their boundaries blurred. She flowed into him. He washed through her. They circled together, revolving, spinning, slowing, weaving until she was not sure where she ended and where he began. Pleasure like nothing she had ever experienced before flowed through her. Heady as wine. Sweet and smooth as syrup. He touched her everywhere at once. Each nerve ending strained to feel him. He caressed. Her body throbbed. Pulsed. Pulsed.

She shattered. Into a million pieces. Exploded into the universe. Scattered like the stars. And then brought back, piece by piece. Until she was whole again.

Dolcezza, she heard him sigh in her head.

A last brush across her mind. And then he was gone. Instead, his solid, warm form stood before her. His fingers still wrapped about her wrist. Her forehead rested against his chest. Those two points of contact kept her upright, for her knees could easily be made of pudding.

She filled her lungs, raised her head, looked up at him. "You gave me *la petite mort*," she said.

"*Sí.*"

"Just with your mind."

"*Sí.*" He gave her a pirate smile.

"How did you do that?"

"A trick." He shrugged as if he had done nothing.

"More than a trick."

He dipped his head. "If you wish." His fingers slipped away from her wrist and covered her hand, pressing it against his chest. "Are you feeling better?"

Better. The word did not seem adequate. The need that had chafed her for the past two days was gone. In its place was an ease that comforted. She felt better than better. Yet, she still was not satisfied.

Antonio's heart thumped beneath her hand. She remembered feeling his heartbeat when he was Shadow. Making love with him then had been incredible, like nothing she had ever experienced. But she wanted to feel the man as flesh and bone. She wanted to feel his weight on her, the brush of skin against skin. The pressure of him inside her.

What she wanted was foolish, a mistake. Then why did she want it so much? Her gaze dropped to her hand against his chest. His hand, larger, darker, stronger, covered hers. As if it protected. And that said everything. He would protect her. She knew that. He had already protected her. Deep in her heart, she realized he would keep her safe. Always.

Something expanded in her chest, something sweet and poignant.

She loved him.

The realization swept through her. She drew in a steadying breath. She could not let him know. Revealing that would give him power over her. It would tip the delicate balance of their association. Their agreements would no longer be cool barter. Emotion—love—would be his bargaining chip.

"Solange?"

His voice recalled her to the moment. She raised her eyes, met his golden gaze.

"I am better. *Merci*," she said. "But you have not finished."

"No?"

"No." She spread her fingers against his chest. "I want you to make love to me."

* * *

Antonio stared down into those turquoise eyes, eyes that were as fathomless as the sky. Eyes that held secrets. Eyes that had shed tears. He wanted to make love with her as flesh and bone, more than he ever had as Shadow. He wanted her to want him, not because of his seduction, but because she truly wanted to connect with him, soul to soul. Her request was real. He had seen that. Whatever her reason, he knew there was no deceit in it. He needed this once to believe her, trust her. Whatever came after, he would deal with then. Now, her offer was too enticing to pass by.

He drew the hand that lay against his chest up and around to the back of his neck. She swayed closer. His other arm slipped around her waist, bringing her into full contact with him. Slowly, he lowered his head until his lips brushed against hers.

Her eyes slipped closed.

He felt her surrender in the softness of her muscles, the suppleness of her lips. He had no need for wily seduction. She gave herself freely. His heart danced.

He took possession of her mouth, and she accepted him,

kissed him back. Her compliance was evident in every part of her body.

Easing her around, he backed to the bed, sat, and pulled her to stand between his knees. "Are you sure you wish to do this, *dolce mia*?" he murmured.

"*Oui.*"

"Ah. Well, then." He swept his hand across her cheek, down her neck, to her shoulder. "Do you know how long I have wanted this?" He pushed her coat from her shoulders and stripped it from her arms. "Since you first walked toward me at your salon." He unbuttoned her waistcoat. It fell on top of her coat.

A tiny line appeared between her brows. "But when you were Shadow. . ."

"*Si.*" He pulled her shirt from her breeches, ran his fingers up across her ribs. She had not bothered with the bindings. *Bene.* "But as wonderful as it was to make love to you as Shadow, I desire to feel your skin against mine." He cupped her breasts, brushed her nipples with his thumbs.

She sucked in a breath.

He smiled. "Skin against skin is a delightful sensation, *si*?" He pulled her shirt over her head and let it drop. Before she lowered her arms, he caught one and let it lay in his hand. He circled the inside of her upper arm with his thumb.

She shivered.

He replaced his thumb with his mouth and imitated the action of his thumb with his tongue.

She stopped breathing.

"There are so many places where I want to touch you, *dolcezza.*" He ran the first finger of his other hand down between her breasts, across her middle, to the buttons on her breeches. Slowly, he unbuttoned each one, letting his knuckles brush against her each time, lower and lower.

Her breath released in a puff.

"I think, perhaps, you wish to touch me, too, *si*?"

"*Oui*," she whispered.

Wrapping his arms about her, he fell back onto the bed, taking her with him.

* * *

Solange was so focused on his touch that she was surprised to find herself falling on top of him. In a blink, he rolled her beneath him. He knelt between her knees, and a small smile played around his lips. His eyes gleamed. He was a dark lord, exuding power. He was a seductive lover, promising pleasure. Both aroused her. Both frightened her.

He yanked off one boot, then the other. Resting her foot on his shoulder, he ran his hand down her leg, then back up. The material of her breeches was a barrier to his touch. She wanted more. As he said, skin on skin was so much better. She pushed her breeches from her hips.

He tsked. "Patience is a virtue, *dolce mia*."

Turning his head, he circled her ankle with his tongue, then trailed it across the arch of her foot. It tickled, and she tried to wriggle away. He nipped gently with his teeth.

"No escape, *dolcezza*," he warned.

He turned his attention to her toes, sucking on each one. At the same time, his fingers traced her ankle, trailed across her instep, around to her arch. The sensations were incredible, intense. Solange never imagined her foot could be such a source of pleasure. She lay still, closed her eyes, and enjoyed.

He moved to the other foot and showered just as much attention on that. By the time he tugged off her breeches, she was purring. He ran his hands up the outside of her legs, down the inside of her thighs. He touched and caressed along the smooth planes, around each curve. She spread her arms, waiting, wanting him to feel every inch of her.

His fingers slipped higher, across her hips, along her ribs, to her shoulders. He brushed his hands down her arms, trailing his fingers back up again. Back and forth, up and down, to her wrists, her palms, her fingertips.

Solange drifted under his spell. His mouth replaced his fingers. His lips, his tongue made her aware of every inch of her skin. The pleasure of his gentle touch banished any apprehension about trusting him. He would never hurt her. He would always protect her.

When his mouth fastened on her breast, surprise and desire combined to make her moan. His fingers traced down until they tangled in the curls between her thighs. She opened to him. Pleasurable tension built. She writhed beneath his touch. Her release came in an eruption of sensation and a wild cry.

She opened her eyes to his soft gaze, the tender touch of his fingers stroking her temple. Tangling her fingers in his hair, she drew him down to taste his mouth. She wanted to explore every inch of him. Wrapping her arms about him, she forced him to his back. She straddled him, in the same position as when she had awakened him. Her need was just as strong now as it was then, despite the fact that he had twice already given her release.

"I'm going to devour you," she said, gazing down into those golden eyes.

One corner of his mouth slid up. "I will relish every moment."

She touched that corner with her fingers, traced down to his jaw, lower across his neck, to the hollow at the base of his throat. His eyes drifted closed. She followed the trail of her fingers with her mouth, stopping at his pulse, where she sucked gently. He tasted delicious, like almonds, freshly roasted. She left butterfly kisses across his chest, circled his nipples with her tongue. A low rumble sounded in his throat.

Moving lower, she followed the thin trail of dark golden hair that pointed the way to his erection. She caressed it, licked it, took it into her mouth, teased it with her tongue. He groaned.

"Ah, *dolcezza*, you drive me to madness," he said.

His fingers clutched her hips, and with little effort, he lifted and impaled her. She gasped her delight. The feel of him inside her was glorious, better than when he was Shadow. His warmth, his solidity was comforting. Exciting. Wanting to feel every inch of him, she spread herself across him. His arms closed about her.

He smiled, slyly, intimately. "*La petite mort?*" he murmured.

"*Oui*," she agreed. "*La petite mort.*" She sat up, snuggling him deep inside her.

He began to move, slowly at first, then faster, until her world was only him, until her universe was his. Tension built, higher and higher, until she reached a peak, tipped, and plummeted through space until she floated safely to earth and collapsed on top of him.

* * *

Gradually, Antonio returned to consciousness. A soft, warm body sprawled across him. Solange. Her breath came and went quietly through her parted lips, riffling along his skin. They had both achieved *la petite mort*. And had fallen immediately unconscious. He had never experienced anything like it.

He brushed the hair from her face and tightened his arm around her. Her pliant weight on top of him made him smile. She had yielded to him. Everything. Even if she was not aware of it. She was his now. Whether she knew it or not.

She stirred. Her eyes opened. She sighed and smiled.

"*La petite mort*," she murmured.

"*Si.*"

She bent her knee, drawing her leg up along his thigh, an unconscious movement of invitation. He wanted her again. He felt as starved for her as if he had never tasted her. Running his fingers down her back, he was rewarded with her shiver. She burrowed against him. She was ready.

"May I bring you back to life?" he asked.

"*Oui, s'il vous plaît.*"

Chuckling at her polite response, he flipped her to her back and proceeded to make love to her all over again.

* * *

False dawn lightened the room by the time Solange awoke. She snuggled beneath the covers while she tried to decide what had awakened her. Her body felt loose and pleasantly spent. But something nagged at the edges of her mind.

She peeked beneath her lashes. This was not her bed. And what had once been warm and comforting was cool and empty.

His room. His bed. And he was gone.

She glanced around. There, at the window. Wearing a blood-red brocade dressing gown, he stood with his hands clasped behind him, staring out at the city. The pale light reflected off his solemn features. Even serious, he was the most captivating man she knew.

He turned to her, and his features relaxed into a smile. "*Buongiorno*," he said. Good morning. "Did you sleep well?"

"*Oui. Merci.*"

"*Bene.*" His smile faded. "Today, I will search for your brother."

"I will come with you." She threw back the covers and sat on the edge of the bed.

"No."

She was about to get up, but his single word stopped her. "Why not?"

"It will be too dangerous."

Irritation made her frown. "I can take care of myself."

He shook his head. "Not in this."

She bounded off the bed and strode to him. With her hands on her hips, she glared. "I can throw a knife, shoot a pistol, and wield a sword as well as you. Gide is my brother. I will look for him if I wish."

His hand snaked out and grabbed the nape of her neck.

His gaze was intense. "You will not," he said, staring down into her eyes. "Gide is no longer the brother you knew. He has touched the Crystal Dagger. It was created with powerful magic. Dark magic. Its sole purpose is to kill. It has taken him over. There is no telling what evil he is capable of now."

"I will talk to him, convince him to give it up."

"Don't you understand?" He gave her a little shake. "He may not recognize you." He paused, then said much more gently, "I might be forced to kill him."

Solange gaped at him as the weight of his words fell on her. His fingers brushed across her cheek.

"Solange," he said, his tone soft, "I would not have you harmed by your brother. You mean a great deal to me." He drew her to him and kissed her tenderly.

His mouth against hers conjured up visions of the night before, when they had tangled together, losing all thought of where one ended and the other began. His words made her melt. She meant something to him. More than a body to use. More than an agent of thievery.

Raising his head, he pulled her close, holding her against his shoulder. "Tonight you may help me," he murmured.

"*Oui?*" she asked, seduced by his tender touch.

"Tonight," he said, "I want you to take me down into the Catacombs."

She jerked away from him. "No. I can't. Le Chacal—"

"Le Chacal will not even know we are there."

Fear coursed through her. She knew how ruthless Le Chacal could be. Now that he wanted her dead, the idea of invading his lair made her blood run cold.

She shook her head. "I won't go back there."

He said nothing for a moment, merely stared at her with those incredible golden eyes. The sun was just above the horizon and lent its gilded glow to the room, to his face. Finally, he said, very quietly, "I will always protect you, Solange. With my life."

She let her gaze slip away, humbled by the sincerity of his statement, then wondered if she should believe him. No man had ever been truthful to her. But this man had never lied. He might have kept secrets, but he'd always spoken the truth.

The silence stretched out. She was afraid. Afraid of what might happen if they were caught by Le Chacal. Afraid of how her relationship with Tonio would change once he had the piece of the Sphere. Afraid of what his statement implied.

"Will you honor our bargain?" His words reached out to her.

Would she? Yes. This time, she would do as he asked. Because she loved him, as frightening as that might be. She gave a nod and punctuated it with a single word. "*Oui.*"

"*Bene.*" He released a breath, then stepped closer. "I will come for you at midnight. Do not deceive me."

Irritation tightened her mouth. "I keep my word."

He huffed a laugh. "Of course you do."

Irritated that he knew her so well, she stalked to where her clothes were heaped on the floor. "It is *my* life that is in danger if I take you down into the Catacombs." She yanked her shirt over her head. "It is *my* brother who has surrendered to the Crystal Dagger." She jerked on her breeches. "If I wish to protect myself and Gide, then that is *my* right." She pulled on her waistcoat and coat, then glared at him.

"I never said it wasn't." Although his expression was solemn, an undercurrent of amusement ran through his words.

She stalked to him and poked him in the chest. "Do not laugh at me."

He caught her finger, then placed a kiss on her palm. "I would never laugh at you, *dolce mia*, but you are adorable when you are angry."

The feel of his lips against her palm cooled her ire. His words fueled it again. Snatching her hand from his grasp, she said, "How adorable would you find me with a blade in my hand?"

At that, he did laugh. "I think, if we crossed swords, you would be a formidable opponent."

Somewhat placated, she narrowed her eyes at him, then swung away to find her boots. "Deliver me from arrogant men," she muttered.

His arm came around her from behind. His hand slipped beneath her unbuttoned waistcoat and cupped her breast. "If I were not so arrogant, you would not have had such pleasure last night." He placed a kiss below her ear.

The feel of him made her want to melt. His words annoyed her. She shoved an elbow into his ribs and forced him to release her. "Villain," she snapped.

"*Si*," he said agreeably. He swept her hat from the floor and plunked it on her head. "May I get you some hot chocolate before you leave?"

She turned on him. "You *may* expect to find me waiting for you at midnight." Stalking to the window, she dropped her boots to the ground two floors below. "Do not be late, *Monsieur le Duc*. I do not like to be kept waiting." She stepped up to the windowsill and began climbing down to the ground.

"I would never keep a lady waiting," she heard.

Chapter 20

Antonio stood with Solange at the mouth of the Catacombs. Despite her promise of that morning, he was surprised she was with him. When he arrived at her house to collect her, he had expected to find her gone, not patiently waiting for him. Bemused at her sudden compliance, he watched her stare down into the gaping black void that led underground. In the moonlight, he could see apprehension etched as a line between her brows. This foray into the Jackal's lair was not going to be easy.

He was placing her at risk by forcing her to accompany him. Le Chacal held her death warrant, issued by Nulkana, and Antonio regretted not killing the thief when he'd had the chance. He had promised to protect her with his life. He would not back away from that promise. Even so, guilt twisted in his chest.

Solange sighed and gazed in his direction. "I don't suppose you've changed your mind," she said. "We could just leave now, return to my house. I could pour some wine for you."

The implication of what might occur after she poured the wine was an enticement, but Antonio did not succumb to her temptation. He could not. The price was too high. He remained silent. She knew his answer.

Her mouth tightened. She gave a single nod. Turning back to the entrance, she took a step forward. Antonio caught her hand, halting her.

"You are very brave, *dolce mia*," he said. "*Grazie.*" Twining his fingers with hers, he kissed the back of her hand.

She pulled away. "You may thank me by keeping me alive, as you promised." Resolutely, she reached for the torch just inside the opening and turned back to him. "And then you may keep your part of our bargain, *Monsieur le Duc*."

Of course. His promise of freedom from Vernoux for both her and her brother. That meant sending them far away from Paris. He could hide Solange in Auriano, which was very appealing. But Gide was a danger now. Antonio could not expose the people of Auriano to such a risk. Of course, his other option was to kill Vernoux, which became more tempting the more he thought on it. He could salve his conscience by forcing the marquis into a duel.

He met her narrowed gaze. "I will protect you always," he said.

Solange accepted his statement in silence. After lighting the torch, she stepped forward.

Antonio followed her down the stone stairs. They moved through the dirt tunnel that took them farther below ground and crossed chamber after chamber. Solange held the single Silver Arrow that she had hidden from Vernoux. Its point gleamed with a faint blue glow. Antonio sensed an answering, faint hum in the walls that indicated a piece of the Sphere of Astarte was near. He might have found the piece eventually on his own by following the hum, but the twists and turns of the tunnels were confusing. The Silver Arrow would lead them directly to it. And then, once they found the piece, he needed Solange to help him return to the surface. He did not want to die wandering the maze of tunnels as he tried to find the way out.

Occasionally, Antonio would trail his fingers across the amazing, intricate designs on the walls created by the bones to feel the thrumming emitted by the piece of the Sphere of Astarte. He knew the closer they came to the piece, the stronger the sensation would become.

His heart sped up in anticipation. Soon, part of his curse would be broken.

* * *

Solange made her way carefully through the tunnels. She spoke rarely, only an occasional quiet murmur to warn of obstacles. Sound did strange things in the Catacombs, sometimes reverberating through the passageways and chambers, sometimes dying into quick, muffled silence. Although Antonio had promised to protect her, she had no wish to risk discovery by Le Chacal's outlaws who patrolled the tunnels.

Antonio moved as quietly as she did, but she was very aware of him behind her. Every time he traced his fingers across the walls, she sensed the energy building in him. His eyes began to gleam with a dark fire. At each turn they took, the gleam became more intense. She told herself it was only a trick of the torch light. But she knew his golden eyes, and that gleam was not normal. She was not afraid of him, but apprehension of what would happen to him once he had the piece of the magical Sphere tiptoed up and down her back like a spider. The thought of Gide's transformation sat like a hulking gargoyle in the back of her mind.

As she followed the glow of the Silver Arrow, she realized they were headed through the back tunnels that led to the Great Room, the room where Antonio had first met Le Chacal. These were not the same tunnels they had followed that time. These took them first through Le Chacal's private chamber, his underground lair, a path rarely traveled by any of the guards. She did not want to go near either place.

She watched for the traps that Le Chacal had set. She pointed out the first one to Antonio, a mat disguised with dirt and stones that covered a deep pit. Anyone stepping on the mat would fall on razor-sharp sticks that Le Chacal had planted in the earth. They edged around it. The next was a stepping stone that triggered an avalanche of rocks. She hopped across it. Antonio did the same. The one that came after was the most deadly. A silk thread stretched across the tunnel, so thin it was invisible to anyone not looking for it. If it was pulled or broken, it released a series of five armed crossbows with arrows dipped in poison. If one of those arrows pierced anyone, that person would die a horrible, agonizing death. Solange handed the torch to Antonio, then carefully ducked beneath the silk. After taking back the torch, she watched as he did the same, except he was much bigger than she, and the back of his coat caught the thread. She hissed a warning, and he froze in a crouch.

She stuck the torch in the empty eye socket of a skull. Her heart butted her ribs as she gingerly eased the silk from the fold of his coat. Something clicked behind the bones lining the walls. Before she could think, Antonio grabbed her about the waist and threw her to the floor. His weight landing atop her knocked the air from her lungs. The snap of the crossbows releasing their deadly ammunition cracked through the tunnel. The bolts whooshed over them, one coming so close she could feel the rush of air across her cheek.

Three frantic heartbeats passed before she heard Antonio's whisper.

"Are you unharmed?" His breath feathered across her ear.

Relief swept through her. The bolts had missed him. He had saved her life, protected her as he had promised.

"*Oui,*" she replied. "And you?"

"*Si.* I'm grateful for the cushion of your delightful body."

His teasing words made her aware of the stony floor

of the tunnel beneath her and the bruises she would have the next day. She was also acutely aware of the sensuous weight of him. With a huff of exasperation, she pushed him off. He gave a low chuckle, rose to his feet and offered her a hand. She ignored it as she scrambled up.

"What is this?" he murmured. "No thanks for putting myself in danger and saving you?"

"*Merci, mon seigneur*," she said tartly, as she pulled the torch from its makeshift holder and handed it to him. "Perhaps next time, you will be more careful, since you were the one who triggered the bolts."

All he did was smile, showing that devastating dimple. As she turned on her heel, pretending she was not in any way affected, she said, "We must hurry. Le Chacal's guards may have heard us." She hoped she was wrong.

* * *

The entrance to Le Chacal's private chamber was an opening on the left side of the wall. Except for a gargoyle leering from the lintel and dim light spilling out, it looked like any other tunnel opening in the Catacombs. The Silver Arrow began to glow brighter and pulse. As Solange moved the artifact away from the opening, the glow faded. She glanced back at Antonio. His eyes gleamed as he stared at the bright tip. His gaze rose to meet hers. It was alight with anticipation.

He glanced toward the opening. The piece he wanted was within. If it would dispel the ravages of his curse, then she would retrieve it for him. As she stepped forward to enter the chamber, he wrapped his hand around her arm and stopped her.

"He's in there," he whispered in her ear, his words barely a breath. "We'll not do this tonight."

Even through the material of her coat and shirt, his touch tingled. She shook her head, both to answer him and to throw off the enticement of those tingles. "He's not," she said quietly. "He always leaves a lamp burning."

He studied her a moment. She knew he was deciding if she were deceiving him. She met his gaze openly. He released her arm and gave a nod to go ahead. She took a quick peek into the chamber. It was empty. Boldly, she stepped forward.

Antonio followed. He stopped in the middle of the chamber, raised the torch high, and slowly turned in a circle. From the other side of one wall, through a hidden door into the Great Chamber, she could hear the muffled sounds of the outlaws. Le Chacal would be holding court out there among his thieves and murderers as he always did at this time of night. She hoped he would not suddenly decide to change his schedule.

Solange watched Antonio examine the space, the large canopied bed, the table with a glowing lamp, two chairs, a brazier, a shelf lined with books, a tapestry hanging on one wall, on the one opposite hung a sword, knives, and pistols. On another wall were the ubiquitous bones, this time formed into a circular, odd, unrecognizable design, a skull in its center.

He peered at the Silver Arrow, glowing steadily, but it gave no indication where the piece of the Sphere might be hidden. He glanced around the space once more, then strode toward the bones. "It's here," he said.

Solange trailed after him. He stuck the torch into a holder on the wall, grabbed the center skull and pulled. It shattered in his fingers. He muttered an oath and began digging at the bones lodged in the wall with his bare hands. Solange retrieved one of the knives and handed it to him. When he turned to take it, his eyes were dark, fiery, and not entirely focused on her. That gleam she saw earlier had turned to something feral. She fell back a step.

A frown flickered between his brows, but he said

nothing. He took the knife and used it to dig the bone fragments out of the wall. The last of the skull popped free. A small hollow was behind it. Antonio reached forward, then stopped. He placed his hand flat against the wall and appeared to sag.

"What's wrong?" Solange asked.

His face went pale. He dragged in a breath, then another, as if he had run far and long. His head drooped. "I can't—" He gasped another breath. "Take it for me. Please. Quickly." His legs buckled, but he caught himself and turned to lean his back against the wall.

Frightened, Solange reached into the hollowed-out space. Her fingers closed around a small object wrapped in cloth. She pulled it out and unwrapped it. It was an oddly shaped piece, dusty, made of amber. It was small enough to fit in her hand. Curved, it seemed to be part of something larger. A piece of the Sphere of Astarte. She was surprised it looked so ordinary. She held it out to him. He turned away as if it made him sick.

"Keep it for me," he said, his voice thready.

Confused, she pushed the piece closer. "Isn't this what you came for?"

He nodded. "Please, put it away," he said. "I don't know what it's doing to me."

She quickly rewrapped it and stuck it in her pocket. As soon as she did, Antonio's breathing returned to normal, and his eyes cleared, although he still seemed a bit shaky. He smiled and ran his fingers along her jaw.

"You will hide it for me, *si?*" he murmured.

She gave a short nod. "*Oui.*" Her word was a promise.

He took the torch and led the way out of the chamber. Solange tried to make sense of what just happened. Even though the artifact was supposed to break his curse, it made him ill. Despite that, she would keep it for him until they could unravel its mystery and use it to turn him whole. She vowed to herself that Vernoux would never get it as she trailed Antonio back into the labyrinth of the Catacombs.

*   *   *

Gide wandered through the black tunnels of the Catacombs. He had no need of a torch, for the Crystal Dagger pulsed brightly in his hand. Around him, the bone-covered walls reflected the Dagger's colors. Energy coursed up his arm from the weapon. He had never felt anything like it. All his senses were sharper than they had ever been. He could taste the different elements of the dust kicked up by his steps. He could hear the worms burrowing through the earth. He could see shades of black in the darkness. He could feel the minute vibrations of the rats as they clambered over the bones. He could smell the unwashed bodies of Le Chacal's thieves deep within the caverns, hundreds of yards away.

He did not want to eat or drink, sleep, have sex. His desire was for one thing.

He wanted to kill.

Ever since he had picked up the Dagger, he was driven by that one urge.

Nulkana.

The name whispered constantly in his brain.

He could not find her. She shielded herself too well. But he could smell her dog, her jackal. Le Chacal.

And if he could not have the sorceress, he would have her lackey.

*   *   *

Antonio followed Solange back through the maze of tunnels toward the entrance of the Catacombs. He was bewildered at the sensations that ran through him when he tried to pick up the piece of the Sphere, as if he would transform into Shadow at any moment. He remained farther behind her than he would have liked because of the effects of the piece that she carried. Ahead of him, her torch flickered along the bone-encrusted walls, creating the illusion of undulating movement. It made him dizzy. Why did something that was supposed to break the curse make him so ill? Alessandro never mentioned any such severe effect when he found his piece of the Sphere. Perhaps Piero would have an answer.

Solange rounded a corner of the tunnel and disappeared from view. The torch light reflected back, so he was not left in darkness, but he hurried ahead nonetheless. Just as he reached the turn, he saw more light and heard voices. Solange's in answer. Instinct made him halt, remaining out of sight. He risked a peek around the corner. What he saw made his blood curdle.

Solange was surrounded by ten of Le Chacal's men. The King of the Thieves himself stood directly before her. How had he found them? That question was buried under the clench of fear that tightened in Antonio's chest. Le Chacal would kill her for Nulkana. Antonio searched for any opening, any way he could help her escape. Even if she used her power, she would not be able to subdue all of them. He had his stiletto up his sleeve but had left off his rapier. If he attacked, the element of surprise was on his side, but even with that, they were outnumbered, eleven to two, not the best odds.

He backed out of sight to consider his options. As he did, he heard the sounds of a struggle, the snap of Solange's power, a cry of pain, yells. It was over by the time he bounded forward two steps to help her. Before him, one of Le Chacal's men lay groaning and writhing on the ground, a burn mark across his chest. Solange's torch lay on the floor some distance away, its flame sputtering. The Silver Arrow had been kicked aside and

277

was covered in dust-like debris. Solange was on her knees with one of Le Chacal's henchmen on either side of her, each holding one of her wrists, her arms pulled back and away from her body. She was bent forward in obvious discomfort. Le Chacal stood before her.

Antonio's first impulse was to dash forward to her rescue, but common sense curbed that. Since no one had noticed him, he stepped back into the shadows to consider the best way to free her. Focused on the scene before him, he did not immediately register the odd pulsing light on the walls near him. The sharp point of a blade pricking his back diverted his attention. An arm circling his neck from behind and the rough rasp of the voice in his ear confirmed his danger.

"Don't move, Auriano," Gide warned. "Your death isn't my strongest desire, but I won't weep when your blood feeds my knife."

Antonio froze. He saw the pulsing colors washing the walls and knew the source. "Gide, don't do this. It's the Crystal Dagger that makes you want to kill." As he spoke, he wrapped his hand around Gide's wrist.

The point dug deeper. "I don't like you, Auriano, and I don't trust you," Gide growled. "You've seduced my sister and put her life in danger. The Dagger is the only way to be rid of you."

Antonio heard the fear and jealousy in Gide's words, coming from the man's affection for his sister and his desire to protect her. He hoped he could reach those gentle feelings now before his sister became an offering to Nulkana.

"Gide, Le Chacal has Solange," he reasoned. "Release me so we can save her."

"Do you think I'm stupid enough to fall for your trick?" Gide snapped.

The knife tip pierced Antonio's skin. He sucked in a breath at the pain, heightened by the Dagger's enchantment, and felt warm blood trickle down his back. He realized he only had one option to convince him. Pressing his fingers against the pulse in Gide's wrist, he entered his mind. He found himself in the eye of a maelstrom, a calm surrounded by swirling, pulsing energy. But the energy was discordant and disturbing. Tendrils of malice caressed like a lover. With an effort, he ignored the evil seduction and placed his truth in the middle of Gide's mind.

I care for Solange, he said.

The energy stopped swirling for a moment as Gide registered his surprise. Then it circled again with greater speed. *Liar.* The word spat at him in a pulse of purple energy.

Solange is in desperate trouble, Antonio said.

You can't deceive me. The energy in Gide's mind swirled darker.

I need you to help me save her. Antonio tried to use Gide's affection for his sister.

At Gide's silence, Antonio said aloud, "Look for yourself if you don't believe me." He gestured at the curve of the tunnel.

Solange's brother shifted so he might peek around the corner. He immediately ducked back. "Le Chacal has her prisoner," he murmured in disbelief. Then his words and his mind turned black. "I'll kill him."

"*Si,* but not yet. We are outnumbered. Even using your powers, there are too many of them. We cannot risk getting Solange hurt or worse."

Antonio tightened his hold on the young man's pulse and sent calm into his mind. He could not overcome the effects of the Dagger, but at least he could counteract some of it. When the poisonous swirling in Gide's brain quieted, and Antonio felt some of the tension leave Gide's body, he said, "I have a plan." Then he planted it, full-blown, into Gide's mind.

* * *

Solange struggled against the two thugs who held her wrists in their grimy hands. She was on her knees, bent forward, with her arms held behind and away from her body, and unable to use her power. She had been stupid to walk into his trap. She should have known Le Chacal would be aware of her in the Catacombs. Her focus on Antonio and his distress in the presence of the piece of the Sphere had distracted her. All she had wanted was to get him out of the Catacombs as quickly as possible. That had been careless of her. She jerked once more against the grip of Le Marteau and Roux, the oafs who held her fast.

Le Chacal shook his head regretfully. "*Ma petite vache*, you know you are well caught. Don't make me hurt you more than I have to."

"You are a snake, Jean-Jacques. If you hurt me, Vernoux will come after you." That was an empty threat. The last person who would save her would be Vernoux, and he was the last person she wanted to come for her. What had happened to Antonio? Was he hiding somewhere planning a rescue? Or had he fled? No, she would not believe he would abandon her. He had already saved her life once this night.

The King of the Thieves smiled, twisting the scar down the side of his face. "Once this is done, I will no longer need the marquis. Although, he might need me."

She felt the slight weight of the piece of the Sphere of Astarte in her pocket. She hated what she was about to say, but she needed to delay to give Antonio time. And perhaps give herself a few more minutes of life.

"There is something that Nulkana wants more than my life," she said.

As if in response to her statement, Antonio stepped into the chamber. Her heart swooped at the sight of him, and she regretted her last words to Le Chacal. Shame flooded through her for trying to bargain with Le Chacal.

Gide was right behind him. Her brother's eyes were cold, cruel, murderous. He had a hand wrapped about Antonio's throat, and she caught the flicker of pulsing light from the Crystal Dagger held against Antonio's back. Oh, *mon Dieu.*

Gide stopped just beyond the reach of the outlaws. "Le Chacal." His voice held an odd note, deeper, darker than usual.

Suspicion replaced the initial surprise on Le Chacal's face. "What do you want, pup? Are you sure you want to watch me kill your sister? And why have you brought this one here?" He jerked his chin at Antonio.

"Go away, Gide," Solange pleaded. "Please. While you can."

Her brother ignored her, and Roux jerked on her arm. "Shut up," the thief growled. Solange gasped at the pain that exploded in her shoulder.

Ignoring her, Gide said to Le Chacal. "I've brought the Italian duke in exchange for my sister."

Cold washed through Solange. Her brother had never been so ruthless.

Le Chacal smiled. "Why should I take him? I already have what I want."

Her brother remained grimly focused. "Give Solange to me, and I won't kill you."

The outlaw barked a laugh. "So, the puppy is showing his teeth. And you dare to threaten? You are outnumbered, Gide." Le Chacal swept out his arm to indicate his group of cutthroats.

Gide pulled Antonio around to show the Crystal Dagger pressed against his back. "Do you see this? It wants the death of the sorceress, but it will take yours just as well since you are her dog."

Heat flashed through Le Chacal's eyes, then they cooled.

Patricia Barletta

"So, you have come to negotiate," he said. "Very well. I'll indulge you. Tell me why I should want this Italian duke." He flipped his stump in Antonio's direction.

Antonio finally spoke. "Nulkana is here in Paris because of me. She wants something that I have, and then she wants my death, more than she ever wanted the death of some little thief." He jerked his chin insultingly in Solange's direction.

A tweak of pain jabbed at her heart. Was he pretending or did he actually mean those harsh words? Then his eyes flicked to her, warning her to silence.

The outlaw turned a speculative look on Solange. "Nulkana has already promised a very handsome reward for *ma petite vache.*"

"Give me to Nulkana in her place," Antonio said, exuding authority and assurance. "You will be doubly rewarded."

"No!" The word burst from Solange. She knew what Nulkana could do to Antonio. She had seen it that night the sorceress had sent her projection to the hut in the woods. She would not let him sacrifice himself like that.

A cruel smile curved Le Chacal's lips. "Ah, Solange," he purred. "I believe you have some feelings for this man."

Zut. She had given herself away. Almost. Thinking quickly, she gave Antonio a disdainful look. "He is a liar," she spat. "Why would the sorceress want an Italian duke? He is nothing. He has no power like mine. You've seen my power, Jean-Jacques. I can use it to steal for you and make you a very wealthy man. Wealth can buy you influence. Think of what you could do to Vernoux."

Le Chacal narrowed his eyes. "What else would you do for me, *ma petite vache?*" His suggestive question taunted.

Solange swallowed. The thought of becoming Le Chacal's whore made her skin crawl. She forced her voice to remain steady. "Whatever you want, Jean-Jacques."

"Solange, no!" Gide's words exploded.

Solange ignored him and kept her gaze on the King of the Thieves.

The outlaw gave a humorless chuckle. "If I did not think you would kill me the first chance you had, I might accept your very attractive offer, *ma petite vache*." He turned his attention to Antonio, strolled a step to the right, then strolled to the left. He turned to Solange and studied her. "This is very touching. Each of you is willing to sacrifice for the other. So. Which of you is lying? Why would Nulkana bother herself over an Italian duke who has no power?"

Gide spoke up. "He had the moonstone. He knows what it can do, and he knows much more. He can do magic."

"Magic." Le Chacal repeated the word as if he were not quite sure of its meaning. "What sort of magic? Can he make things disappear and then appear someplace else?"

"Of course not," Solange scoffed. "He is no sorcerer. If he were, do you think he would have allowed himself to get caught by my brother?"

"But I can do other things," Antonio said. "You remember, don't you Le Chacal?" His words seemed to lure.

The outlaw turned his attention to him. Antonio gave him a level stare. Solange watched Le Chacal's eyes widen, and she knew Antonio spoke silently into the outlaw's mind. Le Chacal glared at Antonio and hissed a curse. He paced away a few steps, stopped, then turned back to Gide.

"You are outnumbered, puppy," Le Chacal said. "Why shouldn't I keep both your sister and the duke, and perhaps you, as well?"

"You don't want to do that," Gide said.

One of the thieves had edged close to him. Gide slashed out with the Dagger. It sliced cleanly through the man's elbow in a burst of light and heat. The thief howled, clutched at what was left of his arm and stared in horror as his hand and lower arm twitched on the chamber floor. Blood formed in a pool at his feet, then he keeled over.

Le Chacal tsked into the stunned silence. "You have just destroyed one of my best pickpockets."

"Make the exchange." Gide's demand was ice.

"Don't, Jean-Jacques," Solange said. "You'll be making a mistake."

The outlaw ignored her and gave Gide a long look. His gaze slid to Antonio and back to Gide. Le Chacal nodded his agreement. He waved his stump at Solange. "Tie her hands behind her," he ordered the men holding her.

"You'll regret that you've let me go." She made one last desperate attempt to get Le Chacal to change his mind as the outlaws bound her wrists with someone's filthy neckcloth. "The sorceress will come after you."

The outlaw grinned at her. "Not if I bring her a prize, *ma petite vache.*"

Le Marteau and Roux dragged her to her feet and brought her to Le Chacal. "I will miss you, *ma petite vache,*" he said. He took her arm. The cocking of pistols clicked loudly in the silence. "Release the duke, puppy," he said to Gide. "We will make the exchange." With a shove, he ordered her, "Go to your brother."

Solange lurched away from Le Chacal and toward Gide. Toward Antonio. He kept his eyes on Le Chacal. He would not look at her as he stepped forward. He appeared relaxed, composed despite the number of pistols aimed at him, but his eyes were hard, cold as gold. This was not the same man who had fallen weakly against a wall when confronted with the means of breaking his curse. This was not the same man who asked her to safeguard the piece of the Sphere of Astarte. This was not the same man who made sweet, hot love with her only the night before.

This was the Italian duke, aristocratic, self-assured, honorable, willing to bargain himself to free her.

Please, look at me, she pleaded silently. *You can't do this.*

His gaze remained on his goal—Le Chacal. She would not plead aloud with Antonio before Le Chacal. That would give the outlaw another weapon to use against them. But Antonio's refusal to meet her eyes stabbed at her. She loved him. Even if she had not spoken the words aloud, she wanted him to see it in her eyes. Just as they passed, his eyes flicked to her and away. Those beautiful golden eyes. That was all. One last glance.

He passed beyond her. To Le Chacal. Three more steps. Four. Five. Eight. Ten. She reached Gide. A flurry of movement behind her meant Antonio had reached Le Chacal, that the King of the Thieves took him prisoner. She would not think what that meant. She would not look. She would not imagine the horrors that awaited him.

I will see you again, dolcezza.

His sweet words made her stumble and gasp. She glanced over her shoulder. Antonio was already being pushed roughly in the opposite direction. The last glimpse she had was of the back of his head, of the torchlight highlighting a bright golden streak in his hair.

A hole opened in her chest where her heart should have been.

Then Gide took her by the arm.

A frisson of energy ran through her, unsettling, uncomfortable, near pain. It was dark, wild, terrible. She hissed in a breath. Before she had time to recover, Gide dragged her toward the tunnel leading out. She staggered along beside him. The energy pounded through her and distorted everything. In the pulsing light of the Dagger, the bone-covered walls around her closed in, writhed, then vanished into nothing. The floor beneath her feet turned to mire, then air. Only the dark of the tunnel before her remained constant. Solange fought to keep her sanity, not to scream the madness that threatened.

The stone steps leading up to the street finally appeared. Fresh air teased her nose. She gulped it in and forced her brother to stop.

"Gide. Let me go." Her voice emerged thin and barely audible even to her own ears.

Gide looked at her in surprise, as if he forgot she was with him.

"Gide, release me." Her voice was stronger this time.

Slowly, he unwrapped his fingers from about her arm. As soon as he dropped his hand, her surroundings returned to normal. That horrible, black energy receded. She blinked and stared at her brother. His eyes were no longer a clear turquoise, but dark, muddy. In their depths was something cold and vicious.

"Please, cut the bindings," she prompted.

He hesitated as if he were not sure he could trust her. Then, with a single swipe, he slashed the Crystal Dagger through the neckcloth binding her wrists. It hissed as it cut through the cloth. His expression was cold and cruel.

"What has happened to you, Gide?" Solange reached to touch him but remembering that monstrous energy, she pulled back.

He grinned, baring his teeth. "I have power, Solange."

"You've always had power."

He shook his head. "Not like this." He swished the Dagger through the air. "This has made me see things in a new way." He stepped closer. "Between us, we can do anything. We can take whatever we want. We'll be wealthy and powerful."

The look in Gide's eyes frightened her. This was not the brother she had known all her life.

"No, Gide," she said. "The Dagger is evil. You have to get rid of it."

Anger suffused his face. "I won't. The Dagger is mine. You don't understand."

"I do understand." She put her hand on his arm. The dark energy slammed into her, staggering her.

"You see?" Gide said. "You can't fight it, Solange. It wants you, too." His voice sounded far away.

With an effort, she dropped her hand. Once again, she felt normal. "No, Gide. I won't let it have me."

"You have to, Solange. We're brother and sister. It wants both of us." He took her by the arm again. "Come."

As the wave of darkness pulsed through her brain, she forced it back long enough to ask, "Where are we going?"

Her brother remained silent as he dragged her up the stone steps to the street.

She felt as if a sword stabbed her heart. Despair and fear clutched at her. Her brother had turned into a stranger, and Antonio was to be an offering to Nulkana. But that thought whirled away as her brother gripped her arm. The evil embracing Gide embraced her as well. The black energy of the Dagger threatened to take her sanity. Like a puppet, she followed Gide wherever he wanted to take her.

*　　*　　*

Antonio allowed himself to be shoved forward by one of Le Chacal's thugs. But when the point of a blade pinched his back, he turned with a snarl on the outlaw who wielded it. The man fell back a step. Antonio wanted to rip him to pieces, but that would be foolish. He would only wind up dead himself. And he needed to remain alive.

To save Solange.

Pain gnawed at his heart. He had not realized when he quickly devised the plan and planted it in Gide's mind that he would feel such torment. At the time, all he wanted was to protect her. Not until he saw the anguish on her face, not until he heard her silent plea to look at her did he realize what he had done. He had broken their agreement, sent her back to Vernoux. Betrayed her.

He had not been able to look at her, except for that one, quick glance. Even that had nearly broken him. He could not reach out to her, comfort her, as they passed in the exchange. If he had, he would have crushed her to him, revealing his feelings, and sealing both their fates. At least now, he could hope to escape and snatch her from Vernoux's clutches. She would stay alive with Vernoux, a member of the Legion of Baal and an enemy of Nulkana. Better that than a cruel, painful death with the sorceress. As for him, he would be Shadow in another two days. All he had to do was remain alive until then.

The distress he felt at giving Solange over to Gide tore at him. He knew Gide would bring her to Vernoux. Gide was in league with the Legion and under the power of the Dagger. But the devastation he felt shocked him. It was more than regret at sending her away, and more than remorse at giving her back to that monster. He wanted to kill for her. The thought of never seeing her again tore at him like the teeth of some rabid animal. As if that animal ripped away a dark membrane covering his eyes, he suddenly saw clearly what had been before him all along. He loved Solange. He would keep the promise of his last words to her. He would see her again. And he would save her, even if she hated him for what he had done.

Le Chacal led him to a small, bare chamber. No bones decorated the dark stone walls. A trickle of water came from one corner. Beneath Antonio's boots, the floor was rough dirt and stones.

The Jackal snapped his fingers, and one of the men brought two chairs. One was wooden, roughly made, with a plain seat and straight back. The other was delicate,

plumply upholstered, incongruously covered in pale
pink silk, and placed opposite the first. The outlaw sat in
the soft chair, leaned back, and studied Antonio.

"So, *mon ami*," Le Chacal said. "We will have a little
chat, you and I. You will tell me what I wish to know. About
the wondrous moonstone. And perhaps about other magical
objects. This can be a pleasant conversation, or not so
pleasant. That is up to you. I do not think Nulkana will mind
what condition you are in when I give you to her, *oui?*"

Antonio smiled. "I think Nulkana would be disappointed
if you delivered me dead. She might not be so generous with
her reward if you deprive her the joy of killing me."

"Almost dead is not the same as dead." The outlaw
shrugged. "And who knows? Perhaps what you tell me will
be so wondrous that I may keep you myself. That is up to
you."

He was interrupted by two of his men gingerly carrying
in a glowing brazier. They placed it near enough that Antonio
could feel its heat. One of them stuck a poker into the hot
coals, within Le Chacal's reach. The outlaw took hold of
the poker and twisted it in the coals. The embers sparked
and hissed. He turned back to Antonio.

"I think you should remove some of those splendid
clothes you are wearing," he said. "It would be a pity to
ruin such fine garments."

One of the outlaws curled his hand into the back collar
of Antonio's coat. Antonio succumbed to the inevitable,
knowing he was outnumbered, and removed it. With
prompts from Le Chacal, he also removed his waistcoat,
stock, and shirt. His boots and stockings went next. When
he was left wearing only his breeches, he was shoved into
the bare, uncomfortable chair. His arms were roughly
pulled behind him and his wrists tied. Each of his ankles
was bound separately to a chair leg. Then the criminals
left, but not before one of them handed Le Chacal a very
large, double-edged knife.

289

Patricia Barletta

Le Chacal and Antonio were alone.

· The outlaw smiled as he tested the edge of the blade with his thumb. "I like to keep my guests comfortable. Are you comfortable, *Monsieur le Duc?*"

"Quite," Antonio said agreeably, ignoring the ropes cutting into his wrists and ankles. He tested the knots, probed with his mind to see if he could untie them. They remained stubbornly tight. Untying them would take a great deal of time and quite a bit of concentration, neither of which he would have after Le Chacal began his torture. But at least his body healed quickly. Resigned, he accepted what was to come. He would be suffering for saving Solange, for breaking his agreement with her—a fair penance.

"*Bon.*" Le Chacal's smile turned nasty. "Then let us begin."

* * *

Gide dragged Solange through the streets, and all she could do was stumble along with him. The Dagger held her as much as it held her brother. She lost track of time. Her surroundings were only a blur in the night. He pulled her up some stairs and through a doorway. His shout cut through the black fog in her head.

"Vernoux!" He took another few steps, pulling her with him.

Solange glanced around. The pulsing light of the Dagger revealed the black and white marble floor and pale walls decorated with priceless paintings in the empty entry hall of *L'Hôtel de Vernoux*. Rather than taking her home, Gide had brought her to his master. Anger rose up in her like some wild thing.

"Why did you bring me here?" She forced the words out from her clogged throat.

"He told me."

290

"Vernoux?" she choked out.

Gide shook his head.

He. Antonio. He had betrayed her. Gide had not brought her here on his own. Antonio had told Gide to bring her here. Hurt swirled inside her, spinning with a hundred claws. He had saved her only to send her back to her cruel master. Her heart felt shredded. And then her sense of betrayal became something else, black and glutinous, fueled by the Dagger. Fury. Rage.

"No," she said. Even through the dark fog that eddied in her head, she knew she did not want to be here. "No." She struggled against Gide's grip on her arm.

He shook her. "Shut up." His words hissed at her. There was no brotherly love in that tone. "Vernoux!" he called again.

She heard the commotion of servants roused from their sleep, voices raised in alarm. The marquis appeared at the top of stairs. He wore a deep purple silk dressing gown. He was wigless, his short-cropped hair a silver fuzz in the dark. He held his bandaged hand against his chest as if protecting it. He did not look pleased.

"Your visit had better be important, Gide, for I detest being roused from my bed in the middle of the night." Vernoux's tone dripped ice. His valet, flustered and straightening his own wig, rushed to his side with a lit taper. Vernoux took it, then with a sharp gesture, sent him away.

Gide finally released Solange's arm. The dark swirl that clouded her brain receded, but the overwhelming anger remained. She wanted to punish—Gide, for bringing her here; Vernoux, for his past sins against her; Antonio, for betraying her. Most of all, Antonio.

"I've brought my sister," Gide said.

"I can see that." Vernoux's words were clipped and chillier than before.

Solange punched her brother in the shoulder. "You should have taken me home," she hissed.

Gide shrugged her off and took two steps away from her, two steps nearer the sweeping staircase, two steps closer to Vernoux. "I took her from Le Chacal. He would have killed her and given her to Nulkana."

Vernoux raised a sardonic brow and slowly descended the stairs. "Are you looking for my gratitude?"

"I am looking for you to protect her," Gide said. His tone held an authority that Solange had never heard before.

Her brother's words caught her attention. *Mon dieu!* Like a flash of lightning, the truth appeared. She knew without a doubt that Antonio had suggested that Gide bring her to Vernoux because he was Nulkana's enemy. *This* was Antonio's protection. Her rage at where Fate had brought them made her brave. He was saving her life. She would save his.

Vernoux reached the bottom step and stopped. "Truly?" He sounded only mildly curious. "Why should I do that? Your sister seems to prefer the company of the Italian duke. She has become expendable, especially because I have you, and you have the Crystal Dagger."

A sliver of fear pierced Solange's anger. It made her reckless. She stepped forward, ready to bargain anything—*anything*—to save herself and her brother. And Antonio. "Do you think so little of someone who can lead you to a piece of the Sphere of Astarte?" She was not about to reveal she had it in her pocket.

Vernoux's gaze cut to her. Those eyes, so cold, studied her. "Do you bargain with something you have, or with nothing but empty promises and air?"

"I know where it is." She threw the words down like a challenge.

"Where?" Although Vernoux kept his façade of cool remoteness, his question revealed his interest.

Solange smiled, knowing she had him hooked. She was relieved her brain had begun functioning again. "Do you think I'd give it up so easily, *mon seigneur?*"

Vernoux stepped off the last stair and paced closer. "Do not be coy, *ma petite putain*. I know many ways to make you tell me where it is. None of them are pleasant."

Solange suggestively cocked a hip. "But I will tell you for a much lesser price."

Vernoux, ignoring her attempt at seduction, raised his brows in a silent question.

She prayed what she was about to suggest would work.

"Le Chacal has the Italian duke." Her bland tone belied her desperation. "Free him, bring him here, and I will get the piece of the Sphere for you." She took a step closer, reached out and placed her hand in the middle of his chest. She allowed her fingers to caress. "You want to kill him yourself. I know you do. Tell me that is not so."

In a flash of movement, Vernoux backhanded her with his heavily bandaged hand, knocking her away off her feet. She was weightless for a heartbeat before she fell heavily to her side and skidded several feet across the smooth marble floor. Pain exploded in her cheek, her shoulder, her hip, and dark spots danced in her vision. The taste of blood flooded her mouth. The ache of bruises to come throbbed.

Gide jumped forward, the Crystal Dagger raised. His eyes blazed in fury.

The marquis glared at him as he cradled his injured hand. "You will not raise that weapon to me, Delacroix."

Dazed from her fall, Solange watched as some sort of silent battle raged between the two men. Finally, her brother stepped back and ducked his head. His hand with the Dagger fell to his side. She watched in shock as Vernoux raised his arm, and with a single gesture, forced Gide to his knees. Her heart broke as she watched her brother succumb to the control of the marquis. She could do nothing to reach him. Somehow, she had to get the Dagger away from him, or he would be lost forever.

Vernoux turned his chilly eyes on her. "Do not presume to know my mind, *ma petite putain*," he said. He strolled closer and stood over her, stilled sprawled on the floor. "So. Why have you suddenly become concerned about what I want?"

Vernoux was too cool, too quiet. And that was when he was the most dangerous, the most vicious. What had she just done? Solange swallowed.

Sitting up, wiping the blood from the corner of her mouth, she said, "I am always concerned for your welfare, *mon seigneur*."

"Ah." A smile crossed Vernoux's face, turning him crueler than before. He crouched before her. "A woman who cares for me." Reaching out, he brushed a strand of hair from her cheek, took hold of her braid and wrapped it about his hand, a mockery of affection. With a sharp jerk, he brought her to within inches of his face. "How much do you care for this Italian duke, *ma petite putain*? How much are you willing to gamble to keep him alive?"

His hold on her hurt. "No, Vernoux, you misunderstand." Solange tried to keep the panic from her voice, from her eyes.

"Do I?" His eyes narrowed, searching deep into hers.

Solange fought to keep her gaze steady so he would not see her lies. "*Oui.* I do not want him alive. I want him dead. With his capture by Le Chacal, he is easy prey. You can blame his death on the outlaw while having the satisfaction of killing him yourself." She prayed he would believe her. All she needed was to get Vernoux to bring Antonio here. Somehow, she would keep Antonio alive.

"Hmmm." Vernoux stared thoughtfully into her eyes. "An interesting idea, but I think not. I think I have a better plan. It is so much more . . . creative." He spoke the last word as if he were savoring a sip of the smoothest brandy. "I will have Le Chacal bring your Italian duke here. And then—" He chuckled. "And then, you and Auriano will duel. To the death."

Solange stared at him as his statement congealed in her mind. "But—" She tried to find words to argue against his evil idea, but her brain was frozen in horror.

Vernoux raised his brow. "You do not like my idea, Solange?" He tsked. "I thought you cared." He shrugged. "Well, if you can think of a better idea, then I am willing to listen. But, you see, there is the matter of your brother."

He glanced back over his shoulder at Gide again, made a twisting motion with his hand. Like a puppet, Gide raised the Dagger and placed the point against his own throat. Solange's heart seemed to stop.

"No," she said, grabbing Vernoux's sleeve. "Please."

The marquis turned back to her. "So then, you approve of my idea? Very well. You will retrieve the piece of the Sphere and give it to me before the duel. Otherwise, I will have to sacrifice your brother." He unwound his hand from her braid and smoothed her hair. "I do not wish to do that, you see, for then I will have to force you to carry the Dagger, and I have a much better use for you." He stood, turned, and headed back to the stairs. "You and your brother will remain as my guests until all this is finished." He started up the stairs. "And then I will decide if I shall give you to the Lord High or Nulkana."

Chapter 21

Solange stood in the middle of the great ballroom of *L'Hôtel de Vernoux.* Hundreds of candles lit the space. They were not needed now, as the sun had just set and its refracted light still filtered through the doors and windows. But twilight would soon follow, and the ballroom would blaze with the candlelight. But instead of the kaleidoscope of many dancers moving to the musical airs of an orchestra that should fill the space, the room would be used for another reason entirely. In the empty room, one incongruous item signaled what that reason was. A rack of rapiers stood against one wall.

At one end of the ballroom, doors were open to the garden, but no fairy lights lit the walkways. This was not an evening for lovers to stroll, for gentlemen to linger while they made wagers or exchanged secrets. This was a night for subterfuge, for a farce to be performed, for a desperate plot to unfold. This was the night she would duel with Antonio.

The irony nearly made her break out into hysterical laughter. Once, she had thought to have Antonio duel with Vernoux in the hope the Italian duke would do away with the man who tormented her. The Italian duke was so much more to her now. He was Tonio. Shadow. And not. He was the man she loved.

A breeze shifted the filmy curtains framing the open doors. The air was warm and muggy. She was glad she had decided against wearing the waistcoat and jacket. Her shirt and the cloth strips binding her breasts would be drenched by the end of this night, however it ended—either in her sweat or her blood. Despite the warmth of the air, she shivered.

Footsteps echoed in the hall beyond the ballroom, and Vernoux appeared in the doorway. The bandage on his hand was bloody. It had been bleeding ever since he had backhanded her.

"Solange," he said with a cruel smile. "I see you are anxious to meet your opponent."

She did not bother to answer as he stepped into the room. Gide followed, and she was surprised to see the man known as The Messenger enter behind.

"Why are they here?" she asked Vernoux.

"Because I wish them to be," Vernoux snapped.

"Why not invite all your cronies, like Gravois?" she snapped, her anxiety overcoming her good sense. "Especially Gravois, since he so enjoys tattling tales to you."

Vernoux glowered and his mouth twisted in distaste. "Gravois is nothing." His gaze turned chill and vicious. "Beware what you say, *ma petite putain.*"

The Messenger took a step forward. "I am witness to the proceedings, *mademoiselle,*" he said quietly, diffusing the tension. His clear blue gaze pinned her for a moment before his dark lashes swept down as he gave a slight bow. "The Legion of Baal has great interest in the life of the Duke of Auriano."

Of course. The Legion wanted the pieces of the Sphere of Astarte as much as the members of the House of Auriano. The Legion would be very interested if one of their rivals were eliminated.

The Messenger spoke again. "The Lord High has forbidden the members of the Legion from doing away with any of the House of Auriano. Because the Marquis de Vernoux is not himself dueling with Auriano, I have allowed this duel to proceed on that technicality. If you do not kill the duke, then I must bring him before the

Lord High so that he himself may have the satisfaction of the Italian duke's death."

Solange felt her stomach clench and turn over at the implications of the man's words. She nearly vomited. No matter the outcome of this night, both she and Antonio would be dead. She had not known that the head of the Legion of Baal wanted his death. Even if by some miracle both she and Antonio managed to stay alive, they would still have The Messenger to deal with. She surmised the man was much more deadly than his mild manner implied. Despite the fact that he had warned her against touching the Crystal Dagger, she did not think he would hesitate to kill her if she attempted to thwart his intent. Something about him spoke of cool ruthlessness.

She turned from those clear blue eyes and looked to Gide, whom she had asked to stay away. He stood beside Vernoux and did not appear to notice her presence at all. His gaze was focused on something beyond the confines of the room, as if he watched a scene in the distance, or as if he could sense something coming and was merely waiting for it to arrive. The Crystal Dagger was stuck into the waistband of his breeches and pulsed softly as if it also waited.

"Gide," she said, wanting to draw his attention, have him acknowledge her.

His darkened eyes flicked to her, then away, as if he did not know her. The Dagger had him tight in its thrall.

The sound of more footsteps approached the entrance to the ballroom. One set stumbled as if being rushed and pushed off balance. Le Chacal and Antonio. Solange caught her bottom lip between her teeth as a twinge of apprehension slid through her. She was reluctant to see what condition Antonio would be in when he appeared. She wondered if he would even be capable of holding a rapier, never mind dancing in a duel.

Her question was answered when he appeared in the doorway. He stood straight, tall, relaxed as if he had never been Le Chacal's prisoner. Of course. She should have known he would be able to survive and outwit the outlaw. She remembered he had once mentioned he healed very quickly. His tormentor, Le Chacal, stood smugly beside him with Le Marteau and Roux looming behind.

Antonio's wrists were bound at his back. He met her eyes and bowed awkwardly. "Solange," he murmured, her name a caress.

His voice curled around her and surrounded her heart. He had saved her by giving himself up to Le Chacal. She loved this man and would do anything to keep him safe.

"Ah, we are all here," Vernoux said grandly. "Wonderful. Then let us begin. We will watch from here."

He had already moved to the low raised platform where normally the orchestra would be situated during a ball. The Messenger stood slightly apart from him. Gide stood on Vernoux's other side. Le Chacal untied Antonio's wrists but kept a hand wrapped around his arm. With a jerk of his head, he dismissed his two thugs. He and Antonio remained just inside the entrance to the ballroom.

"So, Solange, Auriano is here, ready to fence with you," Vernoux said. "I believe you have something that belongs to me."

As Antonio rubbed circulation back into his wrists, he glanced at Solange. His brows went up in a silent, surprised question. Le Chacal had evidently not told him the reason for his presence, and Solange could not bring herself to inform him.

The small bundle stuck in the back waistband of her breeches suddenly seemed much larger and heavier than it was. She could feel Antonio's gaze, but she would not meet his eyes. Her mind scrambled for a reason to delay, to keep possession of the piece of the Sphere of Astarte. It belonged to Antonio, not Vernoux and his Legion of Baal. She had brought it not because she knew Vernoux would ask for it but in the hope of being able to pass it to Antonio.

At her hesitation, Vernoux made a sound of impatience. "Come, come, Solange. I know you have it."

Still, she made no move to give it to him. She desperately wanted some way to refuse. If she relinquished the object that would cure Antonio, she would hate herself more than she already did for what she was about to do.

Vernoux frowned in displeasure. He stretched out his arm toward Gide. Solange watched, appalled, as her brother pulled the Crystal Dagger from his waistband and turned the point toward his chest.

The marquis focused his attention on Solange. "I would prefer not to have to kill your brother, *ma petite putain*, and I am sure you would prefer to have him alive."

Horrified chills swept down her back. She did not dare use her power against Vernoux, for she was afraid of what would happen to Gide. "Don't," she croaked. "Please don't." Hoping she could find some way to get the piece of the Sphere to Antonio, she took the small bundle from its hiding place.

While Vernoux kept one arm extended toward Gide, he held out his other hand to her. Avarice glittered in his eyes. "Bring it here," he ordered.

Slowly, Solange stepped forward. Perhaps she could slip the piece of the Sphere to Antonio as she passed. She headed in his direction as if she merely wished to speak to him. As she neared him, his face paled, and his lips tightened. She remembered his severe reaction to the piece when they had been in the Catacombs. She wondered again why something that was supposed to cure his curse could have such an adverse effect on him. Her steps faltered. If she passed the piece to Antonio, she feared it would weaken him too much to be able to defend himself.

"Solange." Vernoux's voice, threatening in its deadly calm, echoed across the open space.

She halted. Vernoux's hand twisted, and Gide pushed the Dagger towards his chest.

"To me, Solange," Vernoux ordered silkily. "Don't force me to kill your dear brother prematurely."

Reluctantly, she turned her footsteps toward the platform where he stood. She did not dare look at Antonio, but she could feel his stoic dismay as she passed. As much as the piece made him ill, it was still his legacy and should be in his possession. His gaze felt like chilly fingers on her back.

Sorrow bled through her. She wanted Antonio to do something, say something, reassure her that he understood. He remained silent.

She placed the bundle containing the piece of the Sphere in Vernoux's outstretched hand. He unwrapped the cloth to reveal the intricate piece of amber.

"Why, that's—" Le Chacal exclaimed, obviously recognizing it. "You stole it." He flung his angry accusation between her and Antonio. Then he clamped his lips together when Vernoux aimed his cruel gaze at him. The King of the Thieves fell back a step.

Before Vernoux could close his fingers around the piece, The Messenger swept it from his palm. "I will keep this to be sure it reaches the Lord High," he said.

Vernoux swung to The Messenger. Fury mottled his cheeks.

The Messenger pocketed the piece and calmly met the rage of the marquis. "It is, after all, at the pleasure of the Lord High and for our common goal that we search for it," he said.

Vernoux visibly struggled to contain his anger. Finally, with a swallow and a breath, he nodded once. "Of course," he said smoothly. "Please convey it with my compliments to the Lord High." He scowled at Solange. "Let's get this farce over with," he snapped.

Solange wiped her palms down the sides of her breeches, then turned in the direction of the rack of rapiers. "Come," she said to Antonio with a small gesture. "Please choose a weapon."

She kept her attention on the blades, but she heard his footsteps trail her across the polished floor of the ballroom. Those steps sounded different somehow, not quite so sure and strong as usual, but perhaps that was only her imagination. She sensed his presence, commanding and confident, next to her as she pulled one of the weapons from the rack.

"What is this about, Solange?" he asked quietly.

"Didn't Le Chacal tell you?" she said, keeping her tone light. She risked a peek at him. Now that he was so close, she could see the lines of pain around his eyes and mouth. What horrors had he endured? She did not want—could not—think on that. She could show no compassion, not with Vernoux watching so carefully. "We are to duel, you and I," she said flippantly, for their audience.

"What madness is this?" he hissed.

"Choose a weapon," she hissed back.

He pulled out one of rapiers, bent it to test its flexibility. "Did you bargain with the Devil, Solange?" he murmured.

What answer should she give? Yes? She bargained because Vernoux held her brother in his thrall and would kill him if she did not play out the farce? That dueling with Antonio would postpone his death, either by Vernoux or the Lord High? That dueling with him allowed her one more glimpse of him before one or both of them died? That she loved him more than her own life and planned to die on the tip of his weapon? No, she could not say any of those things, because Vernoux watched, and Antonio would not allow her to die.

Besides, if the marquis discovered her true feelings for Antonio, Vernoux would kill him slowly, painfully before her eyes to punish her, despite the prohibition that the Lord High of the Legion of Baal had placed against killing members of the House of Auriano. She had to push Antonio away. To save him.

"You gave me back to Vernoux," she accused.

"*Si*," he agreed.

"You betrayed me." She was careful to keep anger a thread through her words.

He replaced the rapier and pulled another. "I gave you back to Vernoux to keep you from becoming a sacrifice to Nulkana," he replied.

His words, spoken so calmly, sent a point of painful sorrow through her chest as effectively as if he had plunged his rapier through her. She had not wanted *him* to save *her*. Her intent was for *her* to save *him*. She needed to stoke his rage so that he would fight her.

"That was so thoughtful of you, *Monsieur le Duc*," she sneered. "You kept me from death only so that I might remain in this living hell." Before he could reply, she slapped him across the face. "That is what I think of your heroics," she spat.

Something—was that hurt? —flashed through his eyes, then they turned stony. "My apologies for trying to save your life, *Madame* de Volonté. I assumed you wanted the chance to remain breathing, but I was evidently mistaken."

"Choose a weapon," she repeated in a growl. Even as she said the words, remorse twisted through her for hurting him.

He tapped the tip of the rapier against the parquet. Looking down at it, he said, "This one will do as well as any other."

The resignation in his voice made desolation open in her chest like a bottomless pit. She steeled herself against the pain. She would sacrifice herself to save Antonio. The reward—knowing that Antonio lived—was worth this torment. Turning away, she strode toward the center of the ballroom.

*   *   *

Antonio watched her resolute steps. Her back was straight, and her long braid swung provocatively between her shoulder blades. She seemed determined to punish him for an imagined wrong, but something was off-kilter. He glanced to the platform where Vernoux stood with Le Chacal and the Englishman, who had so elegantly swiped the piece of the Sphere from Vernoux's grasp. Insight flashed through his brain, obviously muddled by Le Chacal's torture. Solange was in a dire situation, one he had placed her in by giving her into her brother's care. Gide gazed off into space, the Crystal Dagger held by his side, but with the point up rather than down. The Dagger had him in its thrall, and Vernoux seemed to be able to control him through the weapon. By threatening Gide, Vernoux controlled Solange.

Antonio studied her as she approached the middle of the ballroom and faced him. Her mouth was drawn in a tight line, and her eyes were downcast, hiding any emotion. A tiny tremor in the hand holding the rapier revealed her agitation. The anger she had shown him and her cruel words had pierced his heart. His dismay at her betrayal when she gave over the piece of the Sphere to Vernoux sat like a rock in his gut.

The burns and slices across his abdomen, chest, down his arms, and along the bottoms of his feet stung and throbbed at every move. He had suffered the torture from Le Chacal gladly, knowing that Solange was alive. But he had made a mistake giving her to Gide. He should have taken his chances in a fight with Le Chacal and his men in the Catacombs.

He swished his rapier through the air several times as he tested its balance, then stepped toward the center of the room. Delaying this foolish duel, even for a few moments, might give him an advantage. Very soon, the moon would rise, and he would be Shadow. Then he would have the opportunity to spirit Solange away.

He faced the platform with its array of members, each present for a different reason. "My apologies, gentlemen," he said. "Perhaps in my befuddled state I have missed something, but I would like to know why I should bother fencing with *Madame* de Volonté."

"I understood that you enjoyed the sport," Vernoux said.

"Quite, but I find I am not in the mood." He yawned and made a desultory motion with his hand.

Vernoux's eyes turned calculating. "Perhaps knowing that Solange would be desolated if her brother came to harm might encourage you." He made a twist with his hand, and Gide brought the point of the Dagger against his own throat.

"Ah," Antonio said, feigning comprehension. "And at the outcome of this duel? What then? Will we both be allowed to go our separate ways?"

"Oh, no, *Monsieur le Duc*," Vernoux said with a cruel chuckle. "One of you will most certainly be dead."

"I see." Antonio cast a quick glance at Solange.

He saw fear and desperation in her eyes, then she turned away. His heart clenched. This brave, glorious woman was forced into this duel by the man who had controlled her since she'd grown into womanhood. Because he had wanted to save her from the other man who had controlled her since she was a child. He understood what she intended. And he knew what he would do. His heart unclenched and swelled. He loved this woman. More than life. He would fight her but he would not win. He would sacrifice himself to save Solange.

Turning back to Vernoux, he said, "If Solange lives, you will set her free, along with her brother."

Vernoux shook his head. "You are in no position to bargain, Auriano. If you are dead, you will have no way to enforce your little bargain. And if you live, you will be going with this gentleman to meet with the Lord High, who is most anxious to make your acquaintance." He motioned to the stranger at his side.

The Englishman bowed. "I'm afraid we have not had the pleasure, Your Grace. I am called The Messenger."

"*Si*, I've heard of you," Antonio said.

"Then I am flattered," The Messenger said.

Vernoux made an impatient gesture. "This is wasting time. You have no options, Auriano."

Antonio glared at the Frenchman. "There are always options, Vernoux." He swished his rapier. "Come, Solange," he said, "let us, as *Monsieur le Marquis* so delicately put it, get this farce over with."

* * *

Solange watched him approach his mark opposite her. He was a study in nonchalance, but she could tell that beneath his casual surface, he was in tight control, more deadly and dangerous than any heated rage. She was frightened but resigned to her fate. By the end of this duel, nothing would matter.

Antonio shrugged one arm out of his coat. At the edge of the armhole of his waistcoat, a bright red stain had seeped into the white of his shirt. He was injured. Of course. That was the reason he had moved with less than his usual grace. Guilt, shame, and remorse were an ugly tangle in Solange's chest. She could not imagine what Le Chacal had done to make him bleed so. He should not be dancing in a duel with her. He had sacrificed himself to save her. She glanced down at the rapier clutched in her fist and could see no way to extricate them from this terrible situation.

When she looked up again, across the middle of the ballroom, Antonio waited, his blade held lightly, its tip dipped to the floor. He stood in shirtsleeves, bright and dark patches staining the white—fresh blood and dried. Solange wanted to gently peel that shirt from him, bathe his wounds, kiss away the pain. Instead, she gripped her rapier more tightly and faced him, prepared to die at the end of his weapon to save him. At least if he lived, he would have a chance to escape. If she had reckoned the days correctly, he would soon be Shadow.

They saluted each other with their blades. Solange could tell nothing about what Antonio was thinking, for his face was devoid of expression. Anxiety tightened her muscles. She wanted to drop her sword and step to him, place her hands against his cheeks and put her lips gently on his mouth. Instead, she gripped the hilt of her blade harder and took her stance.

Antonio echoed her position. They lightly touched blades. And then he did nothing. She realized he was waiting for her to make the first attack. He raised a cool brow. His composure nettled her. After her slap, he should have been furious with her. Instead, he calmly invited her to begin her assault with his passive attitude. She was not about to let him sacrifice himself. She had already decided that he would be the one to walk away.

She attacked in a flurry of movement.

He parried with barely a shift of his wrist. His counter attack invited her to engage. They lunged, parried, attacked, feinted and counter-attacked. Solange could see that he was a master swordsman as their duel danced them over the parquet. Sweat ran down her back. Antonio looked cool and focused. But she sensed he was biding his time, waiting for the moment when he could step into the point of her blade. She was determined that was not going to happen. In desperation, she executed a riposte, inviting his attack. He lunged, sliding his blade down the length of hers until their guards locked and they stood inches from each other.

"Do not think you can lose this duel, *dolcezza*," he murmured. "You will walk away, and find some way to escape and live your life."

Solange sucked in a lungful of air. The scent of his sweat and that faint aroma of rosemary and lemon that was all him filled her nose. She savored it even as she glared at him.

"You've had your way too often, *Monsieur le Duc*," she snapped. "Do not think you can sway me to do your bidding." With a mighty shove, she pushed him away and attacked once again.

Solange had no idea how much time passed. She began to tire, the light rapier becoming heavier and heavier. Even injured, Antonio was stronger and faster than she was. She knew he was holding back, but he was losing strength as well. His mouth was drawn tight with concentration. Pain showed on his face with every step. She decided it was time to end this drama.

During a disengage, he glanced across her shoulder to the open doors behind her. His gaze settled back on her and his lips curved in a tiny smile as if he had learned some bit of information. Solange understood. The moon was beginning to rise. He would be Shadow soon. And then he could escape. A tiny spark of hope lit in Solange's heart. Time to end this evil dance.

He feinted and invited, leaving an opening. She lunged, fully expecting him to parry. Instead, his sword dropped away. Off balance, she fell forward. Her rapier plunged into his chest.

Horrified, she froze. Afraid to move, afraid to breathe, she stared at the spot where the point of her rapier disappeared into his flesh. A small red circle seeped onto his shirt around her blade. Stricken, she met his gaze.

His eyes were soft, despite the pain he must have felt.

"It's all right, Solange," he said.

She gave her head a little shake. No, no, it was not all right at all.

Wrapping his hand around the blade piercing his chest, he gave it a little tug, but the rapier remained firmly embedded. He winced, then smiled. "You are an excellent swordsman, little thief." His words were strained as if trying to control his pain.

Solange shook her head again. She could not think. Her hand still held the hilt of the rapier that pierced his chest. She should pull it out. She was afraid to pull it out.

"I love you," he murmured.

Her eyes widened. Had she heard him correctly?

His dimple appeared, then he stepped back, at the same time wrenching the blade from his flesh. He swayed for a moment. A large bloom of bright blood on his shirt marked his wound. His eyes slipped shut. Then he collapsed.

Solange stared at his crumpled form. No one moved. No one spoke. The silence in the room pulsed from its walls. Her mind could not make sense of what she was seeing. She still clasped her rapier, and from its point hung a single drop of blood. It balanced there for a moment, then fell to the floor with a tiny plop. She watched it spread into a rosy blossom on the parquet.

Blood.

Antonio with her rapier lodged in his chest.

Blood.

Antonio smiling, wrapping his hand around her rapier.

Blood.

Antonio saying he loved her.

Blood.

Antonio pulling the blade from his body, falling.
Blood.

So much blood.

She screamed as her mind and body finally connected what had happened. She dropped her rapier, fell to her knees beside Antonio, and pressed her hands over his wound to try to staunch the flow of blood.

"No-no-no-no-no," she chanted, denying what she knew was happening. "You're not dead," she mumbled. "You can't be dead. Please don't be dead."

Someone knelt beside her. A hand closed around one of her wrists and gently tugged. She flung it off, pressed down against that horrible rush of blood. The hand captured her wrist again.

"*Mademoiselle*," the Englishman said next to her. "Please stop. You can do no more."

He pulled her hands away from Antonio, then spread the coat Antonio had discarded across that beautiful face.

Numb, Solange knelt beside Antonio. He was gone. How could he be gone? So vibrant, alive, passionate, and then . . . nothing? She stared at the blood on her hands, unable to comprehend what she was seeing. Silence filled the ballroom.

Two heartbeats of silence.

"Well," Vernoux said briskly. "That was an interesting development."

Something snapped together inside her when Solange heard his words. She surged to her feet. She was done with him. She was finished with his control. She had been so afraid of him. Her entire life she had lived in fear of two men. Le Chacal and Vernoux. Two men who had controlled her every moment of existence. Afraid to break away. Afraid to use her power. No more.

"How dare you," she growled. "How dare you!"

She advanced toward him, raised her bloody hand,

and let her power fly from her fingers. Vernoux's arm swooped up and diverted the energy to the side, where it flashed and cracked against the wall, leaving a black splotch. Le Chacal inched away from him, and Gide merely gave him a stoic glance.

Vernoux laughed coldly. "I have wondered when you would decide to use your power. It is very impressive. But it is no match for this." He showed her the glowing frog glyph on his wrist.

"That is nothing," she spat and threw her power at him again.

Once more, he deflected it.

Solange could feel the energy coursing through her. Perhaps even Antonio's blood strengthened it. And she realized she was more powerful than Vernoux. Enraged, she threw her power at him again and again. At first, he was able to block it, but after a while, it began to spatter against his body, across his face. Vernoux yelped when one vicious blast scorched his cheek. Solange smiled grimly, knowing even if she lost this battle, he would be scarred.

The pent-up rage, the fear that she had lived with under his dominion fed the force running through her. Without thought, she attacked, slowly moving closer, intent on destroying him. The room echoed with the impact of her blasts. The chandeliers above her head sang with the energy. One particularly intense blast ricocheted from one of the silver buttons on Vernoux's coat and hit Gide on the arm. His head jerked and his eyes cleared. Solange paused, amazed to see the awareness in her brother's eyes. She watched understanding click through him. Before she could gather another bolt of power, he threw himself at their tormentor and stabbed him with the Crystal Dagger. Vernoux screamed. A blinding green flash filled the ballroom.

By the time Solange could see again, Gide was pulling the Dagger out of Vernoux's chest. The marquis was a limp body slowly oozing blood from a blackened hole in his chest. Gide wiped the blood from the Dagger on the dead man's coat and calmly stuck it in his belt, where it glowed with a dull, purplish gray light. It seemed sated, having fed on death.

"He's dead, Solange," Gide said. "I killed him for you."

"For us," she gently corrected.

As soon as she said the words, she realized they were still in danger. Not from Le Chacal, who was cowering against the wall out of the way, but from the man called The Messenger who stood behind her, near where Antonio lay. She swung to face him.

"I will not challenge you, *mademoiselle*," he said, turning his palms out at his sides to show they were empty. "I have the piece of the Sphere of Astarte, and the Marquis de Vernoux has received his punishment for forcing you to kill a member of the House of Auriano. The Legion of Baal and the Lord High have their satisfaction."

Before Solange could respond, an owl flew in through the doors open to the garden and perched on the mantle of the fireplace. Immediately, she felt the cold creep of evil invade her insides. Nulkana was close. As she had the thought, a column of cloud appeared at the far end of the ballroom, and the sorceress stepped forth onto the parquet.

"Well," she said, "this is a cozy group."

She smiled, but it was far from comforting. Solange felt as if a claw had settled in her chest.

"How were you able to get inside this house?" Solange asked. She had no doubt that Vernoux had placed protections on his *l'hôtel*.

The sorceress smiled and gestured at Vernoux's body with a jangle of many golden bracelets. "The master of the house seems to have died."

Solange surmised that with Vernoux's death, his protections no longer worked.

Nulkana turned her attention to Antonio. "Is this who

I think it is?" She tipped her head with curiosity. "Did misfortune visit one of the Auriano whelps?"

Solange backed closer to Antonio. She would not allow the sorceress anywhere near him.

"Why are you here?" she demanded.

"I've come to claim what is mine," she said.

Solange edged nearer to Antonio and held up her hand, prepared to defend him even in death. "There's nothing here for you."

Nulkana sneered, "Do you truly believe your paltry power can protect you?"

"She's not alone, bitch," Gide said and stepped from the dais. "I have this." He held up the Crystal Dagger.

Nulkana circled away from him. "You don't even know how to use it."

Gide gestured at Vernoux's body. "I honed my skill on him."

Nulkana shivered delicately, a pretense of revulsion. "You have done me a favor by ridding the world of him." She drifted closer. "Did it feel good to kill, boy? Do you want to do it again?" She enticed slyly. "Come with me, and I can let you do whatever you want." She licked her red lips. "Come with me and learn the real power of the Dagger."

Gide's body leaned toward Nulkana, even though his feet remained in place. The sorceress was so strong that even with the opposing force of the Crystal Dagger, he was being drawn to her. Solange could feel the pull. She backed one more step until she felt the comfort of Antonio's body against her foot.

"You're not taking him anywhere," she declared.

Nulkana's gaze fell on her, and Solange felt a shaft of cold like an ice pick through her chest. Then the sorceress's gaze flew to The Messenger who stood behind Solange. With a hiss, she fell back a step. Immediately, the shaft of cold dissipated.

"What is your purpose here, Priest?" Nulkana demanded.

Priest? Solange wondered.

The Messenger gave a casual shrug. "I came merely to observe. But I can do more if you wish."

Nulkana's eyes blazed. Then dismissing him, as well as Solange and Gide, she turned her attention to the dais once more, where Le Chacal was attempting to become part of the wall.

"Jean-Jacques," she purred. "How nice to see you. I believe we had an agreement, you and I." She gestured at Solange. "But the little witch is still alive."

Le Chacal pushed away from the wall. "I would have brought her to you, but—"

Nulkana sliced her hand through the air and the outlaw choked. His face turned red, and he struggled to breathe.

"I do not like my requests denied," the sorceress said.

With another swipe through the air, she released the King of the Thieves. He dropped to his hands and knees as he drew in great gasps of air.

"I didn't . . . I would never . . ." He gestured vaguely in Solange's direction. "They dueled. I thought he would kill her. She won."

Nulkana scowled. "But that doesn't excuse you, Jean-Jacques. You have disappointed me. I wanted *her* dead."

As Nulkana spoke, Solange felt the icy evil expand in her chest, then it wrapped itself around her. She saw Gide go pale and stiff. Le Chacal yelped and began to hop around as if the floor had become too hot to stand on. Then he stopped as if glued to the parquet. Horror crossed his face. Flames erupted around his feet, spread up his legs. He screamed and swatted at them. The flames rose higher and engulfed his body—all except for his face. His agonized shrieks bounced from the walls.

Solange watched in shock. But despite what he had done to her and Gide and Antonio, she could not bear to see him in such torment.

"Stop it!" she commanded and threw her power at Nulkana.

The energy staggered the sorceress, but it seemed to go right through her.

"She's a projection," The Messenger murmured. "And she's hurt."

Solange remembered when Nulkana had appeared at the shack in the woods, and how her own power had passed through the sorceress then as well. She saw the small black stain at Nulkana's side that looked like blood. If the sorceress were injured and merely a projection, perhaps she could force her away.

Once again, she threw her power at Nulkana. She aimed at the seeping spot on her side. Again, and again. Each time, as it passed through Nulkana, her image wavered, but then refocused. Le Chacal still howled in agony, the flames still burned, but they seemed to fade.

Nulkana laughed, the evil curling malevolently inside Solange's chest. "Do you truly believe you have the power to hurt me, little slut?"

The sorceress clenched her hand, and in a furious burst of flame and an agonized howl, Le Chacal incinerated. The flames snuffed out, and all that was left was a pile of ash.

"That is what I do to those who betray me," she announced. "But I have something much more interesting for you." Her hand moved in a strange pattern in the air.

Solange could not breathe. She felt as if her heart were being ripped from her. Gripping her chest, she dropped to her knees and fought for air.

"Stop!" Gide yelled. He jumped forward and sliced through Nulkana with the Crystal Dagger.

The sorceress's image parted where Gide had cut, but when it reformed, it was a bit askew. The owl hooted and whooped and ruffled its wings. Through her pain, Solange realized the bird was somehow vitally connected to Nulkana. Solange summoned all her power and shot it at the owl. Her aim was off, but the energy grazed the bird's wing. It shrieked and screeched. Nulkana screamed and clapped her hand to her shoulder. The owl jumped from the mantle and dragging its wing, hopped across the floor to its mistress. With a *pop*, they both disappeared.

In the silence, Solange's ragged breathing seemed very loud. Before she could catch her breath, The Messenger lifted Antonio as if he weighed nothing, as if he had already turned to Shadow. He dipped his head in a small bow.

"Well done, *mademoiselle*," he said. "The sorceress will not bother you for some time. I suggest you and your brother hide yourself someplace far away." He turned and took a step toward the door.

"Wait," she said, barely able to gather enough breath to speak. "Where are you taking Antonio?"

The Messenger turned back, raised a cool brow. "He is no longer your concern, *mademoiselle*."

Solange surged to her feet. "He is my concern. I love him. I wish to return his body to his brother so . . ." She was forced to stop and swallow the tears that choked her. ". . . so he may be buried properly."

"I'm afraid that isn't possible," he said. Those clear blue eyes turned frosty.

"Why not?" she demanded, stepping forward and raising her hand in threat.

"Don't force me to hurt you, *mademoiselle*." The Messenger's level tone indicated how serious he was.

"How can you hurt me?" she challenged. "Your hands are occupied."

The corner of his mouth tipped up with humorless amusement. "Some of us do not require our hands to inflict damage."

As Solange took another step forward, Gide grabbed her by the arm. "Solange," he warned. "Let him go."

The Messenger swept his gaze over them both. "Be glad I am not taking either of you to the Lord High." He turned on his heel and left.

Solange listened to his footsteps echo as he crossed the space to the outer door. Then he was gone. Once again, silence hung in the room.

Solange drew a breath, but she could not fill her lungs. She tried again, but the muscles of her chest had locked tight. Her legs gave out. As she grabbed for Gide, she sank to the floor. He followed her down, his arm about her shoulders, but she felt no warmth from him. Something human, something elemental had been taken from her brother. But at least that dark power did not overtake her. It had been satisfied for now with Vernoux's death.

Even as she had the thought, the loss of Antonio slashed across her consciousness and landed with piercing anguish in her chest. It gouged out a spot that left her hollow. She had killed him. In her stupid, reckless plan to save him, everything had gone wrong. She wanted to cry but found that no tears would come.

"I'm sorry about the Italian duke," Gide said. "It was an accident. It wasn't your fault."

That ache in her chest constricted, and she gave a dry sob.

Gide's arm hugged her closer. "Vernoux is gone. And Le Chacal."

She glanced over to the dais where Vernoux lay, and Le Chacal's ashes were stirred by the breeze. She should be rejoicing that both their tormentors were dead. Instead, she felt nothing.

"We're free, Solange," he said.

She gave a little nod.

"We can leave here."

As soon as Gide said the words, Solange knew she could not leave. Something held her as surely as Le Chacal's

demands or Vernoux's threats. She had no idea why that should be. She hated this place, this city.

She shook her head. "No."

Gide's stillness indicated his surprise. He rose to his feet. "Why?"

She turned dull, dry eyes up to him. "I can't."

Her brother stared down at her, his face expressionless. She expected some argument, anger, some wild reaction. Instead, all he said was, "Very well."

She thought he was agreeing to stay, so she folded herself into a ball and let her head drop to her knees. All she wanted was to turn back time, to replay that duel, to rewrite the end. All she wanted was to drift in her agony.

"I'll be leaving in the morning," Gide said.

Solange's head snapped up. "What did you say?"

"I'm leaving." His mouth firmed into a resolute line.

"But . . ." Unable to voice the stunned thoughts that bounced inside her head, she lapsed into silence.

"I can't stay, Solange." Gide's gaze met hers in a tortured plea to understand. "Something's wrong. With me." He wrapped his hand around the hilt of the Dagger stuck in his waistband. "Ever since I took this, I haven't been right. I have to find out why."

Solange rose to her feet. "But can't you stay here to discover the reason?" To lose Gide now when she had lost everything else in her life terrified her.

"I can't." His words echoed hers. "I'm a danger to you now. And whatever is making you stay here is making me leave."

"But Nulkana," she argued. "She'll come after you."

Gide shook his head. "You heard The Messenger. He said to hide far away. I think we'll be safer if we part." He gazed at her. His eyes were hard, old, not the young, trusting eyes of the brother she knew so well. "You should leave the city, too, Solange. You're not safe here."

Solange noticed he did not encourage her to accompany him again. He was leaving her, not just physically, but emotionally. She was on her own now, with no little brother to care for.

"I'll leave in a few days. Maybe I'll go back to our village," she said, but her words had no substance behind them.

Gide gave a short nod. Then his gaze softened, and he reached out to touch her cheek. Her little brother was still here. The thought made her eyes sting.

"Be safe, Solange," he said.

She covered his fingers as they lingered on her cheek. "You, as well, Gide."

He turned and walked away.

She was alone.

Chapter 22

Solange slowly climbed the front stairs of *L'Hôtel des Vénitiens*, Antonio's city residence. A sad stillness hung over the mansion as if it could not quite understand that its master was gone. She did not know if Antonio's brother, the prince, was in residence, but she needed to complete this errand before her courage failed. Three days had passed since that horrible night of the duel. She had spent the time in bed in a pit of despair, and then in a fit of energy, she discarded all the clothes she had worn as *Madame* de Volonté. That life was over, and she wanted no reminders of it.

She pulled up her long black kid gloves, straightened the skirt on her black linen gown, and smoothed the chignon beneath her small black straw hat. Taking a breath, she raised the knocker on the door and let it fall. It echoed hollowly. She identified with that sound, for she felt just as empty.

The door opened, and the majordomo appeared, looking forbidding and grim.

"I've come to see His Excellency, the Prince of Auriano," she said.

The majordomo swung the door wide. "Please, come in, *mademoiselle*."

She was surprised that the prince would be willing to receive her. She trailed the servant across the black and white marble floor of the foyer to a small door in one corner. He knocked, announced her, and bowed her through.

Solange stepped into a room darkened by closed drapes. This was a very different room than the one she had been in before when she met the princess. The walls were paneled in dark wood, which added to the dimness, and the furniture was heavy and masculine. The only light came from what seeped between the panels of draperies where they did not completely meet. A large desk sat in one corner with two wooden armchairs before it. Two other chairs, high-backed and upholstered, framed the unlit fireplace. Although the air outside was warm and humid, the room was cool. She caught a murky reflection of herself as she passed a pier glass, but quickly averted her eyes. The mirror was too much of a reminder of her salon and the life Vernoux had forced on her. It was too much a reminder of Antonio and the infinite, beautiful reflections of him on that wonderful night he had taken her out into the city.

A man stirred in one of the fireside chairs and stood. The Prince of Auriano. Even though she knew he was a twin to Antonio, still the shock of seeing someone so like Tonio shook her. The pain of seeing him made her avert her eyes.

Solange curtsied. "Your Excellency, thank you for receiving me. I know this is a very difficult time for you."

"I do not often receive those who have mortally wounded members of my family, *mademoiselle*," he said.

"I am so sorry." Her voice barely above a whisper, she kept her eyes lowered. "I didn't mean to do it. It was an accident."

"Nevertheless." His single word, his tone implied forgiveness would not soon be forthcoming.

Solange fumbled in her reticule and pulled out the second moonstone pendant. She had found it among Le Chacal's ashes. She stepped forward and held it out. "I came to return this. I know it is too late to help, but—" Her voice faltered.

He did not move to accept it. Several heartbeats passed. Finally, when she thought he would humiliate her in some way, he held out his hand. A gold band circled his thumb. Solange nearly cried out upon seeing it as she thought for a moment that Antonio stood before her. Then reality swiftly returned. The prince was merely wearing his brother's thumb ring as a remembrance of him. She dropped the pendant into his palm.

His fingers closed around the pendant.

"*Grazie*, Solange," he said.

She gasped. Her eyes flew to his face. Those soft golden eyes caressed her face. No, not possible. This could not be Antonio. She had seen him fall, had watched the blood and life seep from him. She had watched as The Messenger had carried his lifeless body from Vernoux's ballroom. If he had lived, he would have been Shadow, not this vibrant, healthy man of flesh and bone standing before her. Grief and guilt overwhelmed her, and her knees gave out. As she began to collapse, the man before her grabbed her elbow and steadied her.

"Solange," he murmured.

At the sound of his voice, visions erupted in her head like scenes from a play. The night she had awakened to find him as Shadow standing in her bedchamber. The night she had gone to his chateau in the country and seen him during the Hunger. The night she had gone to him to ask for his help in finding Gide and wound up making love with him.

"Solange," he murmured again. "Do you not know me?"

"Tonio," she whispered, afraid to speak his name aloud lest he vanish.

"*Si.*"

That single word convinced her. Surging forward, she flung her arms about him. She knew as soon as she connected with his solid body that this was Antonio. This was *her* Tonio. His arms wrapped about her, crushing her to him.

"I thought I'd lost you," she choked through her tears.

"No, *dolcezza*, I'm here," he said against her hair.

She remained very still, absorbing the feel of him, drinking in his scent of rosemary and lemon. His solid form assured her that she was not dreaming. She felt his lips at her ear, the trail of his mouth down her neck. She shivered. He could arouse her with barely a touch. Then something niggled at her. Something pricked at her joy at finding him alive and well. She leaned back in his embrace.

"Why did you pretend to be your brother?" she asked. "Why have you remained silent for three days? Why did you let me believe you were dead?"

At each question, her anger grew. Jerking from the circle of his arms, she backed four paces. No word had come from *L'Hôtel des Vénitiens* to say he was alive. He had let her grieve, had left her alone in her miserable guilt and despair. He had abandoned her, and now he thought he could have her by merely nibbling at her neck. That was not going to happen.

He tipped his head and raised a sardonic brow. "You stabbed me, Solange. Through the heart, if I recall. It was painful. As I remember, you were quite irate with me."

She looked away, unable to meet his eyes. Her guilt still twisted in her chest. "I didn't mean to stab you. I lost my balance. It was an accident."

"I know."

She went on as if he had not spoken. "Vernoux had Gide in his control through the Dagger. I had to fence with you."

"I know."

She shook her head, ignoring him still. "I had to pretend to be angry so you would duel with me."

"I know, *dolcezza*."

His quiet words caught her attention. Her anger resurfaced. "But you let me think you were dead! For three days!"

"I *was* dead." His lips twisted sardonically.

Her mouth dropped open. "But—How—?"

"It appears the man known as The Messenger has his own agenda," he said. "He brought me back here and left me at the door with this." Tonio reached into the pocket of his coat, pulled out a small object and showed it to her.

Solange's eyes widened when she saw the piece of the Sphere of Astarte sitting in his palm. "I thought he was taking it back to the Lord High of the Legion of Baal," she said.

"He must have changed his mind." A corner of his mouth tipped up in wry amusement.

She shook her head as she tried to make sense of everything. Tonio was alive, not dead. The Messenger left the piece of the Sphere with him instead of stealing it away. In fact, The Messenger had brought him back to life. And Tonio was not Shadow.

She turned her gaze to him. "Are you . . . well?"

He nodded gravely. "As well as I can be after being dead."

"I thought . . ." Her throat closed and she was forced to swallow before she could go on. "I thought I would never see you again."

He opened his arms to her. "Come here, *mi amore*."

Without hesitation, she walked into his embrace. Having his arms about her, feeling his vitality reassured her she was not dreaming.

"I couldn't come to you, *dolce mia*, because I was healing," he explained. "My brother refused to send word to the woman who had stabbed me. He can be a bit difficult."

She remembered the cool, dangerous man she had met on several occasions. "I should apologize to him, explain what happened." Her words were brave, but she was not looking forward to that interview.

Antonio cupped the back of her head. "There's no need.

He'll come around after he learns we are to be wed."

Relief swept through her, then his last words registered. "I beg your pardon?" She looked into his face.

He gazed at her with those glorious golden eyes. A small smile curved his lips. "Will you marry me, Solange?"

Her breath caught. Joy bubbled like champagne in her head. To be Tonio's wife, to see him every day, to make love with him, to bear his children. That was more than she had ever dreamed. But she could not. Carefully, she disengaged herself from his embrace.

"I would like nothing more than to marry you," she said, "but I can't."

Hurt and confusion wrinkled his brow. "If you're concerned about your brother, he can live with us in Auriano," he said.

Solange took a breath. "Gide is gone. He left the day after the duel. I don't know where he is."

"I'm sorry."

Tonio's simple words brought tears to her eyes. She would not cry again. She had cried enough in the last three days. Blinking them away, she raised her chin.

"I can't marry you, Tonio. As much as I love you, it wouldn't work. You are a duke, while I'm a —" She took a breath, gaining courage. "I am a whore."

"No, you are not." Antonio's contradiction was fierce. "You are not what Vernoux forced you to become." He reached out and placed his finger on her chest above her heart. "In here, you are a lioness. In here, where it counts, you are a woman of courage and grace, and the only woman I know who would stab me to make a point."

Caught between another bout of tears and laughter, she stared at the beautiful man before her. "But what of Nulkana and the Legion of Baal? Nulkana wants me dead as well as you, and the Legion will be after me because of Gide. I'd be bringing both of them to your doorstep."

He shrugged off her arguments. "Nulkana has wanted me dead since I was born. Gide is gone so the Legion will be busy trying to find him. He's the one with the Dagger." A dark brow curved up. "Do you have any other excuses?"

Solange searched her brain, but she came up with nothing. She gave her head a little shake.

He opened his arms a second time. "Then come here."

After only a heartbeat of hesitation, she walked into his embrace, the only place she wanted to be.

"Will you marry me, Solange?" he asked again.

Bubbles of joy popped in the vicinity of her heart. How could she have known on that fateful night she had robbed him that he would become the most precious person in her life? She looked up into his glorious golden eyes. "*Oui.* I will marry you."

He smiled a heartbreakingly beautiful smile. "*Bene,*" he said and kissed her.

EPILOGUE

Antonio led the way down the ancient stone steps. He held a torch aloft in one hand, and with the other, he guided his new wife. Solange. She was beautiful in her pale blue silk gown. She had chosen to wear a wreath of lavender twined through her hair, and the scent surrounded her like a cloud. He had gifted her with a large sapphire pendant upon arriving in Auriano, part of the family jewels. She had twisted the chain through her hair to allow the stone to lay on her forehead, like an exotic princess.

He still could not believe they were wed. Behind them, beyond Alessandro and Sabrina who trailed them on the steps, the sun was setting on the wedding celebration, still going on. At one time, he would have been disgruntled at being pulled away from the festivities. He would have still been dancing with the young beauties of Auriano and quaffing wine with the young men. But not today. Today, the celebration was for him and Solange, and he was happy to have her to himself. Or nearly all to himself. As soon as this task was done, he would spirit her away to their chamber in the *castello*.

Antonio smiled at his wife on the step above him. Shyly, she smiled back at him. Her modesty, after the horrific life she had lived with Vernoux as her master, awed him.

Sandro cleared his throat. "We're tottering on the steps here. Could you do your lovemaking after we have completed this task?"

Tonio chuckled. "You're impatient because you want to get to your own lovemaking."

He watched a blush creep up Sabrina's cheeks as Sandro gave her a heated gaze. Even with Sabrina in her delicate condition, he knew his brother could barely keep his hands off her.

His brother turned back to him. "I noticed *Signore* Pastore's youngest daughter looked a bit put out during the wedding."

Tonio's lips twisted wryly. "I never should have danced with her so much at your wedding."

"So that is how you learned to dance so well," Solange teased.

Tonio ducked his head. "We are here for a much more serious reason," he grumbled and swatted away a heavy cobweb with his torch.

Solange let go of his hand to brush the tail of the cobweb off the deep blue satin coat of his wedding finery. Then her fingers brushed his jaw. Her delicate touch reassured him. Her sweet smile warmed his heart. With a returning smile, he recaptured her hand and continued the descent down the stone steps.

In her other hand, she clutched the ragged cloth that held the piece of the Sphere of Astarte which they had stolen from Le Chacal's lair in the Catacombs. It was the piece that The Messenger of the Legion of Baal had swiped from Vernoux's grasp. It was the piece that had brought Tonio back to life. And it was the piece that had partially broken his curse. Like Sandro, he now remained flesh and bone during the day, no matter what phase the moon was in. Only at night did the curse take him over, when he turned to Shadow at the full moon. They had come to this deep chamber to join this piece with the other, which Sandro and Sabrina had found, and place it beneath the Castello Auriano.

After descending many more stairs, they emerged into

a small circular chamber. Tonio and Sandro placed their torches into wall brackets, then approached a large, round, flat stone in the middle of the floor. It was too heavy for even twenty men to move. The twins positioned themselves on opposite sides. With a nod to each other, they held out their hands over the stone and closed their eyes.

With huge mental effort, Tonio concentrated on moving the stone. He could feel his brother doing the same. The stone lifted and hovered several inches above the floor of the cavern. With a flick of his hands, it shifted sideways, then settled with a thud on the ground. Beneath where the stone had lain, the stones looked like the rest of the floor of the chamber, but Tonio knew otherwise.

Sandro stepped back. Tonio stretched out his hand over the space and walked around it in a counterclockwise circle. A round spot in the paving stones turned, following his movement. He flicked his hand, and a vault opened which had been carved into the bedrock. Lined in gold, it held an intricately fashioned golden pedestal, created to hold the assembled Sphere of Astarte. One piece already lay there, the piece that Sandro had placed on the pedestal only several weeks before, after his marriage to Sabrina.

As Solange handed Tonio the piece she held, Sandro stepped forward and picked up the section from the pedestal. The twins fitted the two together, then Tonio placed the partial Sphere on its stand and stepped back.

Solange laid her hand on his back, her fingers gently caressing, comforting. They waited. Two breaths. Three. Four. Tonio became anxious. When Sandro had returned his piece of the Sphere to the vault, the wait for it to work had not seemed quite so long. He glanced at his twin, who tightly clutched Sabrina's hand. Sandro met his gaze and gave a little shrug as if to say he had no idea why the extra piece had not added its magic.

Tonio let out his breath, unaware he had been holding it. Disappointment washed through him. They had all been sure that adding the next piece to the Sphere would boost its magic, and help crack the curse even more. Then he felt Solange's fingers grip his coat. She gasped. The pieces of the Sphere glowed. Tiny beams of energy shot out. The two pieces grew brighter as if the energy heated them. Then slowly, they fused together. The beams of energy died back but left the partial Sphere a rich, translucent amber that emitted an inner light. It pulsed—once, twice. The pulse rippled out, encompassing all of them. It flowed through Tonio in a potent wave of power. He gasped as it surged through him, He heard Sandro's echoing gasp. It spilled beyond them, into the stone walls of the chamber, into the bedrock below Auriano. A heartbeat reverberated in the stone, followed by another.

Silence.

But the partial Sphere still glowed softly. Its magic was working. Their efforts to retrieve it had not been in vain. Besides, he now had a beautiful wife. He smiled at her and was warmed by her answering smile.

Alessandro distracted him with a silent comment. *We have to go to Allegra.*

Si. Tonio gave a nod. *Our sister will have to find the next piece.*

But we will find her a husband, Alessandro said sternly.

Sabrina and Solange erupted into laughter.

About Patricia Barletta

Patricia Barletta always wanted to be a writer. That was right after she realized that becoming a fairy ballerina or a princess wasn't going to happen. But being a writer meant she could go places in her head and be other people as much as she wanted. She could even be a fairy ballerina or a princess!

As a native of the Boston area, Patricia has been inspired by its history, which influenced her stories, and probably had an impact on her decision to become a high school British Literature teacher so she could pay the bills. She received a Master of Fine Arts in Creative Writing degree at the fabulous Stonecoast program in Maine. And now she's an author writing about dark heroes, feisty heroines, magic, and other fantastical things.

Find out more about Patricia and her books at:
www.patriciabarletta.com.